Augusta Trobaugh has achieved a perfect balance of richness and delicacy. Whether she's describing little birds' feet or the s... ing never sh... from the st... found some... me on ever...

Natio... Author...

Trobaugh g... with salty d...

Augusta Tr... insightful w... my second...

Aut...

I do not exp... year more e... than *Praise*... tifully, poet... another ab... rich fields o...

...e White Dog

From its very fi... *Jerusalem!* had r... Trobaugh has gi... ...mpany of ...Smith.

—John H. Timmerman
...e *Jerusalem Journeys*

...werful story. ...
...ative makes this ...ead, and readers ...ing message of ...lity before God

—*CBA Marketplace*

...e art of Southern ...realistic characters ...ous dialogue to ...eness. She subtly ...tside our comfort ...e lives of others ...are all connected ...uffering.

—*Aspire*

...eeply moving ...pe, and salvation. ...gh's writing is ...nd she creates a ...real and familiar ...is seeking solace

—Philip Lee Williams
Author of *Jenny Dorset*

The author with her revered friend and caretaker,
1946.

PRAISE JERUSALEM!

Augusta Trobaugh

And the city had no need of the sun, neither the moon, to shine in it; for the glory of God did lighten it, and the Lamb is the light thereof.
The Revelation of Saint John the Divine
The Holy Bible

 **Baker Books**
A Division of Baker Book House Co
Grand Rapids, Michigan 49516

© 1997 by Augusta Trobaugh

Published by Baker Books
a division of Baker Book House Company
P.O. Box 6287, Grand Rapids, MI 49516–6287

Cloth edition published May 1997
Trade paper edition published October 1997

Second printing, March 2000

Printed in the United States of America

Library of Congress Cataloging-in-Publication Data

Trobaugh, Augusta.
    Praise Jerusalem! : a novel / Augusta Trobaugh.
       p.   cm.
    ISBN 0-8010-1147-7 (cloth)
    ISBN 0-8010-5814-7 (pbk.)
    I. Title.
    PS3570.R585P7   1997
    813'.54—dc21   96-52628

For current information about all releases from Baker Book House, visit our web site:
http://www.bakerbooks.com

For
Merle—
ever gentle
ever kind
ever courageous

1

Looking back on that evening, especially knowing I had to tell Maybelline she'd have to find someplace else to live, I have to wonder why I was so surprised at what happened. Because the truth of the matter is that I should have expected all sorts of unusual things. But I didn't. Shows you what a fool I was.

After supper, we washed up the dishes and went out to sit on the front porch, just like always, and Maybelline started right in with her mumblings like she always did—evening prayers, I guess, but I never did know for sure because I'd never been able to make out much of whatever it was she mumbled. Except, every once in a long while, something like "Sure do praise Your name!" or "shed Your precious blood!"

I was thinking of that cold January day when she came up my front steps, grinning and hollering, "THE LORD DONE SAID FOR ME TO MOVE IN WITH YOU!" with a big wad of chewing gum in her mouth and carrying all those hatboxes and wearing that awful Shirley Temple wig! And what a bitter cold day it was, right in the dead of winter, and her not even wearing a coat, but only that moth-eaten old bunny-fur jacket she set so much store in and black rubber galoshes and her trying to balance the umbrella and the hatboxes and working that gum with a vengeance. And me wondering what on earth I'd gotten myself into!

Knew before that, of course, about Maybelline not having had any advantages. Knew it just from listening to her, something I had done every Thursday morning when I went to Edna's for my shampoo and set. Because Edna had taken Maybelline in—like a stray cat—one summer when, as Edna told it, Maybelline's "husband"—Edna hesitated over the word just enough to let me know she hadn't seen any ring on Maybelline's finger—stopped his pickup truck in front of the Gulf station at the corner of the highway and Main Street, opened the passenger door, and pushed Maybelline right out. The truck had Florida plates and a bumper sticker that read "I love my dog and my woman—in that order."

"Threw her suitcase out after her and drove off just as neat as you please. Never even turned around to look behind him, so I hear." That's what Edna said, later. And old Dove, who was working at the Gulf station back then and saw it happen, called Mr. Charlie—Edna's husband—who'd been Chief of Police for as long as anyone could remember. By the time Mr. Charlie got there, Maybelline was sitting on her suitcase beside the highway, watching up the road like any minute the truck would come back. Edna said she bet he'd done it to her before. Put her out on the highway and then come back and gotten her when he cooled down some.

But this time, he didn't. Mr. Charlie went out to the side of the highway and stood there and talked with her for the longest kind of time. Later on, he told Edna that one of the first things he thought was that this woman was no spring chicken, sure enough. Probably in her late forties or early fifties. Old enough, anyway, to have more sense than to take up with a man who'd treat her like that. They talked for a long time, and then Mr. Charlie just took her elbow real easy-like and she stood up, like a child doing whatever it was told. He carried her suitcase and walked her back to his patrol car, and then, because he didn't know what else to do with her, he took her home to Edna.

That's how Maybelline came to live with Edna and how Edna taught her how to cut and style hair and put in permanents, so she'd have a way to make a living and be able to take care of herself. So she wouldn't have to worry about being thrown out of any man's truck again. I always thought that was a good, Christian thing Edna did for Maybelline, taking in a stranger like that. Better than I could have done.

One Thursday morning, when I went to Edna's to have my hair set, I heard Maybelline talking to someone she was working on in the other chair, and listening to her is how I knew for a fact that she didn't have any education or upbringing at all. And, too, that was about the time Maybelline started in to wearing that terrible-looking wig all made up of plastic-looking blonde curls. The Shirley Temple wig, we all called it, but not so Maybelline could hear us of course.

"That's an unusual name—Maybelline—isn't it?" someone getting a permanent inquired of her.

"Yes, ma'am, it sure is." Maybelline was most amiable about it. "My real name is Maybell, after my mama and her mama before her. But when my mama up and run off like she done, my daddy took to calling me Maybelline, 'cause he said all my mama left behind her was me and a old eyebrow pencil."

That's another way I knew she hadn't had any advantages, saying something like that right out and not having sense enough to be embarrassed about it. What I didn't realize, though, was that Maybelline sometimes listened to what I was saying, even when I was speaking in a very personal way and only to Edna. Or so I thought. That's how it all got started that Maybelline came to live with me.

Because it wasn't long after Maybelline first came to Edna's that I began to realize just what a bad fix I was getting into, financially. Certainly seemed like a gracious plenty back when Henry took out insurance and made all our investments, but it wasn't going to last. Interest rates were bad, and the house was eating up what little I had. The roof had to be replaced and then all the plumbing work one winter when the pipes burst from the cold. And the taxes. Goodness! So that's when I thought of having someone to come live with me, to ease my expenses. At the time, it seemed to be a truly fine revelation, and given the right mood, I could pretty well envision some nameless but very genteel lady, just about my age and with soft, wavy hair and polished nails, who would sit with me on the front porch in the afternoons, the two of us sipping iced tea from frosted, crystal glasses and talking together in the cool shade and maybe reading poetry to each other on long summer evenings.

One day, I happened to mention the idea to Edna, because it was a natural thing to talk in a thinking-out-loud way in the beauty parlor. Everyone did it, sort of trying out ideas that way, see what Edna thought about them. She always did have such a good head on her shoulders, Edna did. So I told her I was thinking about finding a nice lady to live with me—just for the company, I told her, because I wasn't about to tell anyone I was having financial difficulties, not even Edna. And Maybelline must have been eavesdropping, so that before I could even get all the words out, she popped that awful-looking Shirley-Templed head up over the divider screen and shouted, "I'LL COME LIVE WITH YOU, MISS AMELIA!"

Well! How embarrassing for her to yell it out like that! Because it was years before I was finally able to convince her that I'm not one bit hard of hearing. But back then, Maybelline hollered everything to me.

Of course, Edna picked up on it right away that Maybelline had jumped the gun, because I was sitting there, as rigid as a corset and completely stunned by that turn of events, staring straight ahead at my reflection in the mirror—didn't know what to say—and Edna standing behind me, watching my face in the mirror.

"Well, Maybelline!" Edna started in with a little laugh. "I think Miss Amelia was just sort of musing over the idea. Goodness! I don't think she means she's really going to do anything like that; not right away, at least."

So that was how Edna tried to save me, and it almost worked. But not quite.

"Oh, that's okay. Why, I don't mind one little bit waiting while she makes up her mind," Maybelline said to Edna. And to me she yelled, "YOU JUST LET ME KNOW, MISS AMELIA. YOU JUST LET ME KNOW WHENEVER YOU MAKE UP YOUR MIND."

Edna was still watching me in the mirror and she said not a word, but pursed her lips just the least little bit and shook her head—no—to my reflection. But not so that Maybelline could see her do it.

Of course, Edna couldn't say another thing right then and there, but I knew she'd call me on the telephone just as soon as she could, so she could come right out and say whatever it was she had in mind to say. And she did.

"I don't think it would be a very good idea," Edna started out, and her words were slow and careful, like someone tiptoeing through broken glass. "Why, she's the sweetest thing you'd ever want to know, but . . ." Edna stopped talking, waiting for me to say, "What?"

"What?"

"Well, for one thing she's been going to every single one of those tent revivals out at the edge of town, and I think she's getting all caught up in the hallelujah thing, if you know what I mean."

"Yes," I said. "And I really had someone entirely different in mind. Someone more . . ."

"Appropriate," Edna interjected, before I could find the right word.

"Yes," I agreed, because it was a good word, a kind word for saying what needed to be said.

"Well, she's a sweet thing, and she'd do anything in the world for you, but of course, she hasn't had advantages, you know."

"I know."

"Just don't say anything else about it, and let's see if it won't blow over. Maybe she'll forget all about it."

That sounded like a good idea to me, and so every Thursday morning, when I went for my shampoo and set, I was just as polite as could be to Maybelline, of course, and she always chirruped a greeting and studied my face, but I certainly didn't say another word about finding someone to come live with me, at least not in front of Maybelline. So I spoke in low tones to Edna and only about very safe things—how my tomato plants were coming along and what kind of fertilizer I'd used on them—and all the while, keeping an eye on Maybelline, who hummed revival songs in the other booth.

Then the time came, as I knew it would, when I had to watch my expenditures even more carefully than I had been doing. So I stopped going once a week for a shampoo and set, and went only every other Thursday. To Edna, I explained, "Now that I'm older, my hair is too dry to take a shampoo and set every week." And Edna understood perfectly, without my saying another word.

The whole time, I was growing more and more certain that I'd have to find someone to come live in my house with me. There just wasn't anything else I could do. Trouble was, now that Maybelline had plunked herself right into the middle of the situation, it was going to be hard having someone else. And there were other com-

11

plications, too, because Edna had said something to me one time about wanting to bring her very own sister down to live with her and Charlie, now that her sister was a widow and living all alone in Macon, and that maybe it was time for Maybelline to find a place of her own. Edna had even gone so far as to try and arrange for Maybelline to go live with Mrs. Hodges, who sometimes rented out her front bedroom, but no—Maybelline was set on being with me—and I still didn't know why. Not back then, I didn't.

Finally, I'd just about resigned myself that there was nothing else I could do but have Maybelline move in with me, for Edna's sake, if for nothing else, but it certainly wasn't something I wanted to do. Just something I was beginning to feel I didn't have any choice about. But before I could even say anything about it, Maybelline jumped the gun again.

One morning about that time, I started down the front steps and had a most excruciating pain to come in my hip. It was so bad, I had to call the doctor, and he said I should try and stay off my feet as much as possible, just for a few days. Of course, everyone in town heard about it, because that's the way it is in small towns. The story going around was that I had taken a terrible fall down the steps and even had grabbed a jardiniere of begonias on my way down, which of course, wasn't true at all. Still, when Maybelline heard it, that was all she needed.

"She's on her way to your house right this minute!" Edna called and warned me. "And she's got everything in the world she owns with her. I think this is it."

When I hung up the phone, my mind was racing; I was trying to think of something, anything, I could do about it. But just then, I suddenly realized that this way, no one would think a thing of my having someone move in with me—because of my hip and all. So it wouldn't get all over town that I was financially embarrassed and had to have someone share my expenses. And just as I had that comforting thought, I looked out of the window and saw Maybelline coming up the front walk.

"THE LORD DONE SAID FOR ME TO MOVE IN WITH YOU!" Maybelline yelled out that day as she clambered up the steps, juggling the umbrella and the hatboxes. "YES, GOODNESS! PRAISE THE LORD! HE HAS SENT ME TO BE WITH YOU!"

That's what she said, anyway, and so that explained her stubbornness about it. She was on a "mission from God," or so she thought. And after a time, I felt almost inclined to agree with her. Long years during which she rearranged all my kitchen cabinets so I never was able to find a single thing, and put her glass of iced tea on my grandmama's mahogany Queen Anne table without using a coaster under it, and hung her dripping stockings over the guest towels in the bathroom, and chewed very noisily and almost constantly on huge wads of gum, and took that terrible wig off and sat right there on the front porch with it in her lap, brushing it. Can you imagine? Might as well have a big old hound dog sitting out there, scratching himself. And worst of all, she sang revival songs through her nose all the time, interrupting the singing only for wide-open conversations with the Lord Jesus and holding out her hands palms up, as if something from Heaven just might fall into them.

Finally, I began to suspect that perhaps the Lord really had sent Maybelline to be with me—to place a trial on me in my declining years.

But despite the fact that I had often fantasized joyously about being able to get rid of Maybelline, now that it had come down to saying the words, I knew it was going to be awfully hard.

I took a deep breath.

"Maybelline, you need to start looking for someplace else to live," I said right out. And even though I'd rehearsed it over and over, the words still shocked me. Usually, if I said anything to Maybelline while she was in her "rapture," I had to repeat it several times. But not this time.

"What?" It was exactly the question I anticipated, and so I went ahead with my carefully rehearsed litany.

"It's just that my funds are running out."

"I don't understand," she whined at me. "Why can't I stay here with you?" She was serious, of course, and I shouldn't have expected anything else from her. There wasn't much of anything else I'd ever seen register in her face except confusion. I just sat there, looking at that familiar, infuriating face—the improbable circles of orange rouge she always wore on either cheekbone, and pencil-thin, drawn-on eyebrows, and that terrible Lilac Lavender Lovely eye shadow smeared on puffy eyelids above pale blue eyes— a tacky, crayoned setting for the ravages of age. I wondered what made me think one bit of it was going to be easy.

Maybelline could be so simple-minded!

"Because," I tried again. "I'm not staying in this house, so you certainly can't stay with me." Maybelline blinked a confused tattoo, and my cool resolve threatened to crumble.

"I can't afford the upkeep any longer, can't pay the taxes on it, even. So you have to find someplace else to live." Those last words almost caught in my throat, but at long last she looked as if she understood a little of what I was saying. And it was all so hard for me, especially because Maybelline was so convinced that the Lord Jesus Himself had planned everything out for us.

In Person.

She had more questions, of course. Maybelline never did know when enough was enough, but I answered them the best I could, telling her that Henry's investments weren't bringing in the return we'd planned on, and that such a big house was awfully expensive to keep up. I gave her all the details of everything that needed to be done to the house, though it rankled me to do it, and when I was finished, I thought perhaps she had settled down a bit and wasn't going to keep on prying. I was thinking that we'd both gotten over the initial shock of it—of me saying it and of her hearing it.

She went right back to her praying, and I sat there on the familiar porch, feeling more tired than I had ever felt in my life, listening to her familiar mumbling and looking out at the front yard, watching for that exact moment of twilight falling. Because in summer, the dark happens so suddenly, almost in the blink of an eye. Always reminded me of the old Fox Theater in downtown Atlanta— that big, purple curtain coming down, and the light still flickering out of the projector. So much like twilight coming down in the summertime, with a big bruise coming over everything and the flickering of lightning bugs going in and out of the azalea bushes.

Without warning, a sad feeling came over me, but there was something almost familiar about it at the same time. Well, with what I'd been through and with all the worrying I'd done about it, it was no wonder I felt so sad and dizzy. Then I realized with a shock what it was—the Great Mystery come back on me, come back to haunt me in my old age and jump on me and chew me up, now that I was old and tired and everything was going wrong. That old feeling and my finding out it was still there, even after all those years. Like a cloud that passes in front of the sun.

And as if that weren't bad enough all by itself, I thought I heard someone singing, just as clear as a bell:

Coming home to Jerusalem, my Lord,
Coming right on up the front steps
To my Lord!
He will wipe away my tears,
He will smile away my fears,
Praise Jerusalem!
I'm coming to my Lord!

Nearly scared me to death, that singing did. Because it sounded so close, just like whoever was singing was sitting right there on the porch with us. Thought for a minute it was Maybelline, but it certainly didn't sound like her. Not one bit. And besides, Maybelline was still mumbling to the Lord Himself, and she didn't seem to have heard a thing. So there I was, all alone with it, listening and wondering who was singing that old song, and I must have been wondering so hard that I didn't notice when I started sliding away down those long-sounding words to some faraway place where time was like a wave foaming and curling and slipping backwards down a slanted shore.

Back then, I didn't know it was nothing to be afraid of—only memories. I know that now, and maybe I also know that when we come to a certain time in life, we remember things out of the past that we're wise enough only now to figure out. But back then, I didn't know, and that's why it was so surprising for me to land smack dab in an August morning all those long years ago and me just a child again and wearing that pretty blue cotton frock I always liked so much, the one with ruffles on the bodice and a sash Mama could tie into the prettiest bow.

15

Mama and me riding all the way out to the end of Old Quaker Road to get Tulie, who's coming to help clean up my Great-Aunt Kate's house. Because Camp Meeting starts tomorrow—that's when we all move out to Mount Horeb Camp Ground for two whole weeks—and Great-Aunt Kate says she can't stand to leave the house in such a fix. So that's why she's got Tulie coming.

A special kind of morning, with shafts of light coming through the pine trees so gentle and timid-like and the air so sweet, almost like perfume to breathe, but knowing it won't last, that by afternoon, it will be just another hot, endless day in an unbroken chain of hot, endless summer days. But an August morning in flat-baked South Georgia can fool you like that—starting out like it's going to be something special, but always ending up the same.

Tulie's crooked house squatting under a big chinaberry tree that stands right in the middle of a cornfield, and Mama humming as we drive along, watching for that tree sticking up out of the corn so we can find the tiny road—no more than a path, really—that turns off the Old Quaker Road and then goes back through a field of green corn shoulder-high to a tall man and planted almost all the way up to Tulie's porch steps. The sun just up and light coming through the corn rows so that shadows go all the way across the swept yard. Just like the stripes on a tiger's back.

Tulie standing by the steps waiting for us and wearing an apron and a red rag that's tied around and around her head, and when she sees our car, she jumps a little and starts in to wiping her hands on the apron, just as if she's been thinking so hard about scrubbing Great-Aunt Kate's floors that her hands are already wet.

And children—so many children—on the steps. Little black sparrows on a fence rail.

One little boy just as naked as the day he was born, sitting with his knees spread apart like he doesn't know he's naked at all and with his stomach swollen in a most peculiar way and poking out so far that it hangs down between his knees. A strange-looking plug for a belly button and a funny, fat worm in the shadow below.

And me staring and staring at him, but not saying a word, because even as little as I am—not more than six or seven—knowing already that there are things in this world you don't say anything about and being pretty sure this is one of them. Because Mama sees me staring at him, so she reaches over and pats my knee, and that's how I know for sure.

Tulie gets in the backseat, smiling and bobbing her head up and down and making a laughing sound deep in her throat.

16

Mama says, "Tulie, you be sure and close that door good and hard. We don't want you falling out." Tulie must think it's the funniest thing she's ever heard in her entire life, because she grins so hard she almost wriggles all over, and the whole time, her head nods up and down, up and down, just like her neck's gone plumb crazy.

"Yas'm! Yas'm!" she chortles, grabbing the door handle with both hands and slamming the door so hard that the whole car rocks, and grinning so big that I can see her thick gums and two teeth growing out of them, one sticking down out of the top and one sticking up from the bottom—brown and crooked, like two lonely tree stumps leaning over in red clay. Her head still bobbing up and down, up and down. And the whole time, the children on the steps, watching.

At the first movement of the car, Tulie sticks her head out of the window and waves to the children, who break into wide smiles and roll their eyes, as if they have never seen anything quite as funny and exciting as Tulie riding away in a car.

"Y'all be good!" Tulie calls to them as we drive away.

"Are all of them your children, Tulie?" Mama asks after we bounce our way back down the path and turn onto the road once again. Something about the question sends Tulie into another fit of laughter.

"Nawm," she finally sputters. "Only fo'ub'em. Others grandchirren."

Once again, I glimpse the stumplike teeth and the thick gums before they disappear behind the heavily ridged, black lips.

"How many are there—all together?" Mama asks, prompting more laughter from Tulie.

"'Bout seben, I thinks. Yas'm. 'Bout seben."

"Why, Tulie, don't you know?" Mama's voice sounds surprised, but in such a sweet and gentle way, I know she isn't one bit surprised at all.

"'Bout seben," Tulie says again, and she laughs and laughs.

Mama laughs, too, the softest kind of laugh, and she looks over at me with her pretty blue eyes, but something else is in her glance at me, something I don't figure out until much later that afternoon.

Because right after dinner at noontime, we go and take naps—grownups too—which is the way things are done at Great-Aunt Kate's in the summer. But of course, Tulie keeps on working, because that's what she's supposed to do. She eats her dinner out on the back porch, washes her dishes under the pump in the backyard, and then leaves her dishes in a neat little stack on the back steps before she comes inside and goes back to scrubbing the linoleum that runs the whole long length of the hallway. And while she scrubs, she starts singing that song:

17

Coming home to Jerusalem, my Lord,
Coming right on up the front steps
To my Lord!
He will wipe away my tears,
He will smile away my fears,
Praise Jerusalem!
I'm coming to my Lord!
(I'm coming-g to my Lord-d-d-d!)

Great-Aunt Kate, who is so quiet and cool that she can even take a nap without mussing up a hair on her head, goes to her bedroom at the back of the house. Mama and I go stretch out on the cool top sheet on the high bed in the front bedroom, which is where we always stay when we come to see Great-Aunt Kate.

It was Mama's room when she was just a baby and all the way up until she married my daddy and moved to Savannah. Because her mama—my grandmama—lived here long before Great-Aunt Kate and Great-Uncle Albert came to live with her. Grandmama passed on, but Mama still kept some of her things in the big chifforobe of her room—a little pair of painted-silver dancing shoes, and a doll of hers from when she was just a little girl like me, and letters my daddy wrote to her before they were married. "Love letters," Mama calls them. Whenever we come, she always opens the chifforobe and shows me those things all over again, just as if I've never seen them before, and sometimes she reads some of the letters to me. In one, my daddy says, "If we ever have a little girl, I hope she will look just like you." But of course, that hasn't happened and it isn't going to. But I wish it would, because Mama is so beautiful and so fine, that if only I could look like her, I wouldn't want for another thing in all creation. Fine, bold nose. Soft brown hair. High and very noble forehead and beautiful blue eyes.

But my hair is straight as a stick and a terrible carrot-red color to boot, my eyes are muddy green, and there isn't a single place on me where you can put your little finger and not be touching a dozen freckles. My front teeth are way too big for my face, and they stick out. But Mama is beautiful.

So we are lying there in the front bedroom with all the shades drawn down against the sun and with the fan humming, and we are very quiet so as not to disturb Great-Aunt Kate's nap. And in the drawer of the chifforobe is a letter that says what kind of little girl my daddy really wanted.

But I am also thinking about how glad I am that Carol Ann isn't there, that she has to spend all day long across the street at Miss Dolly's house, getting a permanent. Because things are ever so much nicer when Carol Ann isn't around.

Mama says for me not to worry about Carol Ann, that she's the kind of child a lady has when she waits too long to become a mama, like Great-Aunt Kate did. I've always wanted to ask Mama if that means getting to have blonde hair and real dimples, like Carol Ann has, but I never have. But somehow, it makes me feel a little better that Carol Ann isn't the kind of little girl my daddy wanted, either.

Then I start listening to the sound of Tulie's scrub brush going back and forth across the linoleum in the hallway and to the song she's singing—"wipe away my tears and smile away my fears"—and to the hum of the fan, and somehow, the hum and the sound of the scrub brush and the singing all get to going together pretty well.

The next thing I know, I am waking up. I must have slept for a very long time, because Mama and Great-Aunt Kate are both up and talking in low voices in the other room.

Mama says, "She says there are seven, but that many were sitting out on the steps, and I saw a big, grown girl watching from inside the house—Tulie's daughter, maybe, or granddaughter—and she had a baby in her arms and a child standing beside her big enough to see over the windowsill."

"Yes." Great-Aunt Kate clucks her tongue. "It's downright pitiful. Children keep on coming, and they can't even feed the ones they have."

"Some of them didn't even have clothes on," Mama says. "But I didn't see a sign of a man anywhere. Where are the men?"

"Around somewhere . . . obviously," Great-Aunt Kate sniffed.

"Isn't there anything anybody can do?"

"No, but we've tried. Even got the preacher from AME Church to go out there one time to see about it, but the men came out of nowhere and scared him off. He never even had time to get out of his car. All kinds of bad things going on—still going on. Murders, even. And worse." Great-Aunt Kate's voice drops down to a whisper. "Fathers bothering their own daughters. That kind of thing. And if the women get any money, the men take it away from them and go get drunk with it and come back in the night. Makes it even worse for the women who work and try to have a little something. That's why I always give Tulie some clothes and some flour. Something she can really use and the men won't take away from her. There's children hungry out there. I'm sure of it."

About that time, they hear me opening the bedroom door, and they stop talking right away. But I've heard enough to know what it is Mama's glance said that morning: that Tulie's family isn't like a real family, where there's a real daddy and the children all have pants to wear. But even when I know what it is, it's all just words. Until later.

19

2

Maybelline's voice and words without meaning. Soft vibrations and time roaring back into the breach, sweeping me back to the porch and the deep twilight and the here and now.

What on earth! Hardening of the arteries? A dream, maybe? Even that singing I heard at first?

Something about it so real yet from so very long ago. Even down to knowing somehow that it skipped over some part of what happened. Just like someone bumping a record player so the needle skips over Mama and me taking Tulie back home that long-ago summer evening and bounces over to us *coming back from Tulie's house again and Mama saying not a single word all the way.*

When we get back to Great-Aunt Kate's, the first thing I see is Carol Ann sitting in the porch swing and with her head all-over curly, just loaded to the hilt with springy, blonde corkscrews, and when she sees us drive up, she tosses her head so that all the curls go to dancing, like springs or something.

When we come up onto the porch, Mama says very politely, "Your hair looks very nice, Carol Ann." But I wrinkle up my nose because the smell of Carol Ann's permanent pervades the entire porch—a sharp, acrid smell in the hot, breathless air.

I wait until Mama has gone inside.

"You stink!" I whisper to Carol Ann and then run inside.

That evening, Great-Aunt Kate fixes a cold supper of ham and potato salad and little bitty cheese biscuits with fig preserves. But I can't eat a bite.

And all Great-Aunt Kate wants to talk about is how pretty Carol Ann's permanent turned out.

Later, when I am in bed and they think I can't hear them, Great-Aunt Kate says to Mama, "What is the matter with her?"—and of course, she

20

means me. That's right after Carol Ann sticks her head through the door-
way to the front bedroom, whispers loudly to me, "Baby! Baby! Go to
bed early!" and then disappears.

"I expect she's upset over those children," Mama says. "It was certainly
enough to upset anyone."

"She'll get over it," Great-Aunt Kate said. "It's just the way it is, that's
all. What I don't understand is why she has to be so nasty to Carol Ann
all the time."

I am thinking, Well, I don't know why either, but I do. That's for certain.

Finally, I sleep. But during the night I wake up, thinking I can't breathe.
Thinking I'm one of the little black birds all curled up in a corner of the
dark, crooked room where the windows are open to the night and to all
the things with shiny eyes and sharp teeth that creep around in the sad
shade, lying in wait for little birds whose toes are curled stiff and cold
around invisible branches.

Mama, sleeping beside me, reaches over and pats my back, so soft and
slow, for the longest kind of time.

"It's okay, sugar. Mama's here. Just go on back to sleep."

And I do. All those long years ago.

"What's going on here?" My own voice. "Why, it's just like going
to a motion picture show, only when you try to get out of your
seat, something's holding you down."

Took me a few seconds to realize I'd spoken aloud. Because I
certainly didn't mean to.

But Maybelline didn't hear me, because she was still talking to
Jesus, saying, "Lord, you just gotta help us. Please, Lord!"

What on earth was she babbling about now, I wondered. And
what on earth was happening to me? Was I going to turn out just
like Grandmama did when she got old? Talking about things that
aren't real and wandering around in the yard at night, looking for
people who've been dead and gone for years and years, and always
begging someone to take me back to a house that fell down and
turned to dust years ago?

And who on earth was that naked little boy sitting on my front
steps!

But then I realized he wasn't really there, that he was just flot-
sam from the diminishing wave. Still, it all clung to me so com-

pletely that I thought I could see beams of sunlight coming through the cornstalks and blazing across the deep twilight of the porch.

And out of the light, Maybelline's mutterings suddenly bursting into shouts. Liked to have scared me to death, what with everything I'd just been through. Her shouting like a crazy woman: "PRAISE THE LORD! We'll go to Jerusalem! That's what we'll do!"

Yelling like she'd just stumbled on the secret of eternal life.

"What?" I asked, irritated.

"Jerusalem!" she yelled again. "I been sitting here praying and praying to beat the band, saying, 'Oh, my dear Lord, please tell me what to do!' And now the Lord done give me the answer!"

Before I could ask what on earth she was yelling about, I noticed the 'done give' part, that rapturous, uneducated speech into which Maybelline was prone to lapse in moments of her religious fervor. Of course, I was being polite when I called it that. In truth, I thought of it more as a religious hysteria.

"We'll go to Jerusalem! Find my granddaddy's old house and live there. Hasn't a soul been in it for years and years. Why, no one will even know we're there—or care, if they did know."

"Jerusalem?" *Praise Jerusalem, I'm coming to my Lord!*

"Jerusalem, Georgia, Miss Amelia. Up in Jefferson County."

"Why on earth would you want to go there?"

"Not me," she protested. "We! And we gotta go because there's nothing else we can do. And besides, the Lord's done told us to do it."

"Do it?"

"You said yourself we got to move out of this house. Said we got to find somewhere else to live. Got to," she emphasized and started pulling her chair across the porch and even closer to me than it had been before, so that she was only a few scant inches away. *Oh, please! Not now!* I thought desperately, but she was already jammed right up next to me, eyes glittering and hand descending out of the half-light to rest on my arm.

"Please listen," she begged. "I don't know what on earth the Lord had in mind when He sent me to be with you, but send me, He certainly did. And I'm not about to leave you. Besides, like I told you, He done showed us the way!" Her voice rose in jubilation. "And the Lord will lead us every step!" She finished in something akin to a howl.

Somehow or other, I could picture myself and Maybelline walking down a country lane, marching along in a silent tempo behind a life-sized, cardboard Jesus cut out of a revival fan and with "Granger's Funeral Parlor" written across His cardboard back. And thinking: What? Leave this house? Follow Him down a country lane that cuts between fallow fields baking in the August sun?

Maybelline kept on. "I been sitting here, thinking and thinking, and praying and praying. Thinking about maybe you could go live with that cousin of yours in Covington."

"Carol Ann?" Never!

"But I know you don't want that. So here's the answer. The Lord said for us to go to Jerusalem." She paused for a moment. "And don't you go wrinkling up your nose like that. 'Cause that's what we got to do. Or nothing," she said in finality.

Or nothing? How could that be? I was thinking. Nothing. Never been such a thing in this town as somebody has no kin to go to and no place to live. Except for someone like Maybelline. Why, I'd been thinking so hard just about having to leave this house that I hadn't thought about having to find someplace else to go.

Because I couldn't just live on the streets! The terrible image came then of me, weak and unable to stand, crumpled against the corner wall of that five-and-ten-cent store on Main Street while the good, upstanding people of the town stepped carefully past me, whispering, "She used to be such a fine lady." The sun-heated bricks of the storefront burned into my back, and from under the drooping rim of my hat, I peered obliquely up at the store window where an armless mannequin tiptoed endlessly on a field of dead flies. And all that right across the street from the bank where Henry used to be the second vice president. Right across the street.

Never! I'd rather be dead!

That strange thought burst into my mind just like an imp, shouted "Ta! Da!" and did a deep bow to me. And it was certainly a possibility, that was. They could find me stone cold in the high mahogany bed where I had slept beside Henry for all those thirty-seven years. Find me alone, chaste and pure and cool, and wearing an immaculate white batiste nightgown with lace at the cuffs and the neckline. And my hair deeply waved and neatly arranged. High and pure and untouchable. "What a fine lady she was," they would say. And not even notice the Great Mystery where it crouched on the floor at the foot of my bed, snuffling. And besides, what else was there for me to do? Have someone take me in? Charity? Like Edna did for Maybelline, for Heaven's sake?

"Where is this Jerusalem?" I was so surprised to hear myself asking Maybelline, and at the sound of the words, the delicate image of my body in the high bed faded away like someone turning down a radio in a distant room. And the vision of my being deposited in Edna's parlor like an old child nobody wanted any longer vanished in a shudder of revulsion.

"Jefferson County," Maybelline said. "Only about two hundred, maybe two hundred fifty miles north of here. Just a little bitty town, and my granddaddy's house is out another good three or four miles. It's where I was thinking about going when I came here . . ." Maybelline's voice faltered a little. ". . . when I came here so unexpected-like that time. Thought I'd go on up to Jerusalem once I got enough money together to get me a bus ticket. Find his house and live there." Her face suddenly brightened and the penciled eyebrows shot up. "But when I got saved, the Lord done told me to come live with you." Her eyes swam in tears of remembrance.

And I was thinking: Well, if it's His will to take my very own house away from me and send me traipsing off at my age to some God-forsaken little one-horse town to live in some old deserted shack, I certainly hope I get more out of it than I did out of His getting Maybelline to come live with me! Got nothing but vexation from that!

"How far did you say the house is from town?" Not caring, but it was something to say.

"Not very far. And we would have your car so we could get back and forth to town for groceries and such as that. Best of all, the folks who own the house—all my cousins and me who've inherited it down through the generations—pitch in together to pay the taxes. And they don't amount to much anyway, because it's farmland."

"And you propose that we let others pay for where we'll be living?" I sniffed. Because I was feeling very angry at Maybelline right at that time, but I couldn't have told anyone why.

"Well, I got a little bit put by," Maybelline said. "And we can have a good, big garden and grow our own food. That will save even more money. And I can get work. If there's not already a beauty parlor in town, why I'll start one myself. But whatever happens, the Lord has done made a way for us. I know He has!"

"Then why hasn't He made a way for us to stay here?" I shot back. Because it was really disgusting the way Maybelline talked about God just like He spent all day sitting at the controls of a big machine, working the cables and pulling the levers on every little thing.

"I don't know, Miss Amelia," Maybelline said. "But there's a reason for it. A very good reason."

Well, I certainly recognized that maddeningly patient tone Maybelline could use whenever she spelled out what the Lord Himself had told her to do. Those slow, clear, and distinct words, like she thought I was a deranged child or someone who can't understand simple English.

Nothing to do right then but tolerate that maddeningly patient voice, just the way I had to tolerate it from that simpleton youngster, Little Tommy, down at the bank. Him sitting there behind his daddy's big mahogany desk, all puffed up and trying to act important, and wearing a shirt with a collar too big for him so that he looked just like a little boy dressing up in his papa's clothes. And his tie crooked to boot.

But his papa certainly wouldn't have answered my questions so blunt-like. He wouldn't have had the impropriety to come right out and ask me if I couldn't borrow the tax money from relatives, for Heaven's sake! Besides which, there was no one left. Not a one, except for Carol Ann. God forbid!

No, Big Tommy—Lord rest his soul—would have told me not to worry about a thing. That he'd take care of it out of respect for what all Henry had done for the town for all those long years. But now Big Tommy's gone. And these youngsters! What do they know?

Maybelline was still talking, and I struggled to catch up with her, because the way things were going, I knew I'd better listen or there was no telling what Maybelline would come up with. And whatever it was, I had a terrible feeling that I was going to be stuck with it, because it looked like the only choice was between that and the white batiste nightgown, the quiet bed, and my flesh as hard and cold as stone.

"I haven't been back there since I was just a little girl," Maybelline was saying. "But I sure do remember that house, like it was just yesterday. What it looked like and exactly where it was. Off the state highway a bit, where big chinaberry trees grow in between two plowed fields and a dirt road under the trees—more a tractor path than anything—and it going on back and then curving around until you come to the house."

Maybelline's voice slowed and softened, as if she were dreaming, and I was sitting there listening to her and feeling so dizzy and thinking, how could I leave this house? Leave where I've lived most of my life and go off into the countryside, watching for a dirt road under some chinaberry trees. *Where Tulie's crooked house is waiting and all those children sitting on the steps.*

"What I want to know," I said aloud, "is what happened to those children anyway?" I didn't mean to say it, but there it was, and this time, Maybelline heard it.

"Children? Haven't been children there in a long time. Nobody there, as a matter of fact. Not since Grandpapa passed on. Because you see, it was left to him and his four brothers and sisters in the first place by their mama and papa. And when all those four brothers and sisters were gone, it got divided up betwixt all their children—twenty or so of them, all owning it back then. And then to the children's children. Why, nobody knows how many of them own it now. Hundreds, could be. And I'm one of them, through my mama. I'm one of the people owns it, and I even have a receipt for my part of the taxes. Three dollars and seventy-six cents."

"Oh, Heavens!" My words were no more than a low moan, but enough to set Maybelline's hand to patting my arm.

"It'll be okay, Miss Amelia," she crooned. "Why, it will even be a great adventure for us." The enthusiasm in her voice wasn't quite convincing. "We can be like pioneers and live off the land."

I had a vision of myself wearing a sunbonnet and drawing a great, wooden bucket of water up from a well, pulley squeaking and rope straining so that crystal droplets of water popped off from it and shimmered in the sunlight.

"Besides," Maybelline added, "I don't think you'd want to stay here in this town. Not without living in this big house. But we could, you know. Get us a room at Mrs. Hodges' and fix it up real nice."

Sure, I thought. Hang glass beads for curtains and put plaster clowns from the Dollar Store on the lamp table, and people passing by on the sidewalk looking up at the window and whispering, "She used to be such a fine lady!" No!

"No."

"And, too, if you was to sell this house, why you'd have plenty of money for another house, a smaller one. You'd have money left over."

Stay in this town and not live in this house? Hear them say, "She lives in a little shanty now, out on the highway, but she used to be a fine lady who lived in that big white house on State Street. What a shame about her."

"No."

"Well, then, this is the only way to do it."

And she was right. It was the only way to do it gracefully and in good taste. Go away to someplace where nobody knew me, nobody to whisper about me behind my back and feel sorry for me and say what a great lady I used to be.

"We can do it," Maybelline said.

"Yes," I finally agreed. "We can do it."

Yes, leave my home and go off to goodness-knows-where with Maybelline, of all people, and live in some old shack that's been standing empty for half a century.

Good Heavens! What was to become of me?

3

Well, we certainly made a pretty pair that evening, me sitting there just like a stone, listening while Maybelline hummed "Where He Leads Me I Will Follow," with her head back and her eyes closed and smiling just like she was the happiest person in the whole world.

But I certainly didn't feel happy. To tell the truth, I felt sick as a dog. It had all been too much—saying out loud to Maybelline what I'd been worrying about and then her half-baked idea about us going off together. And especially, the way I'd slipped backward in time. Not like just remembering something but like being there. All over again.

I knew I had to get ahold of myself, else I was going to start crying and get all kinds of unwelcome attention from Maybelline. So I tried not to listen to her humming, listened instead to the sounds I'd heard all my whole life right there on that same front porch. Quiet and peaceful sounds that had always been there and would always be there, even when I was gone: crickets chirping in the grass near the quiet street, and a dog barking far off, and from around back, tree frogs singing in the two big oak trees that stood between the backyard and the Baptist Church on the corner of the next street.

The very same sounds I heard early that long-ago morning when Mama and I came here, that summer of Tulie and the children. And knowing even then that the Great Mystery was coming, just as it always came. But something much more about it that summer than had been before.

It was the first time I started calling it by any name at all, the first time I found out enough about it—even things I didn't want to know—to put a name on it. Because we came here to Great-Aunt Kate's house—this house—that summer, and I didn't even know we were coming. Because if I had, maybe I could have done something—anything—to try and keep the Great Mystery away, keep it from staring at me from behind the dark chifforobe at night. Or keep it from making creaky noises on the hall floor when it came. But never face-to-face with it, never walking right into that deep bruise until that summer when I already knew there was something wrong.

And now having it come back on me, and all because of having to leave this house, where everything happened. Sitting there on the porch and knowing that the day was coming when I would sneak away like a thief in the night. Walk across the porch for the last time and down the three little steps to the porte cochere where the car waits and back it out of the driveway for the last time, being careful not to run over the caladiums Maybelline planted way too close to the driveway. Just as clear as day, I could see it, the time of leaving. See the pre-dawn darkness and feel the night-cool air so sweet before the blazing sun could gain the edge of the horizon and heave itself up and out of the darkness.

Because Mama wakes me before daylight, that day of Tulie and the children. She comes into my room and doesn't even turn on my lamp, but just touches my shoulder, and the first thing I notice is the faint shape of her big, brown suitcase sitting on the floor just inside my bedroom door. That's when I know something's wrong. Again.

"Be real quiet, sugar," she says. Beyond the panes of glass criss-crossed by the sheer white curtains at my window, there is only the darkness.

"But it's nighttime."

"Let's be real quiet," she whispers. "Why, it's not nighttime at all. It's morning, and the sun will be up real soon." And immediately, the old thrill of waking up before the world, to the perfume of sunless air and the expectancy of the light coming.

"What's wrong?"

"Why, nothing's wrong." But the voice is too bright. "You get dressed; we're going on a little drive."

While I put on my socks and shoes, she takes my suitcase out of the closet and in one motion, sweeps my dresses—hangers and all—out of the closet, folds them over once, and puts them in the suitcase. I know then that she's in a hurry, so I slip my dress over my head—the blue dress with the ruffles on the bodice—just as she snaps the suitcase shut.

"Now be real quiet," she reminds me again and opens the door. She carries both suitcases, and I hold onto the back of her dress and tiptoe

29

silently behind her down the long, dark hallway and through the swinging door into the kitchen. Through the window, a glow from the light over the garage makes a shining path for us to walk on, right across the kitchen's black-and-white tile floor. Then she opens the door quietly. We go down the steps and tiptoe across the gravel driveway to where Mama's car is parked under the pecan tree.

The inside of the car is dark and somehow cool and very expectant. Mama closes the door on my side ever so quietly and then bumps it with her hip to shut it all the way. She gets behind the wheel, and her keys make a thin, tinkling sound in the dark, and the engine starts right up. She shifts into first gear and lets out on the clutch so fast that the tires spin just a little bit on the gravel. We roll forward out of the driveway, and then the headlights shine on the black top of Old Savannah Road. Mama lets out her breath a little, as if something important is over and done with.

"Let's go see Great-Aunt Kate," she says, and now I know why her voice is so bright. She's trying to make it sound like a picnic or something because she knows what it means to go there, for me, and when she makes it sound like that, I know she's really asking me not to let it happen this time.

But no matter how hard I try, I know it will happen. Especially when there's trouble again between Mama and my stepdaddy. And, of course, there is. That's why we're so quiet about leaving and why we're going away. I should have known it was coming, because for the past few days, Mama and my stepdaddy have gotten to be so very polite with each other, saying only careful things, like "Please pass the butter," and "thank you." So it's no surprise to me.

But going to see Great-Aunt Kate IS a surprise. And here's that sad feeling, a feeling that allows for all kinds of terrible and nameless things. Groves of trees with deep shade in them, and open fields of gray plants stunted in the hot sun, and the lonely little town with gray buildings, all of them very old and empty and nearly falling down now. Once upon a time, they were places where people laughed and talked together and bought things like cheese and salve and thread for sewing pretty dresses. But now, the insides of the high-ceilinged buildings are cool and dark and empty, somehow more than just very far away from the white glare of the sun. Maybe like a dream someone is having, and you can walk into the dream, even though it's not your own. The old buildings with tall grass growing against the wood outside and the inside filled with some kind of a terrible silence. Or something like that.

But, then, that's why I finally started calling it the Great Mystery. Because I could never tell it exactly the way it really is.

In the dark, Mama reaches out and pats my knee because she knows about the thing I can't say, and I watch through the car window at the quiet houses we pass by, houses that have people in them who are sound asleep. Much more than just memories of people who are dead and gone. And behind us, the dark and silent house we have left.

As soon as we turn onto the highway, the street lights are gone. Only darkness, and weeds on either side of the highway where our headlights shine, and gray-black grass sweeping past the car. Once in a while, a glimpse of glowing eyes in the grass beside the road. Even though I know for sure that it's the beginning of the Great Mystery that's going to come and get hold of me and do terrible things—even knowing that, being awake when the world is still asleep is something so wonderful, I can hardly stand it. The way it is before light, when it's the very first day of creation. And watching it happen.

Stars still out, and daylight coming so fast that the sky is already a different shade of dark from the land, a softer black, almost a gray, and tinged with pink I can't even see unless I blink my eyes at it very fast. The air still night-cool.

By the time we begin getting close to Great-Aunt Kate's house, Mama does just what I know she will do—starts pointing out places where important things happened to her in her girlhood. No matter what she shows me, she always starts it out by saying, "When I was a girl . . ."

First thing is a little white church sitting right beside the highway.

"When I was a girl, I came to this church for all-day-singing-and-dinner-on-the-ground one time. Because my best friend lived on this side of town, so I usually never got to see her except at school. But one weekend, my mama let me go home with her after school on Friday, and I spent the whole weekend with her, and this is where we came to church. Her mama brought the best sweet potato pie I ever tasted. Why, you never saw so much food in your life! Fried chicken and biscuits and high, white coconut cakes, and whole big washtubs filled with lemonade and big chunks of crystal-clear ice for keeping it cold."

Of course, by the time Mama finishes telling me about it, we've long since passed the church, so that when she says, "This is where we went to church," we are passing an open field. And then we come to the next point of interest. Of course, I know all of them by heart because whenever we come to Great-Aunt Kate's, Mama tells me the same things all over again. But she likes telling me, and I like seeing it happen over and over again, so it's all right.

31

"And this old church," she says as we pass another one—only this one is not painted at all, but only weathered, gray old boards and a rusted tin roof—"is where my papa pulled up in his horse and buggy one spring afternoon because he saw a terrible storm coming. The sky turned just as black as midnight, even though minutes before, it was a high, clear noon-time with not a cloud. But a big, black cloud came up out of nowhere, and so fast, he never even saw it coming until all of a sudden, the wind came up and everything went dark and strange-looking. So he whipped up his horse and made for that little church lickety-split, because it was the only building around for miles and miles.

"The clouds boiling in the sky, black and blue and purple and with streaks of green, even. And the wind gusting hard and as hot as if some-body'd opened a big oven door. It was getting so bad so fast, he said he'd already decided that he'd unhitch the horse and lead him right into the church. But by the time my papa got there, the wind was so fierce, he knew he'd never get the buggy unhitched in time, so he drove the horse and buggy right in between the church and that high embankment."

Of course, by now the church is probably a mile behind us, so there's no chance of my seeing the embankment, but I know the story already, so I knew to pay attention to it before Mama got to that part about the storm.

"How the wind did howl and blow that day! A big, black tornado it was, biggest had ever been. Lots of people lost their barns and some of them their homes, but Papa was safe. And his horse and buggy, too."

I shiver every time she tells me that particular story, what with the wind and the purple clouds streaked with green, but these are the things I have to get used to all over again every time we go to Great-Aunt Kate's: the dead things that happened a long time ago and that sit in the back of my mind, growling like a mean dog. And that make the hair on the back of my neck stand up.

Daylight coming full now and grass on the land and eerie strips of white, sandy soil in between the rows of plants in the fields, spokes of a big wheel turning. And a low, soft, gray cloud bank on the horizon that looks like a mountain far away. Looks so much like a mountain that I wonder who lives there and what they are doing so early this morning.

Then, a little farther on, we pass an old store that sits far back in a field, and I almost miss seeing it because it's all covered over with kudzu vines. But it's another one of Mama's important places she needs to tell me about.

"When I was a girl, my mama and I walked to that little store one time, and she bought us johnnycakes and cheese for a picnic, and we ate right

32

out there under a big live oak tree that used to stand directly in front of the little store. And my mama told me that when she was a little girl, she used to walk past that very store on her way to school and go in to trade two eggs for a new pencil."

I see my grandmama, and she's a little girl, walking along with two white eggs in her hand and wearing a pink dress with a white pinafore over it and her hair in long braids down her back.

When we get to Great-Aunt Kate's, I find out two terrible things: One is that it's time for Camp Meeting. And the other is that Carol Ann's going to be just as nasty to me as she always is. Finding out that it's time for Camp Meeting is a complete surprise, but Carol Ann's being so nasty certainly isn't. She always starts right in on me first thing, because she acts very grown-up and snooty about everything. Of course, Carol Ann's only about four or five years older than me, but everybody acts like she's already a grown-up young lady. But I know better.

"You're crazy as a bedbug," she always hisses at me.

And sometimes, I almost believe her. Because for some strange reason, every time we come to Great-Aunt Kate's or to Camp Meeting, I stop behaving. But I don't do it on purpose. It just seems to happen—like I'm living in a story somebody has already made up, so that no matter how much I say I won't cause trouble, I do it anyway and don't even realize it. And the next thing that comes in the story is Mama wringing her hands and saying to Great-Aunt Kate, "What on earth am I going to do with that child?" And rolling her eyes up to the ceiling as if the answer is something that will drop into her lap if only she can see it floating around up there.

And then Great-Aunt Kate will say, "Well, she's like her father. Got a streak in her so high-blooded and dreamy, can't anybody do a thing about it. Blood will out, I tell you. Blood will out."

Then they shake their heads and smile that strange, sad-but-happy kind of smile they have when they're talking about how difficult I am. Because that's written into the story, too, and what it all really means is that I'm not like them, and my not behaving and my not paying attention and my being what they call "dreamy" all the time is proof positive of that. Because young ladies who know how to behave themselves and how to pay attention are the stamps of my mother's family.

Except for Aunt Nell. She ran away to New Orleans one time and stayed there for two whole weeks before her papa found out where she was and went and brought her back home. That's what makes me think Aunt Nell knows exactly how I feel and probably knows everything there is to know, *too, about the Great Mystery. I tried to talk to her about it once, but I didn't know then what a hard thing it was to say, and Aunt Nell just looked at me in a strange way and then went back to talking to her two little dogs, Nikki and Honey, asking if "Mama's babies" wanted some supper. So I knew right then and there that I couldn't try to talk with her about it either. That maybe she was just as afraid of it all as I am.*

Because all Mama's family is like that—not wanting to talk about things that are hard to talk about. They can go on and on forever about how much mayonnaise to put in the potato salad or whether Mrs. Stone will be at Camp Meeting this year, but as soon as I try to tell them anything out of the ordinary—like how the old store buildings make me feel so sad and empty inside—they just stare at me for the briefest, startled kind of a moment and then scurry back to talking about potato salad or Mrs. Stone again.

"You're crazy as a bedbug," Carol Ann hisses at me that morning as soon as we get there, when Mama and Great-Aunt Kate are in the kitchen, taking the biscuits out of the oven. "Always saying weird things nobody can understand. My mama says it's because your mama has spoiled you rotten."

But that isn't it. Carol Ann is wrong about that. And about other things, too. Because that's right before Mama tells Great-Aunt Kate that we'll be glad to go and pick up Tulie for her. And later on, when Carol Ann hears about what happened, she says Tulie's children are disgusting. But I just think they're sad. Their mama having to go away all day long and leave them sitting on the steps without any pants to wear.

"I wonder whatever happened to those children?"

Goodness! I had done it again. Started in to talking out loud, but not really meaning to. Somehow the way everything was coming back to me like that had gotten me all confused, but I certainly didn't want Maybelline to notice, because she had a way of blowing everything all out of proportion and making every little thing seem like it had something to do with how much I needed "God's redeeming grace," or so she said.

But Maybelline's humming stopped. So she'd certainly heard me.

"Miss Amelia," she said, with that kind of important tone in her voice she always has whenever she's about to tell me what the Lord wants me to do about something. "That's the second time this evening you've said something about some children. What you got on your mind?"

34

And of course, it was a very good question. Sure wished I knew the answer to that myself. Because I really didn't have an idea of what it was making it all come back to me so clear. But I did know that if I wasn't careful in how I answered, she'd take whatever I said and store it away somewhere and use it against me later on, whenever she got another bee in her bonnet about how I needed "saving."

"Oh, some children I saw one summer when I was a child. Colored children." I tried to sound very casual about it, but even then, I knew it wasn't casual. Not one little bit.

"Colored children?" Maybelline repeated, as if she had never heard of such a thing. "How come you thinking about colored children?"

"Oh, I don't know. Just something I hadn't thought of in a long time."

Still trying to sound very off-hand and casual about it.

"What kind of something?"

"Something that bothered me one time. Nothing important."

"You want to let's pray about it?"

So here it was, then. Maybelline's solution to everything.

"No, thank you," I said stiffly. "I certainly don't want to 'let's pray about it.' It was just something that happened one summer when I was a child."

"Well," Maybelline went on, watching me so hard that I knew she was hoping I'd change my mind about the praying. "When I was a little girl was the first time I went to my grandpapa's house in Jerusalem. And that's how I know about it. The one we're going to," she added, unnecessarily. "Big, old house, too," Maybelline went on, leaning her head back and staring up at the porch ceiling. "Two stories. Used to be a stagecoach stop for travelers on the run between Savannah and Augusta. And sometimes, if the weather turned real bad—like in the spring, when storms came up fast and all but washed away the road—travelers had to stay over. That's why my great-grandpapa built such a big house in the first place. Had to have room for the family, of course—seems to me they had five or six children—and then a big room for all the lady travelers and another room for the men travelers. Why, when I went there, all the beds were still in those rooms—three or four double beds in each one. And that's where us children stayed. We had so much fun, me and my cousins, laughing and jumping from one bed to another. And none of the grown-ups said a thing to us about it, except for once when my cousin Sarah fell off the bed and hit the floor—ker-BLAM! And Grandpapa hollered up the stairs, 'Y'all be careful of splinters in that floor.' And that's all anybody said to us, no matter how much noise we made."

I was thinking that probably, they were so deep in moonshine, none of them cared. But beggars can't be choosers, and a beggar was what I was going to be. If I went and lived in someone else's house and probably nothing more than a big shack at that. Just like the tents out to Mount Horeb Camp Ground used to be. Big, old, ugly shacks with cracks in the walls and nothing but sawdust on the floor.

It was just one of the reasons I never liked going to Camp Meeting. Never. But, of course, it wasn't something I ever had any choice about doing. Because everybody in Mama's whole family always went out to Camp Meeting the last two weeks in August.

Back then, I found out it was time for Camp Meeting just about the same time we had all the trouble about Carol Ann the morning we got to Great-Aunt Kate's house.

Because as soon as we get there, Carol Ann gives me the typical, hissed greeting: "You're just as crazy as a bedbug!" Of course, she makes sure to say it only when her mama and my mama can't hear her, and she lets me know she doesn't have time for fooling up with such a baby—that's me—because as soon as breakfast is over, she's going across the street to Miss Dolly's Beauty Parlor to get her a real permanent. She waggles her shoulders when she tells me about it and juts her chin high in the air.

Miss Dolly is the only lady in town who does hairdressing, and of course, she stays very busy with all of it. So getting Carol Ann an appointment, especially in time for Camp Meeting, was like pulling hen's teeth, or so Great-Aunt Kate says. I sure don't care anything about Carol Ann's permanent, but I DO care about having to go to Camp Meeting. First chance I get, I look at Mama, and she has that look on her face that says for me please not to make trouble about it. Great-Aunt Kate doesn't notice this exchange, because she's too busy reminding us that Carol Ann has naturally curly hair, of course, but it just won't behave, and that's the only reason why Carol Ann is getting a permanent. I don't know why, but just knowing that something—anything—about Carol Ann doesn't behave is absolutely wonderful. So we are all sitting at the breakfast table and Great-Aunt Kate is talking about Carol Ann's not-behaving hair, and I just glance at Carol Ann—don't say a single word—but it sets Carol Ann to fuming. She turns as red as a tomato, so red that her eyes shine just like blue neon lights. And I'm not doing a single thing to her, not even crossing my eyes or sticking out my tongue at her or anything, but she just keeps getting redder and redder until all of a sudden she claps her hands over her face and bursts into tears.

"Make her stop staring at me, Mama!" she yells. And then, so fast that we can't even see it happen, she jumps out of her chair and runs from the room. And I haven't done a single thing to her. But to tell the truth, I love it more than anything, seeing her all upset like that. So I know right then and there that the story I'm in is all in place and that I am already not behaving.

We all jump a little when we hear Carol Ann's bedroom door slam shut all the way down at the end of the hall.

"What on earth!" Great-Aunt Kate says, glaring at me like she'd just love to pull my head off. Just like I saw her pull the head off a chicken out in the backyard one summer so she could make a chicken pie out of that poor, scared old hen.

"I didn't do anything!" I protest loudly, and Mama gives me one of her "freezing" looks—a terrible, stone-still, paralyzing stare that can absolutely make time stand still and nail me to the floor right in my tracks.

"Honey, watch your tone of voice," she warns. "You speak to your Great-Aunt Kate with respect."

"Yes'm," I mumble, for I would rather die than to embarrass Mama. "I didn't do anything to Carol Ann," I repeat, speaking softly but hoping that my voice has a kind of dangerous softness to it—like a tiger growling.

Great-Aunt Kate must be satisfied about my innocence, because she stops staring at me, splits open her biscuit, and spoons a great mound of preserves into it.

"Well, I think Carol Ann's getting ready to become a woman." She speaks very slowly, looks at Mama, and raises her eyebrows. "So sometimes she gets a little touchy about things."

"Really?" Mama seems very interested, and now that neither of them is looking at me, I can relax and smile and watch in my imagination where mean old Carol Ann becomes a woman—screams in agony and splits wide open from the head down, just like a July-fly, and a grown woman, big and fat and ugly, steps out, holding her arms up just as if she's done a trick in the circus.

37

"Isn't she a little young for . . . that?" Mama asks, and I can tell that she's trying to sound very casual about it.

"Not at all," Great-Aunt Kate says. "Why I became a woman when I had just turned twelve years of age. And your own mama was only thirteen when it happened to her. So it usually happens very early to the women in our family. We always mature early, you know."

"What is IT?" I venture, and Mama reaches over and pats my knee.

"Never you mind," she says. "Just never you mind." So I don't find out what "becoming a woman" really means, not right then anyhow. But I know from the way Great-Aunt Kate looks at me when she says "in our family" that clearly, it won't be that way for me.

Just then, Carol Ann comes back into the dining room, looking very calm and pale—almost disdainful, I think—and she sits down without a word, puts her napkin back in her lap, and goes to buttering her biscuit just as if nothing happened.

"You all right, sugar?" Great-Aunt Kate asks in a voice that's so soft, it's almost like a cloud.

"Yes'm," Carol Ann manages to whisper, all the time looking fragile and quite sad, and she keeps her head down and doesn't look at any of us. "But you better go to the drugstore and get me . . . something . . . before we go out to Camp Meeting."

Great-Aunt Kate nods almost imperceptibly, and that's the end of it. Because Mama shoots a glance at me that says I'd better not ask, and so I don't.

It's only after we finish breakfast and Carol Ann and I are clearing the table that she looks right at me and smiles what is absolutely the meanest smile I've ever seen in my life.

"What do you have to get at the drugstore?" I ask. "Ugly-Cover-Up Cream?"

"No, stupid," she hisses. "You're too young to know, so just never you mind, baby!"

And when Carol Ann goes across the street to get her permanent, we start getting everything all packed up and ready to move out to the Camp Ground the next day. And then Great-Aunt Kate says she's got Tulie coming to clean the house because she can't bear to move out to Mount Horeb and leave her house in such a fix, and she's still got to run over to the drugstore for Carol Ann, and how on earth is she going to get it all done?

So Mama offers to drive out the Old Quaker Road and get Tulie.

4

"You're falling asleep right in your chair, Miss Amelia." Maybelline's hand on my shoulder was as tentative as if she were afraid my arm might fall off and clatter to the floor.

"We've had us quite an evening, so let's go to bed," she urged too cheerfully. "We can talk more in the morning. I'll tell you all about the house, and you can start thinking about what all you want to take with you when we go."

"Yes," I tried to say, but the word wouldn't come.

Mama waking me up for us to go to Great-Aunt Kate's house? No. Not Great-Aunt Kate's house. This house. Mine. And all that other? A dream? Or is this the dream?

I didn't even have time to get it figured out before Maybelline had steered me inside and to the door of my bedroom.

"You need me to help you?" she asked.

"No, thank you." I tried to pull my arm away from her.

"I think you ought to sell the house," she said, still holding onto my elbow. And that's another completely annoying trait Maybelline has—saying something like that right out of a clear blue sky and then waiting for me to disagree with her so she can come out with some sort of sanctimonious drivel and make it sound like an edict from Heaven. Just like a tacky, old-woman Moses, wearing Pink Passion nail polish and descending the mountain with the Word of God clutched in her hands.

"Sell it?" The words carried no meaning to me. No meaning at all. "Sell what?"

"This house. I think you ought to sell it."

"No. Not sell it. Never sell it."

She surprised me, then, because she didn't contradict me or try to change my mind. I figured she was probably saving that for tomorrow. But her words stayed with me all the time I got on my nightgown and put my shoes in the chifforobe and my glasses on the dresser.

So that when I was finally settled in the high, mahogany bed and lulled by the humming fan that swept the air steadily and rhythmically back and forth in the darkness, the putter of easy days and the peaceful tempo of life came back to me, all wrapped up in the melancholy softness of something that has surely been lost.

No! I couldn't go! Tears threatened to burn holes in the darkness of the quiet room. Old fool! Lying here and crying like a child. Just like a child.

"Sometimes we have to do things we don't want to do." Mama's voice and the soft-spoken but irrevocable words. Because it was exactly what she said to me that summer when I found out we were going to Camp Meeting. But of course, I didn't embarrass her by saying anything in front of Great-Aunt Kate. So I waited until we were in the high bed in the dark room. This room. And I told her I didn't want to go. And she said, "Sometimes we have to do things we don't want to do." I could hear her very voice saying the same thing to me now: "Sometimes . . ."

So like it or not, we all move out to Mount Horeb the very next day. Because it's a tradition for everybody in Mama's family to move—lock, stock, and Bible, Mama says—out to the Camp Ground the last two weeks in August, always the very hottest part of the summer. Me and Mama and Great-Aunt Kate and Carol Ann, of course. And when everything is loaded in the car, and we all pile in, and we're on the way to Mount Horeb Camp Ground, Carol Ann and I are jammed together in the backseat in between all the bed linens and pillows and tablecloths and boxes of pots and pans, and her hot arm is against mine, and she whispers to me, "My mama bought me all new underwear for Camp Meeting. Not a single piece of it's ever been worn before."

I don't answer, because I suddenly realize that the panties I'm wearing that very day have a big hole in them, where the elastic has come away from the fabric.

"Mama says I get all new underwear for Camp Meeting because of you. Because you're so nosy, you'll probably be snooping around in my suitcase, and she doesn't want you telling your mama that I wear raggedy panties."

Still I say nothing, and I try to think something cool and calm so my face won't turn red and reveal to Carol Ann that my own underwear is raggedy. Think of the creek where we get to go swimming sometimes during Camp Meeting, the slow-moving, old black creek that's so deep I don't even know where its bottom is and water so dark, I can't see my feet, even when I'm in water that only comes partway to my knees. And thinking of the creek really works for me, because my face is as cool as can be, even though it's very hot in the backseat of the car, especially with all the pillows and quilts piled high around Carol Ann and me.

She pulls her arm away from where it is pressed against mine.

"You're hot!" she complains.

"What's the matter, sugar?" Great-Aunt Kate calls over her shoulder, and Mama turns her head and looks at me with a look that says for me please not to cause any trouble.

"I'm all hot and sticky, Mama," Carol Ann whines.

"It's just a little ways more," Great-Aunt Kate assures Carol Ann. "And did you remember to bring your new little overnight case Mama bought you?"

Carol Ann smiles. "Yes'm," she chirrups, and then to me she says in a voice level gauged to reach Great-Aunt Kate and Mama, "My mama bought me a overnight case and new bedroom slippers and a jar of Fresh!"

"What's Fresh?" I hate myself for asking, but just that quickly, I forget not to.

"Deodorant," Carol Ann announces in a very self-satisfied and sanctimonious manner.

Mama glances at Great-Aunt Kate and then at me, and almost imperceptibly shakes her head to warn me not to say anything. Because Mama says that Great-Aunt Kate's making Carol Ann "grow up too fast," and that "some day she'll be sorry." And that's what Mama doesn't want me to say anything about.

So I look out the car window and watch the red clay banks along the sides of the road and picture to myself the little wooden shelf in Great-Aunt Kate's and Carol Ann's room at the Camp Ground and see Carol Ann's jar of deodorant sitting on it like a trophy she's gotten for pretending she's a grown-up lady.

41

A few miles farther, and Great-Aunt Kate turns off onto the dirt road that leads to Mount Horeb, looking just the very same way it looked last year and the year before that. And I'll bet it looks just like it did when Mama was a little girl. We go around a curve, and I can see the big cedar trees that grow in the Mount Horeb cemetery and the first wooden "tent" of a long row of them all curved around the hillside and with the tabernacle squatting right in the center, in a shallow valley all covered with fresh-cut grass.

We always come out very early on the first day, because there's work to be done, like airing out the tent and making up the beds and scrubbing out the icebox. New wood shavings are already put down inside the tent and spread outside the front and back doors, and the mattresses all aired out in the sunshine. All the weeds have been cut down and wood stacked high by the cookhouse because Great-Uncle Albert takes care of all that, the week before. But he can't stay out at the Camp Ground like we do, because he works at the mill in town, so he comes out only on Saturday night and then goes back to town on Sunday afternoon.

A small, thin man he is, with a sober face, someone who never says a thing unless somebody asks him something directly, and even then he only nods or shakes his head and keeps on reading his Field and Stream magazine and smoking his pipe. Mama says the only time in her whole life she ever saw him smile was when they all first found out that Great-Aunt Kate was going to have a child. After all those years and her an old lady only a few years younger than my grandmama. Mama says that back then whenever anyone mentioned anything about it around Great-Uncle Albert, he just smiled and smiled around the stem of his pipe and never said a thing, but kept on reading about catching giant salmon in Alaska and hunting wild elk in faraway Wyoming.

I heard Aunt Nell say to Mama one time that she always thought it was positively disgraceful for a lady of Great-Aunt Kate's age to have had a child—meaning Carol Ann. Of course, no one said such a thing to Great-Aunt Kate herself. But Mama said it was all worth it, just to get to see the look on Great-Uncle Albert's face whenever someone said something about it around him.

And now, driving along the narrow dirt road behind all the rickety, old-looking tents and knowing that Carol Ann has a jar of real, grown-up deodorant and that we have to stay for two whole weeks in that funny old wood house—that tent—is almost more than I can bear. Because the tent is like a big barn—with no paint on it and an open hallway all the way down the middle, from the back door right through to the front. And facing the tabernacle, just like all the other tents at Mount Horeb, ten or

42

twelve of them all together, and all built the same way, with rooms like horse stalls on either side of the hallway, and the walls going only partway up because there is no ceiling at all—only the underside of the tin roof way up high, where all the heat gathers and dirt-dobber nests hang that no one can reach. And no floor, except for wood shavings they put down new every year. But the worst of all, as far as I am concerned, is that there isn't even a bathroom, but only a privy, for Heaven's sake. And I don't want to go to Camp Meeting anyway.

It's our family responsibility, Mama says, whenever I tell her I don't want to go. At least, that's what she says whenever Camp Meeting and trouble with my stepdaddy come at about the same time. And besides, coming to Camp Meeting is a tradition, and so it isn't something you have a choice about doing. Because the whole family has always come, even back as far as my great-great-great-grandmother, whose papa was the one who built it in the first place. Ever since then, the tent is always passed down from the oldest daughter of whoever inherited it before to her oldest daughter, and so on. But my mama is her mama's second daughter, so I don't think she will ever inherit it. Not unless Aunt Tyler, who's my mama's older sister, dies without having had any girl babies of her own to pass it to.

But I know that Aunt Tyler is already going to have a little baby, and I am praying hard for it to be a girl so I will never have to worry about owning the tent and taking on all the responsibility of keeping Camp Meeting going on for the family. Because I'm my mama's only daughter and I'm scared to death that it might just all land on ME one of these days.

Because all they ever do at Camp Meeting is go to church all the time, and whenever they aren't in church, then the children are supposed to sit still and be perfectly quiet while the grown-ups talk about the ancestors— people who have been dead and gone for a long time. Talk and talk and talk about them. Sitting around on each others' porches, saying things like, "Your Aunt Bricie's oldest boy was the one they named John Westerly after Bricie's great-grandfather, and he was my husband's mama's oldest brother."

And I just plain-out hate it, with everybody talking about dead people and going to church all the time. Four services every day, starting with the one at seven in the morning and then with another one at eleven. Then some time off for having dinner and a little rest, and another service at three—that's the hottest one of all. And finally, an evening service, which starts at seven and is always the longest. And at every one of these services there's plenty of Bible-thumping and hollering—A-MEN!—and hymn-singing, and the whole time, it's so hot you could just die, and gnats singing in your ears and flying up your nose.

43

And much more, of course. But I'm not sure of what it is, much less of how to say it. Must be it's something more to do with the Great Mystery. Because that's what can't be said.

About the only thing I do like at Camp Meeting is the tabernacle bell. Not that it's a pretty, clear-sounding bell like the one at the church in Savannah—our church. This one is very flat and tinny-sounding, almost like somebody beating on the bottom of an old bucket with a big wooden spoon. Still, there's something in the sound of it I like. How the clanging bounces around in the air, and if the wind is blowing just right, gets lost in the edge of the dark woods behind the tabernacle, and makes me wonder how far away the sound can go into the woods and who—or what— can hear it. Maybe even the Great Mystery, sitting in the edge of the woods and waiting for us all to go to sleep.

But even that doesn't stop me from liking the bell. And too, there's something else about it, something that stays on my skin and makes me remember it—the smell of fresh wood shavings and the odd perfume of oil of citronella, which is what everyone uses for trying to keep the gnats away. Or the pinging sound the tin roof makes when it warms up or cools off, and I can hear that sound again, even when I am in my own bed at my stepdaddy's house and in a room that has screens in the windows and curtains and a real ceiling and a roof that never makes a sound.

And I like getting to see Aunt Nell and Aunt Tyler again. But that's all.

Only I wouldn't let anybody know I like some things about it for anything in this whole world.

About that time, Great-Aunt Kate pulls up and stops the car in the shade of a big chinaberry tree that grows right by the cookhouse at the back of Mama's family's tent. It's the very last one in the long, curving row of tents, except for the "preacher's tent," a newer, painted house with a real floor in it and glass in the windows, sitting off by itself near a big hickory tree. But aside from the preacher's tent, there's not a thing in between our tent and the Mount Horeb cemetery all full of white tombstones, most of them so old you can't even read the writing on them anymore. Almost like somebody trying to tell you something, but you can't understand what it is.

"Let me! Let me!" Carol Ann starts hollering just as soon as the car stops. Great-Aunt Kate smiles and hands her a key that has a string on it, and Carol Ann is out of the car in a flash and running to the back of the tent, to unlock the door and swing it open to where the inside waits for us, dark and hot, like something old and sleepy.

Once inside, Carol Ann bounces from window to window, unlatching the iron hooks that hold down the heavy shutters, and outside, Great-Aunt Kate and Mama lift up the shutters and put in the sticks that will

44

hold them open to the light and to whatever rare breath of air might stray in from where the silent white stones stand in the sun-baked cemetery.

After we unload the car, Mama and I make up the bed in our "room," and I am glad we have a little place all to ourselves, even if the walls only go up a few feet and I have already seen Carol Ann's face pop up over the top of the stall-wall a couple of times. But seeing that Mama is in there with me, her face disappears again. And I ask Mama, "Do I have to go to all the services?" As soon as I ask, I hate myself for having done it because Mama is always so happy to be at Camp Meeting, and she has been humming under her breath and then telling me more "when I was a child" stories about what went on at Camp Meeting when she was just a little girl like me.

Mama probably always liked going to services, but I hate it. Because sitting there on the long, hard, wooden benches makes me feel like I'm in a prison, one all filled with hollering and loud singing and Bible-thumping and hellfire and damnation. And the whole time I have to sit there, I can hear all kinds of things going on in the free places—in the tents behind us. Sounds of dishes rattling and sometimes a voice far away and even the chirping of crickets in the tall grass say "I'm free! I'm free!" But I'm not.

"Well, now that you mention it. . . ." Mama is smiling her secret smile, the one she has only when something good is coming that I don't know about.

"What?"

"Just you wait and see," she says, and smiles and smiles.

So there's nothing else I can do to get the secret out of her, I know. And besides, no matter what the surprise is, I'll like it. Because I always do. And especially if it has something to do with my not having to go to services all the time.

Mama goes out to help Great-Aunt Kate straighten up the cookhouse, and when I finish hanging up my dresses on a big nail driven into the back of our door, I sit on the fresh-smelling straw mattress on the bed and look out of the window at the old hickory tree beside the preacher's tent and at the cedar trees that grow out of the sandy soil of the Mount Horeb cemetery, where the old tombstones stand silently in the already-hot sun of late morning.

Carol Ann's face pops up over the wall just like a mean old sun coming up.

"You aren't supposed to sit on the bed," she announces.

"Can if I want to," I fire back at her.

"Unh-unh," she sing-songs. "You get off or I'll tell Mama."

45

"Go ahead," I say. "'Cause it's my grandmama's tent, and so I can do anything I want."

That seems to stop her, and I make a mental note to remember to use it again. But she moves to another track.

"It's bad luck to stare at tombstones," she pronounces. "'Cause the devil's hiding there and he'll come get you at night in the dark when you're asleep." She speaks real low and makes a tremor in her voice, so that deep in my stomach, something lurches in alarm. I can imagine the room all dark, the way it will be at night, and nothing between the cemetery and the propped-open window except the tiny road and the sandy soil.

"I know something you don't know." Carol Ann's voice is somehow unexpected.

"What?"

"Oh, I can't tell you," she says. "But you won't like it. I can tell you that much."

"What?"

"The crazy surprise your mama's fixed up."

"Don't tell me," I yell, clapping my hands over my ears. Because I can't stand the thought of Carol Ann's spoiling Mama's surprise.

"Don't worry, I won't!" Carol Ann yells. "But you still won't like it. You just remember that when they get out that folding cot from the pantry and set it up here in your room."

Sure enough, Carol Ann is right. Mama and Great-Aunt Kate bring in the folding cot and set it up in mine and Mama's room. And I pretend not to notice it. But I certainly wonder who's going to be sleeping there.

Then I forget all about the wondering because Aunt Nell and Aunt Tyler arrive. I'm so glad to see them, because they both live in Atlanta and are very much like Mama and me—being that they're from a big city and all. And Mama is so happy to see them that she runs outside to meet them, and they all put their arms around each other's waists and dance around in a little circle. Just like happy children.

Aunt Nell and Aunt Tyler are like two beautiful flowers, all fragile and dewy and always with a perfume about them, like violets or some other flower that's small and delicate. So that when I hug them, they are always slender and cool, no matter how hot the afternoon. And when I hug Aunt Tyler, her tummy where the baby is growing—a girl, I hope!—is like a big, surprisingly hard apple that's gotten warm from lying on the ground in the afternoon sun on a fall day.

"Don't muss my hair, sugar," she says to me.

Carol Ann follows Aunt Nell and Aunt Tyler to their room and I know she'll even get to help them unpack, but Mama and Great-Aunt Kate go out to the cookhouse to see if they can get a fire started in the big cook-stove. So I am left standing in the sawdust hallway, listening to Carol Ann's voice from Aunt Nell and Aunt Tyler's room: "And my mama got me a brand-new overnight case and some Fresh!"

"That's lovely, dear," Aunt Nell says.

Lovely, indeed! And I know that as soon as all their pretty dresses are hung up, Aunt Nell and Aunt Tyler will go out and sit in the chairs out front, to nod their heads politely at the other folks who have come to Camp Meeting, and to fan themselves and touch tiny, ivory-colored hand-kerchiefs to their smooth, white throats and their blue-veined wrists. Carol Ann will be right there with them, just like a sticking plaster, tossing her curls and sitting with her ankles crossed and acting all grown up.

From the cookhouse, I can hear Mama and Great-Aunt Kate trying to get the fire going in the stove.

"That's way too much kindling wood," Great-Aunt Kate says. "Fire'll get so hot it'll burn up every stick of wood we have before we can even get the chicken cut up."

"It'll be all right," Mama assures her. "And besides, she'll be here tomor-row to do it for us, so we won't have to fool with it again."

"She's coming tomorrow, then?"

"Yes, ma'am. First thing in the morning."

"Too bad she couldn't have come on out today and saved us this."

"I know. But she's got old folks depending on her at home. So she had to make arrangements for them, you see."

"All I see is you've got too much kindling in there."

So I stand there in the long, empty hallway, absolutely forgotten by all of them—Aunt Nell and Aunt Tyler and, of course, Carol Ann out front, and Mama and Great-Aunt Kate in the cookhouse. And I stand and wait and wonder who "she" is. But I won't ask. I won't ask even if I stand there and die of wanting to know.

After Mama and Great-Aunt Kate get the fire going, they come back inside and they both have beads of perspiration on their foreheads and bright pink cheeks from being so close to the hot stove.

"Hot as blazes out there," Great-Aunt Kate says, and then she and Mama start cutting up the chicken.

When the long, wooden table is ready—covered with a shiny, new oil-cloth and set with the mismatched dishes that we always use at Camp Meeting—we all sit down to fried chicken and fresh butter beans and potato salad and a big platter of sliced tomatoes that have been chilled in the icebox. And because I had watched while Mama and Great-Aunt

47

Kate cut up the chickens, I know there are two wishbones—one for me and one for Carol Ann.

Sure enough, when Great-Aunt Kate passes the platter to Carol Ann, the two wishbones are right up on the top, golden brown and plump. And I sit there and watch while Carol Ann takes both wishbones and puts them on her plate and then passes the platter to me. Of course, Mama and Aunt Nell and Aunt Tyler are all busy talking and laughing together, and they don't notice what's happened. I open my mouth to protest, but just about that time, I look down and discover that Carol Ann has put one of the wishbones on my plate while I wasn't looking. And I sure don't want any wishbone she's had her dirty old hands on.

But just about that time, Great-Aunt Kate says to me, "Well, pass it on before it's all cold!" and I do, passing the platter across the table to Aunt Tyler, who takes it in pale, thin hands that have shiny nails and elegant gold rings on the fingers. Then along come the butter beans and then the potato salad, and the tomatoes, and when I have passed all these over to Aunt Tyler, I look at my plate and the wishbone is gone.

"Hey! Where's my wishbone?" I bellow, without even thinking, and in the next instant, there's such a silence that you could poke your finger in it and pull it out and leave a hole. And all I can see is four startled, open-mouthed faces staring at me—all except for Carol Ann, who is studying her butter beans with a totally expressionless countenance and chewing as methodically as if she is counting the number of times she bites down on each and every bean. Then, as if in a dream, she turns her head and looks right at me.

"You put it right on your plate," she says evenly, smiling. "I saw you."

"Did not!" I yell. "You took both of them and then put one on my plate when I wasn't looking! And now it's gone and you took it!"

"Why, I never!" Great-Aunt Kate has her hand pressed over her bosom as if her heart is trying to jump out through the front of her dress and she must hold it in.

"Oh, lookie there!" Carol Ann exclaims cheerfully, pointing to the sawdust floor. And there is the wishbone, its golden-brown crust coated in wood shavings. "You dropped it," she states in a matter-of-fact voice. And all five faces looking at me.

"Accuse my child of stealing food!" Great-Aunt Kate sputters.

"Well, I'll declare, those butter beans are just wonderful! I do believe I'll have some more, please ma'am," Aunt Nell says.

And that's the way it ends, except, of course, that I don't get a wishbone. But still, within minutes, everything is just fine again, and everyone is talking once more and smiling. Except for me and Carol Ann. She's cutting a tomato slice and not looking at anyone. And that's when I look down toward my lap, where the oilcloth is draped, and without even a second thought, I curl up the edge with my left hand so that it forms a little trough, and I reach up with my right hand and take my almost-full glass of iced tea and in one motion, I pour it in the trough and not a one of them sees me do it.

"You want some more iced tea, sugar? Goodness! You must have been thirsty!" Mama's voice and her pretty blue eyes looking at me, and I am still holding the oilcloth full of iced tea.

"No, ma'am, thank you," I say, just as politely as I can.

Mama smiles that sweet and innocent smile at me, and I smile back. Then I look down in what I hope is an expression of complete piety, but what I am really doing is tilting the trough full of iced tea down toward Carol Ann's unsuspecting lap. And when I'm sure that all the iced tea is right in place over her lap, I let go of the oilcloth and it dumps right smack where I'd planned for it to go.

"MAMA-A-A!!!" The shriek is deafening, and it doesn't stop. Just goes on and on, the "ah" at the end of the word wailing on and on until I'll bet Carol Ann's toes are shriveling up. Great-Aunt Kate has sprung up and grabbed Carol Ann's shoulders and she's shaking her, desperately seeking an answer to the question of what's causing the horrible anguish. Aunt Nell and Aunt Tyler's faces are just white blobs with round O's for their mouths, and Mama's blue eyes are locked on me in astonishment, unblinking and still so purely innocent that they break my heart, right there on the spot.

As it turns out, I have to apologize to everyone at the table, and I also have to rinse out Carol Ann's stupid old dress. But it's been worth it. Definitely worth it.

Especially later in the evening when I happen to overhear Aunt Nell and Aunt Tyler talking out on the front porch: "Do you remember when I did that very same thing to you one summer?"

Aunt Tyler laughs, a silvery tinkle of a laugh, like rain spattering on little green leaves. "I certainly do remember. Except back then, there were lots more cousins at the table, so it wasn't easy to find out who was the culprit. And I never even knew it was you who'd done it until I had appendicitis that time and you were so sure I was going to die, you confessed it to me and begged me to forgive you."

"And did you?" Aunt Nell asks.

"No," Aunt Tyler says, laughing. "Come to think of it, I never did."

5

While I stood just inside the screen door, listening to Aunt Nell and Aunt Tyler laughing together, their voices diminished and then disappeared altogether. I opened my eyes to the early morning light coming through the white, criss-crossed curtains in my own room, with the high bed and the chifforobe in the corner and the dressing table.

The sound of pots and pans clattering came down the hallway.

Great-Aunt Kate in the kitchen? Carol Ann lurking outside my bedroom door, waiting to look in and stick her tongue out at me?

No.

Then who?

Jessie? Yes! Good old Jessie, who came to us the very day Henry and I moved into the house, right after Great-Aunt Kate passed on. Jessie, who never grumbled, even while we had the whole kitchen torn up and redone, and the back porch glassed in for a morning room, and the wide-planked pine floors refinished.

No. Jessie's gone now.

Then who?

That was a hard waking up I did that morning, confused and not knowing who was banging pans around in my kitchen. Thinking first that I was still a child and then a young bride . . . yes, that lovely time!

The early years when I still thought of this house as Grand-mama's house and then Great-Aunt Kate's, because of all the summers of coming here first and then going out to Mount Horeb. And never thinking once in all those summers that one day the house would be mine. And Henry's. I should have thought of it, because I knew it had been left to my mama, even though she would never have asked Great-Aunt Kate to move, and through Mama to me. But it was years and years before it truly felt like mine. And, too, during that time, I was getting used to my new life as Henry's wife and taking my place in the community.

Garden Club meetings, tiny tea sandwiches served on crystal plates, Sunday mornings in church, and Sunday afternoons on the porch with the visitors who came. Come, they always did, to talk about the comfortable things like recipes for chicken salad and new slipcovers for the parlor.

Even after Henry passed on, they came.

Then, the slow and brutal losing of it all—the ones who used to come passing away themselves one by one. Sometimes seeming like all I did was visit the sick and then go to their funerals.

Now the friends all gone, replaced by new people moving into town, especially since the kaolin plant started up. Strange people, some of them with strange ways of talking. And most of them just out-and-out trash. Drifters, like those Deena-Marie and Buddy people and that passel of hollow-eyed children. All my friends gone, the good people who knew how to do things. Most of them sleeping in the Town Cemetery on the hill, and a few down at Sweetwater Baptist, and two of them—Mabel and Andrea—buried in family plots far away. Mabel in Sebring, Florida, because her daughter lived there and she'd been after Mabel tooth and toenail for years to move down there, but Mabel never would do it. Then when Mabel passed on, the daughter had her brought all the way down there for burial. So the daughter finally won, I suppose. And Andrea in Mason City, Iowa, where her father was a town commissioner, long years ago. That's where her father's family had a plot, and they took her out there and not a one of them who were left in the family had ever met her.

A fresh rattling of pans in the kitchen and the shatter of a glass breaking. Maybelline. That's who was in the kitchen. And she was

51

waiting for me, just like a big old spider, so she could pounce on me again about all this going to Jerusalem mess!

Then a terrible thought occurred to me: Where was I to be buried? What would happen if I did go off with Maybelline, like she was saying I should? Disappear for all eternity, so that no one even knew where I was? What would become of my place beside Henry, already bought and paid for and with that beautiful stone made for the two of us? How could it be that I wouldn't have what even Mabel and Andrea had? Someone to remember me? Because even if they weren't buried in the town, we knew where they were. And that was important.

But if nobody knew where I'd gone, there wouldn't be anyone to talk about me and tell folks where I was buried, the way they did about Mabel and Andrea. Because there was no one left to do it. That's what would happen if I went along with Maybelline on a ridiculous trip to some little no-place town called Jerusalem.

But if I didn't go? Why, I had to go. Because maybe my friends were all gone, but their children were still around, and they would say, "Oh, poor old thing. She used to be a friend of my mama's. But she came to such hardship. And her such a fine lady. Or, at least, she used to be." I couldn't let that happen. Because we owed something to each other, all of us, even if all that was left was the memory.

So even if I had to go away, I had to make sure I finally wound up back in that town, right next to Henry, where I belonged. And not like a pauper either. Never like a pauper.

But how? That's what I was wondering while I was lying there.

And what I finally came down to was this: I had to go back and see that despicable child, Little Tommy, once more, if I could stand it. He was a lawyer as well as a banker, and he was bound by an oath of confidentiality, I was sure. Besides, there had to be something of his papa in him. So I could give him what little I had to pay toward the taxes and he could pay that much for me. Later, when no more money came, the county would probably take the house and sell it. But no one would know why, because I would be gone. Vanished into thin air, as it were. And they would never think I needed the money from the sale of the house. But all that only after I'd gone away and no one knew where I was. Because what would people have said?

Oh, what a mess it could have been! Unless I could find a way to do it just right. Maybe I could put the rest of the money away, so that when the time came, it would be there for bringing me back and giving me a proper funeral and putting me next to Henry. And I'd make Maybelline swear on a Bible not to tell anyone where I'd been or why I had to leave. As a matter of fact, I would make her swear—with her hand on the Bible!—not to come to my funeral at all.

Just as clear as day I could see my own grave, banked with flowers, and I heard someone say, "Yes, she was such a fine lady!" How lovely!

So that it all fell back into place, comfortable and secure. The same feeling as all those beautiful mornings over the years, when Henry left for the bank, and I stood at the window and watched him walking, dapper and charming, down the street toward town.

A terrible raucous voice breaking the beautiful image:

> We're mar-ching to Zi—on,
> Beau-ti-ful, beau-ti-ful Zi—on;
> We're mar-ching up-ward to Zi-on,
> The beau-ti-ful ci-ty of God!

"Miss Amelia? You awake? You say something?" Maybelline yelled from the kitchen.

"No," I muttered into the pillow. "Leave me alone."

"You all right, Miss Amelia? You say something?" Maybelline called again.

"NO, I said!"

"No—you're not all right? Or no—you didn't say anything?" Footsteps and the door opening and the comic face appearing, abrupt, penciled eyebrows and Lilac Lavender eye shadow.

How maddening! "Yes, I'm all right, and no, I didn't say anything."

"I sure thought you did," Maybelline insisted. "Thought I heard you say something about waking up. Are you ready to get up? You've sure slept late this morning."

53

What I really meant to say—I thought but did not say aloud, or at least, I didn't think I did—was for you to stop that caterwauling!

Because Maybelline could sing for hours on end, and the dry voice penetrated everything—even dreams—like an irritating, insistent, and unyielding finger of sunlight coming through the edge of pulled-down shades at noon.

As if my mere thought had somehow been transmitted and promptly misinterpreted as a compliment—because Maybelline never understood anything the way I intended it—she smiled at me and nodded her head as if to say, "Well, if you insist!" and she went back down the hall, singing with renewed vigor and a stepped-up tempo:

> We're mar-ching to Zi—on,
> Beau-ti-ful, beau-ti-ful Zi—on;
> We're mar-ching up-ward to Zi-on,
> The beau-ti-ful ci-ty of God!

At the end of the impossibly sustained refrain, I knew Maybelline would close her eyes, thrust out her chin toward the ceiling, shake her head so the curls on that ridiculous wig would tremble stiffly, and then burst out with, "Oh! I surely do praise the Lord!"

And she did exactly as I knew she would do.

I also knew that in only a moment, the terrible, creaking voice would launch into more song. And that I couldn't tolerate for another instant. Not that day.

"This is the day the Lord hath made! I will rejoice and be glad in it!" I yelled.

It certainly wasn't something I intended to say, and the words surprised me—where did I hear that?—though I would try not to show it when Maybelline came back, which of course, she promptly did.

"Why, Miss Amelia! You're quoting the Bible!"

"I know that! I can quote it just as well as anyone. I just choose not to go around annoying everyone all the time by doing so."

But, of course, and as usual, the sarcasm was completely lost on Maybelline.

"Might be right nice if you did," Maybelline said. "I sure wouldn't mind it one little bit. Like it, as a matter of fact." And she went back to the kitchen, still humming, and the humming grew and grew and then finally burst through her lips. Again.

Mar-ching up-ward to Zi-on,
The beau-ti-ful ci-ty of God!

Beautiful city of God, indeed! Tacky little one-horse town, probably doesn't even have a decent church in it. Holy rollers, I'll bet. All of them. And if Maybelline thinks I'm going to start in at my age with her kind of religion, she's got another think coming.

No! It's all wrong, every bit of it! There has to be another way, and I'll have to find it. Call a halt to all Maybelline's foolish ideas right here and now. Because I'm in no condition to go off to goodness-knows-where. Too sick or confused. Or something.

Oh, Jessie! Why isn't it you in the kitchen this morning?

Why couldn't I have my coffee in the quiet morning room and a freshly ironed tablecloth on the table and my coffee served to me in the paper-thin china cup with the violets on it? And the floor fan humming at the end of the long hallway, drawing in the cool air from the shaded backyard and spinning it out like soothing balm throughout the house?

And it came to me so clearly then. What on earth could I have been thinking about? Why, I couldn't leave this house. I just couldn't do it. And that was final! But how was I to get Maybelline turned off now that I had let it all get this far?

I got dressed and went into the kitchen, wearing what I hoped was a particularly cool expression, just to nip any of Maybelline's crazy notions right in the bud and make her leave me alone until I could figure out what to do. Why, even if I thought I could stand to go off with Maybelline, I couldn't abandon this house. Leave it standing empty. Pretty soon, grass would need cutting, and the begonias would die for want of a drink of water. And maybe those awful boys would break out the windows, or worse, get inside and tear up everything! Soil the quiet elegance. Defile it!

I envisioned my grandmama and my mama standing on the porch, waving good-bye to me. Them left to the marauders. A terrible, tearing sob tried to come up in my throat.

No! I'll find another way; if only I can get Maybelline to leave me alone!

But Maybelline didn't have a chance to say another thing about us going off together, because that awful Deena-Marie person started knocking on the door to the back porch before I could even take a sip of my coffee.

"Yoo-o-o hoo-o-o! Y'all in there?" Deena-Marie called, just as loud as she could, even though she could certainly see that we were sitting right there at the table. Because she was one who would come up to the screen door and peer in before anyone even knew she was around. Nosy.

"I'll go," Maybelline said.

Yes, I was thinking, You go on and see what she wants. I certainly can't bear her this morning, though I'm certainly glad something's around to sidetrack Maybelline. Until I can think!

Why, this town used to have such fine and upstanding people in it, and they certainly would have known that it was way too early to be knocking on folks' doors. But of course, I shouldn't have been expecting any such good manners out of that woman and her family. Knew that just as soon as they moved into the apartment old Miss Vera Roberts' daughter had built in the back part of Miss Vera's big old house right across our backyard and facing the next street.

"No need to have all this space, and it going to waste," Miss Vera's daughter said, and that on the very day of her mama's funeral. So in only a week or two, workmen showed up early one morning and started in to hammering and sawing, and the whining of those buzz saws absolutely shattered the peace of the long afternoons and grated my nerves in more than one way.

"Beautiful old house, it was," I lamented to Maybelline. "And them just ruining it. I'm certainly glad Vera's not alive to see it. Can't imagine what it will look like now, with that beautiful, long hallway cut off like that. Used to be you could stand inside the front doorway and see all the way through the house and right through the backyard and all those big old pecan trees casting a hue over everything, just like looking through a piece of green glass."

That's what could happen, eventually, to this house, if I abandoned it. No! I couldn't think about that. Not have this to be like Vera's beautiful old house.

Because only a day or so after all the hammering and the commotion finally stopped, I saw an advertisement in the weekly newspaper: "For Rent. One-bedroom apartment in local home. Private entrance. New appliances."

For days, I frequented my own back porch often and even puttered around in the vegetable garden, a chore that usually fell to Maybelline, watching for any kind of activity, but no one came around that "private entrance" to the back of Vera's house.

I'll bet she can't find anyone who'll rent it, I thought. Serves her right, ruining that beautiful old house like she's done.

When Maybelline and I did the grocery shopping at the Red and White, I kept my ears open to catch any talk I could about the empty apartment. But I never heard a thing, mostly because all the ones who would care about it were gone. Except for me.

Then, on a Wednesday morning I remember it was, I watched through the kitchen window as a pickup truck loaded to the hilt with old mattresses and chairs and grocery sacks spilling over with clothes pulled up by that private entrance. I almost called to Maybelline, who was in the pantry cleaning off the shelf where a jar of peaches had broken its seal and leaked out a dark, sticky liquid onto the shelf.

But Maybelline wouldn't have seen a thing remarkable about the leaning truck and its disreputable contents. So I watched alone, as silent as a ghost, while two thin, stoop-shouldered people got out of the truck and extracted two tow-headed youngsters from among the bags and mattresses.

Oh, my! Children!

And, of course, I could take one look at those people and tell what we were all in for. Months later, when a cat was found dead at the bottom of an abandoned well, I knew that those two children were responsible. That's the kind they were.

Right from day one, Deena-Marie—what a name!—came across to our back door regularly, to borrow sugar, soap, crackers, and even a couple of mason jars for putting up a handful of blackber-

57

ries her "man,"—as Deena-Marie called him—Buddy, had found growing somewhere.

Buddy didn't have a job of any kind, as far as we could tell. Just spent his days scavenging for food and anything else he thought the family could use. Went out regularly, picking up fallen, spotted peaches no one else would bother with and ears of corn left too long on the stalk so the kernels were tough as shoe leather; other things too: bits of plow blade that had broken off and were rusting in the fields and broken bricks from around old chimneys. And from neighborhood trash cans, he took empty Pepto-Bismol bottles and old bread wrappers; it got so that if people had something personal to throw away, they had to load it in the trunk of their car and carry it out to the county dumpster far at the other end of town.

It's a wonder they don't all have some terrible disease, I thought—what with him bringing all that garbage home. Won't be long before there'll be enough cockroaches in old Miss Vera's house to pick it up and carry it off down the street.

Such common people they were. Deena-Marie all pinched looking and without substance, vacant and without a vestige of anything you could call well-bred. Buddy was even worse. He was thin and freckled and with stained fingers, and when he wasn't out scavenging, he sat in the backyard in an old kitchen chair, always leaning forward, with his elbows resting on his spread-apart knees, staring at the ground between his feet endlessly, so that every single thing about him reeked of defeat. No, worse than defeat—of nothing ever having been in him to be defeated.

But like weeds, they were strong and tenacious, and the two children grew taller, but were still scrawny-looking, and Deena-Marie and Buddy, though stooped as always, did their chores, with Deena-Marie hanging grungy, warped undershirts on the clothesline and sweeping off the back steps, and Buddy bringing home scavenged food and, occasionally, some fish he caught in the creek.

"Maybe we should pray for another miracle like the loaves and fishes in the Bible that fed a multitude of people," I said to Maybelline one time, and as if in terrible prophecy of the multitude of which I spoke, Deena-Marie promptly became an expectant mother.

And again after that. And still once again, adding three tow-headed little girls to the family.

Maybelline, being Maybelline, took to knitting sweaters and booties for the babies, often snarling the yarn and muttering to herself as she ripped out the stitches, bending in nearsighted concentration over mistake after mistake and tangle after tangle. So that the sweaters turned out to be lopsided things anybody else would have been ashamed to let anyone see, and booties that reached above the baby's knees.

"You're getting something started you'll regret," I warned her. "You mark my word." But of course, Maybelline didn't listen, and now Deena-Marie turned up regularly at our back door, as she did that particular morning.

"Yoo-o-o hoo-o-o!" she called again, before Maybelline could get to the door. The baby on Deena-Marie's hip fretted, and the other two little girls stood at the bottom of the steps, sucking on their dirty fingers and watching the door with large, sober eyes.

"Come on in, Deena-Marie." Maybelline welcomed her, ignoring the way I was waving my hand at her and shaking my head.

"Cain't, but I 'preciate it. Got to take the baby right on back home." Deena-Marie shrugged her hip forward, thrusting the baby closer so we could see the runny nose and the reddened eyes. "Need to borry some honey, do you got any."

"Sure," Maybelline said. "Fixing some aspirin and honey for the baby?"

Deena-Marie nodded solemnly and stepped inside the screen door. "Come to think of it, I'll take a few aspirin, too, do you got any spare ones."

Spare ones? I was thinking. Whoever heard of such a thing as "spare" aspirin?

At the foot of the steps, the two little girls started to follow their mother, but Deena-Marie waved them back and barked, "Y'all stay put."

Then, in a falsetto voice she probably thought sounded cheerful, she called to me, "How are you this morning, Miss Amelia?"

"Fine. Thank you," I said between clenched teeth. Cool but not distant. Polite but not warm. That was the way to deal with people like that.

"I'm sorry to hear the baby's sick," I added, feeling that some degree of benevolence was called for. I didn't add: But what can you expect?

She jiggled the flushed, runny-nosed child on her hip and smiled into its face. It looked back at her in a slack-jawed stare, as if it had never seen anyone smile before.

"Yes'm," Deena-Marie answered. "Teething, I 'spect." In the pantry, Maybelline was moving jars about, looking for the honey.

"Aspirin and honey will help with that," I agreed. "And with sore throat and fever and ague, too."

Deena-Marie smiled, revealing a row of discolored teeth. I felt something of a mild shock at the sight of them, and from somewhere deep inside, I remembered other bad teeth too: two of them, one sticking down out of the top and one sticking up from the bottom, brown and crooked.

"You sure do know lots, Miss Amelia," Deena-Marie was saying, and I pulled myself away from the terrible image.

"Well, I don't know about that," I protested, but not enough to encourage a discussion. Still, and in spite of my resolve, I knew my face had flushed, whether at the compliment or because it had been so hard to pull myself out of memory, I didn't know.

"Oh, yes'm, you sure do," Deena-Marie insisted. "I heard Miss Vera's daughter saying that about you just the other day."

"You did?" So this was something more than just Deena-Marie's half-baked idea then.

"Yes'm. There was some other ladies, too. They was from the Women's Club or something like that, and all of them talking about how they could raise some money for a new liberry. That's when Miss Vera's daughter come right out and said you'd know how to help them go about it. That you know lots and that everybody in the community respects you so much."

Yes, poor old thing. She used to be such a fine lady! I thought.

"New liberry . . . library? I haven't heard anything about that," I said, trying to think back and see if it was something I'd forgotten. "Nothing wrong with the old one that I know of."

"Too small, they say." Deena-Marie shifted the baby on her hip just as Maybelline came out of the pantry with the jar of honey. "But I wouldn't know about that," Deena-Marie added.

I'm sure you wouldn't, I thought. Probably never been in a library in your life.

Deena-Marie accepted the jar of honey Maybelline proffered and also a folded paper napkin containing "spare" aspirin tablets.

"And here's some peanut butter we aren't using up fast enough," Maybelline said, thrusting an additional jar at Deena-Marie. "It'll go rancid doesn't somebody use it up soon."

Deena-Marie took the peanut butter as matter-of-factly as she had accepted the honey and the aspirin. "Sure do 'preciate it," she said as she started back out.

"Bye, Miss Amelia," she hollered over her shoulder.

At the bottom of the steps, the little girls stood rooted exactly where they had been when Deena-Marie told them to "stay put." Their eyes took on a new light when they saw the jar of peanut butter, but they said not a word.

"Let's go, younguns," Deena-Marie said to them, and the two little girls held hands and stolidly followed their mother across the backyard. Right at the edge of the chicken yard, one of them turned and looked back at Maybelline for a brief moment. Maybelline raised her hand and wriggled her fingers at the child, but it looked away and hurried off behind its mother.

When Maybelline came back into the kitchen, I said, "Wasn't going rancid one little bit. We've only had it a week."

"Yes'm, I know."

"And did you hear what she said about them building a new library?"

"Yes'm, but so what? We won't be here, you know."

"Oh." Just that fast, I had forgotten.

"Maybelline," I began, but she interrupted me.

"I knew it!" she fairly yelped. "You've changed your mind!"

"Well, yes," I sputtered. Then I swallowed hard, feeling tears starting to burn against the back of my eyes. "I can't abandon this house, don't you see?"

There was a long silence before Maybelline spoke again.

"Yes'm, I guess I can see that. It'd hurt too bad for you to stand it," she admitted. She sat down across the table from me. "But if you'd just sell it, you'd know it would be taken care of."

"How would I know that?" I snapped. "Maybe somebody would buy it just to cut it all up into apartments."

Maybelline studied my face for another long moment before her penciled eyebrows shot straight up into the edge of the Shirley Temple wig.

"Wait a minute! Didn't you say as to how your cousin . . . what's her name?"

"Carol Ann," I said wearily.

"That's her. Didn't she try to buy the house from you right after your Mr. Henry passed on? Didn't you tell me that?"

"Yes, I did." I set my jaw, remembering how Carol Ann's letter went. "Now that you're a widow, you probably won't be able to afford keeping up that big house, and I would consider buying it from you. After all, it was *my* girlhood home, not yours. Besides, it should stay in the family."

Then, I could almost imagine her chewing the end of the pen and thinking about the old saying of catching more flies with sugar than you do with vinegar. So she added, "I remember our days at Camp Meeting together with such fondness, Amelia. We were always so close."

Humph!

My letter back to her was a stiff, proud rebuff of her offer, and I mentioned not one thing about her reference to how "close" we were. Close indeed! Pure, unadulterated hate. That's what it really was.

"Well, couldn't you?" Maybelline's persistent question.

"Couldn't I what?"

"Sell it to her. Your cousin."

"I could, I suppose," I admitted reluctantly. "If there's no other way."

But I do believe I'd rather burn it to the ground! I didn't add.

So for the time being, we left the idea sitting there between us, and finally, Maybelline got up and went to the sink and started rinsing out the dishcloth. I finished my coffee, even though I could clearly see Carol Ann's evil face reflected in the surface of it. Then I started toward my room, to make the bed. That felt like a good thing to do. Something usual and typical, having nothing whatsoever to do with my dilemma.

But on my way through the living room, something flashed before me in such dazzling clarity that it fairly stunned me, and it didn't have a blessed thing to do with Carol Ann.

I bumped my knee against the front of a chair and turned as lightly as a dancer or a dying swan and floated down into the chair, just as if that had been my intention all along.

"You okay?" Maybelline calling from the kitchen.

"I'm fine." Ears like a hound dog! And the idea still bumping about in the back of my mind just like I had bumped the chair, and then righting itself and returning to its full and glorious clarity. So that while I watched, gleaming mahogany bookcases appeared around the entire room, massive structures whose upper shelves surpassed even the fourteen-foot ceiling and disappeared into what seemed to be a cloud floating above them. At the far wall, directly under the portrait of Henry, a neat, cool-looking matron sat at Henry's big, ornate desk, surrounded by neat, clean, exquisitely polite children who waited, smiling, while she noiselessly and very carefully stamped a date in each book. Then she smiled at the children and held the books out to them. "Now don't forget that it was Miss Amelia who gave this lovely house to be the new library. What a fine lady!"

I studied the scene hungrily, even as it gradually faded before my eyes. How perfect! Because this way, no one will ever know I left this house because of financial difficulties. And no one will ever say "poor old thing" about me. Ever. And too, no one will ever chop it up into furnished apartments for trash to live in. Like Miss Vera's house.

And best of all, Carol Ann won't get it!

Certainly, this was the solution. If I had to lose my house, let it be this way. And no one would ever know the truth.

So for the rest of the day, I carried the idea around with me like a delightful little secret, and I hummed to myself so that Maybelline glanced at me a few times in puzzlement. She hadn't said another thing about my having changed my mind, and it wasn't until that evening when we were sitting out on the porch that I told her about the solution.

"This way," I finished up my announcement, "I can just slip away quietly, and no one will ever know why I left. They'll be too happy about getting this lovely house to be the new library, and about my giving it to them free."

Then Maybelline embarrassed me nearly to death. She got up out of her chair, came across the porch with her arms held out—just like a tacky, love-story movie where some boy and girl run toward each other!—and she hugged me too tightly and snuffled into my shoulder until I said, "That's enough now."

"Just think," Maybelline squeaked, "Deena-Marie and Buddy's children will be able to walk right across the backyard and come to a real library."

Well, I certainly didn't want to think about that, so I quickly rejected the vision of those dirty, tow-headed little girls fingering the books with their grubby hands or those cat-murdering older boys sashaying through the cool rooms with hands jammed in their pockets and mischief in their eyes.

I won't think about that. I'll only think of it as the perfect solution to all my problems. Because this too will pass.

That's what Mama always said when there was something coming that I didn't want to come, like going to Camp Meeting. This too will pass.

6

Once that was all settled in my mind, I felt pretty peaceful about everything. So peaceful, in fact, that I wondered if maybe I wasn't getting a little senile to be doing something like that. And to be feeling good about it. Reminded me of one summer—long after that summer of Tulie and the children—when Mama first noticed that sort of thing happening to Great-Aunt Kate.

Because Mama had mentioned something that had happened only a few years before, and Great-Aunt Kate looked surprised and came right out and said she didn't remember a thing about it.

"Why, you do too remember that," Mama said, in surprise.

"No, I don't," Great-Aunt Kate said.

"Of course you do," Mama insisted. "That was just about the same time we had to take Mama over to Atlanta to have that mole removed from her back. Surely you remember that."

"Mole?"

Mama laughed, but I could tell that she was really frightened, somehow, over Great-Aunt Kate's not remembering.

"Mole?" Great-Aunt Kate repeated, as if the word were a piece of chewing gum that had gotten stuck to her shoe.

Later, Mama said to me, "I expect she's getting to be just like Sweet Mama." That was Great-Aunt Kate's and my grandmama's mama. "I surely do hate to see her getting senile. But maybe in a way, it's a good thing God does—anesthetizing us in our old age."

Anesthetizing us in our old age. So maybe that's what was happening to me, because none of it seemed very real at all. More or less like some kind of a dream I was having. And, deep down, while I was making all the plans and going through the closets and the drawers, I sometimes thought I was just packing up to go to Camp Meeting for two weeks instead of preparing to leave my house forever.

But that's the kind of strange thing that was happening to me, now that I knew the house would be taken care of. That I wouldn't just be moving out of it and deserting it to be picked and plundered through by someone like Buddy. Or chopped up into dark, little apartments either, for trashy people to live in. And, especially, not for Carol Ann!

So that was a load off my mind. I could leave in peace. That took care of the what-I-was-leaving part, but it certainly didn't take care of the where-was-I-going part. That still worried me.

Frankly, I just didn't completely trust what all Maybelline said about that old house of her grandpapa's, and everything we were planning depended on that. Why, what on earth would happen to us if we actually got there and found the house had fallen down? Or that someone else was living in it?

So finally, after days of thinking about it, I decided that maybe it was enough for Maybelline to go on—she was so convinced anyway that the Lord would be leading us when we went traipsing off into the woods looking for that old house—but that I needed to know more about it before we moved to the point of no return.

No return. That's what it would be when I made my intentions known about giving the house to the town.

"How come you're so sure that old house of your grandfather's is still there?" I asked.

"Oh, it's there all right," she said.

"Well, then," I argued, "how do you know nobody's living in it?"

"Oh, I know," she replied.

"How do you know?"

"Just do, that's all. Besides, if anybody's done anything with it, they'd have to tell me. Because I'm one of the ones who pays taxes on it."

"Oh." So it was really there. We were really going.

"It's there, all right," said Maybelline, just as if she could hear what I had been thinking. And her voice was so dreamy, I didn't say another thing. Just sat there across the breakfast table from her and watched her sipping her coffee, watched her eyes wandering back and forth across the kitchen ceiling, and wondered what it was she was remembering. But I didn't have to wonder for long.

"Used to be an old spring down behind the house," she said. "Grandpapa had a springhouse down there. You know what that is?"

"Of course I do," I answered. "For keeping butter and milk cool in the hot weather."

"Well, that's what he had. Built it himself, too. Why, I used to love going down there to get things the grown-ups wanted. Because it was always so cool and mysterious-like there at the spring. Always felt so funny to me how, when I would start down from the top of the hill, it would be such a hot day. Sweat on my face and crickets singing in the tall grass and gnats singing in my ears. But about halfway down, I'd begin to feel how much cooler it was. Still a few gnats, but mostly dragonflies. Blue ones and green ones with their big, shiny eyes and those wings just as delicate as spiderwebs. And them just darting here and there."

Well, that certainly surprised me, it did. Because I'd never heard Maybelline say anything like that before. Never once thought, in all those years, she was the kind who would remember things like that. Much less be able to describe them to anyone.

"It sounds beautiful," I said, truthfully. And with that, she kind of woke up out of her little dream and smiled and even blushed a little.

"It's right pretty," was all she said. "I'm glad to be going back."

"Well, I guess I have a lot of things need doing, if that's what we're really going to do. Go to your grandpapa's house," I said. "I've finished up all the closets and everything, so today I'll get up into the attic and tomorrow I'll go to the bank and tell Little Tommy to draw up the papers for giving over the house."

"You going up in that hot attic? Why don't you just tell me what you want done up there and I'll do it," she offered in her usual half-baked way.

"I don't know there's anything you can do," I said, trying to sound very firm. "Henry was a very neat and methodical person, and he insisted on keeping things all cleaned out and organized, so there's only one trunk I need to go through. Old letters and photographs I'd just as soon burn and be done with."

"Well, let me do it for you."

"No. I have to do it myself."

So I put on a duster over my dress and started up to the attic to go through the trunk, just to make sure I threw out anything I wouldn't want someone picking through. And, too, there were the boxes of Henry's clothes that I hadn't been able to give away.

"But it's too hot up there for you," Maybelline argued once more.

"I won't be long," I promised her. "Besides, it's way too early in the morning for it to have gotten very hot up there. I'm sure of it." For Heaven's sake, Maybelline, I was thinking. Sometimes I feel like scraping you off of me with a stick!

Finally, she relented and stopped arguing with me about the attic being too hot, but when I opened the tiny door to the narrow staircase, I thought maybe she was right. Because all the confined heat of the long summer days blew against my face. And more than that, too. Almost like the breath of people who'd passed on long ago. Kind of startled me just for a moment. But it was something that had to be done, and I was the only one to do it. Most certainly.

I wouldn't have Maybelline digging around in my mama's things. Just wouldn't have it.

It had been years since I'd last been up in the attic. Only needed to go up there for the Christmas decorations, and goodness knows, Maybelline always took care of that. Would, in fact, have dragged out the Christmas tree balls and lights around the first of October, had I allowed her to do it.

Because at the first faint hint of fall, Maybelline always went into her "Christmas hysteria." Why, it was all I could do to hold her off until it was decently close to Christmas.

"It's disgraceful to even think of Christmas before Thanksgiving is done!" I argued the same argument every blessed year.

"Yes'm," Maybelline always said, crestfallen. But still, before I could blink an eye, I'd see one of Maybelline's dime-store ceramic reindeer behind the candlestick on the mantle, and a few days later, a string of plastic silver bells on the doorknob to the back door. The whole time, Maybelline looked just as innocent as a lamb, and I nursed a headache born of the sure and certain belief that I couldn't win over Maybelline's Christmas hysteria, no matter what I did. So my headache stayed and stayed, and finally was relieved for a little while during Thanksgiving dinner. But the minute it was over, Maybelline absolutely became a whirling dervish—washing the china and putting it away in the cabinet and tucking my grandmother's silver tableware back into its silvercloth bags, and carefully inspecting the kitchen before she happily clambered up the attic stairs and dragged down that box of Christmas ornaments and decorations.

Of course, I had some lovely Christmas things packed away. Crystal candlesticks and tasteful, mother-of-pearl ornaments, and even two strands of candle-shaped Christmas tree lights with colored water in them that would bubble up and down as the light heated up.

But in spite of the lovely ornaments I had available for her to use, Maybelline's decorating taste—like everything else about her—had certainly not been cultivated at all. Because you can't make a silk purse out of a sow's ear. And it was just that simple.

Why, she could run the gamut all the way from tacky to completely outrageous, and so my headache always came back just as soon as Maybelline brought my box of decorations down out of the attic and then a box of her own and started in to singing Christmas carols while she decorated the house. I moaned when Maybelline put a plastic poinsettia on the sidetable, and I groaned at the fat-bellied, fuchsia-pink light-up Santa on the porch, for Heaven's sake! But still, I tried to keep quiet, knowing that if I said a single word, the offending piece would merely disappear for a day or two and then reappear in a different location.

That's what I was thinking about when I started up the attic stairs. And I guess that was one thing we wouldn't have to contend with for Christmases to come. Not with us moving away. In fact, we'd probably be lucky did we have a single ornament or a tree to hang it on.

I was a little out of breath by the time I had climbed the eight steps, as steep as they were, and I stopped at the top, peering around in a hot twilight that was illuminated only by light coming through the small fan-shaped window at the far end of the attic, a window whose only function was to provide a little architectural interest to the front of the house.

I always used to glance up at it every time we came here to see Grandmama or Great-Aunt Kate, because Carol Ann said that a long time ago, a crazy woman had a baby and hid it in the attic. But that she must have forgotten about it, because it just stayed there until it died and there was nothing left of it but a moldering blanket and a tiny brown skull. Carol Ann said that if I looked real hard at the window, I would be able to see the baby looking out of the attic window watching everyone who came into the house and waiting for its mama to come back for it. I knew it wasn't true, but it always made my skin prickle anyway—and that day was no different, as I made my way carefully across that dark and dusty attic, all the way to where the window looked out over the front of the house. I looked down to where the sidewalk was met by the walkway through the front yard, like an enormous white cross. Below, the porch roof slanted away, just like the gentle hillside at Camp Meeting tilted down toward the tabernacle. And me way up high and looking down on everything, and no one even knowing I am there.

Exactly like it was that morning at Camp Meeting when Aunt Valley came for the first time.

Of course, I don't know who she is when I first see her, but the morning she comes, I have climbed pretty high up in the old chinaberry tree next to the cookhouse. I climbed up there on purpose—because I know it's almost time for the eleven o'clock service at the tabernacle, and Mama will be looking high and low for me. "Where did she go this time? I'll declare!"

So that's where I am when I see a rickety old truck come down the road and stop almost under the chinaberry tree I'm in, and this old colored woman gets out of it.

She has a huge bottom, and when she leans back inside the truck to get something, her dress rides up in back so I can see the rolled-down tops of her stockings, even though I'm way up in the tree above her.

That's how high up her dress could go because of her having such a big bottom. She takes a paper sack out of the truck and just stands there looking around, and the truck drives away and leaves her.

She starts toward the back door of the tent, kind of uncertain-like, but suddenly, she stops right in her tracks—like she's been struck by lightning or something. Then she looks up into the tree, shading her eyes with her hand, and I am wondering how on earth she knows I am there. Because I never made a single sound.

"Who's there?" she demands.

"Just me," I answer.

"Oh, yes, I see you now. Thought there was a pretty little bird 'way up there."

"No, ma'am," I say, forgetting that I'm not supposed to say ma'am to a colored woman. "I'm not no bird, sure enough."

"Well then, good morning to you. A glorious good morning, and ain't it just about the perfectest day you ever seen? 'This is the day the Lord has made. I will rejoice and be glad in it!'"

"Yes," I say, remembering not to say ma'am. "It sure is a pretty day and all that other stuff you say. Do you have any children waiting for you at home?"

"Chirren?" she asks, as if she doesn't know what the word means. "No, not chirren, exactly. My chirren is all growed up now."

"You got grandchirren . . . children?"

"I got a few of them, sure enough."

"How many? 'Bout seben?"

"No, goodness!" she laughs. "Not that many, sure enough. But why you asking?"

"I just wondered."

She walks on toward the back screen door but stops again in mid-step and cocks her head to the side, just as if she's listening to something far, far away.

"Your mama home?" she calls back over her shoulder.

"Inside. What you want her for?"

"I come to work here, doing some cooking and taking care of somebody's little girl," she says. "And I got a pretty good feeling it's you."

So that's what all the whispering's been about! Mama's gone and done it this time. Hired a colored woman to look after me. Because she's always said she wanted me to have that. But as soon as I saw this woman, all I could think about was Tulie and all those children. So Carol Ann was right after all. I don't like the surprise. Not one bit! But I don't really know why. It seems to have something to do with all the laughing Tulie does and the

71

two dirty-looking old teeth. And children like little black sparrows sitting on fence rails. And more.

So maybe because of that, and maybe too because it's just one more thing I didn't know was coming, I decide right on the spot that I won't like this woman and there's not a thing any of them can do about it. It's easy as pie not to like her, because she's old, and she's ugly, and she's just as black as the ace of spades, and an ignorant, country kind of person who doesn't know anything, except how to say "Yes'm" to Mama. And I know already that this woman is scared of Mama, just like she's scared of all white people.

And no matter what she says, I know for sure she's exactly the kind of colored woman who probably has lots of children who sit on her steps all day long, waiting for her to come home. And I don't want to know about that. Not ever again.

Still, there's not a thing I can do to stop her from knocking on the back door of the tent. So I watch from high up in the chinaberry tree, and after she goes inside, it's only a minute or two before I hear Mama calling me. So I climb down and go inside too. Because I figure this colored woman knows I was up in the tree, and she'll sure tell Mama that's where I am, so I might as well behave myself. At least, just until I get the chance to do something about it.

When I go inside, I find out for the first time just how big she is. Not fat—except for her bottom—but big. Legs like oak trees and arms as big as hams. And nothing you could call a neck at all, just a great, square head jammed right down on top of shoulders that are so broad, they're shutting out the light coming in through the screen door.

I glance at Mama, and right then and there I know I'm right about why Mama has hired her. Mama's always had a bee in her bonnet about wanting me to have a "real Southern girlhood," whatever that is. And this is a part of it.

Besides which, Mama likes to "put on airs." And having a hired woman to take care of me is exactly what Great-Aunt Kate expects Mama to do. But she just doesn't understand that Mama's used to living in a city where things are done right, and so am I.

So now here's this woman who's supposed to take care of me, and the whole idea feels funny. Besides which, I still don't like her. But about that time I start remembering what I asked Mama about maybe not having to go to services all the time. So maybe if Mama's gone to the trouble to get somebody to look after me, I don't have to go to every service, like all the rest of them do—Carol Ann included—and sit still and behave, and listen to the preacher hollering all the time.

But what will I do when all the rest of them go off to services and leave me here with this woman? It certainly isn't like at my stepdaddy's, where we have Gus to wait on us, because we don't have much to do with him. Every Friday morning, Mama calls Gus into the library, to where she sits at the desk, making out the menus for the next week. Gus takes off his apron in the kitchen and puts on his snowy white jacket and comes and stands in front of her, and she hands him the menu she's written out, and he takes it and says, "Thank you, ma'am." And that's pretty much the extent of us having anything to do with him, because he just stays in the kitchen all the time. Except, of course, when he serves dinner to us, and when he does that, he wears that spotless white coat and it all starched and stiff and formal-looking, and he doesn't say a word.

The only time I ever heard him say a thing was once when my stepdaddy rang the little bell for him to come back into the dining room. And my stepdaddy asked him, "Gus, is there any reason why the gravy is cold?"

"No, sir," Gus said, and I think he was blushing, except his skin was dark, so I couldn't tell. He certainly looked embarrassed anyway. And he took away the gravy boat, and in a few minutes he brought it back and we could see the steam rising from it, it was so good and hot.

So I already know that being with this woman is certainly going to be different from the way it is with Gus, at my stepdaddy's house. There isn't really even a kitchen here for this woman to stay in, because the tent doesn't have one, except for the little shed outside in the backyard—the cookhouse—and it's nothing but three wooden walls and a sheet of tin for a roof, and boards put down to make a floor and a big wood stove for cooking on. So there's sure no room in there for her to stay.

Besides, I get a strange feeling that she's not going to be exactly like Gus. Or like Tulie either. Because she's got a lot of things she's going to say to me. I know that, but I don't know how I know it. And she's not one to bob her head and grin all the time, either. Because this woman has been with Mama and me for long minutes already, and she hasn't grinned one single time. Hasn't even really smiled very much. Just looked at me with eyes that look like they're trying to bore a hole right through me.

"Now you make her behave, Aunt Valley," Mama says, because it's time for the morning service, and they are all getting ready to go. But I am thinking: Aunt Valley? What a funny name! And why Aunt? Mama is looking hard at my face and she must be able to look right through my skin to where my jawbone is getting ready to open up, so she reaches over just as sweet as you please and puts her hand on my shoulder and pats me a little bit. Just enough to tell me to be quiet. But by the time this happens, I don't really have to ask, because just as her hand reaches for my shoulder, I get it figured out all by myself.

Mama's calling this old colored woman "Aunt" because that's the way all her family talks about colored women. And they call all colored men "Uncle," too. So I know this is just what Mama always does when we get around her family—because as soon as we are with them, she changes the way she talks about things. Sometimes, she even says things like "fixin' to go" somewhere. But she never talks like that when we're at home. And I can't imagine any one of us ever calling Gus "Uncle." The very idea of it makes me smile.

So we're standing there, and Mama's hand is resting on my shoulder very lightly now, because she knows she doesn't have to worry about me saying something embarrassing, and then Great-Aunt Kate and Carol Ann come out of the bedroom all dressed for services. They see this colored woman standing there, and Great-Aunt Kate and Carol Ann glance at each other; so they knew she was coming, even if I didn't. And then Aunt Tyler and Aunt Nell come out of the other room, and they're ready for services too, and pulling on their white gloves.

Aunt Tyler is tall and cool-looking, in a navy blue dress with a wide white collar. And Aunt Nell has on a pale blue, dotted-swiss dress and white, open-toed shoes. When Aunt Tyler and Aunt Nell look at Great-Aunt Kate, I can tell that they knew about this woman coming too. So everybody knew about her coming except me.

Mama is really enormously pleased with this whole thing, because she has a way of fluttering when she likes something a lot. Something like my having a real, honest-to-goodness colored woman to take care of me. So Mama puts her hand over her heart and flutters a little, and she has that look on her face that tells me this is one of those things she's going to remember forever. Already, I could tell you exactly what the words will be on down the road years and years from now: "Why, I'll never forget that day, the way I turned and looked at the two of you just standing there together. It's something I'll never forget for the rest of my life. Indeed, indeed. Not for the rest of my life."

She stands there, looking at us, and we're holding so still, you'd think somebody has a camera and is getting ready to take our picture. Me and this Aunt Valley standing there and not knowing what else to do except to look at Mama and to look at each other.

Coffee-milk eyes is what this Aunt Valley has. Because that's how the whites of her eyes look. Not really white at all, but what Aunt Nell calls "café au lait," because when Aunt Nell went to New Orleans that time, she learned new words like that. And she still likes to say them—words like "café au lait." It means coffee with milk. And that's exactly the color of the whites of this woman's eyes. We stand there for what seems like forever, me studying her and her studying me. And there is no fooling either one of us. She knows who's the boss. And so do I. And she knows that if I tell Mama she's been mean to me, she'll be gone so fast the door won't even hit her on the way out.

Mama says, "Now you behave, you hear me?" And she puts the tips of her white-gloved fingers under my chin, so that I can smell the faint aroma of Ivory soap from when she washed her gloves out last night, and her fingers are warm through the white cotton.

"Yes'm."

But she knows I'm not going to do it. Because it's part of the story for me not to do it. I know that, but I don't know how I know it. And it's part of the story for this colored woman to try and make me behave. But not quite be able to do it. Just enough for her to get paid. And I guess it all sounds pretty confusing, but it isn't. Not really. And even if it is confusing, that's all right. Because we all know the rules.

They all go walking off toward the tabernacle, Carol Ann's pink dress all starched and swaying on her just like a bell, and Aunt Tyler's white pumps rising and falling, as she walks through the grass. Mama's white-gloved hands fluttering as she walks and talks. And they go off and leave me with this colored woman I hardly know.

7

"Miss Amelia? Miss Amelia? You up there? You okay?" The strident voice, muffled and far away, the sound of the door opening at the bottom of the attic stairs, and the thumping footsteps before Maybelline's face appears on a level with the attic floor.

"Where are you?" Maybelline peering into attic gloom that was thrown into even deeper shadows because of the glare from the front window.

"By the window," I said—absently, I suppose—for even as I stood there, I was still watching them walk away down the hill toward the tabernacle.

"There you are!" Maybelline's voice jubilant, just as if she had found me during a child's game of hide-and-seek. "There's some ladies here to see you, Miss Amelia."

But at the same time, Aunt Valley said, *"You wanta help me put my things away?"*

"No, thanks," I say. And then, "What kind of name is Valley, anyway?"

"Just what my mama named me," she answers.

"Why'd she name you that?"

"'Cause valleys is peaceful places, I reckon." She goes into mine and Mama's room, where the little cot is set up against the inside wall and puts her paper sack under the cot. I guess that's what she means by putting her things away.

"What's so peaceful about valleys?" I ask when she comes out.

"Well, there's no cold winds blowing around in them, for one thing—like there is on tops of mountains, and there's lots of sweet grass for little lambs to eat, and clear little streams of water for drinking from."

"Oh." That makes sense to me. I can see a little white lamb who's lost and afraid and trying to climb around on the sharp, black rocks on the mountain. And crying for his mama. An icy cold wind blowing his fleece and he's shivering from the cold. Then far below, he sees a valley, all safe and warm and with the sun shining on green grass. And his mama waiting for him. So he picks his way down off the mountain and goes to the valley, to where his mama is waiting for him and nuzzles against her soft, sun-warmed side. I'm so glad he's found his mama that my eyes fill up.

"You all right?" Aunt Valley's voice intrudes and just for an instant, I'm startled to discover she's there, this old colored woman with the funny name. And besides, I'm not nearly through thinking about the lamb who's found his mama.

"Do you know how to tell stories?" I ask.

"I guess so." She seems a little uncertain.

"Well, tell me a story, then," I say.

"Please . . ." Aunt Valley adds for me, to remind me of my manners, and she looks at me hard and juts out her bottom lip.

"Please," I parrot, tilting my jaw to let her know I'm almost—but not quite—being smart with her. Because she's going to make me have good manners, but I don't think it's very good manners the way she interrupted the story I was thinking.

"Come on, then," she says, and she leads me out to the back porch. Not a real porch, of course, because it's just more wood shavings spread around on the ground right outside the back screen door, under another piece of tin that connects to the roof, but they all call it the porch. And she sits right down in that funny chair that has legs too short for it. Once upon a time, someone must have gotten to sawing off the legs just a little, trying to even them up, maybe, and finally got all of them too short. And they still aren't even. The seat of the chair is an honest-to-goodness cowhide, one that still has the cow's hair on it. It's made from the hide of a brown and white cow. Real pretty, but strange, especially when I stroke the hair like maybe there's still a real cow under it. Only the leather under the hair is all stiff and dead-feeling, and I feel a rabbit run over my grave every time I touch it.

She sits in the chair and the cowhide groans because of it, and she pats her lap, so I have to go and sit in it because that's the only way I'm going to get a story. But I don't lean back against her because her smell is funny and sharp, like copper or something, and she's hot and sweating—probably more from being scared of me than from the hot weather.

> "Chicken in the bread-pan,
> Eatin' fatty dough.
> Granny, will your dog bite?
> No, child. No."

She chants the words and bounces her heel up and down so that the knee I'm sitting on goes up and down too. Like you do for a baby when you play Ride-the-Horsey with it. And I just can't believe that she thinks I'm such a baby!

Silence.

"That's it?" I say. "That's supposed to be a story?"

"That's it," she says. The bottom lip is poking out again. A big, purple roll that's so huge, I'll bet she can jut it out all the way to the cookhouse. If she wants to.

"That's not a story," I protest, jutting out my own lip. But mine is thin and pink and not at all the magnificent and threatening kind of lip Aunt Valley has.

"Is too," she counters.

"Then what's it mean?"

"Mean?"

"Yes. Mean," I insist. Because everyone knows that stories have to mean something. But maybe not to this country kind of person who probably doesn't know much of anything, anyway.

She is fumbling for something to say, and I'm sitting there bolt upright and feeling a strange kind of power surge through me. I don't know what it is, but I like it very much. Because my story is better. And she doesn't have the faintest idea of what that silly thing of hers says. It isn't a story at all; just some old words strung together for saying to a baby who doesn't understand anything anyway. Besides, even if she could tell a story—which I'll bet anything she can't—it would probably be a Bible story, and I don't think much of those because I've had people try to tell me those before, and they aren't very interesting at all. Just about a lot of old, old men and all their "begats."

"What it means is this. . . ." She's still stuck on trying to figure it out, stumbling very slowly over words, drawing out their sounds and stalling and thinking so hard that the skin between her eyebrows looks like little rows of plowed earth, and sunlight glints off the teeny, silver beads of sweat on her forehead.

"You already said that," I tell her, feeling angry at her but not knowing why. "Tell me a story about a little lamb getting lost and looking for its mama."

"What it means is this. . . ."

She just won't leave it alone, and her eyebrows are coming closer and closer together the harder she tries. "What's that about a lamb?"

"I said,"—vexation creeps into my voice—"Tell me a story about a little lamb getting lost and looking for its mama."

She thinks about it. "Well, once there was this little lamb," she begins.

"Lost lamb!" I insist.

"Lost lamb, then!" Vexation in her voice, too.

"How'd it get lost?" I am careful to make my voice so innocent-sounding, and besides, she'd never guess in a month of Sundays what I'm up to. Deep inside, where she can't see it, is the power again. Power over her. And anger, too.

"How'd it get lost?" she parrots.

"Yes, how'd it get lost?" I'm filled with a deep and abiding satisfaction, just being this near her squirming.

She looks at me hard. "It got lost 'cause it was BAD," she pronounces unexpectedly.

"No, it wasn't!" I yell.

"Yes, it was!" She is unyielding. "It was too bad, sure enough, 'cause it went off from its mama after she told it not to. That's why it got lost in the first place."

"Oh." That makes sense. But it also makes the hairs prickle on the back of my neck.

"And when it got lost, it was awful scared, 'cause dark was coming." When she says the word "dark," she says it in a little husky kind of whisper that makes it a lot worse than it really is.

"I hate the dark," I say. Truth! Because all at once, I can see a darkness like when Mama closes the door after she puts me to bed and kisses my forehead, and she turns out the lamp because she thinks I'm asleep, and I crack open my eyes just enough to see her walk along the path of light that comes into the room from the hallway and then her shadow in the doorway, and she always turns and looks at me one more time. Then the door closes and the path of light is gone and dark is everywhere. The kind of dark like it must be at night in Tulie's yard, where something's hiding, but you can't see it.

"Goodness, honey," she laughs. "We sure need the dark. Why, making the dark is just one of the best things God ever did, I expect."

"Why?"

79

"'Cause dark and light is the way He breaks time into little bitty pieces for us. Like your mama cutting up your dinner so you can eat it better. Just right for one bite at a time."

Now that's an idea I like. God cutting up day and night for me. I can see a knife and fork—right out of the top drawer in the buffet in the dining room, the drawer that's all lined with soft gray felt so nothing gets scratched—and just clicking away, and God cutting out shining stars from a slab of something that's just as black and as tough as shoe leather. And putting them on a plate with pink roses on it and a little tiny edge of pure gold all the way around, just like the ones in Great-Aunt Kate's china cabinet.

"What else did God do?" I ask, thinking to go ahead and get her off the lost lamb story. Because I know I can do a better job of thinking that one up myself. And anyway, if I leave it up to someone like this Aunt Valley person, there's no telling what might happen. She might even leave that poor little lamb lost so that he never does find his mama. And once that thought is in my mind, I can't seem to tear away from it.

"Well, let me think up this lamb story first, and then I'll tell you a story I do know. And that's how God made everything in creation."

"No! Stop!" I yell. She is surprised.

"Why, what's the matter?"

"You're going to let the little lamb die." The words catch in my throat.

"Well, sometimes things do die, you know. People, too," she adds. "Didn't you never know nobody what died?" She is sincerely perplexed. And so am I.

"Yes," I mutter. "My daddy died. My real daddy. And I know where there's children gonna die, too. Maybe gonna die right this very minute."

She is staring at me, that dumb old mouth hanging open, and breathing through her mouth and the raspy sound of air going in and going out, going in and going out. It's an awful sound.

Finally, she says, "Honey, I sure am sorry 'bout your daddy. Old Aunt Valley is just sure enough one big old fool sometimes." I can tell she's really sorry. "I'll tell you another story."

This time I lean back against her. "Can I have a wishbone at supper tonight?" I ask. Because this time, I will be sure to get one of my very own, like I always did when Grandmama was at Camp Meeting, because the tent belonged to her and not to Great-Aunt Kate at all, and when Grandmama was here, she always gave me a wishbone.

"Sure you can, honey," she says. "I'll make sure you get a wishbone. All for yourself."

Good, I think. I get a wishbone because my daddy died. "Now tell me another story. But not about the lamb getting lost."

"Please," she reminds me again.

"Please." Not smart. Not one bit of smart this time.

"Well, I'll tell you the story of how God Almighty made the world, 'cause that's the only story I know what's a real story."

A Bible story, I think, but I don't say anything because, after all, I'm going to get a wishbone at supper.

"The way it happened was this: First of all, everything was dark. There wasn't nothing light in all of creation."

That word again. DARK. "Not even the sun?" I venture, hopefully. Because if I think about things like that, about there being no sun, I mean, I go all cold and scared inside, like listening to a ghost story. Then I get pictures behind my eyes that show things I've never seen before, like a world without light of any kind. And that's usually what I'm doing when Great-Aunt Kate clucks her tongue and says I'm "dreaming" again. But the strange thing is that I can really do it. See things, I mean. And feel them, too.

"Not even the sun. Because God hadn't made the sun yet. In fact, He hadn't even gotten around to making Heaven yet. So the Bible says, you know."

I don't know. "Then where did God live?" I ask.

"Blamed if I know," she says. "Guess He lived wherever He wanted to live, that's all."

"But where was that?"

"Now I done told you I don't know. Just listen a little bit now and let's see can we get this story on the road and moving along."

"All right."

"So like I said, everything was dark. Everything. And where'd you hear about children gonna die anyway?"

The question, coming as it does so unexpected-like and right at the end of the sing-song, tell-a-story voice, feels way out of place and strange.

"I don't know. I made it up," I lie. And then, quite suddenly, that's true. I did make it up. I'm sure of it.

She goes right back at the story, without missing a lick.

"And while everything was all dark like that, God made Heaven and earth. But it was still nothing but darkness. Dark on the land. Dark in the middle of the oceans. Dark on top of the highest mountain. Not even a tiny star twinkling. Not a one."

81

I press my head against her shoulder and bend my knees a little, just to tighten my hold on her big lap. And wait for God to cut up day and night for me.

"Then the next thing God done was something wonderful. He just opened up His mouth and said, 'LET——THERE——BE——LIGHT!'"

She says the words in a big, booming voice that makes the hairs on my arms stand up. "And poof! Here comes the light, all over everything, warm and good and clean, like a spring morning when all of a sudden you remember exactly what summer feels like because of that warm old sunshine. And God looked around at all the light and He said, 'That's good.'"

"Oh, I'm glad He made light," I venture, most sincerely.

"Me, too," she says. "Then I guess He got to thinking about maybe it wouldn't do for it to be daylight all the time, and that's exactly when He fixed it so when day's been around a while, dark comes again. That's when the Bible says He separated the light from the darkness, and He called the light day and He called the darkness night."

"I still don't like the dark," I say, and I am thinking once again about God cutting up dark and light on the pretty plate from Great-Aunt Kate's china cabinet.

Carol Ann walks up from out of nowhere, and I am hanging so hard onto the way the plate looks where the Great God Almighty is cutting up day and night for me, that I don't even know Carol Ann is there until her face is right there on the plate among all the stars.

"You leave services?" I ask, incredulously. Because Carol Ann is supposed to be so well-mannered—or so they all say—and everyone knows that well-mannered young ladies don't leave in the middle of services.

Carol Ann doesn't say anything to us, but she starts pumping water into the pan on the wooden counter and dips her fingers in the pan and flicks water on her face and pats it dry with her handkerchief.

"I was fixin' to faint," she says, fluttering her eyelids. "So Mama told me to come on home and stay cool. She said your Aunt Valley was to take care of me."

Carol Ann's face is pasty pale but with two red spots on her cheeks, just like she's wearing rouge.

Aunt Valley lifts me off her knee and stands me in front of her.

"You go on inside and turn on the fan and lie down," she says to Carol Ann. "And I'll bring you a glass of iced tea to drink."

Carol Ann glances at me from under her damp eyebrows and smiles a little. Just a little.

"Wait a minute!" I yell. "You're supposed to take care of me! My mama's the one that's paying you!"

82

"Why, honey," Aunt Valley reaches out and hugs me to her with one of those big ham-arms. *"I'll just be a little minute. Besides, she's sick."*

"She's always sick," I mutter, but it's too late. My Aunt Valley has taken Carol Ann's hand and is leading her inside. Carol Ann looks back at me over her shoulder and sticks out her tongue.

"That's all right," I yell at them. *"I still get a wishbone!"*

"Lord, have mercy! You're gonna faint! I knew it was too hot up here for you!" Maybelline grabbed my arm and practically dragged me across the attic and down the steps. "Let's bathe off your face a little bit. Maybe that'll make you feel better."

She guided me into the cool, blue-tiled bathroom and sat me down on the side of the tub just as if I were a child, and then wrung out a facecloth in cool water and wiped my face.

"What ladies?" I thought to ask.

"Just some ladies," Maybelline said, pressing the cool cloth against my forehead. "But I 'spect we better ask them to come back another time. Why, you just scared me to death, you standing there just like a statue and me hollering and hollering at you and you not hearing a thing!"

"Nonsense!" I protested, pushing away the facecloth. "I feel just fine. I was thinking of something."

"You were talking all crazy-like about a wishbone," Maybelline said in an accusing voice.

"Well," I sputtered, "when you cut up a chicken tonight, I'd like it if you cut a wishbone. I'd like to have one. That's all I was talking about."

"Well, sure I will," Maybelline said, but she was still puzzled.

"Then if that's all settled," I said, "I'll go see whoever it is has come to call on me."

Of course, the minute I went into the parlor and saw the three young women, gloved, hatted, and lined up on my Duncan Phyfe settee like they were waiting for a bus, I knew at once that they must be from the Junior Women's Club. I moved silently toward them across the Aubusson rug and three faces moved upward, like upturned daisies following the sun across the sky. Well, we'll see what the Junior Women's Club has to offer in the way of doing things right, I thought. For certainly, there had to be some young people around who knew their manners. There just had to be.

Instinctively, they stood.

"Good afternoon," I said, as if I were bestowing a blessing upon them, and it certainly was a blessing, what with the gift they had coming to them.

"Please sit down," I said. "May I offer you some iced tea?"

They glanced at each other briefly, as if they were a bit unsure of whether to accept or not, and finally, the one in the middle spoke for them all. "No, thank you, Miss Amelia. We appreciate it just the same."

I sat down and gazed at them openly, without smiling, studying the earnest, young faces for lines of familiarity. Behind me, Maybelline had advanced as far as the French doors that led from the dining room, but she stopped short of entering the living room and turned and began to straighten the silver tea service on the buffet, just as if that had been her intention the whole time.

In the living room, the young woman in the middle, the one who clutched her purse as if she were seeking to draw some kind of comfort from it, spoke in a breathless, nervous tone.

"I don't know if you remember me, Miss Amelia, but I'm Betsy Carmichael . . . Anderson, now, and when I was just a little girl, I used to come visit you on Sunday afternoons with my mama. My mama was Miss Hannah?" The voice rose in hopeful expectation.

Oh—Hannah.

"I remember."

The young woman waited expectantly, as if I would add some niceties, but I didn't. Certainly, I remembered Hannah Carmichael— nosiest woman I ever met in my whole life. Always asking how much we paid for everything. "How much do you pay your yard man? How much did it cost when you had your hardwood floors re-done?" And especially, I remembered the day when she picked up the cream pitcher and simply wasn't thinking . . . turned it over, to see if it was Haviland, I guess . . . and dumped the cream right in her lap! That memory brought a reluctant smile to my lips, which Hannah's daughter promptly took to be friendliness.

84

She grinned at me. "Well, Miss Amelia, these here . . . I mean, these are my sisters-in-law, Mary Louise—and Ruth." She gestured at the pale, smiling faces. "And we're the New Library Committee."

So I was right.

"How may I help you?" I asked, innocently.

"Well," Betsy Anderson—nee Carmichael—sputtered a little. "We're looking into raising funds for building a new library." She fumbled in her purse, drawing from it a paper, which she unfolded and held out toward me. I made no move whatsoever to reach forward and take it. Betsy started to rise to deliver it, but then she realized that the Queen Anne coffee table was in the way, so she thrust the paper clumsily at Ruth, who arose, delivered it to me, and then backed her return to the couch.

"What is this?" I held the paper but made no move to read it.

"That's a list of people in town that we've identified as potential members of a Library Building Committee. We hope you will accept the honor of chairing that committee."

Still, I did not look at the paper.

"I don't think so," I answered and held the paper in thin air until Ruth regained her feet and came to take it out of my hand. Just for the briefest moment, I quite frankly relished the awkward silence and the confused glances among the three young women who looked for all the world to me as if they were only little girls playing dress-up in their mothers' gloves and hats.

And then a small wrenching in me for their awkward good manners and their polite and fragile response to the dilemma in which they found themselves. Because, invisible and silent, their mothers stood near them, chanting the time-honored instructions: Now, sugar, you must have good manners, no matter what anyone says to you. Why, good manners is what separates us from the beasts, you know.

And hearing again the silent charge to duty given by all the mothers who had ever been, including my own, I smiled at the young women, drawing little, fluttering gasps of relief from them. Betsy Anderson, nee Carmichael, actually pressed a gloved hand against her bosom.

Well, well! Maybe it isn't all gone, after all.

"Oh, Miss Amelia, why we're just as sorry as can be if we've troubled you with this," she sputtered prettily.

"No need to be sorry," I assured them, and while they were relaxed and tittering a little, in relief, I carefully prepared the words I would say to them.

"And no need for a committee either."

That certainly stopped their tittering.

"Because I have decided to give this house to the community for its new library."

Three blank faces and three open mouths.

"With all the furniture, of course, though I would imagine you may well choose to hold an auction for some of it—a suitable auction, a tasteful one, mind you—to clear the house a little for shelving and for purchasing more books. And perhaps for having the roof inspected."

Now, they gazed openly around the magnificent room, noting the spaciousness and the high ceiling and the beautiful plaster bas-relief around the chandelier anchored some fourteen feet above our heads.

"Give?" Betsy Anderson managed to whisper. "This beautiful house?"

"Exactly," I responded. "I'm going to live abroad, you see, and I won't need this house any longer."

How on earth those words ever sprang from my lips, I would never know, but I heard a very sharp cough from Maybelline, and of course, it would be just like her to gallop into the living room right in front of everyone and demand to know why I'd said it. So I stood up and moved toward the door, a gesture that would let the young women know that the visit was indeed over. At least, for that day.

"There's only one condition," I said, and they literally froze, right where they were standing. "You will not say one word to anyone about this for ten full days."

"Ten days?"

"Exactly ten days," I said, firmly. "In the meantime, I'll see my attorney and have the papers drawn up. I'll be in touch with you. But mind that you say nothing until ten days have passed."

"Yes, ma'am," they spoke in unison. Then, still shocked, speechless, and smiling in their disbelief, the young women filed through the front door, each one shaking my hand warmly and earnestly. And one of the pale Anderson girls pressed my hand to her cheek before she joined the other two. I watched them smiling and clutching each others' gloved hands as they traipsed down the walkway and then turned and waved at me once more before they tittered their way down the sidewalk.

As soon as I closed the door, Maybelline wrapped herself around my neck just like a mangy fur collar, weeping openly and hiccuping noisily.

"I . . . never . . . saw anything so . . ." she tried to say. "Such . . . a beautiful . . . so generous. . . ."

It isn't for you, I thought, annoyed. It's for our mothers and this town, and all the good people who are clean and honorable and upstanding. And for Henry!

"But what was that you said about going abroad?" Maybelline looked at me in a most accusatory fashion, but I glared back at her so hard that it silenced anything else she might have intended to say.

"I'll go call Little Tommy and set up an appointment for tomorrow," I said, walking toward the dining room. "We'll leave here before ten days are out."

How strange, I thought, to feel already that this house is no longer mine. And the feeling isn't one bit bad!

8

I went directly to the bank the next morning and into the office where Little Tommy sat behind his daddy's big mahogany desk. He stood up when I came in, and I watched him carefully to see if there was anything in his face to betray that he'd already heard about my plans for giving the house away.

But nothing like that was in his eyes, so we sat down, and I told him what I was going to do and asked him to arrange all the paperwork for me. Of course, he was surprised, but he did a good job of tending to business, writing down everything I said on a legal pad. When I finished, I sat there, watching his florid face, watching the eyes that flickered just enough for me to know that he was wondering if I'd had a stroke or if I were going crazy.

"I'm of sound mind and perfectly serious," I said to him while he sat there looking back at me.

"But, Miss Amelia," he sputtered. "Give away your house? Are you sure?"

"Of course I'm sure. Otherwise I wouldn't be here making these arrangements," I said.

"But where will you live?" His question seemed to be a sincere one. So I was right. There was a little something of his daddy in him after all.

"Abroad," I said.

"Abroad?"

"That's right."

"Abroad where?"

"Jerusalem," I answered, without a moment of hesitation.

He didn't ask another thing about where I was going to live, but just kept writing the details in pencil and checking with me from time to time on certain points.

"Do you mean for them to have the right to sell it?"

"No. It will be the new library."

"Okay." He scribbled more words onto the page.

"Do you have any other provisions you want included?"

"Yes," I answered. "I want them to be sure and keep Henry's oil portrait hanging in the front room where everyone can see it. And his mahogany desk, too. Anything else in the way of furniture, they can auction, if necessary, for purchasing books."

Little Tommy scribbled away on the paper.

"And too," I added, "there's extra property with the house, you know. Going all the way over to the next street. They have my permission to sell that, but not for something like a feed and grain store or anything of that nature, mind you."

Little Tommy didn't look up.

"What could they sell that property for?" he inquired, still writing.

"A house," I said. "A nice house. No . . . wait. A church. That's what. Methodist or Presbyterian."

He kept writing, but the smallest possible smile played around at the corner of his mouth.

"You find that to be amusing?" I asked.

"No, ma'am," Little Tommy said. "Not a thing funny about it."

I added, "But put it in writing that I advise them to keep that extra lot. Maybe as the town grows, they will need it for expanding the library. And one more thing," I added. "You are not to say one word about this to anyone until nine days from today have passed. Make the effective date on these papers to be exactly nine days from today."

Again, a brief glance at me, but he wrote it all down and then read back to me all that I had instructed. I nodded my approval, and he called his secretary into the office and gave the handwritten pages to her.

"This is completely confidential," he said. She nodded gravely. That's when I recognized her, and that was nice. Seeing the Clarkston chin again, I mean. A brute of a chin it was, as on all the Clarkstons. But on her, because she was rather large-boned, it was an attractive feature. Gave her a look of complete trustworthiness.

"Would you like me to get you some tea or something while we're waiting for her to get that typed up?" Little Tommy asked.

"Thank you. That would be nice," I replied.

As soon as Little Tommy left the room, I went to the window of his office and stood looking out at the yard that was so familiar to me. At the three enormous water oaks under whose shade Henry and I had sat on early summer afternoons when I used to walk over with a picnic lunch for us to enjoy together.

Henry! Would you like what I'm doing? Like the way I'm protecting our reputation from the old gossips who would pity me and condemn you for not providing well enough for me?

Henry. His eyes such a chocolate brown and sparkling. The little tilt-down angle they had so that he always managed to look just a bit perplexed about something or other. Sitting with me on the quilt in the shade of the trees, a breeze ruffling his hair, laughing with me and then reaching over to take my hand. I always wanted more than anything to love him right there. Right in the wide-open yard, in the shade of the trees, hum together with the music of the earth and. . . .

Behind me, Little Tommy re-entered the office, balancing a fragile cup and saucer in his huge hands, and I turned from the window, praying that he would not notice the flush I could feel on my cheeks.

"Here's your tea, Miss Amelia," he said, depositing the cup carefully on the edge of the desk. "Are you all right? Is it too warm in here for you?"

"I'm just fine, thank you," I mumbled, and sat back down in the chair and took the cup of tea gratefully and in hands that wanted so very much to tremble—but I wasn't going to allow that. Most certainly, I wasn't going to allow that.

Time for only a sip or two of tea before the Clarkston girl returned and handed Little Tommy some legal-sized, typed pages.

After she left and closed the door behind her, he asked me once more, "You're sure?" And while he asked, he was taking the shiny black pen out of its holder.

"I'm sure," I assured him and reached for the pen.

So that was how I made all the arrangements so quickly and surprisingly enough, so painlessly. Like a dream. Just as if it weren't really happening at all.

And now that I knew the house would be loved and cared for, there was no longer a feeling of losing it, of failing to keep something with so many memories to it. Because that was the house where Sweet Mama herself had been born, and my grandmama and then my mama. And the house where my mama and I used to sleep in the very bed where I slept all those years later.

Something about all of that, I suppose, that made me think of myself as a link in a chain. Only there wouldn't be any coming after me. No one to tell the stories to or give the house to when I was gone. No one left.

So the first thing I did that very same afternoon I'd been to see Little Tommy was to get all of my daddy's love letters out of the bottom drawer of the chifforobe, where they had stayed all those years, and I read through them for one last time, even though I knew every one of them by heart and could even hear Mama's voice speaking the words I read.

Then I dragged the cast-iron Dutch oven out of the old chicken house and into the backyard, and I shredded the letters into it, put a match to them, and watched where the flames, invisible in the glare of the sun, ate their way darkly through the thick linen shreds. When only ashes were left, I took them over under the big pear tree in what used to be the chicken yard and put them on the ground.

And I wondered if maybe there were something in the ashes that would be absorbed into the soil and then into the tree. Something that would be in the hard, green pears next year. So that one windy night, when the pears fell with that percussive *bang!* against the tin roof of the old chicken house in the dark and the wind and the rain, something from the letters would be in them. Maybe.

I know now, of course, that nothing is ever lost. It always shows up somewhere. And I guess I knew it then, but I didn't know that I knew it.

The hardest thing to do was to give away Henry's clothes. But I did it anyway. Went over to the Baptist Church and got Thomas, the handyman over there, and brought him right up into the attic and watched him while he brought down the boxes. But I didn't watch while he loaded them into the back of his truck and drove away.

After that, there wasn't really anything else that needed to be done.

Maybelline started in to talking about trying to find room in the car for all those awful Christmas decorations of hers, but I soon squelched that.

"There's no room," I said. "Because I am determined to take my grandmama's Haviland china. So you'll have to leave those decorations." But she looked so crestfallen that I added, "Think how nice it will be for the new library to be able to use them."

And she softened right up to that.

"Why, I never thought about that," she sputtered. "Of course we'll leave them here."

I was going on the assumption that the librarian would have far better taste than to allow those tacky things to be displayed. Still, I sneaked up into the attic later on and marked the box "Throw this out!" in big, bold letters.

The only thing out of the ordinary after that was that I kept on feeling a little dizzy from time to time, what with all the memories still pressing in on me. Once, I even thought for a few minutes it was just Mama and me packing up to go out to Camp Meeting one summer.

But of course, it wasn't.

That's how it finally came to be the morning of our leaving, coming like I knew it would come, but in the end, not quite as hard as I'd thought it would be.

And that was partly because the old thrill of going somewhere before daylight was still there for me, and, too, that none of it felt real. More like a dream.

In the pre-dawn of the morning of the tenth day after I'd given my house to the town, Maybelline finished loading in the car everything we were to take with us. We'd worked late into the night before, loading in the bed linens and the pillows and a few pots and pans and my grandpapa's mantel clock and the big box into which I'd packed my grandmama's Haviland china—and it all fit in just perfectly. Why, there wasn't room for a broomstraw, the way we'd packed everything in so well.

Maybelline wanted to tie some boxes of blankets and clothes on top of the car, but I wouldn't let her. No need to look like a bunch of tramps, for Heaven's sake! Even if we *would* be gone before daylight came. So we emptied the boxes and packed those things in the trunk and under the front seat and anywhere else we could.

The last thing we did was close the front door of the house and lock it and put the key under the mat. Well, maybe I had lost this house, but I knew I had done right by it, and that was a great comfort to me.

When Maybelline and I were in the dark car and Maybelline was ready to put the key in the ignition, she said, "Father, into Thy hands we commend our spirits."

"Good Heavens!" I said, alarmed. "You sound just like we're getting ready to die!"

"Well, I just wanted the Lord to know we're on our way. Going where He said we should."

I heaved a sigh in spite of myself but said not another word, not even when Maybelline put the car in reverse and backed over all those caladiums I told her she'd planted too close to the driveway.

9

There were two things I knew for sure when Maybelline and I left my house forever: The house would be cherished—that was the most important, of course—and I also knew I still loved to be going on a trip and leaving before daylight. Didn't seem to matter one little bit where I was going, just so long as we could leave before dawn. It didn't even seem to matter that I was leaving my house forever and going off to live in some old shack near a town called Jerusalem, for Heaven's sake! But part of it may have been because none of it seemed absolutely real to me, not even when we drove right through the middle of town, along the quiet streets, past the silent buildings and the lazy traffic light blinking yellow at the highway, and turned right, heading north toward this place where Maybelline was taking us.

We drove right past Edna's house. Her porch light was on, of course, because ever since Mr. Charlie passed on—and that wasn't too many years after Maybelline came to live with me—Edna and her sister from Macon had lived alone there, and Edna was nervous about that. Said it wasn't safe for two women to be all alone. Everybody knew that Edna kept a loaded shotgun under her bed, and that she was nervous, and that she really couldn't see very well, even in the daytime. So no one ever dared set foot on her porch after dark, for fear she'd think they were burglars and blow their heads off before she ever found out for sure. In fact, we all halfway expected she'd shoot her own sister in the middle of some night when the sister got up to go to the bathroom. But it hadn't happened. Not yet, anyway.

Maybelline and I had gone to visit Edna one afternoon in the spring, before everything about our leaving town had come to a head. And even though Edna was not that much older than I was, she had certainly gone downhill fast, after Mr. Charlie died.

We knew she was confined to a wheelchair, so that was no surprise. But the way she'd shrunk! Why, she was no bigger than a child, and Edna had always been a good, stout woman. And, too, I wasn't even sure she knew who we were. Napped in her chair most of the time we were there. But her sister seemed to be in good health. Good enough, anyway, that she could take care of Edna.

Later, Maybelline and I talked about how bad Edna looked, and Maybelline cried about it a little. I guess she certainly owed something to her, the way Edna had taken her in when she had nowhere else to go.

Maybe Maybelline and I were both thinking about Edna that gray-dark morning we passed her house for the last time, though we had uttered not a single word to each other, and before I even realized it, we were passing by the roadside park, the last thing we would have to remind us of the town we were leaving.

Before us, the highway stretched away in front of our headlights, and off to the sides, I had glimpses of fenceposts and an occasional dirt road. Ahead of us a good six or eight miles was the road to Mount Horeb Camp Ground, but before I could mention that to Maybelline, she started in to talking.

"I guess I always did like taking a trip, Miss Amelia. Any trip to any place. I just love to be going," Maybelline said, and I thought it was ironic that she was echoing exactly what I was thinking to myself, remembering how Mama and I drove over to Great-Aunt Kate's from Savannah before dawn all those years ago.

"Hadn't been for my knowing the Lord Himself sent me to be with you, I'd have moved on long ago," Maybelline said.

She glanced over at me, and even though it was still dark outside, I could see her face in the light from the dashboard a little. And I could tell that for some strange reason, we'd both thought of the same thing and exactly at the same time—the trip Maybelline had been taking when she was thrown out of that truck all those years ago. I certainly didn't know what to say to her about it, and so the silence grew and grew until it was like a vacuum that needed filling. Because everyone knows how nature abhors a vacuum.

"Be with me, Lord Jesus," Maybelline prayed aloud, and then she took a deep breath and began releasing the words so that they were sucked up in the vacuum cleaner, just like strands of crochet thread from the rug in the big house that was farther and farther behind us with every mile.

"Me and Bobby was going on a trip, but he went on without me. You know about that."

I nodded, uncomfortable with the subject of Maybelline's abandonment and yet delighted at finally being able to learn something about it after all those years. I'll have to tell Edna. That was the first thought in my mind. Then the realization. No. Edna's in that dark house behind us, and I'll never see her again. Home and friends are gone. No one to tell it to. And nothing to keep Maybelline's story away from me any longer.

"Me and him was going up to South Carolina all the way from near Tallahassee, Florida, where we was living. He worked a few hours a week at a fishing camp, and I really thought maybe he was going to be happy there. Pretty place, it was. And the man he worked for let us put our little travel trailer on a knoll with pine trees, right beside one of the lakes. We had a view of the water, and Bobby was even talking about maybe building us a little screen porch. But then one day, he just took it in his head that he had to go see his mama up in South Carolina. He'd do that every once in a while—decide he had to go see his mama like that."

I nodded my head, just to let Maybelline know I was listening, but still, there was something embarrassing about hearing it. And I'd already made up my mind that if Maybelline started coming right out and saying that she and this Bobby-person were not man and wife, I was prepared to stop her. Because I certainly didn't want to hear that.

"I was waitressing at a little cafe just a few miles down the road, but when Bobby took it in his head so sudden-like to go to South Carolina, the manager wouldn't give me any time off to go with him, so I had to quit. That's what set Bobby off, you see—I went and told him about that. About quitting my job. If I'd had more sense, I'd have waited until we got to his mama's before I said anything about it. Because between me and her, we could have calmed him down. But no, I had to go and open my big mouth, and us sitting there at that traffic light right by the Gulf station. Bobby just went wild. I thought for sure he was going to hit me, but he didn't. He reached over and opened the door on my side and yelled at me to get out. And when I sat there—couldn't have moved a muscle if my life depended on it—why, he gave me a shove and out I went. Just like that."

Somehow, I needed to let Maybelline know that I heard what she said, because when someone says something like that to you, you can't just sit there and say nothing. But on the other hand, I was wondering, What on earth can I say to her?

"I'm sorry that happened to you," I finally said, very simply.

"Well, I thank you for that." Then she brightened and sat up straight and flexed her fingers from the tight grip they'd had on the steering wheel. "I guess it turned out to be for the best, you know. The Lord never takes anything away without giving something in return."

I'd heard that old saying often enough, but somehow—probably because I was thinking about my grandmama's beautiful Haviland china that was packed in a big box in the backseat and not sitting in that curved-glass china cabinet back in the dining room, where it had been kept since my grandmama got it from her grandmama—it was hard for me to believe that Maybelline's "Dear Lord" could ever give me something that would make up for what all I had lost.

Maybelline was still hefting up her shoulders and sitting up straighter and straighter, just like an old rooster getting all cranked up for a good crowing. So I braced myself, for I knew from years of living with her what was coming next. And I was right.

"The Lord works in mysterious ways, His wonders to perform!" Maybelline yelled. "Just think—if Bobby hadn't thrown me out, I wouldn't have come to live with you."

From the corner of my eye, I could see Maybelline looking at me, and in the dark, I could imagine the hopeful lift to the penciled eyebrows. The expectancy. So I managed a half-smile and nodded my head, a gesture that seemed to satisfy her, so she put her attention back on her driving. But she had started humming deep in her throat, and once again, I knew what else was coming. Good Heavens!

> We're mar-ching to Zi—on,
> Beau-ti-ful, beau-ti-ful Zi—on;
> We're mar-ching up-ward to Zi-on,
> The beau-ti-ful ci-ty of God!

How maddening!

> Mar-ching up-ward to Zi-on,
> The beau-ti-ful ci-ty of God!

"We get on down the road a bit, we'll find someplace to get us some hot coffee," Maybelline said. "And when it gets to be time for lunch, I got a surprise for you."

And because Maybelline was thinking about food, she changed her hymn:

> Break Thou the bread of life, Dear Lord, to me,
> As Thou didst break the loaves be-side the sea . . .

And me thinking: And where were You, Maybelline's Dear Lord, on that day long ago? That's what I want to know. Maybelline harping all the time about You knowing when every little sparrow falls, and her thinking it's You that gives her everything she's got—hiccups, even, for Heaven's sake. Her getting thrown out of a truck like that, and You supposed to be taking care of her. Somebody please explain that to me if they can.

Then I noticed where we were. "We're coming up on the road to Mount Horeb Camp Ground," I said. "Let's turn in and drive through it."

"What's that you want to do?" Maybelline asked, because she'd still been singing when I spoke.

Before I could say it all again, I saw the familiar dirt road off to the side.

"Turn here!" I yelled, and Maybelline did, throwing up gravel before she finished braking, so that a curtain of all the dust we'd kicked up veiled the road in front of us.

"Here?" she asked, blinking.

"Yes, here." I laughed in spite of myself.

"Where are we?" she sputtered.

"The road to Mount Horeb Camp Ground," I answered.

"Where you used to come when you were a little girl?"

"The same."

"Well, I'm glad to get to see it, but I sure do wish you'd given me some warning," Maybelline said. "As a matter of fact, I always wondered why we never came out here for Camp Meeting some time."

"I just never kept up with it after Mama passed on," I said. But of course, there was another reason, too: I could never imagine spending Camp Meeting with someone like Maybelline. Mercy! She'd have gotten saved four times a day and twice on Sunday! And told everybody all about it—all the time. Hollering and praising the Lord all day long.

"That's a shame," she said.

"What?"

"Your not keeping up with it."

"Maybe." But I was too busy now, looking at the old road that hadn't really changed one bit, so that it was all so familiar to me, even in the still-dim light before dawn.

Just like it was that summer when Aunt Valley promised me I could have my very own wishbone that night at dinner. But I didn't get it. At least, not the wishbone I was supposed to get.

Because when it's nearly time for dinner, Great-Aunt Kate tells Aunt Valley to fix a plate for "Miss" Carol Ann and she'll have her dinner in the bedroom because she still doesn't feel very well, and be sure to put the wishbone on "Miss" Carol Ann's plate. And Great-Aunt Kate gets plenty upset when Aunt Valley looks her straight in the eye and tells her that she's as sorry as can be, ma'am, but she's already promised it to me, and Great-Aunt Kate says to Mama that I'm an opportunist—and Carol Ann should have it because she's the one sick. That's when Aunt Valley starts wiping her hands on her apron in an agitated way and looking at me with those deep furrows between her eyes.

Mama takes my hand and leads me into the bedroom, just like I know she will do, and she says what I already know she will say. That please— just this once, and just for her—let Carol Ann have the wishbone. And I know that's coming, because Mama has a way of asking me to do things just for her, and of course, that makes it a whole different thing than just my wanting what was promised to me. Because I can never refuse her. Not when she looks at me like that, with her eyes such a pretty blue and with little dancing lights in them. Already, I can imagine what a fine thing it will be when I make this noble sacrifice just for her and then she will hug me and say, "That's my fine girl!"

When we come out of the bedroom together to where Great-Aunt Kate and Carol Ann and Aunt Valley are all awaiting the verdict, Mama flutters a little and then pronounces, "Carol Ann may have the wishbone. And we hope it will make her feel better."

Of course, I didn't know anything at all about that last part of what Mama said, and I sure as anything don't hope that my wishbone makes Carol Ann feel better. But Mama's hand is on my shoulder, patting me just a little, real gentle-like, almost like her hand is saying for me please, just this once and just for her, to behave.

Standing there beside her feels so noble and wonderful, I don't think any more about her adding that last part all on her own and without my agreeing to it.

About this time, we hear a car pulling up in the backyard, and it's Aunt Nell. Because she says she just had to go all the way to Savannah today because one of the stores there was having such a wonderful sale. And the yipping little dogs bounce ahead of her through the back doorway and she comes in behind them.

Aunt Nell absolutely refuses to stay out at the Camp Ground at night, so she drives back to Great-Aunt Kate's house in town every single evening after supper and then comes back out the next morning.

She has those two little dogs that are called Pomeranians. Nikki and Honey are their names and they're just about the funniest looking things you could ever see—little, furry pom-poms with legs sticking out of them and tiny, pointed ears. And the legs and the ears are the only way you can tell which end is up. To find their eyes, you have to smooth back their hair, and once, when I did that, I was startled to see angry, little, black eyes that snapped, "Leave me alone!"

But Aunt Nell really loves them and calls them her "babies," and she says they don't like being out at the Camp Ground at night. So every evening, right after supper, she picks all the leftover chicken off the bones and wraps it in waxed paper and puts it in her purse. Nikki and Honey know what this means, and they yip and bounce around like they're on springs until Aunt Nell tells them, "Come on, then!" and they race ahead of her out to the car, yipping and bouncing because they know it's time to go back to Great-Aunt Kate's house for the night. And they know they're going to get to have the chicken Aunt Nell has in her purse.

"I came back for supper," she says when she sees us all standing there. For the briefest possible moment, I can see the question formulating itself behind her eyes: What's going on here? But then I can also see her reject the question. Because she really doesn't want to know. "Oh, look! There's a fly in here!" she says instead, waving her hand in the air above a platter of sliced tomatoes on the table. Nikki and Honey are still bouncing around because they can smell that there's fried chicken around somewhere. Their mouths are stretched into frenzied little grins that show their sharp, needle-teeth. Because they've been shut up most of the day at Great-Aunt Kate's house while Aunt Nell was in Savannah, so they are even bouncier and more frenzied than usual.

Aunt Valley goes back to the cookhouse and we all go in and sit down at the table, all except for Carol Ann, of course. When Aunt Valley comes back inside, she's carrying the platter of chicken, which she sets down in front of Great-Aunt Kate. The wishbone, plump and crispy, is right on top, and Great-Aunt Kate glances at me before she takes it and puts it on a plate for Carol Ann. Then, while the platter is making its way down the table, Great-Aunt Kate splits open a biscuit on the plate and spoons plenty of gravy over it and then she calls to Aunt Valley.

"Take this to Miss Carol Ann," she says, not even adding a "please."

Aunt Valley looks at me hard, but she takes the plate and disappears into the bedroom with it. Under the table, Mama pats my knee. So that's how Carol Ann gets my wishbone.

But right after dinner, Aunt Valley goes down to the Stone family tent, where she says there's a cousin of hers doing the cooking, and she borrows another frying chicken and comes back and cuts it up so there's a wishbone, and she stands in that hot cookhouse with the sweat just pouring off her, and she fries it up just right, and just for me. And so I get a wishbone after all.

Later, Aunt Nell leaves, carrying chicken for the dogs, who bounce around her and smile the whole time she's walking to her car. And then she drives away, and I can see the dogs bouncing around inside the car, bouncing so high, they almost hit the roof. When Aunt Valley finishes doing the dishes, she takes me back to the porch and puts me back in her lap, and she goes right back at the story of God Almighty creating the world, and that without my even reminding her. And she says, "Now, let's see. Where did we leave off?"

"God was cutting up day and night in little pieces."

"Oh, yes," she says, and I lean back against her and I like her smell because it is rich and strong with the smell of sweat and of wishbones frying.

"Well, you know, I guess there isn't much more He did on that very first day of creation, except what I already done told you about."

"First day? You mean He had to make more another time?"

"Sure enough. Took Him six whole days to make the world and everything in it, and on the seventh day, He rested."

"Why'd it take so long?"

"Probably because it's a very complicated place."

"What's complicated mean?" I like the word. It sounds like the clippity-clop of horses' hooves going somewhere lickety-split right in the middle of a dark night when there's thunder and lightning.

"Complicated means there's lots to it. Look at a old dirt-dobber nest sometime, and do you see just how particular it's put together. And the most amazing thing is that there's not no dirt-dobber foreman or nothing like that standing around and telling all the others how to do it. No, ma'am. Because they all know how to work and get along together. And how to stay out of each other's way."

"What's so complicated about that?"

"Because God had to put the knowing how to do it inside every dirt-dobber. And that sure must have took some time. And," she adds, "people is even more complicated than that." I wonder if she's thinking about what a fix she got herself in, telling me I could have the wishbone and then having Great-Aunt Kate make her give it to Carol Ann. But finding a way to get one for me, too, just like she promised.

"You think God likes Carol Ann better than me?" The sound of my voice startles me because I don't know I'm going to say anything.

"Where'd that come from?" She sounds surprised.

"Well, for one thing, she knows how to do things."

"She sure does that," Aunt Valley snorts softly. "But what things're you talking about?"

"Things like how to behave herself and pay attention."

"And you don't know how to do that?"

"I do. But I don't want to do it."

She sits in silence for a few minutes, and all I can hear is her sucking on her teeth.

"Well," she says finally, "you got to keep trying your best. That's the important thing. But I 'spect God put you together just the way He wants. So I wouldn't worry about it none. Just keep on trying."

I twist my head around so I can see her face. She has those old eyes cut sideways and looking down at me, and she's smiling.

"But you know," she adds, "I got a feeling God likes you just fine. Just the way you are."

I have trouble falling asleep that night, because every time I close my eyes, I see Tulie's children sitting on the steps. But I don't say anything about it. Still, Mama knows when I'm having trouble like that, so she sits on the side of the bed in the dark room, humming and with her warm hand on my back. And every once in a while, she gives me a soft pat, always in time to the humming. Until the children disappear again, and there's nothing more in the dark to come after me.

In the middle of the night, I wake up because I hear Carol Ann crying and throwing up in Great-Aunt Kate's room. Mama turns on the light and Aunt Valley, who is sleeping on the little cot in the corner of our room, gets up and says, "Youall go on back to sleep. I'll go see can I help."

So Mama lies back down, but I am still sitting there in the bed and watching while Aunt Valley finds her shoes. And all the while, Carol Ann retching and crying, and the light comes on in Great-Aunt Kate's room and she's yelling, "Not on the quilt! Not on the quilt!"

My eyes meet Aunt Valley's coffee-milk eyes and she looks at me hard.

"I guess my wishbone didn't do much to make her feel better," I whisper.

"Don't you tell me you're glad she's sick," Aunt Valley whispers back. "That's purely wicked. So don't you say one word."

"Please," I remind her and try to hide my smile.

But she doesn't bother to hide hers. She just smiles and smiles, and when she turns out the lamp, I can still see her white teeth smiling in the darkness.

Maybelline's voice: "I said, which one was yours?"

We were passing along the road behind all the wooden tents, and they looked the same, for the most part as they had all those years ago. Except that they were darker and older and some of them leaning a little more. And, too, there was a newer, concrete block building among them—a long, low building with entrance doors at either end and hand-lettered signs that said "Men" and "Ladies." A public bathroom. And probably with flush fixtures in it.

"You want me to stop somewheres?" Maybelline asked.

"No," I said. "Just drive on through. I just wanted to see it one more time."

So we crept along in the grayness of early dawn, and I pointed out things of interest to Maybelline.

"That's the tent where a little girl named Julia Stone stayed one summer," I said. "And there's our old family tent right there."

"Which one?"

"That one. Where the old colored woman's sitting." Dear Lord! Aunt Valley?

"What?" Maybelline asked.

No, I was thinking. No one there. No one sitting in the little cowhide chair on the fresh wood shavings. No one at all.

"You okay?" Maybelline asked, alarmed.

"Of course," I snapped. "Just thought for a minute I saw someone."

"There's no one there," Maybelline said, unnecessarily.

"I know that," I snapped at her again. "I said I just thought so."

Sure enough I had thought so. But I had to get Maybelline off the track or Lord knows, she'd harp on it forever!

"There's the old cemetery." I pointed across the road from our tent, just to get Maybelline's head turned in another direction.

The old white stones still sitting there, just like always, only a little more weather-beaten and nearly all of them tilting a bit, this way and that, where they'd settled over all the years. And a few new ones, sitting straight and tall and dazzling white in the early light.

I laughed.

"Don't remember who it was told me one time that if you come to the cemetery on a moonless night, you can see the devil hiding behind the tombstones. And look." I pointed again. "There's the old tabernacle." It was still there, squatting in that saucer-shaped depression in the ground right in the middle of the Camp Ground.

"I ought to get out of this car and go on down there and ring the bell," I said without thinking.

"Oh, no, ma'am!" Maybelline begged. "Let's not do nothing like that!"

So she sped up, just as if she thought I were about to lunge out of the car and gallop toward the tabernacle like a wild animal. And she bumped us most unmercifully along the dirt road until we'd gone all the way around the Camp Ground and come back to where we'd entered.

Then back to the paved road and a silence between us again. Because I guess she was wondering what on earth she'd gotten herself into, going off who-knows-where with a crazy old woman in tow who was seeing people who weren't really there and wanting to go around ringing tabernacle bells before dawn.

And I was doing some wondering of my own just about that time: wondering if I were really turning into a crazy old woman who was seeing people who weren't really there and wanting to go around ringing tabernacle bells before dawn! And what on earth was happening to me?

"There'll be a place for us to get us some breakfast on up ahead a ways, I expect," Maybelline said, and I was glad the silence was broken. But I wouldn't have let her know that for anything.

"Yes," I said.

"Be coming up on some kind of a town," she continued. "I already saw a sign for a Stuckey's—said it was sixteen miles ahead—so it's got to be a right big town."

"Good," I said, meaning it most sincerely. Because we'd left the house in mint condition, of course, and hadn't wanted to risk messing up the kitchen by fixing any breakfast before we left. So we hadn't had a bite to eat.

It was a long sixteen miles. Fences and fields stretching far away to the indistinct edge of dark piney woods. And something lonesome in it, but I didn't know what. Maybe something as simple as my wanting to be able to know exactly where the boundaries of the field were, what were the edges of things. So I got to watching the fences, seeing if they all joined up together, nice and neat. And whenever they didn't, I held my breath a little, until I could spot another fence up ahead and then wait to see if that one joined up all right. Or something like that.

Finally, we came to the town. Passed the Stuckey's first, but it was a small one, not big enough to have a restaurant in it. And besides, it was still closed, that early. But then we went on into the town itself and right down the main street, and in the middle of the block was "City Cafe," with its lights shining in a real friendly way and a few pickup trucks parked out front.

"That looks good," Maybelline said, and she turned in at one of the parking spaces. By then, I was so hungry, I'd have settled for anything.

When we went in, there were two booths full of men sitting there, and they all turned and looked at us. Of course, Maybelline was wearing that awful old pink-and-yellow-checked dress with rhinestone sandals, so that's why they were staring at us. But the minute we came in, I could smell country ham cooking and good, hot coffee, and nothing ever smelled better to me than that did. Maybelline and I sat down in a booth, and a pleasant-looking woman in an apron came over and gave us some menus.

"How're youall this morning?" she asked rather absently. "Want some coffee?"

"Please," Maybelline answered gratefully.

"Cream?"

"Please."

In a few minutes, the woman returned, bearing two thick, white mugs of steaming coffee for us. Maybelline ordered grits and sausage, and I ordered biscuits and country ham. And when the woman had taken our orders and gone back into the kitchen, Maybelline spoke up.

"I'm sorry did I sound a little sharp-like to you, Miss Amelia," she said, putting an obscene amount of sugar in her coffee and stirring it slowly. "I just worry about you sometimes." She kept her eyes on the cup and stirred and stirred and stirred.

And what could I have said to that? That I was worried, too? That half of me was scared to death of just drifting away one of these days and never coming back? That the other half of me not only welcomed being with Aunt Valley again, but embraced it? And strangest of all, that there was something in it all that bespoke of going back and getting it right this time? But how could I say any of that, without Maybelline being even more convinced that I was absolutely losing my mind?

"And I get scared when you start thinking about something or other so hard that you don't even hear me when I call to you," she continued.

"I'll never let myself be a burden to you," I said, speaking very slowly and meaning every word of it with all my heart.

"That isn't what I mean," she answered. "You could never be a burden to me. I just worry about you is all."

But that's what I was going to be—a burden to her. I could feel it in my bones. What with the way everything between us was so different, now that instead of Maybelline living with me in my house, I was going to be living with her in hers.

But our breakfast arrived just about that time. Wasn't anything else we could have said anyway. And the biscuits were nothing short of heavenly. Hot and tender and with just enough ham in them and it cooked just right. And Maybelline said her grits and sausage were good, too.

After we finished eating breakfast, we each had an extra cup of coffee and then continued our journey, feeling much better all the way around. Because I'd decided I just had to watch myself a little more closely, that's all. Just keep quiet, like Maybelline should have done with Bobby that time.

10

Maybelline made a left turn onto the highway, even though I reminded her that we'd turned right to go to the cafe, so we should turn right again, to keep going north.

"Well, there's a shortcut I know about," she said. "We passed the junction for it a mile or so back, but I didn't take it because I knew there was no town around there where we could get some breakfast."

"How come you know about a shortcut?" I asked. Because I knew for a fact that Maybelline had never driven to this Jerusalem at all. She'd told me that herself. Only time she'd even gone there was when she was just a little girl, anyway.

"I studied a map," she answered. "Wanted to be able to take us straight there and not get us lost or nothing so you'd maybe get scared."

"Me? Scared?" Now this was simply ridiculous, and I wasn't going to put up with it for another minute. "You're treating me like I'm a child!" I protested, but I still wasn't satisfied, so I added, "Listen here. I'm about as helpless as a rattlesnake, and I'm not scared of anything." Of course, that wasn't really true, but it made me feel better just to say it.

"Well now, I didn't mean nothing bad," Maybelline whined. "Just wanted everything to be as smooth and nice for you as I could make it." I could tell I'd hurt her feelings, but I felt I had to make it absolutely clear, right from the very beginning, that just because I'd be living in her house—instead of the other way around—she couldn't go treating me any differently than she'd always treated me. With respect. Always with respect.

But pretty soon, I began to forget about that, because I got to watching the land, and it put me in a different frame of mind. Dark edges of pine thickets on the far side of plowed fields, and sandy trails meandering away from the paved road—going who-knows-where—maybe to the empty yards of deserted farmhouses where people used to live and work and dream.

Something that says the land is our one and only home, that it's always been there and always will be there. Hills that rise and dip, and I'd always wondered what made things like that. Hills and valleys, I mean. Rocks deep down inside the ground? Wrinkles, maybe, in the earth? And the hills always being there. Always. Now something to think about, sure enough. And too, driving through Mount Horeb Camp Ground like we'd done, and my seeing Aunt Valley sitting there just as clear as day, started me to thinking that maybe time isn't really a road that goes off somewhere else—leading to some faraway place, like Jerusalem. That maybe it's more like hills, with layers of rock and soil going far down, and with the top part of the hill getting its shape from what's underneath.

Or something like that.

"You okay?" Maybelline asked, maybe because I was being so quiet.

"Yes, I'm fine," I answered, trying to remember what it was we'd fussed about before I got to thinking about the woods and all. And then trying to go back and find the feeling for the land again, but it was gone, that fragile bubble, upon whose effervescence I'd been floating above the treetops.

"What you thinking about?" she inquired.

"The land," I answered simply.

"Land?" she asked, as if she'd never heard of such a thing.

"Land," I repeated. "What it feels like to look at it."

"Why, you sound just like my daddy," she said. "He was a good one for looking at land. Any land he could put his eyes on."

"Was he?" I asked, purely out of politeness, of course. Because it was hard for me to think of Maybelline's daddy in any way except that he's the one started calling her Maybelline, after an eyebrow pencil, for goodness' sake! So whatever Maybelline could tell me about what he thought or did or said would always be cheapened by that.

"Sure was," she said. "Used to sit in the porch swing with me in his lap and tell me what the land was saying."

"Saying?"

"Yes'm. Oh, I never could hear it, but he sure could."

I imagined her daddy wearing coveralls and sitting in a swing on the porch of a little shack of a house, with a little-girl Maybelline on his lap. And somehow, it was a pleasant thing to imagine. But I didn't know why.

"He'd tell me what the crickets was saying to each other, and the pine trees, and even what the road said to us when we walked on it."

"What did they say?"

"Well, the crickets was talking to each other about what to fix for dinner, and that was always fun to hear about. Because we didn't have much except cornbread and field peas. But you should have heard what all Daddy said the crickets was talking about! They was fussing with each other about fried chicken and gravy and hot biscuits and peach cobbler. And whether they'd like to have honey or syrup on their biscuits. And the trees? Why, he said they was whispering together about what kind of dancing they were gonna do, once we'd turned out the porch light and gone to bed. Because he said that trees never ever danced when anyone was around to see them do it."

"Goodness! What an imagination," I said, wondering why he hadn't had enough sense to curb it when it came to what he'd call his own daughter.

"But what he liked best of all was telling me what the land said."

Well, I thought, this is right interesting! Who'd have thought?

"And what did it say?" I asked, truly interested, for a wonder.

"Oh, lots of things. Especially what it was like during the war."

"War?"

"Civil War."

"You mean," I sniffed, "the War of Southern Independence."

"Yes'm," Maybelline smiled. "That's the one."

110

Once, years ago, when I'd first heard her call it "the Civil War," I'd asked her where she went to school. And she said West Virginia, which, of course, explained it all. "But only through sixth grade," she'd confessed. And of course, that explained it, too.

"What did the land say about the war?" I asked.

"Said it took the blood that was shed and made fine crops grow because of it. Said the blood was honor. Or something like that."

Well, now, that was a strange thing, sure enough. And what a gruesome thing to tell a child! Still, I was thinking of the sacred ashes of my daddy's love letters, working their way into the ground under the big pear tree.

"He knew a lot about the war because my great-grandpapa was in it."

"Which side was he on?" I asked suspiciously.

"The South, of course."

"Why 'of course'?" I asked. "You're from West Virginia, aren't you?"

"No, ma'am," she protested, shaking her head emphatically. "We only went there so's my daddy could find work. We're all from North Carolina, except for my great-granddaddy and my granddaddy. They were from Jefferson County, Georgia."

"He's the one was in the war?"

"Yes'm. In a regiment called the Jeff Grays, so my daddy said. Got killed, though. He was the one built the house we're going to, when he was just a young man."

"And he died in the war?"

"Yes'm. That's why my daddy said the land was talking about it. My great-granddaddy's dying on it. Because he deserted the army and came home to try and save it."

Deserted? Well, so much then for honor. There wasn't any.

"He ran away," I said simply—because I couldn't resist it.

Maybelline glanced at me sharply. "No, ma'am," she said. "He didn't run away; he ran *to* his home to try and defend it. And that's when he was killed. Defending it."

So I couldn't condemn him for that, could I? Not after he'd given his life trying to defend his home. The home I would be living in now.

111

"I'm sorry," I said, and I was.

"Well, I'm sorry if I sounded sharp," Maybelline said. "It's just important to me that you understand about him."

"Why haven't you ever mentioned that before?" I asked. Because after all, Maybelline and I had lived together in my house for years and years, but here we'd been in the car together only a few hours and I'd learned more about her in those few hours than I'd known in all those years.

"Because you never asked me," she replied. And she was right. But then she came out with a question that surprised me completely: "You believe in ghosts?"

"Ghosts?"

"Yes'm. Because my great-granddaddy's ghost may be around sometimes. When we get to the house."

"What do you mean?"

"I mean my granddaddy said his daddy's ghost came around sometimes. He'd seen it."

"Seen it where?"

"In the hall, mostly. But once in the kitchen and another time in the backyard at midnight."

Well, that certainly sounded contrived to me, so I'd bet anything it was just something he'd imagined. Or made up for scaring children so they would stay in their beds at night.

"I don't believe in ghosts," I said. But of course, that wasn't entirely true. Not if that included Aunt Valley, for I was sure she'd been dead and gone for more years than I could count. Still, I believed I saw her sitting in a chair outside the back door of the old tent at Mount Horeb that morning. I was positive. But then, that wouldn't have been what I would have called a ghost, anyway. It was memory. A very real memory.

"Well, I just wanted to mention it to you before we got there," Maybelline said. "And I'm glad you don't believe in ghosts anyway."

The whole time we'd been talking, the miles had been passing under the wheels, and Maybelline was certainly right about there being no towns along that road she'd taken. Nothing for all that time but woods and fields, and once in a while, another of those sandy tracks going off into the woods. But not anything you could call a town, not even a crossroads where there were two or three houses.

The sun getting higher and higher in the sky all the time, and the morning beginning to feel hot and sticky. And once, when Maybelline slowed down for a railroad crossing, I could hear crickets chirping in the tall grass beside the road.

"Another couple of hours or so and we'll be about halfway there," Maybelline said. "We're sure making good time. And goodness knows, there's not a bit of traffic."

But we didn't keep on making good time. Because as soon as the words were out of her mouth, the car broke down.

11

"Lord, help us," Maybelline muttered, and she struggled with the steering wheel as the car lost momentum, and as the tires slowed, the sound of the road gravel crunching under them grew louder. No more engine sound, no hum of working machinery. And after the final crunch of gravel, only the airless noon and crickets chirping in the tall grass and the dead heat of the August sun blistering the earth.

"It's overheated." Maybelline pointed to the temperature gauge, where the little needle pointed itself at a small, rusty screw a good eighth of an inch above the H for HOT. Then from the front of the car came a faint hiss of steam spewing under the hood. In that minute or so since we came to a stop, the heat inside the car had become insufferable—airless and overwhelming, exactly like someone had opened an oven door to take out hot biscuits. Only this was an oven we couldn't shut.

"We have to have water for the radiator and maybe a new hose," Maybelline announced after she'd opened the hood and peered through the steam rising from the engine. "You better get out of that hot car, Miss Amelia. You'll get sick."

Maybelline shaded her eyes against the glare of the sun and looked around. Then she pointed across the road. "Why don't you walk over there and stay in the shade of that big tree. I'll go on up the road a piece and see can I find a house that has a telephone.

We're pretty close to a town by now, I think, so maybe I can even find a gas station where there's someone to help us."

I got out and stood by the car and looked over to where the big tree stood that Maybelline had pointed out. Right at the edge of a fallow field. A big pecan tree, it was, and beside it, a clearing, so that I knew full well a house had stood there once upon a time. Only now, ankle-deep wild grass around the clearing and the tree. And that's all.

Maybelline rummaged around in the trunk and finally found my big, black umbrella, which she opened out into a most welcome circle of shade.

"Go on now and get in that shade," Maybelline ordered, waving the back of her hand at me as if to shoo me along. "I'll use the umbrella and walk on up the road. 'For the sun shall not smite thee by day, nor the moon by night. The Lord shall preserve thee from all evil: He shall preserve thy soul,'" she added. "Now you go on, Miss Amelia, and get in the shade. I don't know how long I'll be, but if you get hungry, you open that suit-box I've got tucked under the driver's seat. I told you I had a surprise for you!"

And because there was nothing else to do, I crossed the road and walked over the uneven ground toward the big tree, stopping only once to turn and watch Maybelline walking off along the side of the highway, the round, black umbrella covering the entire upper part of her body, and below it, the swaying skirt of the pink-and-yellow-checked dress and the rhinestone sandals slapping against her heels.

Maybelline was right about it being nice and cool in the shade of the big tree. I even found two concrete blocks to sit on—left over from shoring up the old house, no doubt. Made me wonder who all had lived in the house and what they had thought about and whatever happened to them when it was gone—when it burned down or fell in or whatever had happened to it. Even some old doodlebug holes near the concrete block I was sitting on.

And what a fix to be in! Stuck out there in the middle of nowhere all alone. Not a soul or a house in sight. Nothing but the hot sun and the rough, gray highway stretching away and with little ribbons of wriggling, hot air over the pavement. And far, far on, a little bobbing black dot that was Maybelline's umbrella.

So I sat there, looking at my shoes and wondering how far she'd have to go to get help for us. I watched the doodlebug holes and remembered . . . *how a few days after the night when Carol Ann got sick off my wishbone, I was squatting around at the side of the tent, playing "Doodlebug" with those perfectly round little holes in the sand. I'd gotten a broomstraw and stirred around and around in each hole real slowly, and all the while whispering what you have to whisper to make the doodlebugs come out:*

> *Doodlebug, Doodlebug,*
> *Fly away home.*
> *Your house is on fire*
> *And your children are alone.*

Every single time, the doodlebug would come out from where he's hiding deep at the bottom of the hole, and he's a gray, fat, ugly little bug with teeny pinchers on his head. And the reason he comes out is that he hears you say that his children are all alone in a burning house, and so, of course, he is very anxious to save them.

That's what I'm doing when I see my stepdaddy's black Packard automobile pulling up in the yard, with Gus driving it and wearing his black jacket and his black chauffeur hat and both hands on the steering wheel and looking straight ahead when he pulls up under the chinaberry tree by the cookhouse. Then Gus gets out and goes around and opens the back door of the car and never even once looks toward the tent.

I can't move or speak. So I just sit there and watch as my stepdaddy's polished shoes step down in the weeds, and then he is standing there beside the car and looking at the tent, holding onto the car door like it had taken too much out of him just to stand up, and his face is gray. Taking his glasses off, wiping his face with a white handkerchief, and then putting his glasses back on again and standing there by the car, staring at the tent just as if he is trying to see can he make Mama know he's there without even going up and calling "Hello." Because he's much older than Mama. In fact, he's probably what people call an elderly man, and he's thin and tall and has white hair, only there isn't much of it, just a fringe all the way around the back of his head.

I'm still squatting there when Mama comes out the screen door and goes to where he is standing, still leaning against the car door, and I can hear her voice, but not the words. From their faces, I can tell they're talking about how me and Mama left without telling him. And he must be very, very sad about that, especially if he's come all the way out here to the Camp Ground from Savannah, because he wouldn't come all the way unless he wanted Mama and me to come back home. Because he's a very busy man.

Mama talking and then my stepdaddy talking, and then Mama nodding her head and going back inside the tent. He doesn't follow her, but gets back in the car and leaves the door standing open. Then I hear Mama calling me.

"Yes'm?" I answer, brushing the sand off my knees and running to the back door. She comes out, and she is wearing her gloves and carrying her purse. So I guess we're going back home with him and won't have to stay here for the whole two weeks of Camp Meeting after all.

"Listen, honey," she says, "I have to go home just until tomorrow, and I want you to stay here."

"Don't leave me here!" I whisper desperately. But the hand is on my shoulder, patting me, and I know she will leave me.

"Aunt Valley is here to take care of you. So you be a good girl and behave yourself for her." Mama looks at me hard, and she can see trouble coming. "Just go to sleep tonight and when you wake up in the morning, you'll know I'm coming back."

Standing just on the other side of the screen door is Aunt Valley, and even through the screen, I can see the furrows in her forehead. She is wiping her hands on her apron in an agitated way, just like she did about the wishbone.

"I'll be back first thing tomorrow morning," Mama says over her shoulder to Aunt Valley, and then she kisses me on the cheek and walks across the yard quickly before I can cause any trouble and gets into the car where Gus is standing by the door. Then Gus closes the door and gets behind the wheel and the car drives away back down the dirt road, just the way it had come, and she's gone.

It's the worst feeling in the whole world, seeing the black car swallow her up and take her away, and it's so sudden and so lonely feeling that everything all around me is suddenly lonely looking too. Like when the sun goes behind a cloud right in the middle of the brightest day and it all looks so different. Even those dumb old doodlebugs who keep falling for the same old lie, over and over again.

Aunt Valley is still standing inside the screen door, just like a statue and with her hands still wrapped up a little in her apron, where she's been wiping them. Then she pushes open the door, and she glances at me, but

117

she doesn't say anything, just goes across the yard and into the cook-house. I think I must be rooted to the ground, because I can't move, and I can see only two things in the whole wide world. One is Aunt Valley's big bottom sticking out, because she's bent over and throwing wood into the stove to get the fire going for dinner. And the other thing is the tire tracks on the dusty road.

I don't even know I've started running until I see my knees pumping in front of me and my face is like a flame, and I'm running and running in the tire tracks, the little crossed x's in the road. Ahead of me, just around the curve, the provocative cloud of dust from the car.

"Hold on, there!" I hear Aunt Valley bellow behind me, but I can't stop, of course. I can't stop. And that's a part of the Great Mystery, too.

I pass the other tents, and snapshot glimpses of white-faced people flash by me, one a frozen image of a lady taking a drink from the dipper by a backyard pump, and another the faded and startled mask of an old lady sitting in a chair with a cardboard-Jesus fan in her hand.

I can't stop. Even when my breath comes in ragged gasps, and I pass the last tent in the row and the grove of pecan trees across the road bobs into view. And the whole world tilting and the solid staccato of the clump-ing feet coming up behind me.

Aunt Valley scoops me up in mid-tilt, and the spinning carries me around and against her hot shoulder. I throw my arms around her as if she's a big, black rock in the middle of a raging flood and I must hang on. Or drown.

The steady hum of the fan, a damp cloth on my forehead, and Great-Aunt Kate's voice, muffled and low. "I knew there was going to be trouble. Knew it just as soon as I knew they were coming out to Camp Meeting."

"Yes'm." Aunt Valley's low mutter answering.

"I declare, that is the strangest child I have ever seen."

Carol Ann pipes up, loud and clear, "She's crazy, that's what."

"Hush!" Great-Aunt Kate hisses at her. "She'll hear you."

On the other side of the stall-wall, they dissect me, resolving in the end the only thing they ever resolve: They don't understand me.

Well, neither do I.

Dinner is late "all because of her" (and that's me, of course), and Great-Aunt Kate and Carol Ann have to leave for service without having a "rest." That's what they do every single day right after dinner. Take off their dresses and stretch out in the bedroom with the fan blowing on them and rest. But they don't get to do it today. And all because of me. When I hear the screen door close, I come out to where Aunt Valley is sitting at the table drinking iced tea out of a mason jar. When she sees me, she stands up.

"Now don't you go saying to nobody 'bout me sittin' to the dining table while they was all gone," she says. Her face is serious and a lot of the coffee-milk whites of her eyes is showing.

"Why?" I ask. Doesn't she understand that everything in the whole world is something I have never seen or known before?

"Promise me," she orders.

"Okay."

"Now, don't you forget."

"I won't."

"So sit down here now and I'll get you something to eat."

I sit there and listen to her chopping ice for the tea out at the counter on the back porch, and I trace the little blue flowers on the tablecloth with my finger and watch while it all turns into a wide, open hillside with the sun shining down on it like a big smile. A wind coming around the flank of the hill and little blue flowers moving in the breeze and letting go a yellow veil of pollen so that . . .

She puts a plate in front of me. A white plate with little spiderweb cracks around the edges, and on it, creamed corn, field peas, cornbread, and a short thigh in gravy. Somehow the aroma of the food tickles me under my tongue and my eyes water. I dig a fork into the short thigh, all the while knowing I'll never be able to finish cutting it because my arm has gone all rubbery, and everything I can see is beginning to swim around in the hot place behind my eyes, piling up and burning and burning more and more.

I am thinking: It's not that easy. Dying, I mean. The old cemetery and all the hot, white, sand. And too-little tombstones, "precious ones" who are "Resting in the Bosom of the Lamb," springing up out of the tablecloth and appearing around the edge of the plate, and the blue flowers all the little bouquets for the graves. Tighter and tighter in my throat and me blinking as hard as I can so it won't all come out. Because it's crazy, just as Carol Ann says, and I know it is, but it's there. In spite of everything, it's still there.

"What's wrong?" Aunt Valley asks, but I have no answer to the question. I wish to the sweet Lord Jesus I did. Just the Great Mystery inside me that keeps saying that the house is on fire and the children are alone. Besides which, even if I did have an answer, I wouldn't be able to say it. Because of all the thickness in my throat. Until I can swallow it away. Until the house finishes burning down and I don't hear the screams anymore.

119

She sits down beside me, and without any effort at all, she lifts me right off the bench and into her lap. And she starts rocking back and forth just a little bit. Something nice about it, so I draw up my knees and try to make myself smaller, because I'm a big girl and not at all like a baby. But there's something in her rocking that makes me smaller than I really am, somehow.

At first, I think she's starting to say something to me, but then I find it's just a sound that doesn't have any meaning. Not like singing, really, but maybe just something so sad, moaning low and wandering around inside her chest and looking and looking for the way to her throat so it can come out and color the air all blue and steamy, so that the outside looks just like the inside feels. And she keeps on doing it for the longest kind of time, and then I guess it finally finds its way out.

"I guess I'll just have to tell you a story to get you cheered up," she says. "And I done started in to telling you the only one I know, how Great God Almighty made the Heavens and the earth and everything else we got. I done told you the first day, so we'll pick up with the second."

I wait for the words to unravel themselves out of the sad-sound, "Second day, Great God Almighty made the firmament."

I move my head just a little, and I don't even have to ask the question because she can hear it in just the twitch of my head.

"That's Heaven. On the second day He made Heaven. And that's where you go if you're good and if you love the Lord and serve Him all your days."

Heaven, I am thinking. Where my daddy is. The sweet-smoke smell of his pipe. A warm cheek with just the barest little roughness to it. Eyes a deep green and dreamy so that whatever the eyes are seeing is something inside and not something outside. And I can see it, too, whatever it is the eyes are seeing. Late afternoon, and whiskers rising out below his pale cheeks, over the smooth jawline, and each whisker just like a bright, little amber rod pushing up and out of the smooth skin. Red whiskers. Like my hair.

"Don't you got no questions about it?" she asks, and the whiskered cheek disappears.

I don't answer.

"You mean to tell me you're just going to sit there and not ask me a single thing about it?"

I nod against her shoulder.

"Well-well-well." She runs the words together so that they look like little bubbles on a string, and in a way so that her voice lifts up right in the middle of the words, almost like they just float up on top of some notes of music and take on their shape and go up and down, singing-like.

120

And then they trail off, sliding right back down her throat and go back to wandering around again inside her chest.

They wander around for the longest kind of time.

When I wake up, I'm lying on the bed, and the fan is humming, with the rusty sound that comes every time it stops turning one way and starts turning back the other way. Through the humming, I can hear singing from the tabernacle.

> *At the cross, at the cross*
> *Where I first saw the light*
> *And the burden of my heart*
> *Rolled a-waa-y . . . (rolled away) . . .*

As soon as I open my eyes, I can tell that I've slept for a long time. Because the light from the square-framed window is shining against the wall in a sharp wedge that breaks where the wall ends, and then disappears into the hot air up under the tin roof.

The three o'clock service. I've slept all that time.

Then I hear something else. Aunt Valley's voice. Who's she talking to? I hear the voice but not the words.

When I stand up, I feel dizzy for just a minute, but I know already that something inside me is all better. I can tell that by the way the sunlight lying across the corner of the bed is just that—sunlight lying across the corner of the bed. And nothing more.

I walk silently across the wood shavings and stand just inside the back screen door. Aunt Valley is sitting in the cowhide chair, and a little girl just about my age and wearing a yellow dress is leaning against her knee. She has dark brown hair, braided, with the two braids tied together in the back with a yellow ribbon. Only one of the loops has come undone, so it's only half a bow. Her elbows are resting on Aunt Valley's leg and she's looking up at Aunt Valley's face with eyes that are such a pale blue, you almost can't tell they're any color.

"So you're Miss Mattie's grandbaby," Aunt Valley says, nodding her head in some kind of satisfaction.

"Yes'm." So she doesn't know you're not supposed to say ma'am to a colored woman.

"You know, once upon a time years and years ago, I took care of Miss Mattie, when she'd just had a little baby. Now let's see. They named the baby Bessie, after Miss Mattie's mama."

121

"Yes'm. That's my Aunt Bessie. My mama's a little younger than Aunt Bessie, I think."

I push open the screen door and they both look at me.

"Well, look who's woke up at last," Aunt Valley says. "Come on over here and see who's come visiting."

The girl is looking at me from under jutting brown eyebrows, and the pale blue eyes are soft. And smiling in the nicest kind of way.

"This is Miss Julia, Miz Stone's grandbaby, and she's come down to play with you." Of course, now I'm wondering whose idea that was, and Aunt Valley sees the question.

"Just this very afternoon, right after I put you in the bed asleep, Lizzie comes walking down here to sit with me a little while, and she happens to mention to me that Miss Julia here is a right sweet little girl, but she doesn't have no other little girl to play with, and I says, 'Why, send her right on down to us. We've got somebody wants to play, too.'"

The whole time Aunt Valley is talking, I am looking at this girl, and I don't know what there is that looks so familiar to me about her. Because I know I've never seen her before. Just that the minute I look at her, I know her. Or something like that.

"Why don't you show Miss Julia how to play 'Doodlebug,'" Aunt Valley suggests.

"You want to?" I ask, suddenly feeling embarrassed about such a dumb thing to show someone.

"I already know how," she answers, smiling. "But I'll show you something I'll bet you don't know about." She walks right over to me and takes my hand and starts leading me off across the yard. I look back at Aunt Valley to see if she's noticed that I'm barefoot, but she just smiles and waves at us.

"Come on," Julia urges, and we start running together down the dirt road, and then we start laughing because we're not running in step, and so our hands jerk against each other and it's hard to hold on. But hold on, we do. And we run all the way down to the Stone family tent.

"Why're we coming here?" I ask.

"'Cause I got to let my grandmama know where we are and what we're doing."

"Oh."

"And 'cause this is where part of it is you have to see."

"Oh."

We pass their cookhouse and go in through the back screen door, into a tent almost identical to ours, except they've got their pump for water inside, and a piece cut out of the side of the wall and a screen over it, for *a little window. Real nice, really, and I'll bet they don't get so many gnats in their dipper, what with the pump being indoors and all.*

Julia calls out, "Grandmama?" and goes into the bedroom, but I wait out in the sawdust hall because even I know you don't go into someone's bedroom without an invitation. But their walls are like ours, going only halfway up, so I can hear what Julia and her grandmama are saying.

"Where'd you say you're going?" The voice is old and creaky, the way a voice always sounds when you've just waked up someone real old.

"Just to see Great-Grandpapa," Julia answers.

"Well, I guess that's all right, but youall stay away from the tabernacle. You know how the preachers feel about children playing down there."

"Yes'm. Can I bring her in to meet you?"

"Why, honey, I'm in my petticoat."

"That's okay."

"Well, give me that sheet to pull up over me then."

"Yes'm."

Julia comes back out into the hall, and I move forward, but she bumps against me and leads me away from the door, and then she cups her hands on either side of my ear and whispers, "Don't say anything about it, but be sure you look at my great-great-grandmama on the far side of the bed. 'Cause she's one hundred and two years old!"

Julia draws back and looks at me with her eyes shining. I nod, and she takes my hand and leads me into the bedroom.

The room is in a kind of twilight, and an oscillating fan that stands on a dresser in the corner groans and hums and swings slowly back and forth. In the bed, a large lady with the sheet pulled right up tight under her chin, so all I can see of her is her round, red face and her hands clutching the top of the sheet.

"Grandmama," Julia's voice is sweet and cool, as befits this formal occasion. "This is Miss Kate's niece." Then Julia turns to me. "This is my grandmama," she says, and I am thinking, My! What lovely manners she has.

"And this is my great-great-grandmama." Julia is pointing to the other side of the bed.

I have already smiled at the face and hands of Julia's grandmama and said, "How do you do," and I look at where Julia is pointing so I can say hello to her great-great-grandmama, but I don't see anyone. I look at Julia and she points again, so I lean a little closer to the bed, peering into the twilight, and then I see her.

All shriveled up and such a little bitty thing, she hardly makes a bump under the sheet. At first, I hardly know what to think, except maybe it's an old doll there under the sheet on the other side of the bed because I

123

saw such an old doll once, in a box way in the back of the garage at home. Such a strange-looking thing it was, and I never did know whose doll it used to be. But now, its face was yellow-brown, like the air had worked at it for a thousand years, and with its hair worn off and most of the stuffing gone out of the body so it was just like a floppy old gray rag with dirty arms and legs and the awful old yellow-brown head.

That's exactly what Julia's great-great-grandmama looks like, except she's got this big nose that's just like a beak on a bird, and it bends down so far, it almost touches the sharp little chin that's curving up. And then that strange-looking, old brown doll lets out the loudest snore I've ever heard, and I almost jump right out of my skin.

"We gotta go," Julia says and pulls me out of the room.

"PLEASED TO MEET YOU," I yell back over my shoulder.

We go out the back door and past the cookhouse, where their colored woman is putting wood in the cookstove so she can bake supper biscuits. And she must be Lizzie, Aunt Valley's cousin, but Julia pulls me on past so fast that I don't even get to see if she's got a square head like Aunt Valley's.

When we get out to the dirt road, Julia slows us down. "Well, what do you think of her?"

"Who? Your grandmama?"

"No, silly," she laughs. "Great-Great-Grandmama."

I fumble around for something to say, because I'm sure not going to say I think she looks like that old doll I saw that time in the garage. But Julia is laughing now.

"I think she looks like a little monkey!" she says. I try not to laugh because maybe I shouldn't. And I can almost feel Mama's hand on my shoulder. But Julia keeps laughing and so finally, I can't help it. We laugh and laugh, still holding hands and staggering against each other as we walk along.

"She's been like that long as I can remember," Julia finally says, wiping her eyes on the sleeve of her dress. "Every time Camp Meeting comes along, she knows it somehow or other, even though I've never heard her say one word. But Grandmama says she knows when it's time, just as good as anything. So we load her in the car and bring her out here. Carry her just like a little baby and put her in the bed, and she stays there the whole Camp Meeting."

"In bed?"

"Right in the bed. And Grandmama always sleeps with her. I'm glad I don't have to."

I am imagining what it must be like to be in the dark and in the bed with the old doll.

"Because she wears diapers!" Julia whispers.

"Diapers?"

Julia nods her head and rolls her eyes. "And that's why I wouldn't want to sleep with her."

"I'd be afraid she'd die, right there beside me," I say.

Julia laughs. "If she died, I bet Grandmama would never even notice it. She'd just load her back in the car after Camp Meeting was over and prop her all up with pillows and take her home and put her back in the bed there. Hey! Maybe she's dead already, and we just haven't noticed it!"

I don't notice which way we've been walking along together until we come to the edge of the cemetery, and Julia is still talking: "I'll bet you didn't know that's why they always wait three whole days to bury some-body after they die. Because they want to be sure they're dead."

I stop so suddenly that Julia spins around, still laughing and with her arms all loose and akimbo.

"What's the matter?" she asks, laughing. And then she sees my face. "Oh, come on," she urges, pulling me by the hand. "Don't be scared of a graveyard, silly."

"I'm not scared, and I'm not silly," I protest. But the sun has gone behind a cloud that is sitting near the horizon, and suddenly the light has gone a little gray and the air cool and strange-feeling.

"Come on," she pleads. "Just a little way. Please?"

Reluctantly, I let her lead me slowly on, past the little granite borders that mark the family plots and bumpy cardboard vases that once upon a time held flowers, but that now are crumbling from months and months of hot sun and afternoon rains. Until she stops in front of a big marble marker with the name STONE carved on it. And she points at one side of it, at the name, Josiah Warren Stone, and the dates: Born January 5, 1820. Died May 6, 1880. May 6th. My birthday. But before I can tell that to Julia, she says, "That's my great-great-grandpapa. He died a long time ago."

Then she points at the other side of the stone. At the name, Eliza Cornwell Stone. And the date: Born March 3, 1832.

"Who's that?" I ask.

"Why, Great-Great-Grandmama," Julia answers. "You just met her."

And then I realize what it is. A tombstone already fixed up for the old brown doll. And with everything all written on it except the date of her death because that hadn't happened yet. Maybe.

"Isn't it creepy?" Julia asks. "Can you imagine seeing your own name on a tombstone?"

125

But I am already backing up, because I can imagine it, and just as clear as day. It's mine all right, but it says Daddy. Julia doesn't even notice, because she's still talking.

"And did you know if you come out here on a moonless night, you can see the devil hiding behind the tombstones?"

I turn and run, leaving her standing there. Run back down the road and the sun coming back out from under the cloud so that deep golden rays come through the chinaberry tree right behind our cookhouse and spread out like gold paths you can run on. I can hear Julia running behind me, and I know I'm doing the kind of running that I can stop anytime I want to. So I stop.

"What's the matter?" Julia pants.

"Nothing," I say. "Except I don't like graveyards."

"Okay. Let's go to the tabernacle. Services are over by now, and we can go play 'church.'" She takes my hand and begins pulling me along.

"But your grandmama said we weren't to go there," I protest.

"It's all right," she says. "Come on."

"But she said not to."

"Goodness!" Julia laughs. "Do you always do everything someone tells you to do?"

I hesitate. "No."

"Then let's go!"

We circle around behind the tents and keep going on the dirt road that comes around full circle behind the tabernacle. It's all so still and quiet, not a sound but crickets in the weeds across the road and a sound of a pot or pan banging against something in one of the cookhouses behind the circle of tents all around. We come into the tabernacle under the sweeping tin roof, the sawdust cool against my bare feet, and sit down in the front pew and make ourselves small, so no one walking around in the front of the tents will notice us, especially the preachers.

Julia picks up a hymnal and ruffles the pages against her thumb. "You know how to play 'church'?"

"I don't think so," I say.

"Well," Julia says, "I'll be the preacher and you be the sinner and I'll tell you how you're going to burn in hell forever. Then you say you're sorry, and I forgive you and pray over you. And then you get to go to Heaven when you die."

"No, thank you," I say.

"Okay," Julia is agreeable. "Then I'll show you a trick. What's your favorite song?"

126

I think for a few seconds. "'Rock of Ages,' I guess," I say finally and think: Rock of Ages, Cleft for me. Let me hide myself in Thee. Hide myself. Hide myself.

"Let's see then." She looks it up in the hymnal. "It's number four hundred seventy-nine. Four-seven-nine. That means you'll meet your future husband in the fourth month—April." Then she laughs. "And he'll be seven feet tall, and you'll have nine children!"

I am seeing myself walking beside a very tall man with all nine children skipping around us. And it feels so ridiculous, it isn't even funny at all. Julia laughs a little longer all by herself, and I try to laugh, but it won't come.

"Why you scared of cemeteries?" she asks right out of the blue.

I am looking at her face, at the kind eyes and the gentle mouth, and I know I'll be safe in telling her. "Because my daddy died," I say.

She looks back at the hymnal in her hands. "I know. My mama died."

"Your mama?" Then how can she stand it? How on earth do you ever keep on going after you lose your mama? And while I am asking this question silently, I remember my own mama, her pretty blue eyes and the smell of her perfume, and something hot comes up behind my eyes.

"I'm sorry about your mama," I say quickly, while I can still get the words out around the thick place that's coming in my throat.

"I'm sorry about your daddy," she says simply and keeps on rubbing her thumb across the edges of the hymnal pages. How silent and still it is under the great tin roof of the tabernacle, somehow so peaceful, even if it doesn't seem quite real, with the pianos standing black and silent and the empty rows of wooden seats stretching behind us all the way to where the blistering sun outside is a dazzling glare that's not any color. "You ever been saved?" she asks, just as suddenly as she asked about the cemetery.

"I don't have to be," I answer.

"Why not?"

"Because I'm Episcopal."

"Oh."

"You ever been saved?" I ask.

"Sure. Lots of times."

I don't really take any stock in this kind of thing, because even though Mama's never said a single word against it, I see a look on her face when services are almost over and lots of folks have headed down the center aisle to kneel at the altar and cry and holler and have the preacher pray over them. And from that look on Mama's face, I know that we don't do that sort of thing. So that's probably more putting on airs, but that's the way she is. And that's the way I am, too.

127

"It's real weird, getting saved," Julia says, looking up at the empty pulpit with her eyes going sort of dreamy. "Like something gets hold of you and you can't do a thing about it. Just makes you want to holler and run around. Like some kind of electricity gets in you."

I know what that's like, but for me, I guess it doesn't have a thing to do with getting saved.

"You ever hear anybody speaking in tongues?" she asks.

"What's that?"

"When the Holy Ghost gets inside folks, and they start talking the way angels in Heaven talk, and can't a soul on the face of the earth understand what they're saying. I think it will happen to me some day, but it hasn't happened yet. I've seen it, though, and right here in this tabernacle."

"What's it sound like?"

"Kind of like they are saying real words, only you don't know what they mean."

Somehow, I am thinking about Aunt Valley, and suddenly, I want to be near her. Smell her smell. A lonely kind of thing coming up in my chest and I want my mama to come back, too. And tomorrow she will. Because she promised.

"I better go on back," I say to Julia. "My Aunt Valley said for me not to be gone too long."

"I didn't hear her say anything about that," Julia says.

"Well, she didn't say it right then," I explain. "But she doesn't like it when I'm gone for a long time. Because she gets lonely." But what I really want is for Aunt Valley to say something to me. And I'll be able to understand what it is.

When I come back to the tent, Aunt Valley is shelling butter beans out back and she says to me, "Well, you didn't stay and play for very long."

"I wanted to come back," I say honestly. "I wanted you to talk to me."

"What you mean, talk to you?" she says, still popping open the hulls and scooping out the beans with her prodding fingers. "Don't you like playing with little Miss Julia? Seems like she's a nice little girl."

"I like her just fine," I say. Then, "Why do they wait three days after somebody dies to bury them?" Because Aunt Valley will tell me. And I can believe her.

She stops shelling butter beans and looks across the dirt road toward the cemetery. "Never thought about it," she admits. "But I 'spect it's to give family time to come from far away, needs be."

"Why?"

"Why what?"

128

"Why does family need to come?"

"Because they does, that's all," she answers. "And why you asking, anyway?"

"I just wondered."

"Of course family comes to a funeral," she adds, as if to think otherwise was something she couldn't imagine.

"But why?" She can tell I'm not trying to be smart with her, that I just want to know. Because no one's ever told me.

"Because family's like fruits off one tree," she explains. "And that's important. Like the Bible says, 'the tree yielding fruit, whose seed is in itself, upon the earth.'"

"That's pretty."

"That's what all God did the third day of creation," she says. "We never have finished that, you know."

But I don't want to hear it that day. Because if what she's saying is true, I'm fruit from my mama's tree and more than anything else in the world, I want my mama.

That's what all I was thinking while I waited for Maybelline to come back. And maybe, in some strange way, feeling exactly like I did when I was missing my mama so much that hot summer day so long ago.

Me sitting there all alone and still, not a soul in sight. But then a pickup truck passed by on the road with a couple of young men in it, and when they passed the broken-down car, one of them whistled and slapped on the side of the truck with his open hand. But they didn't turn around and come back to look at the car or anything. So I just sat there and watched them go on down the road, and of course, I didn't know a thing about what was going to happen to Maybelline on the road up ahead and around the curve until she told me about it later.

Nearly a mile and a half up the highway, Maybelline trudged along the sandy shoulder of the road. Not a car or a truck had passed. Nothing. Her feeling like she was the only living creature on the face of the earth. Nothing else but crickets chirping and the scurrying sounds of something in the dried grass every once in a while. And every time that happened, she thought for sure a big, black snake would come slithering out of the grass toward her.

So she was remembering a story her grandpapa had told her that summer she went to see him in the house in Jerusalem, a story about a snake called a coach whip that would come slithering out of the bushes and wrap its head end around your ankles and throw you down on the ground and then whip you to death with its tail.

"The Lord shall preserve thee from all evil," Maybelline said, and she believed it. But that didn't stop the goose bumps from coming up on her skin.

In the distance she could see something at the edge of the road. And when she was closer, she saw it was a leaning mailbox beside the highway, right where a little rutted clay road came up to the paved road. A mailbox that used to have a bird or something painted on the side of it. Only now, nothing left but an outline and an oversized bird's eye, with a shining white dollop of paint in the center of it making it look so real. Then the sound behind her, almost like the wind coming up, but before she could turn and look, an engine sound and tires whining on the hot, black road— Bobby?—she said that's exactly what she thought at first. Then a blur of wind or metal or wire or something so that she was pushed forward into the mailbox, the umbrella falling away. The last glimpse of a truck roaring past and someone laughing and yelping in delight, "We got us one!"

Her forehead resting against the post of the mailbox and the sun suddenly going down so that the air across her arms was cool and fresh and then cooler and cooler until all that moved was the umbrella spinning around in the middle of the road on its broken ribs.

That's what I didn't know was happening. Just sat there and kept on waiting. Finally, I was so hungry that I went back to the car and got that suit-box like Maybelline said to do and then went right back to the shade of the big pecan tree. And I was thinking that Maybelline was certainly right. That kind of heat was enough to make you sick. So I sat back down in the shade and took the lid off the box.

And wonder of all wonders, sitting right up in the top and nestled down on about a dozen biscuits, were six brown and crispy wishbones.

12

I was so hungry, I sat right there in the shade of that big pecan tree and ate three wishbones and two biscuits, more than I'd ever eaten at one sitting in my whole life. And even though I didn't have a thing to wash it down with, it was the best dinner I ever had.

After that, I waited and waited and waited some more, but there still wasn't a sign of Maybelline. What a terrible feeling it was, being left to sit there and watch the shadows growing longer all around me, and it getting to be that sad time of the day and me waiting there, all alone, out in the middle of nowhere and not knowing why it was that Maybelline hadn't come back for me.

The light beginning to take on that old-gold color, the very kind of light that reflects off the windows of empty houses and makes you think there's a lamp on inside. But there isn't. Just a dying sun reflected on panes of glass.

Then, just as I was feeling more forlorn than I had felt since I was a child, I saw someone coming down the road, away far off. Too far away for me to see them very well, but still, I could tell it wasn't Maybelline. Didn't walk like Maybelline at all. Whoever this was—a woman, I could tell that much—she was taller than Maybelline and walked purposefully and fast. A woman, yes. Mama? Come back for me like she promised? No. Not Mama. Aunt Valley, then? No. Not Aunt Valley. But a colored woman, nonetheless. And me sitting there just like a stone.

Of course, she would see the car, and I expected she'd look all around, to see where were the people who'd been driving it, and that's exactly what she did. I watched her go up to the car and peer inside. And what on earth was I going to do if she started rummaging through our things and taking them? My grandmama's Haviland china!

But she stuck her head in the car window only briefly, and then she looked all around at the pine trees across the road and at the chinaberry trees and then at the big pecan tree where I was sitting.

"ANYBODY 'ROUND HERE CALLED A MISS A-MELIA?" she hollered, and at the sound of my name, all the hairs on the back of my neck stood up.

Should I answer her? How on earth did she know my name?

"ANYBODY OUT HERE BY THAT NAME, THEY BETTER SPEAK UP," she ordered.

My hand went up involuntarily, just as if I were a timid schoolgirl, and I stood.

She saw me right away and came toward me in that same strong, rapid-fire way of walking. Nearly scared me to death, what with how she came tromping up on me so bold-like. That big, sweaty, moon-pie face and the eyes crisp and darting, like black starlings flying this way and that.

"You a Miss A-melia?" she asked.

"Yes, I am," I answered, determined to remain cool and calm.

"There's a Miss Maybelline done sent me to find you. So you come on with me, please, ma'am."

"Where?" I managed the one word.

"Gon' take you to my old daddy's place. Right yonder." Her finger, the size of one of Henry's big Cuban cigars, pointed vaguely down the road. "I 'spect youall's car just needs some water in your radiator or a hose or a new fan belt. Something like that. Anyway, my old daddy will see to it."

"Where's Maybelline? Why didn't she come back?"

"Now don't you go getting yourself all het up," she warned. "She done had a little fall, but she's gonna be just fine. She's waiting for you at my daddy's place. Come on; we'll go see her."

"But how do I know she really sent you?" I asked.

"How else would I know your name?" the woman fumed. "You tell me that!"

Then, in only a slightly gentler tone, she said, "Come on now; let's go."

She held out a massive hand, as if I were a robin that could jump right into it, and I watched in almost detached astonishment as I saw my own hand reach out.

"Who are you?" I asked.

"I'm Mamie, and I'm gonna hep you."

It was a long walk we had, but this Mamie-person kept her arm hooked through my own the whole way, so that she almost carried me along. On and on, and the air so hot we were both drenched in perspiration. Finally, far ahead, I could make out a shack set pretty well back from the road and with a light in its window. I glanced behind me, to see if it might be just a reflection of the setting sun, but the sky behind us was red, and the light in the window was yellow.

Aunt Valley taking me back to the tent? Had I run away, trying to catch my stepdaddy's black car when it took Mama?

But that wasn't it. Because as soon as we got inside the small house, I saw Maybelline lying on a lumpy couch with a cloth on her forehead, but one that didn't quite cover the terrible red and purple bruise above her eyes. When we came in the door, she smiled in an apologetic manner and waved her fingers at me.

"What on earth happened to you?" I could tell this had been more than just a fall.

"It's nothing, Miss Amelia," she managed, but now this Mamie-person spoke up.

"Some of them wild boys from town come up behind her in a truck and thought she was colored. I seen the whole thing right from the porch."

"Thought you were colored?" I mouthed the words, but I couldn't see what that had to do with anything.

"Yes'm," Mamie nodded her head. "Thought she was colored and tried to run her over."

What? "What does that have to do with it? Are you all right?"

Mamie started to say something else, but she changed her mind and reached over to smooth the caseless pillow under Maybelline's head. "Let me wring that rag out for you," she said and took the cloth from Maybelline's forehead.

That was when I saw the full bruise, an angry purpling that went nearly all the way across Maybelline's forehead. Below the bruise, her swollen, red lids almost covered her eyes completely and looked for all the world just like badly misplaced rooster combs.

"Good Heavens!" I sputtered.

"That's sure enough right," Maybelline whispered. "The good Lord in Heaven's taking care of me. Else I'd a been dead and gone."

"But why?" I couldn't unglue myself from trying to understand it.

"Why is He taking care of me?"

"No, of course not. Why did someone try to hurt you?"

"Guess it's what Mamie said. They thought I was colored."

"But why?" My mouth simply wouldn't say anything else.

"Guess there's some what hates 'em that bad is all I can figure."

Mamie came back carrying the cloth, which she replaced none too gently over the purple bruise.

"Youall got some family 'round here I can call?"

"No family," I said. "We're just passing through."

"Well, in that case, I guess we better work on getting your car fixed. If you gimme your keys," she said, "my daddy will walk down the road and get it for you."

"But it's broken down," Maybelline said.

"Probably just a fan belt, Daddy says. Or a hose. He can patch it up enough to get it this far tonight and get a new part for it over to town first thing tomorrow."

Maybelline motioned toward her purse, which was sitting on a straight-backed chair.

"Keys are in there," she said, and then she closed her eyes.

"Needs rest," Mamie said.

Mamie sure was right about that. Because Maybelline slept and slept, right there on the couch. After dark came, Mamie picked Maybelline up in her arms, just like a baby, and carried her into a little bedroom off the living room. When Mamie saw me staring at the lumpy, old bed, she assured me, "I done put on clean sheets for youall. And the bed's clean." But of course, I hadn't said a word.

She put Maybelline on the bed and we worked together to get Maybelline's dress off and put her in a voluminous nightgown that Mamie had brought in, clean and folded.

"Youall can stay here tonight," she said. "But don't you go making no noise. Because my man won't like it that you're here."

"Your daddy?" I asked in surprise, for from what I had seen of the old daddy, he reminded me a lot of my Great-Uncle Albert. Because he was little and thin, and his face, from the brief glimpse I'd had, was as passive and open as a baby's.

"N-o-o-o, not Old Daddy," Mamie laughed. "He wouldn't hurt a flea! No. I mean him. . . ." She motioned her head toward the back of the house. "My man."

"Who?"

"My man," she repeated. "We lives in a trailer back there." Again, she motioned her head toward the back of the house. "And he ain' going like us having no white folks 'round here."

Oh, my!

"White mens killed his daddy," she added simply, all the while rolling up the sleeves of the huge nightgown around Maybelline's pale, quiet hands.

"What do you mean?"

"Just what I says."

"Why'd they . . . kill . . . ?"

"Said he bothered a white lady."

"And did he?" I couldn't stop the question from coming out, but regardless of whether the answer was yes or no, it would tell me something I really didn't want to find out.

"I don't know," Mamie said. "Don't think he knows neither. Just knows he seen his daddy get hung."

"Maybe we'd better leave," I said. "Isn't there a town somewhere? Your daddy could take us there and then bring us the car in the morning, couldn't he?" Anything to get out of there. Away from an angry man I could already envision. A scar on his face and big, strong hands.

But even as I asked the question, I was thinking that first of all, Maybelline shouldn't be moved. And, too, if we went off and left our car there, everything we had in this world would be stolen. I was sure of it.

135

"Nothing near enough," she said. And so that settled it. So I'd really been foolish, I suppose, thinking that leaving home wasn't going to be so bad after all. And, too, I'd been worrying about going to live in some old broken-down house of Maybelline's granddaddy's, but at that moment, I'd have given anything if we'd been there, no matter what it was like, instead of where we were.

After we got Maybelline settled, Mamie heated me up a bowl of soup and made me a cup of tea, and then there was nothing else for me to do but get into bed and try to go to sleep.

I'll have to say one thing: Mamie's old daddy was certainly a polite and most respectful old man, and he wouldn't even sleep in the house that night, not even out on the porch.

"Not fittin'," I overheard him say to Mamie. "Sleep in the yard, thas what I do."

No amount of her persuading could change his mind. So that's the way it was done. And from the very minute Mamie went back to the pine thicket, where her trailer was, the old daddy stayed outside. So Maybelline and I had the little shack all to ourselves, though I certainly didn't see why Mamie couldn't have stayed in the house with us, to help us if we needed something during the night.

Later, I found out.

Because during the night, I woke up with a start. So confusing it was, waking up in such a strange place. And what had awakened me was rain hitting on the tin roof, a sound such as I hadn't heard in years and years. Last time I remember it was out at Camp Meeting. And then, the rain beginning to drip off the roof and onto the bare ground outside the window, and once or twice a little flash of lightning and a deep mutter of thunder.

Then I thought I heard someone crying. At first, I thought it was Maybelline, but it couldn't be. She was snoring ever so lightly and hadn't moved a muscle since Mamie and I put her in the bed.

When I heard the crying again, it sounded in quick beats, almost like a puppy whimpering out in the yard. The sound was coming from Mamie's trailer.

I wondered if she had some poor little puppy chained up out there in the dark and the rain. Wouldn't have surprised me one little bit.

But when I heard it again, it raised the hairs on the back of my neck. Because there was a word in the yelp—"no!"—and after that, I didn't hear anything more, because the rain got heavier, and all I could hear was it drumming hard on the rusty tin roof over my head.

Toward dawn, Maybelline groaned a bit and turned over on her side.

"Are you all right?" I asked in the darkness.

"Yes'm," came the muffled reply. "Got a little headache is all."

And after that, I never heard another thing until someone was stirring around in the kitchen, and I opened my eyes to find morning light coming in the window. Weak light, though, so I knew it was still very early.

Mamie was stoking up the wood stove in the kitchen when I came out of the bedroom, and she didn't turn to look at me, but just kept on feeding light-wood into the stove.

"You sit yourself down, and I'll have some coffee for you in just a few minutes," she said in a kind of gruff way. I sat down as she had directed and quietly waited for her obviously surly mood to work itself out. And it did.

Because a little later on, when she brought the steaming mug of coffee to me, she set it down before me almost gently, and I glanced up at her.

"Good Heavens!" I said, because one of her eyes was swollen almost shut, and a deep purple bruise covered one whole side of her mouth, the rubbery lip swollen and shiny around a deep, red split.

"What happened to you?" I asked.

She didn't answer. Just turned back to the stove and started breaking eggs into an iron skillet. I heard the front screen door open and shut, and the old daddy appeared just outside the kitchen doorway, his hat in his hand. He nodded to me in a quick, bobbing motion and then whispered to Mamie, "Some coffee, daughter. And I'll be on my way." Mamie poured his coffee into a mug and walked across the kitchen to hand it to him. He took it almost reluctantly, as if he were afraid for his hand to extend into the kitchen. Briefly, he glanced at Mamie's face, but not one thing about his expression changed.

When he was gone, Mamie went back to the stove.

137

"He's gon' get youall a fan belt," she said. "Be back in about a hour." And she came toward me, carrying a plate of eggs.

"What happened to your face?" I asked again, and this time she didn't turn away.

"My man beat up on me," she said, simply.

"What?"

"What I said."

"But why?"

"'Cause of youall," she replied. "I done told you he don't like havin' no white folks around."

"He beat you because of us?"

"Thas what he done it for."

"I'm so sorry." The words thin and inadequate.

"So'm I," she said and turned back to the stove. "But being real honest with you, hadn't been youall, woulda been something else."

"He's done it before?"

Mamie snorted. "Lotsa times," she said.

"What does your daddy think about it?"

"Don't think nothin' about it."

"Well, surely he can't approve of it."

"No, he don't 'prove of it, and he don't not 'prove of it. He just don't see it."

"Don't . . . doesn't see it?"

"Don't wanta see it. So he don't."

When she spoke again, it was so low, I almost didn't hear the words. And, too, her back was turned to me because she was still stirring something on the stove, and that made it harder for me to hear her.

"You really sorry?"

Took me a minute to figure out what she'd said. "Why, of course I am. We'll get out of here just as soon as we can, and then you won't have any more trouble."

"Oh, I'd still have trouble," she muttered. "I done told you if it hadn't been youall, it woulda been something else. You really sorry?" she added.

"Of course I am!"

"Then when youall goes away from here, you take me with you."

138

"What?"

"I SAID," she was almost growling, "take me with you."

"With us?"

She turned from the stove then, her hand propped on her massive hip and still holding the pancake turner, so that grease dripped from it onto the floor. But she didn't seem to notice. "Cain't you hear good?" It wasn't a question. It was an accusation.

"I hear just fine," I protested. "You want us to take you with us."

"Thas right." The grease on the pancake turner had dripped slower and slower, and now it stopped. "This time it was because of youall, but he's done it lotsa times. Over and over and over again. Never know what it's gonna take to set him off to beating on me. And sometimes, it don't take nothing at all. He just does it."

"I . . . I don't know what to say," I sputtered, and that was completely true. And her flat, black eyes—especially the swollen one—were fixed on me, unblinking. So I knew I had to say something. "Well, I can certainly understand your wanting to get away from someone . . . like him, but you don't even know where we're going," I offered.

"Don't care where you're going," she spat out. "Long as it's away from here. Away from him. Far away."

"We aren't even going far away," I protested, growing more alarmed every minute at the thought of that huge woman entrenched in the backseat of my car like a great, stone monolith.

"Where you going to?" she demanded.

"Jerusalem."

"Jerusalem? Like in the Bible?"

"I suppose so. Only this is Jerusalem, Georgia. In Jefferson County."

"Jefferson County? Never heard of no Jefferson County. Never heard of no Jerusalem neither, 'cept the one in the Bible."

"That's where we're going."

"Well then, praise Jesus! It's a miracle, thas what it is! I'm going to Jerusalem!" Not a question this time, but a joyous pronouncement. Solid, earnest, and absolutely undeniable. Certainly, I must have looked quite alarmed by that time, for she reached over and patted my hand with her massive paw.

"I'm goin' to Jerusalem," she repeated, almost gently.

Still, something in her eyes snapping and crackling, despite the honey-smoothness of her voice. And the big hand still patting my own, but quite hard. Or something like that.

Maybelline appeared in the doorway to the kitchen with Mamie's oversized nightgown hanging so long on her that it puddled around her feet and made her look just like a little child in her mama's dress. From within the deep purple and green bruise, her swollen eyes blinked at Mamie's nearly equally swollen face.

"What happened to you?" Maybelline asked, looking at Mamie.

"Sit down and I'll get you some breakfast," Mamie said. And Maybelline sat down at the table without another word.

We watched in silence as Mamie reached into the dark recesses of the very back of the kitchen cabinet and fished out a wrinkled doily she—or someone—had made from an old sheet, cutting it into a square and then drawing out threads from around the edges, making a fringe of sorts. I couldn't help but watch her, how she shook it out and then put it in a wooden bowl—hand carved, looked to be—and then piled the biscuits into it. Her way, maybe, of trying to fancy up the breakfast. Something about it making my heart lurch against my chest.

Maybelline waved her hand at me and mouthed the silent words "What happened?" I shook my head at her just as Mamie turned and placed the bowl of biscuits on the table.

"He hit me," Mamie said right out to Maybelline.

"Who? Old Daddy?"

"No." Again, Mamie almost laughed. "Not my daddy. Him." She motioned her head toward the back door. "And I ain't taking it no more. Thas why youall is taking me with you when you go."

Maybelline looked at me in surprise, as if it were an arrangement Mamie and I had cooked up together. I blinked in open-eyed innocence.

"You sure?" Maybelline asked Mamie. And I was sitting there thinking: Dear Lord, was she going to let this Mamie-person do just that?

"Sure, I'm sure," Mamie was leaning against the counter, slurping coffee loudly from a mug. "Sure, I'm sure," she repeated, as if to convince herself.

140

By that time, Maybelline had begun reading the expression on my face, and so she knew this was something I didn't like. Not one little bit. But right away, she got that dying-calf-in-a-thunderstorm look about her. I'd seen that look before. Plenty of times. Whenever she went all soft about someone she thought she could rescue from something.

"I don't know if there's room in the car," I said quickly, not looking at either of them. Because if I didn't say something, and that right quickly, Maybelline was sure to take this strange woman right in. Let her go with us. Maybe even let her live with us.

But Maybelline had closed her bruised eyes and her lips were moving silently, and then her eyes flew open as she pronounced, "We'll have to make room, because the Lord done said for us to take her."

"Now when did He say that?" I snapped. Because if she got it in her head it was the Lord's doing, it was all over. And I knew it.

"Just then!" A passionate expression in her swollen eyes.

"I didn't hear anything," I insisted, desperately.

"It was a still, small voice," Maybelline said. "Maybe I'm the only one what heard it."

"I heard it!" Mamie piped up, her face an absolute picture of honesty and innocence. "He done said for youall to take me with you. I heard it clear as day. He said He wants me to go along to take care of youall," she added as an afterthought. And having struck upon a new and, to her way of thinking, most persuasive argument, she swam all around it just like it was a lifeboat she was trying to grab hold of in a stormy sea.

"Why, I can clean and cook and do for both you ladies, and you don't even have to pay me nothing"—in my memory flashed the image of the little cot in mine and Mama's room at Camp Meeting—"but we gotta do it the right way." Mamie's voice had taken on a low and serious tone. "He sees me trying to get away, he'll kill me sure."

Maybelline glanced at me, a pleading in her face such as I had never seen before. Not for lost kittens or Deena-Marie's vacant-eyed children or for anyone who'd ever come to the back door and asked to rake the yard in exchange for something to eat. And just that fast, I began to fear that it was all settled, and this woman would certainly be going away with us, when we went. That is, if we didn't all wind up with our throats cut.

Mamie leaned forward and planted her hands onto the top of the table, so that with every low word she spoke, I watched the big, black hands against the red-and-white-checked tablecloth. And the pitiful, wrinkled doily in the wooden bowl.

"Soon as my old daddy gets youall's new fan belt and puts it on, and Miss Maybelline here is well enough to travel, we gotta leave real quiet-like."

"You going to run off and leave your old daddy?" I asked, looking for anything I could think of to put an end to this whole wild idea.

"He be all right. He got a widder woman gon' be wanting him pretty soon."

"Won't your hus . . . he . . . get mad at your daddy if you run off like this?" Maybelline asked, and it was all I could do to keep from bursting into applause. What a good question!

"Nome. He won't touch my old daddy," Mamie said. "He don't beat up on nothing but wimmin-folk. Ain't never raised his hand to another man."

But I was sitting there and thinking that if Maybelline kept on encouraging this conversation, somehow or other it would all be settled and accepted that this Mamie-person most certainly would go with us. So maybe the time for good manners was over.

"I'm against it," I said, flatly, and Maybelline and Mamie both looked at me just as if I'd run over a dog.

"It don't matter what you're against," Mamie said. She locked her eyes onto Maybelline's and they didn't even flicker for a second. "It don't matter what she says," Mamie repeated to Maybelline. "The Lord done told us what to do, so it don't matter what nobody else says."

Maybelline was looking back and forth between this Mamie-person and me. And I tried to look at her just as strongly as Mamie was doing, but somehow or other, I knew already that it was no use. So I guessed this was what my life was going to be like now. At the mercy of Maybelline and all her so-called "instructions" from the Lord Jesus.

142

When Maybelline finally spoke, it was to me. "I can't go off and leave her," she explained. "I can't leave her any more than I could have left you."

Well, I thought that was a right sharp argument she'd conjured up. But, of course, she hadn't taken into consideration one little bit that I would have more than welcomed her going off and leaving me alone. That's what I'd anticipated, once I told her she had to move, that she would do just that . . . move on along. And I could have taken care of myself just fine. I could have . . . I could have . . .

"I thank you," Mamie said to Maybelline, and then they both looked at me, Maybelline's face filled with pleading and Mamie's face stone-cold and eyes glittering.

"I ain't gon' forget this," Mamie said. And she was looking right at me, so I figured it meant she'd remember how I'd opposed her going with us. But right at that moment, she shifted her eyes to Maybelline, and so Maybelline thought she had made the statement to her, in gratitude.

"It's okay, Mamie," Maybelline said. "You just tell us how to get it done, and we'll do it."

"First thing is, how you feeling this morning?" Mamie said.

"I've got a little headache," Maybelline said. "And the light hurts my eyes, but other than that, I feel right good."

"Well, we gotta get you well. 'Cause I don't know how to drive," Mamie said.

"I know how to drive," I volunteered, before I'd even really thought about it, and both Mamie and Maybelline smiled at me. Well now, that was really something, how they tricked me into that!

"We still gotta wait, leastwhile 'til tomorrow," Mamie said. "He's gon' go see his brother then, like he does every Saturday, and that's when we can get away."

"You think he'll suspect anything?" Maybelline asked.

"Maybe. But we gotta chance it."

Maybelline just nodded her head and sipped at her coffee. And me sitting there and wondering how on earth it all got turned around so we were now faced with "getting away" and taking chances, dear Lord!

13

For the rest of that whole day, we said not another word about our impending "escape"—almost as if *he* could hear us, even though we were in the house and he was in the little trailer among the pine trees out back.

Right after Maybelline finished her coffee—she couldn't eat much of the eggs Mamie had fixed for her—she went back to bed, explaining that she still felt woozy, and because there was really nowhere else for me to go, I stayed at the kitchen table. But there was certainly an uncomfortable silence between Mamie and me.

She cleared the table and washed up the dishes, and when they were all put back into the cabinet, she turned and went out the back door without a word. So I was left all alone.

I went and peeked into the bedroom first thing and saw that Maybelline was sound asleep. I supposed that was good for her, but still I was worried. Because it seemed to me I remembered hearing somewhere that someone who has had a blow to the head shouldn't be allowed to go to sleep. For fear they would never wake up again. Still, I reasoned that Maybelline had already woke up for what little breakfast she had managed to eat, so probably, she was okay.

I didn't want to sit out on the front porch—that felt too exposed for me, just in case that man of Mamie's would see me and go off on some kind of tirade. So I sat down in the little living room and looked around to see if there wasn't something I could read. But there wasn't a thing. Not a book. Not a magazine. So I just sat there, wondering how we would ever get through this long day stretching ahead of us. And what would happen tomorrow when we tried to leave? Sitting there, all alone, I suddenly realized that I was tired, too. Strange, feeling so tired that early in the morning. But with what all we'd been through, with Maybelline getting hurt and then this Mamie-woman taking advantage of us and getting us all mixed up in her affairs, it was certainly no wonder I was so tired.

So I leaned my head against the back of the chair, just as I heard *Great-Aunt Kate's voice coming through the back screen door: "I don't care what her mama said. You get her bathed and dressed right after supper. She's going to services, and I don't want to hear another word about it."*

"Yes'm." Same yes'm as the one about the wishbone. Then I'm thinking about there being only tonight and I'll wake up and Mama will be back. But what's this about my having to go to services?

I don't go inside until Great-Aunt Kate's voice trails away and I know she's gone on through the tent and out to the front porch. I come in the back door to where Aunt Valley's wiping off the oilcloth on the table and getting ready to set it for supper.

"What's the matter?" I say.

She doesn't look at me, but just keeps wiping and wiping the oilcloth so hard I think the little blue flowers are going to be on her dishrag when she gets done.

"Soon as supper's done, you come in the bedroom and let me bathe you and help you get dressed. Miss Kate wants you to go to evening services with them tonight." She still doesn't look at me.

"Services? She's got no right to make me go when my own mama doesn't make me!"

"I don't know nothing 'bout that."

"She's making me go 'cause my mama isn't here to stop her!"

"I said I don't know nothing 'bout that," Aunt Valley says, and she's still going at that oilcloth as if it's the dirtiest thing in the whole world.

Right after supper, Aunt Valley takes me into the bedroom and washes my face and hands and scrubs the grime off my knees and puts me in my blue dress. And while she is buttoning up the back and tying the sash, I am looking at Mama's pillow there on the bed, and I can see another me—wearing only my cotton petticoat—crawling across the bed and flopping down on Mama's pillow and breathing in her perfume in great tearing gulps. She's not an old doll. She's beautiful and full of life and has sparkles in her blue eyes.

And the hot things behind my eyes and in my throat go all peppery again, and I start swallowing over and over, to keep it all down. I feel Aunt Valley's hands hesitate in tying the bow, and I know she's noticed, but—please, Lord Jesus—don't let her try to say anything to me about it or it will all come out all over everything. Because now I know what it felt like when those children sat on the steps and watched Tulie drive away with us. And the knowing of it was ready to gush out from behind my eyes and throat, great globules of something so red and awful, it'll just never stop.

"Tomorrow, I'll ask Miz Stone can Miss Julia come back and play with you again." And that's all Aunt Valley says.

No, I think. Tomorrow you won't have to. Because Mama'll come back.

When Aunt Valley takes my hand and leads me out of the room, Great-Aunt Kate and Carol Ann are waiting for me, Carol Ann still pale but feeling good enough to stick her tongue out at me. Great-Aunt Kate takes one look at me, and she can see I'm struggling with something. "Mercy!" she mutters under her breath.

We join up with Aunt Tyler, who has been waiting for us on the front porch, and we all start walking through the grass, down the hill, and toward the tabernacle, where it squats at the bottom, light flooding out from under the tin roof, and the pianos already playing—"hot and heavy," Aunt Nell always says—pounding out "When We All Get to Heaven."

Because there are two pianos, and the two women who play them for services are almost as big as the pianos are, and they always wear navy blue dresses with white lace collars on them and smile at each other and perspire something fierce once they get the music going.

Great-Aunt Kate is holding Carol Ann's hand, and Carol Ann gives a little skip every once in a while and looks up at her mama to see if she's noticed how happy Carol Ann is to be going to services.

I am lagging behind them, planting my feet at each step just as if I'm being dragged along by an invisible rope, and I wish Great-Aunt Kate would turn around and see how mad I am. See how ugly I can look when somebody tries to make me do something. But she doesn't. And by the time we reach the tabernacle, I can hear Mama's voice saying "just for me," and so I start "behaving myself"—or trying to, anyway. And just at that very minute, the bell starts clanging and some of the clang bounces back from where it hits the trees behind the tabernacle. The good sound of it.

At the tabernacle, Aunt Tyler goes into a back pew to sit beside Mrs. Andrews, who is also going to have a little baby. But Great-Aunt Kate and Carol Ann and I go on, walking up the full length of the sawdust-covered aisle and sitting down in the third row from the pulpit. Since I'm the last one in the pew, Great-Aunt Kate is in between Carol Ann and me. Because Carol Ann goes right on into the pew, looking back at Great-Aunt Kate to see if she noticed how eager Carol Ann is to get right in and sit down and get right to it. Just like some dumb old cow jumping into the tick-dip and looking around to see if everyone notices how much she loves it.

The preachers come in then, from the side of the tabernacle, three of them, all wearing black suits and carrying big, fat, black Bibles with the covers all worn-out—so you know they've been reading them. Then they sit down in folding chairs on the podium, and all the while, the pianos still going at it—and the preachers slide forward a little in their chairs all at once and sort of crouch there, with their elbows resting on their knees and their foreheads resting on their balled-up fists—and I think it's really interesting how they did it all in one movement, just like somebody blew a whistle or something. After they stay that way for a while, they all sit back at one time and look out at the congregation, just like another whistle blows to tell them when to do it, only we can't hear it.

The pianos start winding down from about the seventh or eighth time through "When We All Get to Heaven," and at the very end of the song, the two ladies nod at each other and one of them stops playing and wipes her face and hands with a white handkerchief she always keeps right there at the end of the keyboard on her piano, while the other lady keeps on drifting along with some chords, kind of slow-like and shifting them all around until she hits on the one that seems to suit her and the other lady. Because they look at each other and nod again and smile, and the other lady joins right in on her piano. And lo and behold, there is "Standing on the Promises," just as neat as you please, and just the way they want it. And it sure sounds nice.

I am wondering how something gets to be something else, but in a natural kind of way, so I start trying to back up through it again, just to see how it works the other way. Back up now from "Standing on the Promises" and hear all the rolling chords going back down and winding up back at "When We All Get to Heaven," because if . . .

Great-Aunt Kate shakes my shoulder and frowns down at me because she is already standing up and so is everyone else in the whole tabernacle, except me. And I jump to my feet and start looking through the hymnal, but of course, it's too late for me to find the right number to the song. Carol Ann leans back a little, so she can see me from around Great-Aunt

147

Kate's back, and she is smiling in her mean way. And in the middle of her smile is her mouth singing:

> Glory in the highest,
> I will shout and sing,
> Standing on the
> Promises of God.

But I know some of the words, the ones coming up now, so I bellow out:

> Stand-ing
> Stand-ing
> Standing on the promises
> Of God my Savior!

Great-Aunt Kate frowns at me again and shakes her head a little, because I guess she thinks I'm singing too loud. And Carol Ann has her hand over her mouth, laughing. Once again I seem to hear Mama's voice telling me to behave, so I do, and just sing the regular way, which I do whenever I know the part is coming that I already know the words to.

Because I am thinking about promises being promises, and Mama's coming back first thing in the morning, and just like Aunt Valley when she promised me I could have a wishbone, and she kept her promise, no matter what. And the way I promised not to tell anyone that Aunt Valley had been sitting at the dining table, though I don't see anything wrong with that. But maybe it's like Mama says—that sometimes you just never know what'll set Great-Aunt Kate off. You just never know.

All of a sudden, Great-Aunt Kate is tugging at the hem of my dress, and I look around and see I'm the only one left standing. So I sit down. Because the singing is over.

One of the preachers walks up to the pulpit and reaches out and grabs both sides of it, jams his eyes shut and points his chin straight up to where the bell hangs in the belfry. His face is twisted up and pained-looking, like somebody's standing on his toes or something.

"Lord!" he yells, and the folks who aren't paying attention jump just a little bit. But then they settle back down and bow their heads, and all their cardboard-Jesus fans settle down to a nice, steady rhythm:—Stand-ing, Stand-i-n-g, I'm standing on the promises of God. I close my eyes.

"Lord!" he yells again, only this time nobody jumps. "We come before you this evening, Lord, just cr-a-a-w-ling on our hands and knees. . . ."

148

I open my eyes, just to make sure I'm not the only one still sitting, while everybody else is down in the sawdust, crawling around on their hands and knees. But they are all sitting. And they all have their eyes closed. Except for Great-Aunt Kate. She's got hers wide open and glaring at me just like she's trying to bore a hole right through me.

So I close my eyes again and try to behave and pay attention.

Pretty soon, the preacher gets all his praying done. About what miserable worms we all are, and how we'll all burn in hell—Doodlebug!—unless we throw ourselves on Jesus. And then he yells "A-MAN!" and sits down. But another preacher stands up, and then he comes to the pulpit and opens his Bible and starts reading.

At first I try to listen, but he loses me after about the first three or four words, once he gets to the first "begat." So I sit with my hands folded in my lap and try not to think about how hard the wooden bench is getting. I look down at my shoes and gently tap the toes together and discover that when I do that, the shoes look like two little black puppies talking to each other:

> Hello, puppy! What's your name?
> Blackie. What's yours?
> Why, mine is Blackie, too!
> That can't be! Your name is Blackie, too?
> Sure is!

I look up at the preacher, and he's getting pretty good into the hellfire and damnation stuff. His face is red, and there's a big vein in the side of his neck beginning to throb. Some of his hair, a piece that was lying very carefully combed right across the top of his bald head, begins to slip down over his forehead and finally sticks there in his sweat, just like a big comma.

But he's still got a long way to go before he gets fired up enough to be worth watching, so I go back to the two black puppies that are both named Blackie. But the puppies won't come back, and the shoes are just shoes, and so the preacher's voice is all there is because I know that if I keep staring at my shoes, they will become nothing. Stop being what they are and get to be whatever has no meaning. Backing all the way down from when they were puppies.

". . . and burn in hell! And burn and burn!" the preacher yells, and the next thing I know, the black puppies that are my shoes spring to life, and, speechless, I float above them and watch them running, skimming across the sawdust and all the way down the long aisle and then a twilight and

149

the dark grass crackling, and they aren't shoes again until they reach the front screen door.

"Aunt Valley?" I yell. "Aunt Valley? Where are you?"

"Out back," she calls.

I run out to where Aunt Valley is standing under the dangling light bulb, talking to another woman—maybe Lizzie, her cousin from down at the Stone tent, because she has the very same big, square head and no neck and a very big bottom.

They look at me and stop talking and nod at each other as if the nod means something, and Aunt Valley's cousin walks away from the light and into the twilight dirt road.

"What are you doing back here?" Aunt Valley asks. But even as she asks, she sits down in the cowhide chair and pats her knee. "How come you leave services?"

And what can I say? That my shoes ran away with me?

"I don't know," I say truthfully. "I just had to run."

She doesn't say anything, and I am busy making up my arguments against her sending me back to services.

She thinks for a few minutes and then she starts nodding her head. "You know, I have a old aunt acts a lot like you do," Aunt Valley says. "Yes'm. A lot like you do. She's my papa's sister."

Here, she falls silent, and I wait without asking for her to go on. For I think that maybe she's getting ready to tell me something that has to do with the Great Mystery, and I don't know how to hear it. For the Great Mystery has always been the thing I can't say, and to hear it spoken will be unbearable.

Aunt Valley slows down in the rocking and finally she stops completely, and I know it's coming. I know I'm going to hear it. And I can't bear it.

"She just feels things so strong and . . ."

"Don't tell me. Please don't tell me!"

For a few seconds, she is silent, and I think maybe she's going to tell me anyway, and I know I can't bear it. But then she says, "All right," and we both heave a deep and relieved sigh. "But you know Miss Kate's going to come in that door any minute, and she's going to expect something from you."

"What do I tell her?" I ask.

"Goodness, I don't know. But we better think of something and think of it quick."

"How about I'm sick?" I suggest.

"How about tell her the truth."

"No."

"All right, then. I guess you better tell her you're sick."

We hear the front screen door squeak open, and "Where are you!"
Great-Aunt Kate calls, the minute she gets in the door. "And what on
earth is wrong with you this time?"

The screen door slams, and I know she's all het up, because she's the
one always after me not to let the door slam because "ladies should know
better than to let the door slam."

Aunt Valley stands me down beside her chair and says, "Go on, now."
And she gives me a little push to help me move along. I go in through the
back door and I don't let it slam, and I meet Great-Aunt Kate about halfway
down the hallway, and we stand there in the sawdust, facing each other.

"I got saved!" I say to Great-Aunt Kate. And when the words come out
of my mouth, I know them for the first time. Because it never once occurs
to me to say them. I just open my mouth and they fall out. And so I'm just
as surprised as Great-Aunt Kate is to hear them.

"Saved?" she mouths the word, incredulously.

"Yes'm." How sincere it sounds! And I feel the surge of power I love to
feel, and so I go on with it. "The Holy Ghost Himself just got inside me
and started me to running before I even knew what hit me. Ran all the
way home before I knew what had happened."

Great-Aunt Kate backs up and sits down on a little wooden chair right
by the door of her bedroom, and when she sits, the breath kind of goes
out of her in a little wh-u-m-ph sound. But she never takes her eyes off
me.

Carol Ann comes in the front door and lets it slam, but Great-Aunt Kate
doesn't say a thing because she's still busy staring at me.

"I got saved!" I say to Carol Ann, and the bright sound of my voice is
strange in my ears.

"Did not!" she retorts.

"Did too," I come right back at her.

Aunt Valley has come in the back door, and I can feel her standing
behind me, feel her bigness and that square head jammed down on her
shoulders, her just as big as a mountain and with her hands on her hips.
So I am also thinking that somehow I'm going to have to explain this to
her, too, as well as to Great-Aunt Kate.

"That's enough," Great-Aunt Kate says to me and Carol Ann. And to
me, she adds, "You come in here and tell me all about it," and she motions
to me to go into the bedroom. So we go in together and sit down on her
bed. Carol Ann follows us into the room, but Great-Aunt Kate says to her,
"You wait out there, sugar. Mama wants to talk in private." And Carol
Ann sticks out her bottom lip a little bit, but she goes away. Only I hear

the springs in the settee squeak a little and so I know she's sitting just on the other side of the wall, listening.

"Now I want you to tell me about it," Great-Aunt Kate says.

"Well . . ." I am stalling a little because it occurs to me that I can come pretty close to the truth about what happened, but not close enough to disturb the Great Mystery. For nothing must ever disturb that.

"I just got this sort of electricity in me, and it made me want to holler and run around." I am looking at Carol Ann's jar of deodorant, where it sits on the shelf.

"Electricity?" Great-Aunt Kate is looking at me hard. "What kind of electricity?"

"The Holy Ghost is what it was," I breathe out the words in what I hope is a sound of complete reverence.

"And it made you want to run?" she asks.

"And holler," I remind her. Then I am remembering what Julia said about . . . what did she call it? Talking with a tongue? Talking in tongues! Oh, Lord, please let what Julia said be true!

"Yes, ma'am." My voice sounds so assured that I'm beginning to believe it all. "Words not a human being knows. Angel-words."

"Like what?"

"Why, I don't remember them, now."

"But you knew them then?"

"Yes, ma'am. I sure did."

We sit there for the longest kind of time, with me looking right into her eyes and blinking a little in what I hope is a gesture of innocence.

Finally, she sighs and shakes her head, and it's just like some kind of a tension is broken. "You go on now and tell Aunt Valley to help you get ready for bed."

"Yes, ma'am."

Aunt Valley is sitting back in the cowhide chair on the back porch, and I go and stand beside her and lean against her. But she doesn't pat her knee for me to come up and sit in her lap. She just sits there, shaking her head just the tiniest little bit and looking off into the darkness across the twilight dirt road. Finally, after what seems to be a long time, she puts her big, brown hand over mine.

"You be careful," she says real low. "You just be careful what you go telling folks about getting saved."

"Yes'm," I say, and it's not an accident that I'm saying ma'am to a colored woman.

Aunt Valley bathes me and helps me get on my nightgown, and she puts me in bed and turns out the light, but she sits down on the side of the bed, and I bet what's coming is a real scolding about me getting saved. So I just wait, and she sits there for a long while, patting the side of the bed, like she can't quite bring herself to pat me, and then she starts in to talking, right out of a clear blue sky:

"The fourth day of creation, God made the sun and the moon and all the little stars. And He put 'em high up in the Heavens to make light for the world. And after that, He stopped and put His hand on His hip and took a long, hard look at everything He'd done made that far. And after He got done looking it all over, He said, 'That's good!'"

I am lying there, thinking that maybe I'm not going to get any lecture after all. But I was wrong about that.

"So don't you never go making fun of Someone Who could do all that just with a blink of His eye, you hear me!"

"Yes, ma'am."

Her hand stops patting the side of the bed and reaches over and pats me on the shoulder for a moment, and then she gets up and goes out of the room, but she leaves the door open so a little glow of light from the lamp on the table comes in through the hallway. And, too, because there's no ceiling, the little light is glowing all the way up to the rafters, to where the big slabs of rusty tin make the roof. Rafters like old black ribs. Like being in the belly of the whale.

I hear her taking the big paper sack of butter beans out to the back porch, where she'll sit in the cowhide chair and shell them for dinner tomorrow.

And there's something nice about it. Being in the cool bed and no old doll beside me. Hearing the fan hum and the snap of the butter bean pods and knowing that all I have to do is go on to sleep, and tomorrow, Mama will come back.

But sleep won't come, and I lie there wondering if I should pray to God to forgive me for my sins. And then I remember how wonderful it felt when I was talking to Great-Aunt Kate and working so hard to make her believe me. And while I am thinking, I hear Carol Ann come in the front door and go into hers and Great-Aunt Kate's room and I hear the little stirring sounds as she takes off her dress and hangs it on a nail and then pulls her nightgown out from under the pillow. Then a scratching, scraping kind of sound, one I don't recognize, and Carol Ann's face suddenly appearing at the top of the stall-wall between the two rooms.

"You lied!" she says in a half-whisper.

"What?"

153

"Said you'd been saved."

"I was," I say. "I was saved."

"Unh-unh," she sing-songs. "And Mama knows you wasn't saved."

"Does not," I murmur, half-heartedly.

"Does so," Carol Ann insists, and then she wobbles around a bit, and I know she's standing on the old rocking chair that has no bottom in it. Then she steadies herself. "My mama says your mama has just spoiled you rotten. And you're probably going to grow up to be a criminal or something."

I don't say a word.

"So there," Carol Ann adds, and with a satisfied smirk, she disappears, her face going down behind the top of the stall-wall just like a mean old sun setting.

I hear the top of Carol Ann's Fresh deodorant unscrewing. Because she wants to remind me that she thinks I'm just a baby.

I'm sorry, Mama, I think to myself. I didn't behave, and I hate them for saying bad things about you. But I couldn't help it. I really couldn't.

Then, just to be sure, I say my prayers before I go to sleep.

Next thing I know, someone's standing by the chair, and first off, I think it's Aunt Valley. But it's Mamie.

"Ain't no way for us to get started together, being mad like this," she said.

And maybe because I'd thought for a minute that she was Aunt Valley, I softened toward her a little, right then and there. Not much, but a little.

"Sometimes it takes me a little bit to get used to new ideas," I said, and she must have sensed that it was about as close as I was ever going to come to saying anything she wanted to hear.

"I did spring in on youall kind of sudden-like," Mamie admitted. "Just that I was desperate. Been looking a long time for how to get away, and seems to me this is just about the perfectest thing's come along this old road."

"I don't see what's perfect about it," I said. "Why, I'm not even sure the place where we're going is there any longer."

"Jerusalem?"

"Oh, there's a little town called Jerusalem, no doubt," I said, and then I lowered my voice—just in case Maybelline was awake and listening to us—"but I'm worried about the house we're supposed to go to; don't even know for sure it's really there."

"House?"

"Miss Maybelline's granddaddy's house."

"Oh, I thought maybe youall already lived there. You ever been there before?"

"No, indeed, and worse, she hasn't even been there since she was just a child."

"That's a long time ago," Mamie said.

"It certainly is."

"You think maybe the house isn't there no more?"

"I don't know. Like you say, it's a long time ago."

Mamie looked as if she were deeply concerned, and certainly, she should have been. Besides, I wanted to let her know right off that she wasn't going to be living in the lap of luxury. Nothing waiting for her like she probably imagined: a big, beautiful house and her own room right off the kitchen and an easy time of it.

"Then what're youall going there for? How come you're going anyway?"

"We have our reasons," I said and made up my mind not to say any more than I absolutely had to. No need for this woman to know our business.

"You going visiting?"

"No. We're going there to live."

"And you didn't never see it?"

"That's right."

"And you not even sure it's there?"

"That's right," I repeated, relishing her deflated voice.

She let out her breath in a slow whistle, and I felt a faint glimmer of hope that she'd change her mind about going along with us. But after a long silence, she finally said, "Well, I guess it's a gamble, sure enough. But if youall are gonna gamble, then Old Mamie can gamble, too. Besides," she added, "better to go to something I don't know what it is, than stay with what I know I got here."

I was just about to remind her of her daddy and how he would miss her, when we heard the engine start up on my car. Mamie looked out of the window.

155

"Daddy's done got your car fixed," she said, and she turned and looked at me for the longest kind of time before she broke out with the most insincere grin I've ever seen.

"See how I can take such good care of youall? Arranging to get your car fixed and taking care of Miss Maybelline like I done? And you just wait 'til you see my ironing! If there's anything I like to do, it's ironing."

I didn't know what to say, so I said nothing.

"Because you ladies sure needs somebody to help you. Do for you. And I'm the one what'll do it."

Still, I said nothing, because somehow and in a way I couldn't explain, it was almost as if she were reading the lines in a play. Or something like that.

"Anyway," she went on. "You just sit here and rest yourself a while. I got someplace I gotta go. But I'll be back soon as I can. You need anything, you call to Old Daddy." And with that, she was gone.

Wherever it was she went, she was gone a long time. Maybelline still slept, the old daddy sat out on the front steps smoking cigarettes, and I sat in the hot living room, thinking that I'd give just about anything for a cool shower and a change of clothes. And that's the way it was for almost that whole, long day.

Toward dark, Maybelline came out of the bedroom, still wearing Mamie's big nightgown, and she looked as if she felt much better. I got right up and went to help her, but she waved me off and made it to the couch all on her own.

"I feel better," she said, smiling. Oh, the bruise was still terrible-looking, maybe even darker than it had been, but beneath it, the swelling in her eyelids was going down.

"I'm right hungry," she said. "Where's Mamie?"

"She's gone somewhere. Been gone almost all day."

"Well, I don't think she'll mind if we go on out to the kitchen and find us something to eat."

But just then we heard the back screen door open on its rusty hinges and Mamie appeared in the kitchen door. She seemed a bit agitated, and I glanced behind her to see if maybe that hus . . . man of hers was coming in the door behind her. Lord, have mercy!

But she was alone.

"Well, look at you!" Mamie chirped to Maybelline too cheerfully. "You feeling better?"

"Much better," Maybelline said. "And I'm sure hungry, if you don't mind."

"I thought so! Got us a whole mess of butter beans be ready in a little bit. But while you're waiting, I'll get you some good hot coffee with a little milk in it."

But as Mamie turned back to the kitchen, I distinctly heard her mutter under her breath, "Lord, forgive me!"

That evening, Mamie fixed us the best, golden-brown cornbread I ever tasted, and fresh butter beans cooked just right, and sliced tomatoes. I made a pig out of myself, I'm afraid, but it was so good! So I got to thinking how maybe it just might be all right, having Mamie with us. Especially if she cooked that well all the time.

As I fell asleep that night, I pictured us—Maybelline and me—sitting on the front porch of a big, old country house that stood on a hill, looking out over a beautiful green lawn, and Mamie, wearing a starched, snow-white uniform, bringing us two tall, crystal glasses of iced tea.

So maybe it wasn't going to be so bad, after all.

Such a peaceful night it was, with no rain drumming on the roof and no crying sounds in the dark. And I slept deeply and peacefully, until Mamie touched my shoulder before dawn and whispered, "Let's go."

14

"He's gone," Mamie said a little louder, still shaking my shoulder. "Left real early this time. And I done made coffee for us."

Maybelline sat up, rubbing her eyes.

"You okay to drive?" Mamie asked her.

"I'm doing the driving," I said. Because after all, it was my car we were going in.

"Whatever," Mamie said.

"I'm fine," Maybelline said. "'Cept for being hungry. And I do feel good enough to drive."

Whatever.

Mamie went into the kitchen and made biscuits while Maybelline and I got ready to go. I glanced out of the window once, to where my car sat in the front yard, its black finish shining in the light from the porch. And Mamie's old daddy sitting on the steps, smoking a cigarette.

We ate the hot biscuits and drank our coffee, and then Mamie washed up the dishes and reached behind the door to get a brown paper bag—with her clothes in it, I supposed—and a big, black felt hat, which she plunked onto her head and secured with a monstrous, evil-looking hatpin.

We went out to the car, passing right by Mamie's old daddy. Mamie bent down and hugged him, but he didn't say a thing. Didn't ask where we were going. Didn't ask why Mamie was going with us.

As soon as Maybelline opened the back door of the car, we both realized that there was absolutely nowhere for Mamie to fit in. Not a prayer in this world of getting her into the backseat.

"Let's us all ride up front," Maybelline suggested.

"What?" I couldn't help but be completely appalled. Whoever heard of such a thing? Mamie should ride in the backseat, by herself—like she was our maid, which, of course, she was going to be. But all of us crammed together in the front seat? Utterly ridiculous!

"Doesn't matter how we do it," Maybelline said. "But we better go ahead and get out of here."

And, without another word, she reached into the backseat and started pulling out the big box with my grandmama's Haviland china packed in it.

"Now wait just a minute!" I yelled. "That's my grandmama's, and I'm taking it!" I guess I'd never before spoken so roughly to Maybelline, but how dare she?

"It's this or sitting together, Miss Amelia," Maybelline said, and even though I thought and thought, I couldn't figure out that there was any choice other than what she said.

"There's not enough room for all of us in the front seat anyway," I said. And it was true. Mamie was a very big woman.

"Then we have to leave this box," Maybelline insisted, and for some reason, I couldn't say another word nor could I move a muscle. I just stood there like a stump while Maybelline pulled the box out and set it on the ground.

My grandmama's Haviland china!

"Daddy?" Mamie called to the old man where he was still sitting on the steps. "You put this box in the shed for us, will you? We'll come back and get it sometime."

He nodded, absently.

"It'll be okay," Mamie said, and she reached over and patted me on the shoulder, then she scrambled into the backseat and sat there, all puffed up just like a big old black turkey, plunked right down in the middle of the seat among all the pillows and the blankets.

So that's how we drove away from Mamie's house and left her old daddy sitting on the steps and my grandmama's china sitting in the yard.

Such a strange feeling it was, too, leaving something that mattered that much to me. Something that had been entrusted to me to take care of. Riding once again before good daylight, but it all feeling so very different to me. And, too, with Mamie's voice shattering the peace.

"I am so glad that Jesus loves me . . ." she started in to singing, and Maybelline joined right along with her.

> Jesus loves me,
> Jesus loves me.
> I am so glad
> That Jesus loves me,
> Jesus loves even me!

Just exactly the way Aunt Valley's cousin sang it that day when I left Camp Meeting and went home with Aunt Valley.

Because the cook from the Public Tent is knocking on the back screen door before a one of us is awake the next morning after I get saved.

"Hello, in there," she hollers, still knocking. "Phone call—long-distance—at the Public Tent."

I hear Great-Aunt Kate's feet swishing through the wood shavings in the hallway, and I notice that Aunt Valley's cot is empty, so I figure she must be fixing breakfast. I come out of the room just in time to see the screen door slam shut behind Great-Aunt Kate, and I watch her hurrying off toward the Public Tent, with the fat cook trotting right behind her.

But while I am watching Great-Aunt Kate and this woman go hurrying off down the road, all of a sudden I know it's Mama on the other end of the telephone wire. She's in what my stepdaddy calls the "sitting room" that's right off their bedroom, and I can see her just as clear as day, wearing her pretty gray satin robe with the pale pink collar and cuffs, sitting on the chaise lounge and holding the phone, waiting for Great-Aunt Kate to get to the telephone at the Public Tent.

As soon as I can imagine her like that, I know what the phone call's about. She's not coming back today. Even though she promised.

And of course, I'm right. When Great-Aunt Kate comes back, she goes straight to where Aunt Valley is standing in the cookhouse, stirring the boiling grits and turning the fragrant slices of country ham for breakfast. I watch while Great-Aunt Kate says something to Aunt Valley, and Aunt Valley says something back to her. Finally, Aunt Valley pushes the black skillet with the ham in it right to the back part of the cookstove, and she puts the lid good and tight on the pot of grits. The whole time, Great-Aunt Kate stands there and waits, and then they both come toward the back door.

Aunt Valley comes right to me, where I am still standing in the bed-room doorway, and Great-Aunt Kate slips on past us and into her room.

"Your stepdaddy's real sick, honey," Aunt Valley says. "And your mama can't leave him right now."

"She's not coming back today."

"That's right."

"Oh."

"So get yourself dressed and come on and have some of this good breakfast Aunt Valley has fixed for you."

I go into the room and start getting dressed, but I am really waiting for the Great Mystery to happen, because I think I can feel it coming. But it doesn't come. And I don't know why.

At the breakfast table, Great-Aunt Kate glances at me because she's expecting me to cause trouble about Mama not coming back. Just me and Great-Aunt Kate sitting there because Carol Ann's sleeping late and Aunt Tyler doesn't eat breakfast—just a cup of tea a little later on—and Aunt Nell hasn't come yet.

But I just sit there, eating the good hot grits and the salty ham and thinking about what it's like at my stepdaddy's house, especially if he's sick. Because his head hurts so bad, he can't stand having light anywhere because it makes his headache much worse. So the whole house is in that soft kind of darkness you get when it's daylight outside, and the blinds are shut and the drapes pulled together, and no playing allowed. Or laughing.

I can tell by the way Great-Aunt Kate and Aunt Valley keep glancing at each other that they still expect trouble out of me, but I know that it isn't going to happen. Not this time. Not unless the Great Mystery has fooled me and comes on so suddenly and makes me run and run so that I can't stop.

Aunt Nell arrives toward the end of breakfast, and then Aunt Tyler comes out of the bedroom, and that's how the day gets started. Carol Ann has a glass of ginger ale over chipped ice for her breakfast, and Aunt Tyler goes to services by herself because Great-Aunt Kate doesn't want to leave Carol Ann, and Aunt Nell stays home with Nikki and Honey. After services, Julia comes to play, and we fix up make-believe horses out of some tree branches that have fallen, and we gallop up and down the dirt road behind the tents on our horses until dinnertime, and make up a very

161

complicated story so that she's the hero and I'm her helper, and we are trying to save a lady who's lost in a gold mine in the snowy mountains.

After dinner, Aunt Valley says to me that I should have a good rest because it's so hot and Julia and I have been playing so hard. Great-Aunt Kate and Carol Ann are already resting, with the electric fan blowing on them, and so are Aunt Nell and Aunt Tyler in their room, and with Nikki and Honey lying on a towel that Aunt Nell's put across the foot of the bed, and the fan in that bedroom is humming, too, and blowing Nikki and Honey's long, fluffy hair. And I can hear Aunt Tyler and Aunt Nell talking low to each other and laughing a little bit from time to time.

So Aunt Valley turns the fan on in mine and Mama's room, and she fixes the sheet nice and smooth and cool and sits on the side of the bed while I try to fall asleep.

Usually, when I'm trying to get to sleep, she doesn't say much to me, but this time she does.

"You gonna be okay about your mama, aren't you?"

"Yes, ma'am," I answer.

"Well, I'm sure glad of that," she says. "Don't know much about what happens with you sometimes, but it scares me a little bit, you know."

I am so surprised. Something that scares Aunt Valley? Then the words come without my even having thought them. "Sometimes it scares me, too."

"You wanta talk to Aunt Valley about it?"

"No."

"All right," she says. "But if you change your mind, I'll listen."

"Okay."

"Goodness, if only I could let you meet up with Old Auntie, that would be something sure enough."

But I don't want to hear about it, and so I say, "Tell me more stories, please."

"Well, let's see," she hesitates. "What day of creation was we up to? I disremember this little minute."

"You told me about the fourth day," I reply, hoping that she wouldn't remember it was when she was so worried about me saying I'd been saved. But of course, she remembers, and she cuts those old eyes at me kind of sideways, but then she smiles just enough to let me know she isn't mad with me anymore.

"Then next one's the fifth day, and that's just about my favoritest of all," she says. "'Cause that's the one where God made all the creatures in the whole, wide world—butterflies and birds and mules and cows, and every single kind of living thing, right then and there."

"Tell me about them, every single one of them," I say, turning on my side and getting the pillow comfortable under my head.

"Well, I sure don't think I knows about every single one of 'em," she says. "But I bet He started out with something real simple-like—gnats, maybe."

"Gnats? Why'd God make something like gnats?" Because they were the peskiest things in the whole world, and not a bit of good to anybody, far as I could see.

"My, my, sugar," Aunt Valley says. "You is the biggest one in the whole world for asking questions. Now, I'll be glad to tell you all about it, but first I gotta think about the gnats a little bit. Besides, you're supposed to be taking a nap, and I 'spect we better do like Miss Kate done said, and that's for you to have a rest. But I'll tell it to you later, once I get it figured out. I promise."

"Okay," I say. "But stay with me, please."

And I know for sure that Aunt Valley will do what she says. Remember to tell me the story about God making gnats and stay with me until I'm asleep. So I close my eyes and start right in to thinking about how we don't take naps at home—at my stepdaddy's house. One time I asked Mama why we don't, and she said that instead of going into the bedroom, we usually sit out on the verandah on the shady side of the house for a while. Because I guess going to bed after dinner is maybe a country kind of thing to do.

But I don't mind it, because, usually, I don't fall asleep. Not unless the Great Mystery's gotten ahold of me and tired me all out. And lying there like that, hearing nothing but the humming of the electric fans and the popping of the tin roof, up where the sun's shining right down on it is a very nice thing. Almost like being asleep, but not being asleep, and with my mind just floating around and not thinking about anything in particular, but just relaxing and playing in and around a lot of soft, gentle things.

But just as I am about to relax all the way and maybe even fall asleep, I remember.

"Is my stepdaddy real sick?" I whisper, suddenly finding myself speaking so softly, because I am seeing the parlor in his house and the blinds closed against the light and furniture sitting hushed and still in the twilight room. And we must be very quiet.

"I reckon so," Aunt Valley says. "He might have to go to the hospital."

"Oh."

"But don't you worry about it none," she adds.

She doesn't know that I'm not one little bit worried. Not one bit.

"Your mama says she'll call again tomorrow. To let us know."

"When's Camp Meeting over?" I ask.

"Two or three days, I think . . . yes, that's right."

"What'll I do if she doesn't come back for me?" To see myself alone in the night here after everybody else is gone, I first have to see myself in my own bed in my own room, in my stepdaddy's house in Savannah. See myself there, remembering what it's like here, to make it work.

"Oh, she'll come back for you," Aunt Valley chuckles a little. "You can bet on that."

And then we are quiet, and Aunt Tyler and Aunt Nell are quiet. Lying in their white petticoats on the cool white sheet and the fans humming and the tin roof popping just a little in the afternoon sun.

The next day, Mama calls again, just as she said she'd do, but she says my stepdaddy has taken worse and is in the hospital. And I get to talk to her this time, after Great-Aunt Kate talks. Mama's voice sounds a little too cheerful or something, and the velvety tone makes me miss her all over again.

"Honey," she says, "you go on home with your Great-Aunt Kate, and I'll come and get you just as soon as I can."

"Why can't I come home?"

"Because we're at the hospital all day, and there's no one to look out for you."

"What about Gus?"

"He doesn't know how to take care of you," Mama's voice has a little edge to it.

"Then I'll bring Aunt Valley home with me," I say, suddenly having found the perfect solution.

Mama hesitates. "Let me talk to Great-Aunt Kate again," she says, and I give the telephone receiver back.

Great-Aunt Kate listens for a few minutes, and then she says, "Well . . . we're going to Folly Beach on Wednesday, and . . ." another pause. "No, I can't change my plans. Carol Ann's looking forward to it, and I hate to disappoint her." Another pause and then, "No, Tyler's going back to Atlanta with Nell first thing in the morning. Well, now, please don't be that way about it. If she weren't so . . ."—Great-Aunt Kate looks down at me— ". . . so d-i-f-f-i-c-u-l-t, maybe it would be different, but—"

Mama must have interrupted her, for she stops talking. Great-Aunt Kate puts her hand over the receiver and says to me, "Go get Aunt Valley." I run back to the tent and tell Aunt Valley my mama wants her on the phone, and Aunt Valley lumbers behind me back down the road to the Public Tent, wiping her hands on her apron and breathing hard.

164

Great-Aunt Kate gives her the receiver, and Aunt Valley takes it in her hand like she's never held a phone before, and then puts it to her ear in a very tentative way, like she's scared to hear the sounds coming out of it.

"Aunt Valley?" I hear Mama say, and then Aunt Valley has the phone to her ear, so I can't hear Mama's voice any longer.

"Yes'm," Aunt Valley says. And again, "Yes'm." The brows draw together.

"Nome. Nome," she is shaking her head, as if Mama can see that.

"Nome," she repeats again. "'Cause I gots family needs tending to, that's why. I only come out here to work for youall 'cause I needs the money so bad. And I can't go to no far-off place like Savannah. How'd I get myself home if somebody in my family needs me?"

Then silence, because Mama's talking. Aunt Valley cuts those old coffee-milk eyes at me.

"That so?" she mutters. "I sure am sorry to hear it. Yes'm. Why, yes'm. I guess that'd work all right."

I am bouncing up and down and raising my eyebrows. Is Aunt Valley, my Aunt Valley going home with me?

"Nome," she says. "Ain't no men-folks around my place. 'Cept for my old daddy."

Her place?

"Yes'm. Yes'm. Well, I don't have no phone myself, but my next-door neighbor do. Her name is Alma. And her phone number is 27. Yes'm. Now don't you worry none. Yes'm. That's a plenty, and don't you worry none. Good-bye now." She says "good-bye" in a very stiff kind of way, like she's never said it before and hangs up the phone.

"Why'd you hang up?" Great-Aunt Kate demands. "I wanted to speak with her again."

Aunt Valley ignores that and looks at me and then at Great-Aunt Kate. "She says for me to take this child home with me," she says.

"With you?" Great-Aunt Kate is frowning at Aunt Valley.

"Yes'm. That what she says."

"To your house?"

"Yes'm."

Great-Aunt Kate throws her hands up in the air. "She's gone plumb crazy, that's what. Just plumb crazy!"

Aunt Valley says not another word, but she grabs my hand and walks off fast, sort of pulling me along, and we go back down the road. Behind us, I hear Great-Aunt Kate talking on the phone again. "Yes, operator, I want Central Hospital in Savannah. Third floor. Yes, I'll hold on."

165

Aunt Valley is stomping her old man-shoes into the dust, and I am running beside her. She has a grip on my hand that's just like iron, and her jowls are shaking while she mutters something I can't understand.

"Are you mad?" I ask.

"I'm mad," she answers.

"Are you mad at my mama?"

She slows down and shakes her head. "No, I'm not mad at your mama. There's just things you don't know nothing about yet."

"What things?"

"Just never you mind," she says.

When Great-Aunt Kate comes back from the Public Tent, she goes right to Aunt Valley.

"Well, that's what she wants, so I wash my hands of the whole thing. Never heard of such a thing in my life!"

And nobody says anything else. Except Carol Ann.

Because that night, when I pass by Great-Aunt Kate and Carol Ann's room, I see my mama's jar of cold cream on Carol Ann's shelf. So I go into mine and Mama's room and look, and sure enough, it's gone. So I know it's my mama's, and Carol Ann took it when I was out playing with Julia.

I march right over to Carol Ann's shelf and get it back. But I step on something that's on the wood shavings on the floor. It's a pair of Carol Ann's panties, all rolled up like a doughnut on the floor. And then I stop dead-still. Because there's blood on them. Not a lot of blood, but a reddish-brown smear, and I prickle all over but I say not a word.

Later, when I am almost asleep, Carol Ann comes into her room and climbs on the old rocking chair and sticks her head over the wall between our rooms.

"My mama says your mama's going to let you go live with nigras!" Her voice tilts up at the end, in a sing-song, taunting chant. I don't answer her, and she folds her arms on top of the wall and rests her chin on them.

"My mama says that's the craziest thing your mama has ever done."

Still, I say nothing. Because Carol Ann's panties get blood on them, and I'm afraid she's going to die and fall over the wall into my room.

"My mama says your mama's done lots of crazy things, but this is the craziest."

Still nothing.

"You eat off their dishes, you'll get a disease," Carol Ann pronounces in a voice that has a hopeful note to it. "And die."

I say nothing. She's the one who's going to die. Not me.

166

"Didn't you know that?" she persists. "That's why my mama won't let the dishes Tulie eats out of even come into the house."

Nothing.

And finally the face disappears. I can hear Carol Ann unscrewing the top of her Fresh deodorant.

The next morning, we have only cold biscuits and milk for breakfast, because the dishes are already washed and packed away, and besides, Great-Aunt Kate doesn't want to leave a fire going in the cookstove. So after I eat my biscuit, I go and get my clothes together and strip the bed of sheets, and the last thing I do is take Mama's jar of cold cream and take off the lid and smell of it—of her—before I put it in my suitcase.

Aunt Nell and Aunt Tyler pack up their things, and they hug everyone and then drive away together, with Nikki and Honey bouncing around in the car and Aunt Tyler and Aunt Nell laughing and waving good-bye. It's always such a lonesome thing when they leave, because I'd give anything if I could go with them. Because I can see what they will be doing by late this afternoon, when they have gotten all the way back to Atlanta, and they'll be sitting at that little wrought-iron table on Aunt Nell's pretty patio, drinking iced tea and laughing together. And with Nikki and Honey laughing up at them with their needle-teeth laugh.

Great-Aunt Kate goes around the outside of the tent, removing the support sticks and letting down the big wooden covers over every window, and when she closes the one to mine and Mama's room, I'm suddenly in a twilight, one that has all the familiar smells shut in, too—the sweet, dusty smell of the straw mattress and the old wood of the walls and, incredibly, even the smell of sunshine on the tin roof overhead. Carol Ann is coming around to lock each big window shutter from the inside, forcing the iron hooks into the metal eyes screwed into the windowsills. She crawls across the bed to the window, deliberately kicking my suitcase, and as she struggles with the hook, she mutters through her clenched teeth, "You eat off nigra dishes and you're gonna die."

Then, hook secured, she crawls back across the bed, kicking my suitcase again. On purpose.

"Y'all come on!" I hear Great-Aunt Kate calling, and when I come out into the sawdust hallway, it's like being in a long tunnel, all dark and hot and only the blinding, dazzling light at the end, where Great-Aunt Kate's silhouette is against the glare, so that it looks just like she's standing in a very real and all-consuming fire.

"Come on, I say!" Great-Aunt Kate raises her voice.

Carol Ann rushes past me, hitting my suitcase. "Die!" she whispers as she passes.

"Come on, honey." I hear Aunt Valley's deep and resonant voice. And I come.

> Just as I am, without one plea
> But that Thy blood was shed for me.
> And that Thou biddst me
> Come to Thee,
> Oh, Lamb of God, I come.
> I come.

I can hear the familiar hymn from the tabernacle as clear as if it's like any other Camp Meeting morning and services are going on. But this isn't any other morning, and Camp Meeting's over, and things that are over and done with are the saddest things in the whole world. Even if they're things I don't like in the first place. Like Camp Meeting.

Aunt Valley comes walking down the dazzling shaft of light from the open front door to meet me, her big feet sending up little explosions of sunbeams from the sawdust, and when she reaches me, she is so big, it's just like an eclipse of the sun. A huge, black mountain between me and the fire-sunshine Great-Aunt Kate is standing in. Without a word, she takes my hand and leads me into the light.

"I declare!" Great-Aunt Kate mutters as we come out. She bangs the wooden door shut behind me, rams the hasp over the iron ring, and then clicks shut the lock. Without a word, she goes toward her car where all the quilts and pillows are piled in the back and Carol Ann is sitting in the front seat, fanning herself with a cardboard-Jesus fan she's stolen from the tabernacle.

Aunt Valley carries my suitcase and keeps holding my hand. We walk in silence toward the same pickup truck that dropped her off under the chinaberry tree that first morning she came. Her cousin from the Stone tent is sitting behind the wheel. Aunt Valley heaves my suitcase into the back of the truck and then she opens the door for me and I get into the middle of the front bench seat.

"Hurry!" Aunt Valley says to her cousin in a rough-sounding whisper, and she crowds in beside me so hard that her thigh is hot against my leg, and it's like I'm squashed between two big, strong, black bears. Aunt Valley's cousin races the engine and lets out on the clutch so that the truck jerks forward. I am wondering why we have to hurry. Wondering if there's

something for us to be afraid of in the empty tent behind us in the red, dusty cloud the truck raises from the road.

"It don't matter what she says." Aunt Valley speaks right out of a clear blue sky, so that it takes a minute or two before I realize she's talking to me. "You won't get no disease off'n my dishes."

"I know that," I say.

"Good. You just remember it."

I don't look at Aunt Valley, but I can tell she's looking over the top of my head at her cousin.

"HU-U-MPH!" is all her cousin says.

When we reach the paved road, we turn right—instead of left, which is the way to go back to Great-Aunt Kate's house. In a little bit, I turn and look through the dusty rear window, and I can see Great-Aunt Kate's car coming out of the cloud of red dust and turning left onto the paved road. And I'll bet you anything Great-Aunt Kate and Carol Ann are both covered in all that dust. And I hope they are.

"Don't you say a word," Aunt Valley warns me, just like she knows exactly what I'm thinking. And when I look at her, she's smiling.

"I am so glad that Jesus loves me!" the cousin starts in to singing, just as loud as she can, and she laughs in between the notes, a big, booming laugh. Aunt Valley starts laughing, too, and then so do I. And I don't even know what's so funny.

But I expect it has something or other to do with Great-Aunt Kate and Carol Ann being all covered with our dust.

> Jesus loves me,
> Jesus loves me.
> I am so glad
> That Jesus loves me,
> Jesus loves even me!

15

I almost laughed out loud before I caught myself and realized I wasn't in the truck with Aunt Valley and her cousin at all, but riding along in my own car with Maybelline and Mamie. And I was lucky that time because it looked as if neither one of them had noticed a thing.

Maybelline was saying to Mamie, "I'll bet you waited a long time to get away like this."

"Sure did," Mamie replied. "And the right thing for getting it done was a long time in coming. Still, though, I probably couldn't have gone anyway until the widder Jenkins' old mama passed on."

"Who's that?"

"Somebody lives a few miles away. Goes to our church. Wouldn't have been nobody to look out for my old daddy 'til then. But would you believe it? The widder's old mama passed on just recently—Praise Jesus!—and now the widder, why she'll be all over him, just like a fly on a melon. 'Cause it was the old mama what wouldn't let the widder even get started with him. Said HIS daddy was a low-down piece of trash, that's why. But I know for a fact that she didn't even know my daddy's daddy. I know it for a fact, because my mama told it to me. The old mama just wanted to keep her daughter around for waiting on her hand and foot. So now the mama's gone at last, my old daddy'll be just fine. Why, I'll bet right this very minute the widder's on her way over to my daddy's house with one of her sweet potato pies, and she'll be letting him know what she's got in mind. Scare him to death at first, but he'll get used to it."

Sitting there listening to Mamie, I'd had a terrible thought: Well, that was certainly convenient, wasn't it? Recently? Maybe it was just yesterday. And did she die a natural death, the old mama? Easy for me to imagine a pillow over the old woman's face when no one was looking, and Mamie's powerful arms holding it until . . . Because after all, Mamie had been gone that whole afternoon, and she'd seemed awfully nervous when she came back. And I'd heard her say "Lord, forgive me!"

"You didn't help that old woman along, did you?" I asked, without even really thinking.

Mamie grabbed the back of the front seat and used it to haul her massive weight forward out of the sunken springs. I jumped, involuntarily.

"No, I sure didn't!" she sputtered. "You thinking such a thing about me, and here I been sitting, trying to be polite and figure out how to tell youall I done lied to you," Mamie said. "Me thinking I cain't bear to take another breath without I tell you the truth. But it shore ain't got nothing to do with the widder's old mama!"

"You lied to us?" Maybelline asked. But I am thinking: Who do we have in the backseat? Someone who killed the old mama? Even if she denies it?

"Yup," Mamie said easily. "Lied like crazy 'bout how I was going to be youall's maid and take care of youall and do for you all the time and such as that." Then Mamie put her massive black hand on my shoulder, and once again, I jumped. "I done told you I didn't do nothin' to hurt the widder's old mama. 'Cause I wouldn't do nothin' like that. And yes, I was kind of upset when I come home. 'Cause I ain't never in my whole life stolen nothing, but I done it yesterday. Stole butter beans out of somebody else's garden so's I'd have something to fix you to eat!"

"I don't understand." Maybelline adjusted the rearview mirror so that the perspiring, sober, black face filled it. And I was thinking: Yes, Maybelline, watch her. Because if there's a razor blade going to come across our throats, better if we can see it coming!

171

But I was surprised to see that Maybelline didn't seem one bit upset. Just sitting there looking in the rearview mirror at Mamie's massive face and with a completely relaxed expression, as if Mamie were merely telling her about a recipe for pound cake.

"What I lied about is that I ain't gon' wait on youall. Ain't gon' be no maid at all. I just told you that so's you'd take me with you."

"I don't understand," Maybelline repeated. But I certainly did. False pretenses, that's what it was. Her pretending she'd go along with us, only now that she'd gotten away from that crazy man, she was going back on what she said she'd do.

"I can't believe I gave up my grandmama's Haviland china and left it sitting back there in the yard, just to make room for you," I said. "And now you're treating us this way. And not even going with us anyhow." Somehow and for some strange reason, I felt like laughing, but all the same, I was close to crying.

"Oh, I never said I wadn't going," Mamie protested. "I'll go anywhere to get away from that devil." She jerked her head toward the rear of the car and toward the long, gray ribbon of narrow highway that could lead right back to the leaning house and the swept yard, the old daddy sitting on the steps, and him in the trailer, waiting. "I sure am going with you! 'Cause I like your company . . . for the most part," she added, shooting a glance at me. "Just that I'm not gon' take care of youall." After a moment of silence, she added, "Though I certainly 'spect youall don't need no taking care of anyway. No, ma'am. Unh-unh. Gon' take care of me for a change." Her eyes took on a dreamy quality. "Gonna get me some store-bought teeth. Gonna get me a high school diploma. Gonna get me a job. Gonna be called MRS. Johnson." The litany came out with the measured rhythm of a long-rehearsed chant.

"Mrs. Johnson?" I asked, smiling—because after all, it was quite amusing.

But I certainly made her mad with that.

"That's right," she insisted. "Mrs. Johnson. No more Mamie-this and Mamie-that. 'Cause everything's gonna be different from now on. And I sure ain't about to be no maid and no old mammy to a old white lady don't know enough to wipe her own nose! And trash she done took up with."

Mamie released her grip on the back of the seat and sank back into the springs with a grunt. I turned my head and stared at her openly and incredulously. Why, I couldn't imagine any colored woman ever talking to me like that. And Maybelline was certainly surprised, too, because her mouth was hanging open and red streaks were coming up the side of her neck.

"Miss Amelia is NOT trash!" Maybelline said, evenly.

What? Me? Are you crazy? I was thinking.

"Ain't nobody trash, as a matter of fact!" Maybelline's voice was rising.

"Is too!" came Mamie's retort. "Is too trash. I knows trash when I see trash. And I ain't talking 'bout her, anyway. I'm talking 'bout you."

Maybelline hit the brakes so hard and so fast that she threw me over against the door. She pulled the car over to the side of the road in a cloud of dust, and Mamie grabbed the door handle, just as if she were ready to bolt from the car. Even as angry as I was, I could tell from her face exactly what she was thinking: Everybody knows these white-trash women carry razor blades! Every last one of them!

I was wondering what on earth was going to happen, too, but Maybelline certainly had brought all this on herself. The minute she got the car stopped, Maybelline turned in the seat to face Mamie, who was poised to flee.

"Nobody's trash to the Lord," she said in that patient voice that was so familiar to me. "Nobody's black and nobody's white. And I gotta work hard to remember that, because I got to love you, no matter what kind of hurtful things you say. The Lord said I got to, and that's what I'm gonna do. No matter what."

"Don't you go telling me about the Lord," Mamie retorted. "My old daddy used to be a preacher, and I done heard all of it from him. But no matter what He say, I sure don't love you. And I don't love her, neither." The massive head indicated me.

"Leave me out of this," I said. "I'm Episcopal, and I don't have to love anybody." So there!

"Oh, yes, ma'am, you sure do," Maybelline contradicted me.

"What you yes-ma'aming her for? If we're all the same? And if we're all loving each other so much?" Mamie's eyes were gleam-

173

ing with delight. I suspected that was because she was actually sparring openly with a white woman, and she was winning. Of that, she seemed to be sure—even though, as she put it, it was "trash" she was winning over.

"Why, because I respect her," Maybelline said.

"You gon' say 'Yes, ma'am' to me?" Aha!

"Why, I don't know you that well," Maybelline protested.

"You don't know me? And I'm the one what scraped you up off the road and took you into my own daddy's house and nursed you back to health? The one what took youall in when you wasn't fit to travel . . . I'm the one got beat up for doing it?" Mamie's voice was heavy with bleak accusations.

"You're right," Maybelline said, blushing. "I hadn't thought about it that way."

"Well, you better think about it," Mamie said accusingly. "And let's just settle for you calling me Missus Johnson." Mamie crossed her massive arms across her chest and nodded her head in a most satisfied manner. Unh! Unh! I want to hear this! she seemed to be saying.

"All right, Mrs. Johnson," Maybelline said easily. "We'll be glad to call you that, always."

We? That Maybelline! Making all kinds of promises, and how was it any of her business anyway, what I called Mamie? I'd call her anything I wanted to call her, that's what I'd do.

"Well, you two can work out anything that's agreeable to both of you, but I'll call her Mamie," I said.

"And I'll call you Amelia," Mamie shot back.

"What?" I sputtered.

"Thas what I'm gonna do," Mamie pronounced.

"And if I were to call you . . . Mrs. Johnson," I stumbled over the words—"then what would you call me?" I couldn't believe I was having this conversation!

"Melia," Mamie said.

Why, no one ever called me that but Aunt Valley. No one!

Aside from that, none of this surprised me one little bit, of course. It's only what you could expect, once someone like Maybelline got to messing around with the way things have always been done.

"I'm not trying to be ugly to youall," Mamie said in a somewhat softer tone. "Just I been waiting such a long, long time to be called that. Been dreaming about it. Been waiting seems like my whole life long to have a new start in a new place and have everything be different for me than what it's always been."

"Well, Miss Amelia," Maybelline said. "How about it?"

"There you go," Mamie complained. "Still calling her 'Miss'!"

"I have to do that, Mamie . . . Mrs. Johnson," Maybelline said. "Why?"

"Because I do," is all Maybelline would say.

Mamie started laughing. Crazy as a coot! I was thinking.

"Well, what's gotta be has gotta be," she said. "So you just take us right on down the road, Missy," she said to Maybelline. "Mrs. Johnson gon' show you what it's really like to be born again." Her booming laugh filled the car, just like someone beating on an enormous drum.

And the strange thing was, I felt like laughing, too. But I couldn't have said why, for Heaven's sake! Maybe just because it had been so many years since I'd heard anyone say "Melia," just like that.

Maybelline was sitting there with that same blank expression she always had, and then the laughing from the backseat made the corner of Maybelline's mouth turn up, so that she looked almost as if she were trying not to sneeze.

Oh, my Heavens! I thought. My grandmama's Haviland china!

After that, we drove for quite a ways in silence. Still, we all seemed to relax a little bit, and after a while, we heard Mamie . . . Mrs. Johnson . . . snoring peacefully in the backseat. She was sagged heavily in a deep sleep, hands clutching the big paper bag in her lap and face concealed by the black felt hat. As the car went around the curves, her big, square-looking head rolled gently from side to side.

"We'll go back and get your china, Miss Amelia," Maybelline said in a low voice. "I promise you that."

"I don't think that will ever happen," I replied, suddenly able to imagine the widow putting a piece of her sweet potato pie on one of the delicate plates and setting it in front of Mamie's old daddy, where he sat at the kitchen table with the fringed, wrinkled doily tucked into his shirt-front.

"No, ma'am," Maybelline said, as if to erase the image. "It will happen. I promise," she repeated.

"Well, I guess we've got more to worry about than just that," I said, making sure to keep my voice low.

"I know you're thinking maybe my granddaddy's old house isn't there anymore, but it is. I know it is," Maybelline said.

"I know so, too," I agreed.

"You do?" Maybelline was surprised.

"Yes," I said. "Because if it isn't, what on earth's to become of us?"

We drove for a long time without saying anything more. Just the two of us thinking the same thing: It has to be there!

And Mrs. Johnson snoring in the backseat.

Soon, Maybelline was inching the big car through the hot sunshine in a nondescript little town that was built along a one-block main street, and moving so slowly that it was almost like we were trying to sneak through town without anyone noticing us. Ahead, a truck stopped to let a long-haired dog amble across the pavement, and the dog, red tongue lolling, glanced at the truck and waved his plumed tail once, as if in thanks.

"I declare! That there's a moving pitcher house!" Mrs. Johnson had waked up, and she craned her neck to look at the marquee of a theater, sandwiched between a hardware store and a vacant building that had "Hadley's Market" in faded letters on the empty front window.

"I been to a moving pitcher once, all the way over to Waycross," she went on, her voice husky from sleep. "A good one, too, what's called *Carmen Jones*—nothing but coloreds in it. We was all sitting in the balcony—that was the colored section back then—and you could've heard a pin drop, we was all so surprised at there being a movie like that. Guess the white folks who come to it was surprised, too. Mostly high school children, you know, and what a ruckus they made over it. Throwed popcorn at the screen and slurped so loud on they arms whenever the people on the screen kissed each other. And hollered, 'Nigger lips!' But that's the only moving pitcher I ever seen."

176

Maybelline and I exchanged glances, and I couldn't help but flinch when Mrs. Johnson said that word, because the only time I ever heard it spoken was from trashy whites who spoke it with venom. And I would have bet anything that Mrs. Johnson was going to go on and on about that movie.

"What town is this?" Mrs. Johnson asked. So I was wrong about her going on about it.

"I'm not sure," Maybelline answered. "Why?"

"Seems to me it was someplace around here pretty near that my granddaddy come to from Savannah. Come up here and worked for a old, old lady named Mrs. Johnson." She stopped and laughed. "Same name as me, 'cause that's where he got his name. She was a old lady needed someone to help around her place. You know . . . keep the chicken house from falling in and chop a little stove wood, and such as that. And she couldn't afford no young man. Besides which, she was scared of young, strong ones anyway. So my granddaddy was just right. Turned out, it was real lucky for her. And for him, too. 'Cause she was a nice old lady and good to him. And right next to that old lady's place there was a big farm, and my granddaddy met my grandmama because her mama was a cook over there. And when they got married, my grandmama was only fourteen years old." Mrs. Johnson chuckled to herself.

"Fourteen?" I'd heard of such.

"Thas right." Mrs. Johnson was shaking her head and laughing.

"And him already in his sixties."

Goodness!

"And she got seb'n chirrens by him, and he lived to ninety-two years. The last child they had was my old daddy. And when he was born, his daddy was eighty-two years."

"Goodness!" I said. But ringing in my ears was another voice saying, "Seb'n. Yas'm. 'Bout seb'n."

"Thas right. 'Cause you know, men can cause babies right on up until the day they die."

"Cause babies? Oh . . . my goodness!"

"Didn't you know that about men?" Mrs. Johnson asked most sincerely.

"Well, I . . . guess I never . . . thought about it, actually," I admitted, drawing a somewhat startled glance from Maybelline.

"Didn't you never know no men?"

"Well, of course I did," I said, feeling my face flush and immediately regretting I'd even answered such a vulgar question. "I'll have you know that I was a married lady for thirty-seven years. Until my husband passed on. Seventeen years ago September seventeenth."

"Well, then you know men don't never get too old for that."

This time, I said nothing, but I could feel my cheeks getting hotter. What a conversation, for Heaven's sake!

"How about you?" Mrs. Johnson said to Maybelline, and I was glad she'd gotten off the topic of what I did or didn't know about men.

"How about me what?"

"Whatchu know 'bout men?"

Maybelline kept her eyes riveted on the highway ahead. "Only thing I know is most of 'em's no good . . . except for the Lord Jesus," she added hastily.

"Amen!" Mrs. Johnson yelled happily.

"There it is! The sign I was watching for," Maybelline said. "There it is. I was scared we'd missed our turnoff."

Waynesboro, 84 miles. And under that, Jerusalem, 94 miles.

"What's it say?" Mrs. Johnson asked.

"Right there," Maybelline pointed.

"I see it," Mrs. Johnson's voice was impatient. "But what's it say?"

"It says Jerusalem! Praise the Lord! He's leading us to Jerusalem!"

"The little bitty old sign say all that?"

"It says 'Je-ru-sa-lem.'" Maybelline pronounced each syllable and then she repeated it. "Je-ru-sa-lem. That's what the sign says. I said all the rest myself."

"Onct is enough," Mrs. Johnson said, with disdain in her voice. "I can catch it with just onct."

Maybelline took the right-hand fork of the road, and the tires bumped softly onto the macadam surface of a county-maintained road while the broad, smooth pavement of the highway curved away to the left. No centerline here. No smooth shoulders. Just pavement like a thick slab of biscuit dough all dried out and hard.

Uneven edges like it had melted in the August sun and run into the knee-high grass growing at the side of the road. Slowing down the car, as Maybelline had done, let a wave of hot air blast in through the open windows to shock our skin, and a new sound—of tires growling against the road surface and the singing of crickets in the tall grass. Ahead of us, the road stretched away endlessly, not a house in sight. Or a barn. Or another car. Only endless kudzu mounded up against wire fences and the land low and flat and with all the life baked out of it.

"I'll be glad to learn you how to read, do you really want that high school diploma." Maybelline's words were as unexpected as a sudden snowstorm.

Talk about the blind leading the blind! I thought.

"Learn me?" Mrs. Johnson asked suspiciously.

"Learn you to read," Maybelline said, and I couldn't stand it for another minute, that kind of talking.

"Teach you to read," I sputtered.

Maybelline smiled. "Yes'm. That's what I meant. I'll *teach* you to read. How about that, Mrs. Johnson?"

"I can read," Mrs. Johnson said, and then she went silent, staring out of the window, massive shoulders squared and jaw hard, looking for all the world like a frowning idol carved out of ebony.

"I'll teach her," I said without thinking.

"Nothing of the kind!" Mrs. Johnson's voice was deep and petulant. "Ain't come away from what-all I come away from to have nobody bossin' me around no more."

"There's a big difference between bossing and teaching," I said, though I was frankly wondering why I was bothering about it.

"No, there ain't," Mrs. Johnson contradicted. "I done been taught by white women all my life and I ain't never been taught without being bossed. How to iron the clothes. How to wash the dishes. How to make the bed."

"This isn't like that," I said, simply.

"I'm too old." Mrs. Johnson fired the words as if they were an undeniable volley.

"We'll see," I declared. "You said you wanted to finish high school."

179

"Said I wanted me some store-bought teeth, too, but I don't see you opening up your pocketbook to that. Besides which, you is sure one hardheaded old lady, you know that?"

I know that.

Ahead, the road stretched endlessly, and we fell silent. I was thinking that I had absolutely no idea of how to teach someone to read.

Maybelline hummed softly under her breath, so she was probably imagining herself standing in the doorway to the big old house, smelling its aromas and feeling the house wrap itself around her, shutting out all the night and the deep sadness.

Please, Lord—it has to be there!

Mrs. Johnson had fallen asleep again, and I'll bet she was dreaming that she stood in front of a mirror, her wearing a black hat with a blood-red ostrich feather rakishly angled across her broad forehead and smiling with big, strong white store-bought teeth. Big teeth, like a horse's teeth. And strong enough to bite a corncob right in half!

16

When Mrs. Johnson waked up, she said, "I think we should celebrate. Stop somewheres or other and get us some white bread and
bologna and a Nehi orange. Don't that sound good?"

"Celebrate?" I asked, and the mere thought of a tall, frosted
bottle of bright orange Nehi was completely appealing—a bottle
covered with crystal beads of chilled moisture. And it was well past
time for lunch anyway.

"That's right," Mrs. Johnson said. "Celebrate."

"Celebrate what?" I retorted, because once again, I'd been thinking of what I'd left sitting in the yard at her old daddy's place. All
Mamie's talk about what she did for us. Let her think about what
we did for her, too. The big box and the delicate, oyster-white china
plates inside it, resting securely against the crumpled paper.

"Why, celebrate starting a new life," said Mrs. Johnson, as if
she were completely astounded that such a thing had not occurred
to either Maybelline or me. "'Cause that's what we're doing, ain't
it? Every one of us starting a brand new life."

"I think that's a good idea," Maybelline said. "We have a lot to
celebrate and a lot to be thankful for, praise Jesus! How about it,
Miss Amelia?"

"Bread and bologna and Nehi orange drinks!" Mrs. Johnson
bellowed, without even waiting for me to answer. "And I got
money," she added. "So it's my treat. For all of us."

So much for reminding her about my china!

181

Maybelline was looking at Mrs. Johnson in the rearview mirror. "You needn't act so surprised I got money," Mrs. Johnson protested. "I done ironing enough for white folks, I could be a rich lady. Only I ain't. And you, missy," she added to Maybelline, "you better keep your eyes on the road. Ain't gon' find no Nehi's in the ditch."

"I guess we should of thought about doing that before we got off the main highway," Maybelline said. "Gonna be hard to find someplace around here." She was right, of course, and we looked at the flat, black highway shimmering in the August sun and stretching away in front of us through the endlessly flat countryside. And then, miraculously, a hand-lettered sign: "Randy's Gas and Food: Two Miles Ahead."

Mrs. Johnson was digging around in her big paper sack, mumbling to herself and lifting out two large, shiny eggplants and half a dozen yellow crookneck squash before finally finding an old black purse at the very bottom of the bag. She unzipped it ceremoniously and drew from it a single bill.

"See?" Mrs. Johnson waved a twenty-dollar bill in the air. "I got money for sandwiches and Nehi's. Let's us just find a place what has 'em."

"There's a place up ahead. I saw a sign for it," Maybelline announced. "And we better get some gas, too, while we're at it."

"I ain't said I'd pay for no gas!" Mrs. Johnson's protest was abrupt and final. "Don't see why I should," she went on. "Youall was coming this way anyhow. I'm just along for the ride."

Perhaps, I thought. But if you weren't "just along," all my grandmama's china would be where it's supposed to be—right there where you're sitting. Instead of left behind in the yard. Goodness knows, I'll never see it again, and I wonder what will happen to it? Will Old Daddy really remember to put it in the shed? And maybe one of these nights, some old tramp will come walking along and slip into that shed to sleep and find my grandmama's china and wonder how on earth someone came to leave something so lovely behind them.

"That's okay, Mrs. Johnson," Maybelline said. "I think it's right nice of you to treat us to lunch and to Nehi's. I got gas money."

Even though Maybelline parked under a sprawling pecan tree, the afternoon heat still surprised me. Because I guess I'd gotten so used to the wind blowing in through the open windows of the car.

"Randy's Gas and Food" was about what I'd expected. A small, concrete-block building out in the middle of nowhere, a gas pump, and a big wad of cotton wired onto the center of the screened door, for keeping out the flies.

When we went in, it took a while to become used to the dark, because the only light inside came from the screened door and one small, grime-covered window. Maybelline went straight to the linoleum-covered counter behind which a young man—Randy?—was sitting in a rocking chair.

"You have any bologna?" Maybelline asked him. He nodded, reached behind him to open the door of a small refrigerator, and took out a bologna roll that had never been cut.

"Got a good, fresh one here for you," he said. "How much you want?"

"Half a pound?" Maybelline asked, as if unsure of how much it would take to make three good sandwiches.

"Half-pound it is." He stood up and began slicing from the roll.

I found the loaves of white bread in a white-enameled, wire stand and put a loaf on the counter by Maybelline. Mrs. Johnson had been heading toward the cold drink machine, but a colorful display of fishing lures had caught her attention, and she was standing there in wonder, poking her finger on a cellophane package of rubber worms.

"Feels just like they is real," she exclaimed in a loud voice, and Randy—or whoever he was—stopped slicing the bologna.

"Ma'am, is your maid gonna buy something?" he asked me, indicating Mrs. Johnson.

"What?"

"I just don't like her putting her hands all over everything. So maybe you better just tell her to go on back out and wait in the car."

Reminded me once again about how hard the old ways die, but I wasn't about to argue with him.

Not so with Maybelline.

183

"She's with us," Maybelline started to protest, but even while she was speaking, we heard the screen door close and saw Mrs. Johnson retreating stiffly to the car.

Randy said not another word, but finished slicing the bologna, weighed it, and then wrapped it in white butcher's paper. Maybelline opened her purse.

"And three Nehi orange drinks and five dollars' worth of gas," she added.

Randy added up the purchases, gave Maybelline her change, and followed us out to the car and pumped the gas. And he never once looked at the car, though Mrs. Johnson's expressionless face was only inches away from him, on the other side of the glass.

When we drove away, Mrs. Johnson said, "Makes me mad as fire, that does. But I ain't so dumb as to cause trouble. Not after what I just got away from this very morning. Away from the very devil hisself!"

She took a deep breath, almost a sigh, and then, without warning, she yelled, "Low-down! Shiftless! Meaner'n a old snake! So mean he couldn't even stand hisself, and that's why he beat up on me. Couldn't beat hisself, thas why. And had to beat on somebody!"

We knew then that Mrs. Johnson was talking about "her man," and not about that Randy-person at all. Still, it seemed as if that's what had set her off.

Maybelline kept her eyes on the road, and I sat silently, the bag of groceries in my lap. Mrs. Johnson hesitated just long enough to issue forth two disgusted, disgruntled grunts—UNH! UNH!—and then she went right back at it.

"Tell you what I shoulda done," she said. "Shoulda took a razor blade to him a long time ago, thas what I shoulda done."

"No, Miz Johnson, you shouldn't have done anything of the sort." Maybelline looked into the rearview mirror and braced herself for Mrs. Johnson to grab the back of the seat and heave herself forward to protest. But Mrs. Johnson said not a word.

"You shouldn't have done anything of the sort," Maybelline repeated, as if she thought maybe Mrs. Johnson hadn't heard her. "Because the Bible says, 'Thou shalt not kill.'"

Somehow, the very sound of the words seemed to soothe Mrs. Johnson, and I relaxed my shoulders a bit. Goodness! She can sure get mad! I was thinking. Still, Mrs. Johnson said nothing, so finally, I glanced over my shoulder at her.

The broad, black face was frozen into a solidified grin, and it was an unnerving sight, so that I looked at Maybelline and then right back at Mrs. Johnson. The face exactly the same, the eyes unseeing and the lips still pulled back from discolored teeth and as rigid as molded asphalt.

What on earth! I thought desperately. Has she worked herself up into an absolute fit?

But then two sudden, fat tears racing over the round cheeks and down on either side to the waiting, terribly curled lips. The shuddering intake of breath.

"I'd a done anything for him." The whisper was just as terrible as the grimacing smile. "I'd a done anything," she repeated. "'Cause I loved him." The last words were almost a howl.

The black ribbon of highway I was looking at began to swim in uncertain undulations, and I was vaguely aware of Maybelline slowing down the car and pulling off to the side of the highway.

"Thank goodness!" I said. "I was wondering how far we had to go before we could stop and eat. Bologna's going to spoil in this heat. And the drinks won't be cold."

Perhaps it was a strange thing to say, right at that moment, but I figured someone had to get hold of the situation. Change the subject. Get Mrs. Johnson to thinking about something else.

A little way from where we'd pulled off the road was an abandoned shack with a tin roof and leaning porch and an overgrown path leading to it.

"Let's go get in the shade on that porch over there," Maybelline directed. "But watch out for wasp nests." She took the grocery bag from my lap and helped me out of the car while Mrs. Johnson clambered out of the backseat, wiping her nose on a not-so-fresh handkerchief she had fished out of the black purse.

I shielded my eyes from the sun and looked at the shack. "This your granddaddy's house?" I asked in alarm. Because just for a minute, I was all confused.

"Oh, no, ma'am," Maybelline said, looking at me in the strangest kind of way. And I knew she was thinking, Could be the heat. Could be losing her grandmama's dishes. "We still got a ways to go to get there, and his house is in better shape than this one. I hope!" she added.

Still, I stared and stared at the house. "This isn't Tulie's house, is it?" Because, you see, I had to make sure.

"No, ma'am, it sure isn't. I don't think. But who's Tulie?"

I didn't answer, so Maybelline followed me as I moved up the path, and Mrs. Johnson brought up the rear, still muttering under her breath, "Shoulda took a razor to him. Shoulda done it, thas what."

"I know whose house it is!" I shouted.

Aunt Valley's little gray house sits right up close, with only a drainage ditch filled with tall weeds between the house and the road. It's got a swept yard and white-painted rocks around a flower bed in front of the porch, and a rusted tin roof just like the one on the tabernacle. And an old woman who's sitting in a painted-green metal chair in the deep shade of the porch and staring at us as we drive up.

"Here we are," Aunt Valley says as the truck stops.

"You going to prayer meeting?" her cousin asks. "Do, I'll come by for you."

Aunt Valley thinks for a minute or so. "I 'spect so," she says, nodding. She heaves my suitcase out of the back of the truck, and I slide across the seat and step down into the bare yard.

"Let's have you meet Old Auntie sitting over there."

Aunt Valley takes my hand again, and we start across the yard.

"She the one like me?" I ask.

"Sure is," Aunt Valley says. "And I bet she's gonna be mighty happy finding out there's somebody else in the world like her."

Of course, I still don't know quite what she means by that, but if I set my mind to it, I can make it just pass. And that's what I decide I'm going to do. Make it pass on by me, no matter what. But when we get almost right up to the porch, and I look up at the old woman sitting there, I see that she's smiling to beat the band. Like maybe I'm somebody she already knows.

And I am rooted to the ground. Can't take my eyes off of her. Because this colored-woman Old Auntie of Aunt Valley's is white.

17

Aunt Valley's hand is on my shoulder, doing the same kind of hand-on-the-shoulder talking Mama's does when she's telling me to keep still, behave myself, and say not a single word. Right at that moment, I resolve myself to do all that for Aunt Valley. So I say nothing and try not to stare at the funny-looking, smiling old white woman sitting there—strangest chalky white. Like nothing I've ever seen before.

Aunt Valley's hand moves gently, urging me forward, and we come up the steps, closer and closer to where this woman is sitting, and me keeping my eyes down so I won't be staring at her. So that as we come up the steps, the first thing I see is her shoes—bright blue, felt ones like you get at the dime store, with little Indian-looking beads sewn to the toes. And above the shoes, two skinny, yellow-cotton-stockinged legs with the stockings rolled down just below bony little knees no bigger than my own. Hands spider-webbed with blue veins and so small, they look just like a doll's hands resting in her lap, and a cotton dress that flaps over and ties at the side. A little bulge just below her waist, just like Aunt Tyler's.

Like maybe this old, old woman's going to have a little baby, too.

Then a wrinkled neck the same chalky white and some big, bumpy looking freckles or something on it. And finally the face and more bumpy freckles, one very light but absolutely monstrous and covering the whole eyebrow and lid and even going down a bit onto her cheek. She looks just like a little brown and white dog I have seen around the neighborhood at home, one that has such a spot on his face exactly like this old woman.

But then I am thinking that maybe she's a colored woman, after all, because her yellow-white hair is wiry and all done up in tiny little braids all over her head. Still, she's certainly a white color, and her scalp, where

187

it shows between the rows of braids, is bright pink, like she's blushing about something or maybe getting ready to cry.

When Aunt Valley leads me to stand right in front of this strange little person, I finally look at her eyes. Blue. But not a warm and pretty blue like my mama's. Something different. A vacant, sleepy look somehow, or something milky-looking just a bit.

When I stop looking at all the various parts of her and see the face all put together, it's absolutely the kindest I've ever seen. Something glowing behind the giant freckle and the milky blue eyes. Like there's a good loud laugh just waiting to happen. Or a hug coming. Something like that.

"Auntie," Aunt Valley says to her. "This here's the little girl I been taking care of. She's gonna stay with us 'til her mama can come over from Savannah and get her."

Then to me she says, "This here's my Old Auntie I been wanting so bad for you to meet."

One of Old Auntie's blue-veined doll-hands flutters a little and lifts from her lap, rising until it is close to me but not touching me. Waiting suspended in the air for me to reach out.

"She can't see, honey," Aunt Valley whispers to me. "You have to take her hand yourself. She can't see you," Aunt Valley repeats.

But even before I hear her words, I see my own hand—as small as Old Auntie's but pink and very smooth—moving toward her with a mind of its own. I barely touch the tips of her fingers, and it's like some kind of a spark or something jumps from her to me.

And those milky eyes that aren't supposed to be able to see anything look inside of me and see the Great Mystery where it lies sleeping. She takes in a quick breath.

"Daddy doing okay?" Aunt Valley asks, but Old Auntie doesn't answer. I take my hand away.

"How do you do?" I say, remembering my manners. But those eyes—those strange milky eyes are still frozen and staring at the Great Mystery. After a few moments, the eyes go so deeply sad that they almost tilt down at the sides, the cloudy-look in a deeper mist.

"Melia."

Old Auntie whispers my name in a voice so faint and wavery, I can hardly understand it.

"Well, I'll be!" Aunt Valley speaks low. And that's when I remember she's even there. "I'll be!" she says again and sighs deeply and with what seems to be great contentment.

Then to me she says, "You stay here with Old Auntie a few minutes while I go see to Papa." Aunt Valley looks at me and at Old Auntie for

188

another moment, smiles and shakes her head, then picks up my suitcase and goes inside, letting the screen door slam behind her.

I sit down in a big rocking chair beside Old Auntie, who starts right in to saying something, but I can't understand what it is. And besides, I realize she's not talking to me, because she's not looking in my direction at all, but out toward the yard, to where the tall weeds grow in the ditch beside the road. She talks and talks, and I can't understand a single word in those wavering, wobbling tones, so I sit there, looking out across the yard just like she's doing and with the wordless sounds like baby birds cheeping.

So I finally stop thinking about how I can't understand what she's saying and start thinking about her being white—sort of. But not white like white people, so I am wondering if I should say "yes" to her or "yes, ma'am"? That is, if she ever says anything I can understand well enough so that I can answer her. And I wonder, too, what happened to her that made her not be able to see anything.

For the longest kind of time, I sit like that. Until Aunt Valley comes back out on the porch, and even then, Old Auntie keeps on talking, just like she's been doing all along.

"What's she saying?" I whisper to Aunt Valley.

"Dunno," came the matter-of-fact answer. "Don't nobody know. First thing I ever heard her say what I could understand is what she said just now."

"What?"

"Your name."

"Why?"

The whole time Aunt Valley and I are talking, Old Auntie just keeps on with her sounds.

"Why she say your name? Dunno. Don't even know how she knows what it is, 'cause I sure never told her. And you didn't, neither."

"No, I mean why can't she talk right? And . . ." I use my finger to motion Aunt Valley even closer to me so I can whisper to her—because not saying anything to hurt someone's feelings has nothing to do with her being black or white, and I don't know how I know that, but I do—"Why's she . . . white . . . sort of?"

"She's a albino. That's somebody what's not any color at all. Born that way and that's one of the reasons she's so special."

"If she's so special, why can't she talk right?" I ask again.

"Oh, she's talking right. It's us can't hear it right."

"But why?"

Aunt Valley cuts her eyes at me. "Because she's talking in tongues. And what you're hearing right now is what it really sounds like."

189

I can hear Julia's voice just as clear as a bell saying, "When the Holy Ghost gets inside folks, and they start talking the way angels in Heaven talk, can't nobody on the face of the earth understand what they're saying."

"Besides which," Aunt Valley goes on, "she was born with a caul, you know." She nods her head up and down.

"A what?"

"A caul," she repeats. "You never heard tell of that?"

I shake my head.

Aunt Valley looks at me for a bit, as if she's trying to decide exactly what to say. Finally, she says, "It's when a baby gets born with a sort of veil over its little face. Means it's special."

Well, that doesn't make a bit of sense in this world to me, and so I think of Aunt Tyler and her little baby that's going to be born, and the baby I imagine is a real pretty little girl baby. But with a veil over its face. A lavender veil, like the one Mama wore in her hair when she was the matron of honor at Aunt Tyler's wedding that time.

"Don't worry about it none," Aunt Valley interrupts what I'm thinking.

"And what's that big mark, that freckle on her face?" I ask.

Aunt Valley looks at me the same way she looked when she was trying to piece together that story about the lost lamb. Finally, all she says is, "She got hurt."

"How?"

"In a fire. A long, long time ago."

"Oh."

Doodlebug!

"So how did Old Auntie know my name?" I ask, glad to change the subject, and besides, I really do wonder about that.

"Dunno, honey. Just plain dunno. Come on," she says. "Let's go inside and I'll show you where you're gonna sleep."

So we leave Old Auntie sitting on the porch talking in tongues and go inside the house.

After being out on the porch where there's so much light, I can hardly see inside the dark, little house. A small living room that has a wood stove in it and a couch with a crocheted granny-square afghan across its back, and a big wooden rocking chair and a rickety, round table with a lamp on it. And the room is very hot, even this early in the day.

I follow Aunt Valley through to a kitchen, and she opens a door into another room, a pantry or storeroom, but big enough that there's a single-bed cot in it. My suitcase sitting at the foot of the cot, and a tiny window way up high, and along the walls, lots of narrow shelves with all sorts of jars of pickles and peaches and green beans in them, and some cans of

190

pork and beans and a sack of rice and one of grits. And the whole little room smelling good, like warm milk or corn or something like that.

Aunt Valley pats the cot. "This is where you sleep," she says.

"Where do you sleep?" I ask, suddenly able to imagine this little room in the dark and maybe with something making scratching sounds in the night against the side of the house.

"I'll be near," she says and leads me through the kitchen and onto a back porch where there are two doors, one that Aunt Valley opens to show me another room, a bigger room with two double beds in it. "I'll be right here," she says as I peek in. "You won't even be able to turn over at night without me hearing you."

"What's the other door?" I ask, and she opens it to a tiny little room just big enough for the single bed that's in it. And a little three-drawered dresser with a big black Bible on it. And nothing else. The barest room I have ever seen. Not a picture on the wall, not a mirror, nothing. Just the bed with a faded blue quilt on it and the dresser and the Bible.

"This is Old Auntie's room," Aunt Valley says. "Used to be a Preacher's Room long, long ago."

"What's it called a Preacher's Room for?" I ask.

"'Cause a long time ago, preachers was what they called circuit riders and that means . . ." she anticipates my next question . . ."they had to travel around from one church to another. So they had to have a place to spend the night before movin' on."

"Is Old Auntie a preacher?" I ask. I mean, it makes sense, doesn't it? If this is a Preacher's Room and it's hers?

"Mebbe," Aunt Valley says. "'Cept nobody can understand her if preaching's what she's doing."

"And why can't she see anything?"

"Same thing as that scar. A fire."

"Tell me about it," I say, and my heart bumps one time hard against my ribs.

"You sure?" Aunt Valley asks. "Don't want you having no bad dreams, now."

I nod because the words won't come out.

Aunt Valley heaves a deep sigh, a sound like wind whipping the trees just before black clouds open up and dump big, warm raindrops onto the flat-baked earth.

"It was a fire," she starts out and stops. Another sigh, and I look right at her because I mean for her to tell me, no matter how long I have to wait for it.

191

"The house caught on fire one night and she got me out, me just a little thing. She took me outside and then she went back in and got my mama and brought her out, too, and by then the whole place was blazing and roof timbers beginning to fall. My mama picked me up and hugged me and cried, and we all stood there with that terrible heat burning our faces. Then all of a sudden, Old Auntie—and of course, she was just a girl herself back then, only twelve or thirteen years old—started screaming, 'My dress! My dress!' And before Mama could stop her, she ran back into that burning house."

Aunt Valley stops talking, but the memory in her is so strong, I can almost imagine the flames reflected in her eyes.

"Go on," I croak. "Why'd she go back in there just for a stupid old dress?"

The flames I see in Aunt Valley's eyes suddenly flare up even higher. "'Cause it was her baptizing dress!" she says. "It sure wasn't no stupid dress at all."

I say nothing. Her chastisement is complete.

When she speaks again, her voice is soft once more. "It was her white baptizing dress she'd been sewing on for the longest kind of time."

I am ready to ask more, but while we're standing there, a very old man starts coming up the back steps very slowly, just as if he can barely make it, and when he pulls open the screen door, it hits him right in the chest and knocks him halfway down the steps again. So that he clutches the door handle with one hand, while the other hand is cupping two big tomatoes, and he's leaning backwards at an alarming angle. Aunt Valley reaches out, grabs him right in the middle of his green plaid shirt, and hauls him to the porch.

"This here is my papa," she says to me. "Who ought to be more careful coming up those steps!" The old man smiles a completely toothless smile and thrusts the tomatoes at me.

"Good tomatoes," he says in a dry voice that sounds like dead leaves rustling against each other.

"Papa's a farmer." Aunt Valley explains, nodding her head and winking at me.

"They're beautiful tomatoes," I say, taking them from him. "Thank you."

Aunt Valley smiles at me and nods in satisfaction, and after her papa toddles to the living room and sits down in the wooden rocking chair, we go into the kitchen.

"Let's us make some tomato sandwiches. Bet you're hungry, only having a cold biscuit for your breakfast."

So I help her make the sandwiches and iced tea, only there's no ice to go in it, and when it's ready, Aunt Valley helps Old Auntie into the kitchen and gets her into the chair. And we all have a nice late breakfast together, eating mostly in silence, except for when Aunt Valley says to her papa, "Y'all okay doing for each other while I was gone?"

But her papa doesn't answer. Because he's stuffed a whole tomato sandwich into his mouth at one time, and he's been chewing on it for the longest kind of time and with a little dribble of mayonnaise on his chin. He doesn't have any teeth, so when he chews, it seems like the whole bottom half of his face almost disappears—goes up and down and in and out in the strangest kind of way. Then I remember it's not polite to stare, so I look at Old Auntie, and she's not eating a bite, just looking in my direction with that strange smile. Aunt Valley looks at both of us and nods her head.

"I thought you two would probably hit it off," she says in a very satisfied way. But then I remember not to care what she means by that, so I look down at my tomato sandwich and at the plate it is resting on and think of what Carol Ann said about me getting a disease and dying.

"Good tomatoes!" old Papa shouts, having somehow accomplished the chewing and swallowing of the whole sandwich.

"That's right, Papa," Aunt Valley says. "You grow the best tomatoes there's ever been." Then again, she said, "Y'all get along all right while I was gone?"

He looks at her, puzzled.

"Where you going?" he asks in a loud voice, as if Aunt Valley is hard of hearing and with his neck getting long and alarmed-looking.

"I'm not going anywhere, Papa," she assures him.

"You not?" He relaxes a little.

"I'm not, and that's a fact."

"Oh, that's good." The neck goes back down into the collar of the green plaid shirt, and he is content.

I guess Aunt Valley finally decides to give up trying to find out how they got along while she was gone, so she looks at Old Auntie, who is still looking toward me, her sandwich untouched on her plate. Aunt Valley reaches over and pats Old Auntie's arm, and stupidly, I am seeing the black hand on the chalky white arm.

"Try and eat a little something," Aunt Valley urges, but Old Auntie just sits and smiles.

After Old Auntie is once more settled in her green chair on the porch and Aunt Valley's papa is sitting out on the back steps, watching to make

193

sure that no crows get into his garden, Aunt Valley and I are alone. She is washing up the plates and I am still sitting at the table.

"Tell me everything about the fire," I say, waiting for that single alarmed bump of my heart. But it doesn't happen.

"Why you so interested in that?" Aunt Valley asks.

"I don't know," I answer most truthfully.

"Well, the rest of it is this—and then I don't want you asking no more about it, you hear?"

"Yes'm."

"The rest of it is this: She went back in that house to try and save her dress, her baptizing dress. And one of them burning timbers fell on her. And my mama put me down on the ground and went in after Old Auntie. I remember seeing Mama dragging her out by the feet and then putting out the flames in her hair with her hands. And about that time, my papa come running across the yard to help us."

She stops talking, and I wait a long time for her to start back up, but she doesn't.

"That's it?" I ask, because I want to know it all.

"That's it," Aunt Valley says. "Except Old Auntie was never the same after that. She never did talk again so anybody could understand her. And of course, she was blind."

"She didn't get the dress," I say. It isn't a question.

"She didn't get the dress," Aunt Valley repeats after me.

"What'd you say Old Auntie is again? Why she's white, I mean," I ask, changing the subject, because I feel my throat trying to go tight on me and my feet beginning to twitch.

"Bino . . . albino," she corrects, but in a distracted way, because I can tell she is still thinking about the fire.

"Am I a albino?" I ask, looking down at my smooth, pink arms against the red-checkered oilcloth.

"No, you're not." Aunt Valley laughs a little and looks directly at me.

"But I'm white," I argue, wishing that I were special, like Old Auntie and that I talked in tongues all the time so nobody could understand a thing I was saying. And that I could have been born wearing a beautiful lavender veil. But I wouldn't want to be blind.

"And besides," I say to Aunt Valley. "You're the one said she was like me." Because just that fast, I forgot not to wonder.

"That's what I said. But it don't have a thing to do with color."

"Then what's it have to do with?" I ask, because no matter how hard I try, I always have to know things I don't know already. "Us talking in tongues?"

Aunt Valley wipes the last dish and puts it away. Then she spreads the dishcloth out to dry and comes and sits down at the table with me.

"You wasn't talking in tongues," she says.

"Oh, yes, I was!" I insist, wanting with all my heart to believe it.

"Oh, no, you wasn't," she says. "You can fool your Great-Aunt Kate mebbe, but you can't fool me."

"Why not?"

"Never mind about that. Just can't, that's all. And besides, that's not what I meant 'bout you and Old Auntie."

"Then what?"

She looks at me for a long time, and we sit in silence, with only the far-away sound of Old Auntie talking and talking on the front porch.

"I don't exactly know what to call it," Aunt Valley finally says. So she's trying to talk about the Great Mystery again. But I'll never tell her what it's called. Never.

"Some kind of real deep feelings about things. Other folks' pain, 'specially. Mebbe as simple as the two of you being so compassionate. But that must be awful hard on somebody what's just a child."

Real deep feelings about things . . . that's what she said, and I am thinking: what things? But I don't ask, because once again, I've decided I really don't want to know.

"You know exactly what I mean, don't you?" Aunt Valley is still looking at me hard.

"How come Old Auntie's a albino?" I ask.

"Dunno," Aunt Valley confesses, and I am thinking that it's really pretty easy to get her off track. "It's just how she come into this world. And my mama said her being a albino meant other things about her is special, too."

"Like talking in tongues?"

"Mebbe."

"But what good is it to talk if nobody can understand what she's saying?"

"Dunno," came the answer.

"Maybe it's like the gnats," I say. "Like what you're trying to figure out about them?"

Aunt Valley laughs. "Mebbe so."

"Well, when you get the gnats figured out, maybe you can start figuring on Old Auntie. And then tell me."

"I don't know about that," Aunt Valley says, drawing her eyebrows together and shaking her head. "Don't pay to try and figure out too much."

"Why not?"

"'Cause of something we got to have—faith."

195

I've never thought of that before. Not just like that anyhow. But it would certainly explain why Aunt Valley couldn't get it figured out about why God made gnats. And maybe that's the way it is about the Great Mystery, too.

"Old Auntie going to have a little baby?" I ask.

"What on earth!" Aunt Valley laughs. "How come you to ask such a thing?"

"'Cause she's got a round tummy," I say. "Like my Aunt Tyler, because she's going to have a little baby."

"No, honey. That's not no baby, sure enough."

"What is it then?"

"Sickness. It's sickness makes her fat."

"Oh."

"So don't you go saying nothing to her about no baby, you hear?"

"I hear."

"You not going to say nothing?"

"I'm not," I say. But I wonder what kind of sickness it is, would make it look like there was going to be a baby.

"What's inside her?" I hear myself asking.

"It's a growth," Aunt Valley says. "Something growing . . . down there." She raises her eyebrows and looks at me hard, to see if I know what she means by "down there."

And, of course, I don't. Not exactly. But I think at once of the funny-looking, pink, knit-cotton bloomers my grandmama wore, and I can remember her whispering to my mama, "Only kind I can wear that don't hurt me. Because I never did heal up right, you know."

And the terrible brown-blood smear on Carol Ann's panties. "Down there."

So something's growing in Old Auntie's panties. That much I can figure out.

"Oh," I say, and Aunt Valley closes her eyes and nods her head up and down slowly.

"Okay, then." Her massive hand reaches over and covers my own. And it happens right then and there that I feel completely joined with her. Because even without my knowing quite what has happened, something has changed between us. Because Aunt Valley and I have talked with each other about "women-things," and that's what has made everything different.

18

"This kind of thing happen to her before?"

Whose voice?

"Aunt Valley?" I croak.

"I ain't your aunt anything!" Mrs. Johnson growled.

"Praise be!" Maybelline yelled. "She's back!"

Maybelline's face filled my whole field of vision.

"You okay now? You feel better?" she asked anxiously.

"I'm all right," I managed to say. Then I looked around at the porch of a little shack, with weeds growing right up to it and the dazzling-hot sun all around on the outside.

"You've had a spell," Maybelline said. "Maybe we better find a doctor to take a look at you."

"Nonsense!" I shouted. "Can't I even sit somewhere and *think* without you making such a fuss about it?"

"Give her some of this," Mrs. Johnson said, holding out a Nehi orange drink, and Maybelline tried to take it and hold it for me, but I took it from Mrs. Johnson myself and drank and drank. It was the best thing I ever tasted.

"Don't drink it so fast. Make yourself sick in this heat," I heard Mrs. Johnson say.

"Better take little sips," Maybelline added.

"This kind of thing happen to her before?" Mrs. Johnson asked again.

"Yes," Maybelline added.

"Stop talking about me as if I'm not here," I snapped. "I don't know why you're so worried. Sometimes I get to thinking and remembering things, that's all. And I wish you'd just leave me alone."

I didn't say anything else, but I wanted to. I wanted to tell them that if they would just stop bothering me so much, I could get all this taken care of. Go right back into the old memories and stay with them until it was all fixed the way it was supposed to be. But I couldn't have told them in a million years what it is that needs to be done. Just a way to curl up with something and rest for a good, long time. And let it get all warm and relaxed with me. So that I don't have to fight so hard ever again. Or something like that.

"It's just that you scared me half to death, Miss Amelia," Maybelline said.

"I wish you'd just leave me be!" I retorted. "I need time to think about things. Now where are those good tomato sandwiches? I'm right hungry."

Because I'd been feeling hungry ever since I remembered Aunt Valley's papa chewing on that tomato sandwich.

"Bologna sandwiches, you mean," Maybelline said, and she got busy putting the sandwiches together, and my! they were certainly good. Not as good as sandwiches made with homegrown tomatoes, but good anyway. There always had been something I liked about soft, white bread and fresh-sliced tomatoes.

Afterward, I felt very refreshed and happy, despite the fact that Maybelline and Mrs. Johnson glanced at me from time to time, as if they were waiting for me to have a fit at any moment and wallow around on the porch, frothing at the mouth. Such as that.

But in spite of everything, there was something peaceful about the little porch and the abandoned house, good to sit there and look out over the weeds and over to where the car was parked at the side of the road.

"Youall want any more of this bologna?" Mrs. Johnson asked, and when Maybelline and I shook our heads, she ate the rest of it almost in one big mouthful.

"Old tooths holding out just fine this day!" she announced, as if she had accomplished something wonderful just by chewing.

"You sure you're feeling okay now?" Maybelline asked once more before we went back to the car.

Mrs. Johnson didn't even give me a chance to answer, but she just spoke right up, "Sure, she's all right now," she pronounced. "See how pink her cheeks are? She's fine! Just upset about them old dishes she's so fond of, is all."

And I thought, How I wish that were it. Something that simple.

When we piled back into the hot car, I could see dark clouds coming up in the west.

"Storm coming," I said.

And so we started driving to Jerusalem and whatever was waiting there for us.

Sure enough, the dark clouds came up fast, throwing black veil-shadows over the countryside. A storm coming like always on late summer afternoons. Because when the land had soaked up all the heat, it started breathing back that blistering heat that rose up and up until the undersides of the white clouds were singed, dark with the heaviness of moisture. After a few mutters of thunder, the inevitable downpour would come.

"It's catching us," Maybelline said, looking in the rearview mirror. Mrs. Johnson and I both turned to look through the back window, and sure enough—coming along the gray road right behind us was a silvery curtain of hard rain. Getting closer every instant.

We rolled up the windows and Maybelline turned on the windshield wipers just as the first, heavy plops of fat, warm raindrops sounded on the roof of the car, and then in an instant, we were enveloped in the drenching rain. The steady sweeping thump of the wipers and the inside of the car just like an oven.

Maybelline peered through the rapid sweepings of the windshield wipers, her knuckles white where she gripped the steering wheel. And then, just as suddenly as it had come, the rain was gone, like dancing, twirling water from a lawn sprinkler stopping in mid-leap and falling to earth in startled silver droplets. Maybelline's shoulders relaxed, and we rolled the windows back down, to the

199

thick plumes of steam coming up from the hot pavement beneath our wheels.

The miles seemed to go by ever so slowly and I'd begun to wonder if we'd ever get where we were going. And now, dark was beginning to come on, too. But in spite of that, there was still a peacefulness in me. Something I hadn't felt in a long, long time. Not since before Henry's last illness. Knowing I could close my eyes for a few minutes and go right back in my memory and sit down at the table in Aunt Valley's kitchen and be with her a while longer. And talk to her and listen to her and maybe even figure everything out, once and for all.

But I didn't get the chance to do that, because Mrs. Johnson kept up a steady stream of chatter for hours. Talking and talking and talking until I thought I'd just die. Even Maybelline had begun to look a little droopy from it. On and on and on, all about her mama and her brothers and sisters, how there were thirteen of them—goodness!—all living in a one-room house and how her mama worked as a maid and how Mrs. Johnson was the oldest girl, and so she had to take care of all her little brothers and sisters while her mama worked.

"Where was your daddy?" I couldn't help but ask. Because I was remembering about Great-Aunt Kate saying, "Fathers bothering their own daughters. That kind of thing. There's hungry children out there, sure enough," all those long years ago.

"Daddy took awhile," Mrs. Johnson said, as if that explained everything.

Then she went on, telling us about each and every one of her sisters and brothers, all eleven of them. And after that, about some old lady she used to work for and how mean and impossible she was, and after that, starting in on how she got mixed up with "the devil"—her "man." And I certainly didn't want to hear anymore at all, especially that.

"I wish we could have gotten there before dark," I said, jumping right in when Mrs. Johnson had to pause to take a breath. That was the only way I was going to be able to say a thing, and I was beginning to feel worried. Dark when dawn is coming is one thing, but dark at the beginning of night is something else. Something that makes me want walls around me. To keep out the beasts.

"Maybe we should try to find a hotel or something, just for tonight," I offered. That would certainly be an improvement over trying to find our way around an abandoned house in the dark.

"Don't think there'll be a hotel any closer than all the way to Augusta," Maybelline said. "We'll be all right," she added. "Just you wait and see."

So I sat quietly for a few minutes, watching the road ahead of us and noticing how rapidly darkness was coming.

"Suppose we get there in the dark and find out there's tramps or hoboes living in the house?" I asked and felt goose bumps come up on my arms.

"I'll git 'em out, if there is," Mrs. Johnson said. "Just the 'scuse I needs to bust some men's heads wide open."

"No one's there. I'm sure of it," Maybelline assured Mrs. Johnson, yet at the same time, I believe Maybelline and I both had some kind of a strange thrill at the thought of Mrs. Johnson's massive hands attaching themselves irrevocably to the scrawny neck of some malicious-looking derelict. And Mrs. Johnson must have been envisioning something quite similar, for she emitted a series of soft grunts and then muttered under her breath, "Bust 'em wide open!"

It's almost exactly word for word what Lizzie, Aunt Valley's cousin, said the afternoon of the same day we first came to Aunt Valley's house.

Because while Aunt Valley and I are still sitting at the kitchen table together, we hear Lizzie's truck drive up and then her yelling and hollering all the way around the side of the house, until she reaches the back door. "Somebody stop me 'fore I go over there and bust his head wide open!"

"What on earth?" Aunt Valley goes to the screened door and gets to it just as Lizzie comes storming up the porch steps and yanks the door open so hard she almost pulls it right off its hinges.

"What on earth?" Aunt Valley repeats.

"What he did!" Lizzie yells. "My younguns just told me about it." Aunt Valley motions her head toward the kitchen where I am sitting, and so Lizzie says not another word, but sets her jaw hard and clamps her lips

201

together while she and Aunt Valley go down the steps and out into the backyard.

I tiptoe across the kitchen and stand real still, near the door to the back porch, listening. Lizzie is mad as fire, saying something about "up to no good," and then putting her hands on her hips and looking out across Old Papa's garden while Aunt Valley says something too low for me to hear. And the whole time, Old Papa sitting on the steps, smiling vacantly and looking all day-dreamy, just as if nothing is happening.

"Already said he hated to stand by and do nothing see her not get to go to Heaven," I hear Lizzie say, and Aunt Valley turns to Old Papa.

"Why didn't you tell me, Papa?" she demands.

"Tell you?"

"Tell me the new preacher'd been here while I was gone."

"Preacher coming?" Old Papa says. "Good! Give him some tomatoes."

Aunt Valley shakes her head and shrugs her shoulders. "Not gon' get nothing out of him," she says.

"Preacher must think we're lying about her," Lizzie snorts. "Thas why he waited 'til we was gone to come 'round. Come to see for himself."

"Well, I guess it's time we tried to do something about it, once again," Aunt Valley sighs.

But Lizzie was getting worked up to mad all over again. "Him taking advantage like that! Like we was bad peoples! Oughta go bust his head wide open!"

"Said he thought it might be the devil keeping her from it," Aunt Valley says. "But he just don't understand. Been mighty hard on all of us."

"You still wanta go to prayer meeting tonight?" Lizzie asks with a glint in her eye.

"Yes, I believe we better," Aunt Valley says. "Can't have him taking us for heathens and thinking we're telling lies about her."

"Okay. Let's do it, then."

Lizzie walks away across the yard, but I can tell by how she's walking that she's still mad about something. But not as mad as before.

I run quietly back and sit down at the table.

"What's wrong?" I ask Aunt Valley when she comes back.

"New preacher," she says, as if that explains everything.

"Y'all help me watch for a sign," Maybelline broke in. "Should be around here somewheres." And sure enough, our headlights reflected on a small sign far ahead, and Maybelline eased off on the accelerator. Around us, the deep twilight had become complete darkness that threatened to envelop the car as it lost speed.

"That sign up there say Gough?" Maybelline leaned close to the windshield and peered intently. On either side of the car, the high weeds that had been passing in a blur for so long became distinct blades and stalks, and the crickets chirping nearby went silent.

"Cough?" Mrs. Johnson asked, leaning forward a bit.

"No. Gough," Maybelline said, still peering ahead. "It's a town."

"Thas sure a funny name," Mrs. Johnson said suspiciously. "You sure 'bout it?"

A few miles more and Maybelline slowed down where there was a road to the left. More a break in the steady march of weeds than anything else.

"This is it!" Maybelline said, but I could tell that she was trying to sound more confident than she really was. Then she took a deep breath and turned onto the dirt road. "At least I think this is it," she muttered. Then "Dear Lord, please lead us. Please lead us to my granddaddy's house. I got others depending on me here."

That unnerved me a bit, and I glanced around at Mrs. Johnson, whose wide, round eyes were distinctly visible in the darkness.

Maybelline's face almost right up against the windshield now, her eyes peering intently into the cone of illumination from the headlights. Ahead, only dark bushes on either side of the road, and I was beginning to feel more and more alarmed, especially when I noticed that the road hadn't even been scraped—a sure sign that it probably wasn't used anymore.

Sure enough, as we crept along, the road got bumpier and with deep ruts coming in from the edges, closer and closer to the wheels. So that it finally narrowed into nothing more than a path, with grass and bushes crowding in and reaching out and touching the big black car like strange fingers.

"This isn't it," Maybelline moaned.

"Nothing but a old path," Mrs. Johnson added, hoisting herself forward to lean over the front seat and squint nearsightedly through the windshield. And indeed, she was right. Nothing but a path, one that now tilted sharply downhill, so that when Maybelline finally put on the brakes, the tires slid a little before the car stopped.

"Sand," I said. "Must be a creek down below, for it to be sand. We better back out of here while we can."

Maybelline glanced at me uneasily and eased the gearshift into reverse. But when she stepped down on the accelerator, the back wheels zizzed fruitlessly in the sand, and to our alarm, we felt the back of the car sink a few inches.

"Stop!" I shouted. "You'll dig us a hole we'll never get out of!"

"Needs to find us a old board or something like that to put under the wheels," Mrs. Johnson suggested, but not one of us made a move to open the doors, get out, and start looking for such a thing. Because the dark was wrapped around us like a vise, pressing at the windows like the hide of a big black bear that was scratching himself against the car. Oppressive and heavy and so dangerous that I could almost smell the rank indifference of it.

"What're we going to do?" Maybelline asked no one in particular.

"Gonna stay put, that's what," Mrs. Johnson said. "Leastwise 'til morning." And she spoke with a finality in her voice that suggested complete authority over the situation. So much authority, as a matter of fact, that Maybelline switched off the ignition and turned off the headlights, almost without thinking.

Simultaneously, the living hum of the engine ceased, and the dark and the terrible silence bore down upon us so hard and so fast that we sat absolutely silent and motionless—the way deer crossing a highway at night freeze in blinding headlights. Only we were the opposite—creatures of light stunned by the blinding dark.

"Oh, good Heavens!" I breathed. "We're stuck in the woods in the dark!"

But even then, I felt a strangely exhilarating surge of excitement. So that I, who thought I would have been yearning for the high, cool mahogany bed in my own safe and quiet room, instead was exhilarated by the long-forgotten thrill of challenge. The nape of my neck prickled most pleasantly in wonderful and dreadful fear of the dark wrapped around us.

All those eyes shining out of the grass beside the highway when Mama and I went to Great-Aunt Kate's. And now, I'm the eyes.

"Lock the doors," Mrs. Johnson commanded, and we did. Then absolute silence for long minutes and crickets resuming their chirping and then the deeper, pulsating call of tree frogs.

"Well, we're stuck, sure 'nough," Mrs. Johnson said, as if she were telling us something we didn't already know.

"Nothing to do but stay put. Until daylight, at least," Maybelline echoed what Mrs. Johnson had said, as if she had just then thought of it herself. "Then we can find some tree branches or boards or something to put under the tires and give them some purchase."

"Certainly don't want to go tromping around the woods in the dark," I added, just in case Mrs. Johnson was taking it into her head to commandeer us into doing something like that. "Could be snakes, especially this time of year."

"Cain't we have the lights on?" Mrs. Johnson asked.

"Run down the battery," Maybelline said. "We're just stuck here 'til morning. Nothing I know of we can do about it. I sure am sorry," she added.

I sat staring straight ahead, the flush of excitement wearing off a little and the sounds of the deep woods all around us growing louder and louder. My head ached, and for no reason at all, my eyes teared up.

"Sounds . . ." My voice was husky, and I cleared my throat and tried again. "Sounds just like it did out at Mount Horeb Camp Meeting at night when I was a child. Crickets and tree frogs singing, and something—-coon or possum—rustling around in the weeds. Like I used to hear when I was safe in bed with my mama beside me, patting my back so I could get to sleep."

Maybelline must have been trying to imagine me as a child, but it was hard for her to do. "What was she like, your mama?" she asked, maybe looking for an image she could hold onto and also maybe grateful for something to talk about besides the mistake she'd made about the road.

"Very beautiful," I answered. "Very fine and fragile."

"My mama," Mrs. Johnson interjected, "was a great big woman. Chopped firewood just like a man. Coulda' chopped down all the woods in the whole state of Georgia, did she ever take a mind to."

More silence, and a scurrying in the dead leaves. A lizard maybe. Or a snake. I rolled up my window.

205

"My mama," Maybelline began, "run off when I was just a little thing."

"Run off and left her own child?" Mrs. Johnson asked, incredulous.

"Sure did. But she always meant to come back and get me. She just never got the chance to do it. But she loved me anyway."

I could see the little girl, Maybelline . . . no . . . Maybell. Freckled hands with the nails bitten down, solemn eyes staring out from under uneven bangs. A bleached-out, tow-headed little girl with nobody in the world to teach her a thing. Except for a daddy who had no more couth than to call her "Maybelline," after an eyebrow pencil, for goodness sake!

"My Aunt Valley was like another mama to me," I said and wondered only briefly how I'd gone from imagining Maybelline as a child right to thinking of Aunt Valley. Except maybe I was wishing that little girl could have had someone like Aunt Valley in her life.

"Aunt Valley?" Maybelline asked. "I never heard you say one thing about a Aunt Valley. Not until this very afternoon, and us together all those years. Told me about your Aunt Tyler and Aunt Nell one time, but not a Aunt Valley."

"Oh, she wasn't my real aunt. Just someone who took care of me one summer a long time ago."

"A colored kind of aunt?" Mrs. Johnson asked, suspiciously.

"As a matter of fact, yes. Since you ask."

"Humph!"

"Now don't you go saying anything against her." Strangely, my voice was tremulous. "She was too important for me to hear that."

"Sure she was," Mrs. Johnson said. "Washed your clothes and wiped your nose and put up with your sass."

"I sure could sass her," I admitted. "Only grown-up I ever could sass and get away with it." In the backseat, Mrs. Johnson nodded her head, satisfied at what she evidently regarded to be a confession on my part.

"Only reason you could sass her was she was colored and you was white."

"Maybe." For a moment, I considered that possibility. But it didn't fit. Not at all.

"Maybe," I amended. "But it was more than that. Much more."

"Listen!" Mrs. Johnson interrupted. "What's that noise?"

From out of the darkness directly ahead of the car came a loud rustling. Something in the bushes. Footsteps, maybe. Coming closer and closer.

Maybelline and Mrs. Johnson rolled up their windows. "Help us, Lord!" Maybelline mumbled. The inside of the car growing hot and stuffy so quickly but not a one of us willing to crack a window the least little bit. Not with something making all that noise out there in the dark. So we sat stone-still, holding our breath and staring into the deep night.

"Turn on the lights," I said to Maybelline. "Quick!"

She fumbled for the switch and suddenly the headlights blazed out beams of white-light, arrow shafts that caught in their lightning-glare a big raccoon with unholy-looking eyes gleaming and blinded. Standing motionless at the edge of the narrow path.

"A coon!" yelled Mrs. Johnson in delight. "Thas all it is. One great big old granddaddy coon!"

Maybelline turned the lights off, and we blinked blindly in the dark until once again, we could finally see the different levels of darkness in the bushes and in the sandy path and farther ahead, the deepest darkness of all, where the land tilted downward, to a creek.

"I gotta go," Mrs. Johnson announced. "That old coon done scared me so bad, I gotta go. But I shore ain't going out there by myself."

"I'll turn on the lights and we'll all go," Maybelline said. "Better now than in the middle of the night."

"You'll do no such thing," I protested. "I'm certainly not going to 'go'—as you put it—in the glare of headlights. Just leave the lights off. So we can have some decorum."

"Whatever that is, I don't want none. I wanna see where I'm going," Mrs. Johnson grunted most emphatically. "You the very one what said they's snakes out there."

"But . . ." I sputtered, and Maybelline interrupted me.

"Let's do it this way—I'll turn on the lights so we can see where we're going, and we can each of us get behind a different tree so we can't see each other. How 'bout that?"

Mrs. Johnson nodded enthusiastically, and finally, so did I, but reluctantly.

So that's the way we did what needed to be done, and the only thing the least bit strange about it was Mrs. Johnson asking in a most sarcastic voice if she had to find a tree that said "Colored Only." Because I guess we were all thinking about the old ways of doing things, the way we had been talking together about them. Maybelline and I didn't know what to say, so we pretended we didn't hear her. So each one of us found her own particular tree. For decorum.

Afterwards, we got back inside the car, locked the doors, rolled the windows up nearly all the way, and settled in to try and sleep while we waited for a dawn that was going to be a long time in coming. I closed my eyes and listened to Mrs. Johnson's steady breathing that, within only a few seconds, had become resounding snores. And to Maybelline's evening conversation with Jesus.

The leaves rustled a little, where the old granddaddy coon was moving off through the underbrush, and just as I was about to fall asleep, another sound, too. From very far away. Folks singing, sounded like, but so faint and so far away that even the crickets' chirping could drown it out. Almost.

"I gotta go to church again?" I whine at Aunt Valley.

"Yes ma'am, you sure does," she says, buttoning my dress up the back and tying the sash. "Lemme brush your hair, and what you done with your hair ribbon?"

"I don't know," I say. "Besides, I hate it."

"You hates a little bitty old hair ribbon?" she asks, brushing my hair so hard that she lifts my eyebrows up almost to the very top of my head. "You gots the prettiest hair," she says. And I am surprised. It's not one bit pretty. It's ugly. Stupid and red. "Looks like the sun going down on a hot summer evening," Aunt Valley adds.

"I hate it," I say, hoping she'll say more nice things about it.

"You sure do hate lots of things today," she comments.

"I hate going to church again," I say. "That's what I really hate. Camp Meeting's over, and I thought I was done with having to go to church all the time!"

"You'll like this," she assures me. "It's not like your church."

"My church?"

"White folks' church," she says easily.

208

So now I'm wondering what it will be like, so I don't say anything else about not wanting to go. Just "OUCH!" while she keeps on brushing my hair. And I hear Carol Ann's voice just as clear as day: "You eat off their dishes, you'll get a disease. And die." So I wonder what she'd say will happen to me if I go to their church?

Lizzie comes to pick us up and we drive away, leaving Old Auntie sitting on the porch, still talking up a storm and Old Papa sitting on the front steps, smiling up at the sky. I don't say a word as we drive along, and soon, above the hum of the engine and the sound of the tires on the dirt road, I can hear singing—faint and far away, but singing just the same.

"We're late!" Lizzie mutters. And the singing gets louder and louder just as we go around a deep curve and come upon a little white-painted church with yellow light in the windows and singing coming out of it so loud that the walls are almost bulging with it.

Lizzie parks the truck in the weeds, and Aunt Valley has her door open before we even come to a complete stop. The three of us go running across the bare yard to the front door, Lizzie clutching one of my hands and Aunt Valley the other, so that with some of the steps they take, my feet don't even get to touch the ground. Opening the big double doors, and I am wondering why they have double doors. To keep people from crushing each other when church is over, and they're all trying to get out at one time?

And the singing's begun to wind down a little bit, but not all the way. Because there's a thread of it left hanging up in the air, stuck there. A note-moment that will last forever. And more sounds, too. Clapping, but not all together, and hollering: "A-MAN!" Strong, solid words, like how Aunt Valley's feet sounded when they were clumping in the dust behind me when I couldn't stop running.

"A-man!"
"Praise Jee-sus!"
"Tell it, brother!"
"A-man!"

The air is very hot inside the church and when we come in, people turn and look at us. Mostly women. Big women. Square shoulders and strong arms and cardboard-Jesus fans waving the hot air across broad, black faces with eyes that stare at me openly. Aunt Valley standing taller now by a good six or eight inches, looks like, and turning her shoulders sideways, like a big black cat that puffs up and swaggers around with its head low and its ears flat and its yellow eyes glowing.

209

Up at the very front of the church and behind a plywood pulpit with a white cross painted on it stands the biggest man I have ever seen in my whole life. So big, he looks like he's a thick, black tree that's tall enough and strong enough to hold up the entire roof all by himself. And when he sees us come in, he smiles so broad that light flashes off a honest-to-goodness solid gold tooth he has right in the front of his smile.

"Praise GAWD!" he shouts in a voice like a bass trombone—massive vibrations that rise up from the very soles of his feet and curl through the barrel-sized chest and blossom into the hot air, leaving great, golden circles above his head and all around, like shining wreaths.

"Come in! Come in to the house of the Lord!" he booms, holding his arms wide open as if he's standing in front of an invisible cross, and with Lizzie and Aunt Valley still holding my hands, we go all the way down the aisle to the very front bench and sit down close together.

It only takes a minute or two for me to realize that Aunt Valley's sure right: This isn't like my church at all.

For one thing, the people say things right back to the preacher, out loud. Things like "A-man!" and "Praise Jee-sus!" and "Tell it, brother!"

And the preacher doesn't just stand around shouting all the time, either. He prances back and forth and throws his voice around in a way that makes it just like some kind of music he's dancing to. Marches around like a soldier to words that are big and strong and dances on his toes like a ballerina to words that are little and soft.

Why, it's the most wonderful thing I've ever heard of. Because what he's saying isn't something he's memorized, like I have to do for school, but just whatever comes into his mind to say. And somehow, it all fits right in with the music he walks and talks.

And more.

Because while I'm sitting there, looking and listening, I begin to see how the words get rolled up into round, shining sounds like great, golden balls that go bouncing and spinning from the preacher out to the people and then from one to another of them for a little while and then they throw it back to him. Some of the golden ball-words plumping into the wall above his head so he has to speak out another one real quick and then reach up and grab that one and set it to bouncing and spinning again, too.

It's just like being right in the middle of all creation, with "Let there be light" spinning around so happy and so beautiful, I can hardly stand it.

I don't even know what's happening when all of a sudden I hear my own voice yell "Tell it, brother!"

Because I just have to catch one of the golden balls and toss it back, too, like the other people are getting to do. Aunt Valley and Lizzie look at me with the most surprised faces I have ever seen, and then they look at each other across the top of my head and start in to laughing, and Lizzie shuts her eyes and grins and goes to clapping her hands, and Aunt Valley hugs me and says, "Praise the Lord!"

And all those people sitting behind us—why, I'd forgotten they were there!—clapping too and saying Praise the Lord! and the big preacher sweating and laughing and smiling right at me and with his shiny gold tooth gleaming.

Church is so much fun that I'm surprised as can be when it's over so soon. And I look around toward the back of the church to see if the big double doors are open wide so people can rush out. But no one moves a muscle to leave. Only all these smiling faces looking back at me and nodding and "Praise Jesus-ing."

"Come on," Aunt Valley says to me. "They's waiting on us all to leave first 'cause you're a special guest."

"Me?" I ask. Me special?

I walk all the way back down the aisle with Lizzie on one side of me and Aunt Valley on the other, and the whole time, people smiling and nodding their heads at us, all the way down to where the preacher is waiting at the door.

"And who is our blessed little guest tonight?" he asks, smiling and flashing the big gold tooth. "The little one who got so filled with the Spirit!"

"This here is little Miss Amelia," Aunt Valley says, and I can tell by the way she says it that she's proud of me. So I remember my manners, and I hold out my hand to him.

"How do you do?" I say, and Aunt Valley beams.

"How do you do?" he says, taking my hand in his, which is big and soft and very warm. "Suffer the little children to come unto me and forbid them not, for of such is the kingdom of Heaven!" He rolls the words out like a mighty flood and looks at me as if they're supposed to mean something.

"Hallelujah?" I say hesitantly, and he throws back his head and "Praise Jee-sus!" he shouts. And I'm all set to say Hallelujah again, just to see what he'll do this time, but Aunt Valley's hand pats my shoulder.

"I hear you came out to see Old Auntie while we was gone," Lizzie says, and her voice is cold-sounding, like a tinkle of ice in a glass on a hot, summer day.

"Yes, indeed!" the preacher says, nodding his head and smiling even more. "Went out to see everything was all right in your absence. Took a fine peach pie out there, too."

211

Lizzie glances at Aunt Valley and then casts her eyes sideways at the preacher. "You didn't come out to see if she was really . . . like she is?"

"No in-deed," he says, still smiling, but with a slightly offended tone in his voice. "Although it would certainly be a blessing could we have a baptizing," he adds.

Lizzie is completely disarmed, so Aunt Valley speaks up. "We want it, too, but you know what we're up against."

"I do indeed," he says. "We'll just have to keep praying, sister." He takes both of Aunt Valley's hands in his. "Just keep praying. Running out of time, I do believe, though," he adds, looking deeply sad and serious.

"That's the truth," Aunt Valley agrees. "We have to find a way."

"Have faith," he says. "God will make it happen."

"What's a baptizing?" I ask on the way back to Aunt Valley's.

"When you're taken down to the creek and dunked good and proper so your sins is all washed away."

I am seeing the creek out by Mount Horeb Camp Ground, the slow-moving water dark as ink and the squishy, terrible feeling of the sand under my toes down under the black water.

"Where you die in the Lord and rise back up with Him," she adds.

"What you want to do that for?" I ask.

"So you go to Jesus when you die."

"Oh. Who's getting baptized?" I ask.

"Nobody. Yet. It's a long story," she says. "I'll explain it one of these days."

"Is this another one of those things like the gnats?" I ask, and Lizzie looks at Aunt Valley as if to say, What on earth!

"Mebbe," Aunt Valley says.

I don't say anything more. Just sit there thinking that if my shoes ran away with me in Aunt Valley's church, I'll bet no one would get mad with me about it. And thinking too how good it feels to sit kind of squashed like this in between Lizzie and Aunt Valley and riding along the dark road.

Because if this was a moonless night and if we happened to pass near a cemetery where the devil was waiting behind a tombstone to try and get me, I'll bet anything Lizzie and Aunt Valley would bust his head wide open.

Hallelujah!

19

When I started waking up, I thought Aunt Valley and Lizzie were still sitting on either side of me, for I could smell their good smell and feel their strong hips and hot arms against me as we drove along down the road.

But I opened my eyes to find that I had been sleeping in my own car, deep in a ravine out in the middle of goodness-knows-where. And all I could see was a multitude of green leaves, just as brilliant in color and as perfectly still as if they were painted onto the windows of the car and each leaf glowing in the morning light and with a coating of fine mist.

Maybelline was sound asleep in the driver's seat, mouth slightly agape and emitting faint and peaceful snores, and Mrs. Johnson was curled up in the backseat, having made herself into an almost impossibly small ball among the quilts and pillows, her sonorous snores muffled against the massive forearms curled protectively about her head.

At least it was daylight, and everything looked a lot better than it did last night. Maybelline, I thought, how on earth could you get us into such a fix?

As if Maybelline could hear my thinking, she stirred and opened her eyes. Yesterday's lilac eye shadow had impacted itself solidly under her eyes, and when she blinked at me, she looked just like the old granddaddy raccoon from the night before, only her eye mask was pasteled and comic.

I couldn't help but laugh. "Why do you wear all that stuff anyway?" I asked finally, after all those years of trying to keep my mouth shut about her preoccupation with crayoning her face the way she did. "You just cake it on, did that even when your face was still so swollen you hardly had any eyelids to paint."

"Do what?" Clearly, Maybelline was not completely awake.

"Put all that paint on your face." As long as I've started this, I might as well say it all.

Slowly, it dawned upon Maybelline what I was talking about. She straightened up and leaned forward to look at herself in the rearview mirror and then wet her finger and began trying to scrub away the misplaced eye shadow.

"You mean eye shadow?"

"I do indeed."

"What's wrong with it?" More than ever, Maybelline resembled a raccoon, this time washing its face vigorously beside a small stream.

"What's wrong with it is that you don't use it right. Why, if you'd leave about half of that stuff off your face, I think you'd look right nice."

It wasn't what I meant to say, but it's what came out.

"You think so?" Maybelline was studying herself in the mirror. "Well, truth of the matter is I've already made up my mind to wear a lot less of it. Just some powder and a little lip gloss."

"You have?" If I'd known it was going to be that easy, I'd certainly have said something about it sooner. "But why?" I couldn't help but ask.

"Well," she started, still scrubbing off the last of the lilac shadow under her eyes. "Coming to my granddaddy's house is supposed to be a whole new life for me. So I got to thinking about how the Bible says you can't put new wine in old containers. And that's why."

She studied her face again carefully in the rearview mirror. "Nothing much I can do about having a purple forehead though, is there?"

Actually, the bruise had diminished a great deal, and almost all the swelling was gone, only a small abrasion about her right eyebrow still red and angry-looking.

"New wine?" I said, but I must have been thinking out loud, because I didn't even know I was going to say a thing.

"Yes, ma'am!" Maybelline smiled. "New wine, sure enough! Gonna have a new life, I am. Not gonna be known to everybody as the woman who got thrown out of a truck."

"What?"

"That's right," she said. "That's all anybody ever thought about when they saw me. Even you." It wasn't an accusation, merely a stated fact. "And now I'm putting that behind me and having a whole, new beginning."

"I didn't know it bothered you," I said most truthfully.

"Well, not all the time, it didn't. But sometimes I felt like no matter how long I lived in that town, it would never be any different. Like somebody wrote me into a story, and I couldn't change any of it to save my life."

Well, that certainly sounded familiar to me, it did. But I'd never thought of it that way, where Maybelline was concerned.

"Going to be known for something else," she added.

"What?" I tried not to ask, but did anyway.

"I don't know yet," she confessed. "But it'll sure be better than that."

Even though we'd been speaking in low tones, Mrs. Johnson's most recent snore suddenly broke into a rasping gasp, followed by loud smacking and a loud yawn. "I shore do praise the Lord this morning!" she rose up fairly yelling.

"And so do I!" Maybelline answered. I remained silent, but I was thinking: The Lord be with thee. And with thy spirit. That's the way it was supposed to sound.

"How about you, Miss Amelia?" Maybelline asked. And I certainly shouldn't have expected that she was going to miss an opportunity like this one. "Don't you praise the Lord this morning?"

I looked once more at the riotous green leaves pressed against the car windows. And I remembered what it felt like to be safely wedged between Lizzie and Aunt Valley in the dark. Yes, I surely do, I thought.

Tell it, brother!

But I didn't know how to say it out loud.

"Maybe she ain't got nothin' to praise the Lord about," Mrs. Johnson muttered, straightening her dress and pushing aside some

215

of the quilts she'd been resting on. "Look like she sittin' there sucking on a lemon or something."

Maybelline's sharp intake of breath interrupted the matter-of-fact tirade.

"Please don't talk like that this morning, Mrs. Johnson! It hurts me bad, because I happen to love Miss Amelia." Maybelline's soft tone seemed to disarm Mrs. Johnson almost instantly.

I was thinking, She loves me? But what I said was, "Stop speaking of me in the third person!"

Maybelline blinked at me vacantly. "Ma'am?"

"Third person as in 'she,' which is precisely the way you were speaking of me. Just like youall did yesterday when I was just thinking hard about something and youall thought I was having some kind of a spell."

"Who's 'she'?" Mrs. Johnson asked suspiciously. "Somebody else gon' come live with us? Somebody I don't know nothin' about?"

Oh, Heavens!

"Listen, I didn't mean nothin' by what I said." Mrs. Johnson's voice was low and reluctant, exactly the way mine had sounded all those years ago when I had to apologize for dumping that iced tea on Carol Ann's lap. "Guess I woke up thinking how this is the first morning I don't hafta wonder what's going to set that devilman off. And that's when I said 'Praise the Lord!' But then I got to thinking 'bout how many times I done been hit already, and that made it so I had to say something low-down mean about somebody, and I guess you was just standing in the way."

Somehow I believe that both Maybelline and I were expecting her to go on with what she was saying—add an "I'm sorry," at least. But she didn't. So when Maybelline glanced at me, her eyes finished what Mrs. Johnson couldn't say right out—I'm sorry.

"Well now!" Mrs. Johnson's booming voice was back. "Let's us figure out how to get this car unstuck and be on our way. I'm powerful hungry this morning, and I got about three pounds or so of country ham in this here bag and it just calling my name!"

"Ham?" I repeated senselessly, for the mere sound of the word made my mouth water.

216

"Ham!" Mrs. Johnson proclaimed. "I'm the one what raised it and fed it and butchered it and dressed it out and cured it. Wadn't gon' leave all of it behind for the widder to enjoy."

I could imagine thick slices of ham, country-cured, a deep lovely mahogany color. See them in the skillet, hear them sizzle.

See Aunt Valley drop two golden-yolked eggs beside them in the skillet.

"Wish we had some eggs," I said.

"We'll have eggs," Maybelline assured me. "Real soon. Soon as we get chickens."

"Ham ain't gon' be around that long," Mrs. Johnson said. "Now let's us get outta this fix."

"So what are we looking for?" I asked after we had gotten out of the car and stretched a bit.

"A board, I guess," Maybelline said. "Or maybe some small rocks. Anything to put under the back tires so they don't spin in the sand."

We all went off in different directions. Mrs. Johnson through the trees and Maybelline back toward the road we'd turned off of last night. And I went on downhill, toward what would surely be a creek, or even a good little branch. Might be a place to find some rocks small enough for me to carry.

Down and down the little path, curving against the sides of the hill and with the morning sunlight left behind me. A descent into something cool and primitive and somehow, completely familiar to me. So that I knew something was waiting for me. The path a bit steeper than I'd thought, so that my footing was a bit unsteady and . . . I don't even get all the way to the creek because I am going through Aunt Valley's kitchen in a twilight that's made from the light bulb on the back porch shining across the kitchen floor in the middle of the night.

Because I am sound asleep when I think I hear Aunt Valley calling to me.

"MEE-LIA." Up-note, down-note, and calling from far away, sounding just like the cry of a mourning dove and so soft I can barely hear it. So I wait. And sure enough, it comes again.

I go through the kitchen, out onto the back porch and wait again.

217

"MEE-LIA." Why, it's not Aunt Valley's voice at all. It's Old Auntie's. I can tell by the wavering sound of it. And I see the door of the tiny little room and a little line of light coming through the crack under the door, so I push it open.

Old Auntie is wearing a white cotton nightgown and sitting propped up in the plain little bed with the covers all perfect, not a wrinkle in them. And she's so little, she hardly makes a bump under the blue quilt, and the doll-hands folded neatly and she is still smiling that same smile.

"You call me?" I ask.

"Come in," she says, just as plain as day. And I do, and I stand there at the foot of her bed, wondering stupidly how all of a sudden she knows how to talk right.

"MEE-LIA!" Mrs. Johnson's raucous voice bobbles the delicate silence of Old Auntie's room.

"WHAT?" I yell, watching as Old Auntie fades away, still smiling.

"WHATCHU DOIN' DOWN THERE?"

"LOOKING FOR ROCKS."

"COME ON BACK UP HERE! WE DONE FOUND SOME-THING TO PUT UNDER THE TIRES. YOU NEED HELP COMIN' BACK UP?"

"NO!" But for one terrible moment, I wonder if I'm wrong, for the path back up is steep and irregular. No. I'll find a way.

And I do, clutching at anything I can hold onto and scrambling back up the embankment and vowing silently to come back down to the creek to see Old Auntie just as soon as I can.

What Mrs. Johnson had been yelling to me about was that Maybelline had found some big slabs of bark that she'd been able to pull off a dead tree. And even though the bark was somewhat rotten, Mrs. Johnson said it was probably good enough to give the back tires the purchase they needed in the sand. So by the time I got back to the car, Maybelline and Mrs. Johnson were packing the bark as far under the tires as they could, and then Maybelline took my arm and guided me up to the top of the incline.

"If you'll stand right here, Miss Amelia, and watch me, you can make sure I come back out of here nice and straight." Then she went back down the slope to where Mrs. Johnson was standing directly at the front of the car, massive hands placed firmly on the hood, ready to push.

"You get it in reverse and go real easy-like 'til I tells you," Mrs. Johnson ordered. "I'll do the pushing."

"Well . . ." Maybelline hesitated, but a ferocious glance from Mrs. Johnson silenced anything else she might have said. "Well, don't you hurt yourself," Maybelline added hastily as she got in behind the wheel.

From my vantage point at the top of the small ridge, I watched as Maybelline started the car, saw the tailpipe burp a pale blue puff of smoke. Heard the increasing hum of the engine as she steadily depressed the accelerator and saw the right rear tire moving an inch or so on the slabs of rotted bark.

"NOW!" Mrs. Johnson's voice, big as it was, barely reached me, for she'd lowered her head like a charging bull and was pushing on the front of the car with all her might. Slowly, the car was moving backwards, more from Mrs. Johnson's brute strength and abject determination, I believe, than from gears and pedals.

Almost clear! Almost clear!

Inch by agonizing inch, the wheels moved backwards, engine whining and Mrs. Johnson grunting as she planted first one foot and then the other in the ground, until the wheels reached a thick pile of pine straw, spun madly, and the rear of the car slid to the right.

I held my breath as the engine roared louder and a shower of pine straw shot straight upwards from under the wheel. Mrs. Johnson looked up at Maybelline and then thrust her chin skyward, eyes squeezed shut, teeth clinched, and the broad face shining with sweat.

Old Auntie's face still smiling, hands folded over the blue quilt.

The faintest possible bulge under the hands where something DOWN THERE was wrong. Something like a writhing purple wasp nest DOWN THERE.

But not a baby. Never a baby.

"Praise Jesus," she whispers.

"MOVE!!!" Mrs. Johnson's roaring voice and the looming Buick simultaneous. I stepped back out of the way just as the car roared past me in full reverse and at a mighty speed, the right rear fender

219

so close that it fluttered my dress, and then the broad side and the gleaming door handles and, at last, the sloping windshield and behind the glass, Maybelline's white-knuckled hands clutching the wheel and her face centered by the startled mouth. The infinitesimal "O." The car bouncing backward over the bumpy ground and finally sliding to a stop in the middle of the road we'd turned off of last night in the dark. A huge plume of red dust rising from around the car and then, picked up by the morning air, moving off across an empty field like a flaccid and dying dust-devil.

Gone was the roar of the engine and the thrashing of the tires, so that the pure, cool silence descended, and a half-note from a mockingbird whose morning song had been so violently disrupted sounded from far away.

Maybelline still sitting behind the wheel, her face ashen, and the sound of Mrs. Johnson's man-sized shoes trudging up the incline and the rasp of her breathing.

"Whoo-eee!" Mrs. Johnson panted. "You nearly got yourself runned over good and proper that time!"

Now Maybelline getting out of the car.

"You all right, Miss Amelia?" she called.

And I waved off her question as if I were shooing away an annoying fly.

"Let's us go on," Mrs. Johnson said, and she attempted to take my arm. But I pulled away from her.

"I'm just fine! Don't need your help. Don't need your help one little bit!"

But what I am thinking is: What is it, Old Auntie? What are you trying to tell me? And how come you can talk right, all of a sudden?

220

20

The road Maybelline was looking for the night before was only a quarter mile or so farther on, and it, too, was overgrown with weeds, so that at first Mrs. Johnson and I glanced at each other, afraid Maybelline was going to take us down another phantom road and into a ravine at any moment. But the road—more of a wagon track, actually—stayed level and true, winding steadily beside a row of chinaberry trees that followed the irregular perimeter of a fallow field. Weeds slapped the underside of the car and the springs squeaked at the dips in the road. A plume of dust drifted away behind us and broke up against the trees.

Then we came around yet one more gentle curve, and standing right before us was a weathered old house the very same color as the bark on all the trees that grew around it. A big house. Plain. Like old country houses are all plain. And needing some work, sure enough. Still, a good, stout house, a sentinel that had stood through all those years. Empty and waiting.

Seeing it like that so early in the morning and with the light still soft and tender gave me the strangest feeling. Just as if I were coming back to a place where I'd been before.

"We're home," Maybelline breathed almost reverently.

Home?

"Well, I'm glad to be home," Mrs. Johnson exclaimed, scrutinizing the house.

And I am hearing:

Coming home to Jerusalem, my Lord,
Coming right on up the front steps
To my Lord!
He will wipe away my tears,
He will smile away my fears,
Praise Jerusalem!
I'm coming to my Lord!

"Good tin roof. Stout walls. And . . ." Mrs. Johnson added, "no mens inside 'em to give us misery."

"This is where we're all gonna be happy," Maybelline pronounced solemnly, just as if she'd heard the singing, too. "Our very own New Jerusalem the Lord's done led us to. That's what it is."

"Hey!" Mrs. Johnson yelled. "New Jerusalem just like in the Bible! And it right chere in Jeru-sa-lem, Geor-gia."

Maybelline smiled at that, but she was still looking at the house as if she could never get enough of seeing it. "Look up there." She pointed to the second story, a smaller structure that looked like a shotgun cabin perched on the roof of the more traditional first floor that had a wide porch on one side and a similar, enclosed, room on the other.

Whatever the house lacked in architectural beauty, I could only hope it would make up for in strength.

"The second floor is that one big room that was divided in two, for the stagecoach travelers." Then she pointed toward the rear of the house.

"My goodness!" she exclaimed. "There's the kitchen! I forgot all about it."

Sitting back some distance from the rear of the house was what appeared to be a small, one-room cabin, connected to the main house by a narrow, wooden walkway.

"Why, that's a detached kitchen," I said. "Why didn't you tell me? I haven't seen one of those since I was just a child."

"I must have forgotten all about it," Maybelline answered. "Sure don't know how I could have done that. Because us children used to play it was a bridge and that there was alligators in the water under it. Wasn't any water, of course, but sure was water there when we pretended hard enough."

"Well, no need us sittin' here like warts on a pickle," Mrs. Johnson said. "I'm gon' get in that kitchen and find a way to fry up this here ham." She gathered the paper bag in her arms and got out of the car, closing the distance to the house in a dozen or so strong and confident strides.

But Maybelline walked slowly, as if she were entering a dream, and I came behind her, expecting someone to come out on the porch and wave at us at any minute.

"Front steps need fixing," Mrs. Johnson yelled back at us, and she proceeded to bounce most alarmingly up and down on the protesting, half-rotten wood.

I was looking at the pine trees growing in the edge of woods on the far side of the house. "You know, I'll bet we were within shouting distance of this house all last night. Isn't that the strangest thing—to be so close and not even know it?" But Maybelline didn't hear me.

Close enough, anyway, I was thinking, for me to go back first chance I get and find Old Auntie again. Listen to what she has to say to me—this time.

We went up on the porch, layers of dried leaves crunching under our feet. A pale green, nondescript vine that had somehow pried its way between the floorboards stood a good six or eight inches in the air, wavering aimlessly for want of finding something upon which to climb.

Mrs. Johnson and I watched Maybelline reach out for the door-knob as hesitantly as if she expected it to burn her hand, touching it with the very tips of her fingers before she finally took hold of the knob and turned it.

The door squeaked and swung inward of its own volition, revealing a long hall so dim in the half-light of early morning that it disappeared into an indefinable darkness. Off to one side, a leaning staircase going up and disappearing into more darkness.

As our eyes became accustomed to the dim light, we could make out the outline of a doorway at the far end of the hall, a doorway with slats of wood criss-crossing it.

"There's why it's so dark in here," Maybelline said. "Back door's been all boarded up."

223

"Whas' it boarded up for?" Mrs. Johnson asked suspiciously. "Haints done it?"

"Haints?"

"Ghost-es," Mrs. Johnson explained, continuing to look around the hall, but leaning forward from the waist up, as if her feet were nailed to the porch floor. "Whose house you say this was?"

"My granddaddy's."

"He die inside here?" If there were a ghost in the house, Mrs. Johnson meant to know it now. And whose ghost it was, too. Maybelline glanced at me, and I knew she was thinking of what she'd told me about someone seeing the great-grandfather's ghost one time. I shook my head at her. Better not to say anything about it around Mrs. Johnson.

"No, he didn't die here." Maybelline nodded at me, for after all, she'd told the truth.

"Wher'd he die then?"

"In a little house on down the road."

"How come he died there and not here?"

Maybelline smiled and blushed. I was waiting patiently for this absurd conversation about "haints" and "ghost-es" to be concluded. Because I wasn't about to walk into that dark, musty house alone.

"After Grandmama died, he was courting a widow."

Mrs. Johnson's face slowly lost its suspicious look. "Well, then!" she laughed. "Ain't no haint of his in here! Not if courtin's what he died of." Satisfied, she stepped into the hall. "Now come on in here and show me where that thatched kitchen y'all was talking about is, and do we see if your granddaddy happened to leave a frying pan around here somewhere. One big enough to hold these good big pieces of ham." She patted the grease mark on the side of the paper bag. Sure enough a good piece of ham in there.

We went through the dim hall together, looking through a doorway on the right into a large room furnished sparsely with two old, wooden rocking chairs and a wicker settee, all of which were laced over with strings of dust and cobwebs that waved slowly to and fro in the air from the open front door.

"Living room." Maybelline waved her hand toward the doorway as we passed. "And dining room over here." I briefly glimpsed a room across the hall that looked to be of equal size with the living room and with a large, old table, its top covered in shreds of yellowed newspapers and hundreds of petrified watermelon seeds. So old probably, that even the mice didn't want them.

You'd think someone could have cleaned that up before they closed up the house, I thought, envisioning the spotless condition in which I'd left my own house. The gleaming buffet, freshly polished, the sterling condiment set centered on the shining dining table, and all covered over with clean dustcloths. But obviously, whoever left this house behind them didn't care one little bit what people thought about them. I made a mental note for us to take that disgusting mess away as soon as possible.

When we reached the end of the hallway, Maybelline pressed the heel of her hand against the boards nailed over the doorway from the outside.

"Have to find us a ax or something to get those boards off," she said.

"Don' need no ax," Mrs. Johnson pronounced, punctuating her words by kicking off three stout boards with only one hearty thrust of her man-sized shoe. One more kick and the rest of the boards fell away equally as easily. Morning light, thick with dancing, roiling dust from the old boards, filled the hallway.

Stepping over the fallen boards and their protruding rusty nails, we went out onto a back porch from which ran the narrow, two-board-wide walkway to the detached kitchen.

"Y'all stay back," Mrs. Johnson ordered. "Railing's gone, but I can make it." She started across boards that bent ominously under her weight. "Y'all go clean off that table, and I'll fix the ham," she said over her shoulder.

"I thought you said you weren't going to wait on us," Maybelline said.

Mrs. Johnson stopped right in the middle of the walkway and rocked a little back and forth as she balanced herself.

"I ain't!" she shouted back at Maybelline. "But I do like to cook, if you don't mind!"

Maybelline smiled and nudged me with her elbow. "Yes, ma'am!" she yelled happily.

Grumbling, Mrs. Johnson disappeared into the little kitchen, but then popped right back out again.

"Gotta get this kitchen took back from the kudzu! Gotta have firewood 'cause it's a wood stove and some kindling, too! Gotta have water!" she bellowed.

"We need a broom," I offered, thinking of the watermelon seeds.

"I know," Maybelline said almost wearily. "We need lotsa things. Just have to take them one at a time."

"Cain't do a thing without a ax for cuttin' out all them vines done took over the kitchen," Mrs. Johnson insisted. "And water for washin' things."

"Water?" Maybelline frowned. "How on earth did we get water that summer? Because we sure didn't haul it from the spring. I would have remembered that."

She stood for a few minutes, still frowning, and Mrs. Johnson and I stood by, as impassively as if we were watching Maybelline sift through a basket of apples to find the good ones.

"Seems to me I remember cupping my hands under a iron pump and there was one of my girl cousins and her wearing faded pink shorts and pumping a handle up and down. And then icy cold water in my hands. But where? Well, at least I know where there's probably a ax, or maybe a hatchet, anyway. In that toolshed out by the chicken house," Maybelline said. "You go look, Mrs. Johnson, and I'll try to find that pump for us. Back porch? Not in the yard. Because I remember that much."

"We better go ahead to the spring," she said at last. "I know for sure where that is. You see any kind of a bucket out there?" she called to Mrs. Johnson, who was banging around inside the ramshackle toolshed Maybelline's grandfather had built after the barn burned down during a lightning storm one nameless summer.

"See two in here," Mrs. Johnson called back. "One got a hole in it big enough to run your leg through. Other got no bottom. Got a ax, though. Got a good ax!"

Mrs. Johnson came out of the toolshed with cobwebs draped in her hair, grinning and holding up an ax. "Now I'll get them vines," she said. "But we'll find something to haul water in first."

226

Maybelline and Mrs. Johnson went together out to the car, to look for some kind of a container for hauling water, and I waited on the back porch. Stood there looking at the narrow, unsteady-looking walkway to the kitchen and noticing the roll-log base to the little house. Long years ago, that was the way they tried to protect the main house from a kitchen fire. Because the walkway could be chopped out with just a few strokes of an ax, and the kitchen rolled even farther from the house. And iron rings built into the side of the kitchen wall, for hitching mules to it and hauling it off. Simple enough it was, to rebuild a kitchen, needs be. Not so simple to build another house.

Without another thought, I started across the walkway, feeling like a circus lady on a tightrope. But about halfway, the boards quivered ominously under my feet, and I stopped, bobbing like a dry twig in a creek.

How old and stupid I would look if I didn't keep moving along, I thought. And the vision of myself having to be rescued by Maybelline and Mrs. Johnson provided just the inspiration I needed to keep going, take tiny, rapid steps the rest of the way to the kitchen doorway.

Goodness!

A complete jungle of finger-thick kudzu vines invaded every single opening in the room. Coming in through the two screenless windows and the unchinked floorboards, running up the walls every which way, and then escaping back outside through the vent spaces between the top of the walls and the tin roof. The whole room was padded in thick leaves as big as a man's hand, leaves that almost completely concealed a yellow cabinet whose broken-off doors revealed a stack of dust-covered, mismatched plates and a few jelly jars. On the very bottom shelf a black iron skillet as big as a dishpan and without a speck of rust on it. The sight of such a fine skillet filled me with anticipation, and my stomach growled at the thought of the good ham sizzling away. Just think of it—not a speck of rust on that pan after all these years. So whoever seasoned it certainly knew how to do it right. I wondered who it was.

Twined in and around all the kudzu vines were morning glories, purple, trumpet-shaped flowers blooming all over, like they were

227

growing out of the flowerless kudzu. Tendrils of all different sizes and shapes slithering across the floor, tangling up with each other, and some of them going around and around the legs of the big iron wood stove. In through the open damper and out through the burner holes before catching back up with the vines on the wall, so that they were all moving, silently and indifferently, toward the ceiling vent.

So I wasn't the least bit surprised when

Aunt Valley comes bustling in from another, invisible doorway, paying no attention whatsoever to the vines.

"Get us some biscuits made soon as I get a fire going," she says, opening the oven door. And when I say nothing in return, Aunt Valley turns to me. "You want biscuits this morning, don't you?"

Just as she asks, the morning sunlight tops the pine trees outside, coming through the open windows, shining on all the bright, green leaves and the vibrant purple of the morning glories. Colors so sudden and intense that I want to shield my eyes.

"You went to Old Auntie's room last night, didn't you?" she asks.

"Yes, ma'am."

"How come?"

"How come?"

"How come you go to her room?"

"Why, she called to me in the night. So I went to her room. And she said, 'Come in.'"

"What else? Youall talked for the longest kind of time."

But somehow, it's just as if someone turns out a light inside me. Because I can see myself standing in the bare little room, and I can hear her say "Come in," just as clear as a bell. But after that, there's just darkness so I can't see her. Or hear her, even if she does say something I can understand.

"I don't know," I say. "But she was talking just fine."

Aunt Valley keeps working the biscuit dough. I watch while she rolls it out and cuts out the biscuits and puts them on a pan. And just as she's ready to put them in the oven, she stops and looks at me.

"No," she says. "She wasn't talking just fine one little bit. I heard it all. Told you before you went to bed you couldn't even turn over without I'd hear it."

She opens the oven door and puts in the biscuits.

228

"You remember when you asked me why she couldn't talk right, and I told you it was us couldn't hear right? Well, last night, you were hearing her, and she said lots of things to you. Even if you don't remember what they was."

I'm not sure what she means, because I'm still trying to go back and find the exact moment when I can't see Old Auntie anymore. Or hear her either.

Aunt Valley heaves a sigh.

"Well," she says. "Praise Jesus for it, I say. This may be what we been waiting for."

"What we been waiting for?" I am still wondering why I don't remember another single thing about Old Auntie or even going back to my own cot in the pantry-room across the kitchen. Because I did go back. I know that because it's where I woke up.

"What we been waiting for so we can have this baptism, praise the Lord!"

"What baptism?" I ask. And I'm not really sure what Aunt Valley answers to that, because what I'm hearing is what she answered when I asked her last night: "When you die in the Lord and rise back up with Him."

But I think what she says this time is, "Old Auntie's."

"WHATCHU DOING IN THERE?" Mrs. Johnson hollering at me. "GON' BREAK YOUR FOOL NECK, WHAT'S GON' HAPPEN. COME ON BACK DOWN HERE!"

Obediently, I left Aunt Valley standing in the vine-filled kitchen and went wobbling back down the planks to the porch, wondering only vaguely how Aunt Valley even knew we were coming.

Mrs. Johnson and Maybelline were standing on either side of the walkway, and they both reached for me as I tottered down the narrow boards. As soon as I was off, Mrs. Johnson fixed me with a terrible frown, harrumphed loudly, and then, grabbing the ax, went across the boards to the kitchen.

"Please, Miss Amelia, you go sit down somewhere nice and cool while I get us some water." A little vexation in Maybelline's voice, and she held out the bottom of a double boiler she'd gotten from the car.

"No! I want to go back and see Aunt Valley." I turned on my heel back toward the walkway, but Maybelline's hand touched my arm and rendered me as immobile as if I had been stunned by lightning.

229

"No one's in there." The statement was irrevocable. "You dreamed it, Miss Amelia."

Sounds coming from the kitchen now. Not Aunt Valley opening the oven and taking out the biscuits, but Mrs. Johnson hacking off the kudzu vines, the crunch of the ax severing the stems, and the swooshing of the vines being yanked out of the floor cracks and thrown out of the window, where they piled up like tangled rope. Then Mrs. Johnson's sweaty face in the doorway.

"Won't take long. See about some firewood after you get the water."

"I found some pieces of old board will do us," Maybelline answered. "Put it under the porch right about here." Her foot indicated an area a little to the left of where the walkway attached to the porch. "Want me to get you some now?"

"No. Not now. Gotta have water first, then we'll see about gettin' the stove goin'."

"Come on with me then, Miss Amelia," Maybelline said in a voice like you'd use with a child that wouldn't behave itself and so you give up trying to get it to behave and just take it with you wherever you have to go, so you can keep your eye on it, at least. "I'll show you the spring where we'll get our water. Leastways, 'til I figure out where I saw that pump."

"Maybe you dreamed it," I shot back at her, and Maybelline blinked in astonishment.

"I don't think so," she protested, but a waver in her voice betrayed her.

I smiled. "Could be, you know. Gets hard to tell when you're of an age."

"Granddaddy told me his own grandmama came down here to get water when she was a little thing," Maybelline said as we followed the gentle slope downward to where the air was cool, and blue-green, darning-needle flies darted about.

I was about to tell her how my own great-grandmother used to haul water up from a spring down behind the tabernacle at Mount Horeb when Maybelline held out her hand for me to stop.

"Listen!" she whispered.

230

We're close to it, I thought. Don't need to hear it. Can feel it in the air.

The silence around us was almost deafening, only the singing of a few gnats in our ears, and the dampness clammy on our skin. Then the unmistakable sound of water trickling.

Maybelline grinned. "It's still here!"

Don't know where she thinks it would have gone, I thought. Unless she dreamed the spring, too.

At the bottom of the incline was a rusted pipe that looked as if it had been hammered into the side of the hill. The water from the moss-covered end of the pipe fell melodically into a sandy pool and then drained away in shallow rivulets to a nearby branch that ran smoothly away into the underbrush.

Maybelline put the boiler under the pipe and stood back while it filled.

I looked upward toward the canopy of trees high above, feeling a little dizzy. And the clamminess of my skin, I had begun to suspect, was from something other than the high humidity. Maybelline was watching me.

"You're not feeling so good, are you?" And she didn't even wait for me to answer before she said, "Having to wait too long for your breakfast, that's what's wrong." She took the brimming boiler from under the pipe. "It'll be better soon. Here. Take a good long drink of this."

The water was clear and crisp-tasting and icy cold and somehow flavored very faintly with the sweet, fresh green of healthy moss.

This is my blood, which is shed for you . . .

And so strangely, the cold water going down my throat warmed me, so that I thought of my heart as a red, glowing sun.

"It'll be better," Maybelline repeated.

Yes, I thought. It will be better, once I find a way to go back and look for that creek. The one I walked down looking for rocks. Couldn't be far, could it? Because that's where they are waiting for me.

Maybelline took the boiler from my hands and refilled it.

"Goodness, you must have been thirsty!"

"Yes, I was. A little."

The cup of salvation . . . take, drink, for this is . . .

Maybelline took my arm, and I did not draw away. Together, we started back up the incline. We had gotten nearly back to the top when we heard the sharp cackle of a guinea hen nearby.

"Eggs!" Maybelline said, thrusting the boiler of water into my hands and disappearing into the brush, following the guinea hen's cackling. From where she'd left me, I could see the edge of the back porch up on the other side of a stand of sassafras saplings, so I went on toward the house. As soon as I reached the yard, I thought I could smell wood smoke, so I figured Mrs. Johnson had gotten the stove to going after all.

"Sure do smell good, don't it?"

"What?" I ask.

"Why, those good biscuits in the oven," Aunt Valley says. "They be ready in just a bit."

She comes and sits down at the table with me. I'm wondering if maybe she's mad with me about going into Old Auntie's room in the night. And I'm all prepared to protest, "But she called me!"

"We need to get Old Auntie baptized," Aunt Valley says. "But we can't find out does she know what it means. And does she want it?"

"Why?"

"'Cause we can't understand a thing she says, of course, not since that fire when she was just a girl. But you can. And you gotta find out for us." She leans toward me hopefully.

"But why?"

"It was her trying to save her baptizing dress got her hurt, and afterwards, when we couldn't understand what she said no more, my mama told the preacher how Auntie was so happy about getting baptized, and that her going back in that burning house was proof positive that she wanted to be saved. But we never could find out from Old Auntie herself—not for sure."

Aunt Valley turned her full gaze on me.

"You're the first one could ever understand her. So you gotta ask her. 'Cause if she passes on without it, she can't go to Heaven. And I done told you she's got something bad wrong . . . down there."

"You want me to ask her?"

"Yes. Will you?"

"I don't think I know how," I say.

"You just let it happen," she says. "Like you done at church." She gets up and goes and opens the oven and takes out the biscuits. They are high-topped and golden brown, and their aroma fills the kitchen. She puts two biscuits on a plate and comes toward me, holding them out and smiling.

"Will you?"

"I'll try," I say, remembering the golden balls of speaking and singing that went bouncing and spinning all around the church. Is that what she means? And I reach out to take a biscuit.

Mrs. Johnson standing in front of me, trying to take the boiler of water from my hands.

"Gimme the water! We need it for clean cups and coffee to go in them. Whatsa matter with you?" she finally growls. "Gimme the water. And where's Maybelline?"

"Looking for guinea eggs," I answered, finally able to release my grip on the boiler. "Do I smell biscuits?"

"No biscuits. Gonna have ham though, just as soon's I get the pan cleaned out." Mrs. Johnson cast a baleful glance at me and then went back to the kitchen, now cleared of kudzu and seeming to rise out of the pile of chopped and discarded vines she had thrown through the windows.

Twisted green vines, and among them, the purple morning glories, still bright and trumpet-shaped. And while I watch, I think I can hear from each purple throat a sound of singing, very faint and far away.

"I got eggs!" Maybelline came loping across the yard, holding the front of her dress up in the air, just as if it were an apron, so that her whole petticoat was showing.

"Maybelline!" I said. "You're showing your underthings to the whole world!"

"Don't care!" Maybelline laughed. "Lookie here what I got!" And she held out her dress to show me a dozen or so speckled guinea eggs before she went running on toward the kitchen.

"Put on the ham," she yelled to Mrs. Johnson. "We got eggs!"

And how is it possible for anything to taste this good? I wondered briefly. The rich, red ham and the strange, orange-yolked eggs fried in ham drippings. Even the muddy coffee in a blue cup with no handle. Not even a tablecloth on the table, but just brushed off the best we could in our haste to have breakfast. No knives or forks, either. For we had sat down together with the ham and eggs on the mismatched, cracked plates Mrs. Johnson had found and with nothing but spoons for scooping up the eggs.

We ate silently and hungrily, with only the sound of our spoons scraping against the plates and an occasional gulping sound from Mrs. Johnson.

"We forgot to say the blessing!" Maybelline said suddenly. And Mrs. Johnson, who was holding a thick slab of ham in both hands and sucking on it noisily, looked up with ham grease running down her chin.

"The Good Lord knows how much we 'preciate it," she pronounced and went right back at the gnawing and sucking.

Afterward, we sat silently around the table, completely sated and strangely content, at least until Mrs. Johnson grunted, "Uh-oh," and then thrust a finger into her mouth. "Done lost another tooth," she proclaimed.

"It fall out?" Maybelline asked.

"Guess so. Think I musta swallered it," Mrs. Johnson laughed. "So busy chomping ham, I didn't even notice!"

I writhed a little but said nothing. Discreetly, I looked down at the multitude of watermelon seeds on the floor, unwilling to give Mrs. Johnson any attention that might prompt additional comments from her about details of the lost tooth.

"We need a broom," I said. And I was thinking: I need to find a way to go back and find that creek and ask Old Auntie about her baptizing. And without anyone interrupting me this time!

21

Seems like that was all I could think about, and as soon as Mrs. Johnson stacked the dishes and took them back to the kitchen and Maybelline went off, still looking for that pump she probably imagined in the first place, I decided I'd walk on through the pines—see if I couldn't go right back to where we'd been that morning.

But all kinds of things got in the way of that. Because I happened upon a good stand of broomstraw growing not far from the house, and I couldn't pass by, because we certainly needed a broom. I gathered the broomstraw, trying to remember the whole time just how to tie it all together good and tight, the way Aunt Valley taught me to do all those years ago. After I'd gathered all I wanted, I went back to the house and found some string and tied the ends together securely and made a fairly good broom, although I expect that Aunt Valley could have helped me to make a better one.

Since I finally had a broom, it didn't make much sense for me not to go ahead and use it. First I worked at peeling off the layers of old newspapers from the dining room table, and I scrubbed the table the best I could. Then I took that little broom I'd made and swept the shredded paper and the watermelon seeds out to the hall and onto the porch.

Then I had to sweep them off the porch and all the dead leaves along with them. And while I was sweeping, I couldn't help but smile to myself, remembering how I'd pictured us—Maybelline and me, that is—sitting on the front porch and fanning ourselves while Mrs. Johnson—Mamie, that is—dressed in a proper uniform, brought iced tea to us. Well, that was right funny, I thought. Lo! How the mighty have fallen!

But things would be different, I was sure, once we got all settled in. That's what I was thinking about while I was sweeping. When I came to where that little green sprout was sticking up from between the boards, I left it there. I didn't know why.

Then there was the living room needing attention, and Maybelline still hadn't found the pump, so she had to go back down to the spring and get more water so I could wipe down the rocking chairs and the wicker settee, at least. And last thing I did in that room was to go back out to the car and get my grandpapa's mantel clock—a wonder Maybelline didn't leave that sitting in Mrs. Johnson's yard as well!—and take it into the house and set it on the rough mantelpiece above the wood stove.

By then, it was noontime already, and Mrs. Johnson stopped what she was doing—slinging off some of the tallest weeds around the kitchen with a sling she'd found in the toolshed: "Ain't goin' in there tomorrow morning and find no big old snake all curled up asleep in my good, clean frying pan!"—and she cooked up some of the crookneck squash she had brought. Fried it in the ham drippings and my, was it ever good! And this time, when we sat down at the table, it was clean-scrubbed and covered with a tablecloth. Unironed, of course, but still something nice about it.

We had springwater with our dinner and drank it out of some fruit jars Mrs. Johnson had found in that same yellow cabinet in the kitchen. And the water had a wonderful taste to it, an iron taste and good and almost icy cold. But not setting me to glowing, as it had done before.

After we finished dinner, Mrs. Johnson said not a word but went out to the car and took a quilt out of the backseat and spread it out under the pine trees, where there was a good cushion of pine needles and started in on a good, long nap.

Maybelline and I pulled the wooden rocking chairs out of the living room and onto the front porch, to have a little rest out there, and we'd hardly sat down before Maybelline put her head back and closed her eyes and went to sleep, too.

But I wasn't one bit sleepy. Tired, yes—a good kind of tired—but not sleepy. So I figured that as soon as Maybelline was fast asleep, I'd go start looking for the creek.

I sat and rocked on the front porch of my new home and waited and looked at the little green vine thrusting upward and got to thinking about its roots somewhere down under the porch in the cool, gray dust.

"Melia? Melia? Where is you?"

Aunt Valley calling me, and me sitting right under her house and thinking:

> *Rastus! Rastus!*
> *Whur is you?*
> *I's under de house.*
> *Whatchu doin' under de house?*
> *Eatin' raisins.*
> *Whur'd you git dem raisins?*
> *Off'n de dog.*

It's a poem Carol Ann taught me a long time ago, when we were both very young and she was still being nice to me. I thought it was the funniest thing I ever heard. So that if either one of us just said "Rastus" it put us to giggling. And it's what Aunt Valley really sounds like.

"Melia! Melia! Where is you?"

So I yell to her, "I's under de house!" And to my delight, she yells back, "Whatchu doin' under de house?" I'm all set to say, "Eatin' raisins," but I don't, because her big moon-pie face appears right beside the front steps where she is bending down and peering under the house, and seeing her, I stop playing the game because it might hurt her feelings.

"I'm just thinking," I tell Aunt Valley, because I sure can't explain to her what it is I'm really doing, which is simply breathing in the smell of old dust and liking it and wearing the cool, semi-darkness on my skin like a veil.

"Come on out here, sugar, and let's bathe you off. You'll get so dirty under there. And besides, we got some company coming."

"Who?" I ask, crawling out through the cool, powdery dust and into the glare of the sun.

"You'll see," Aunt Valley says, brushing off the front of my dress. "Goodness! Just look at you! Come on."

237

She leads me around back to the hand pump in the yard, and the muscles in her massive arms bulge as she pumps the handle up and down and the crystal, cold water gushes out.

"You been able to remember anything else about what Old Auntie said?" she asks while I'm washing my hands.

"Not a thing," I say, rubbing my hands together under the cold gush of water. "Like a dream I didn't have."

"Well, you wash off good, now," she instructs, keeping a steady flow of water coming. "Feet, too," she directs.

When I am clean enough to suit her, she wipes my face and hands dry with a handkerchief and then leads me around front, where I see two colored women who have come into the yard and are sitting on a quilt on the ground in the shade of the chinaberry tree. They sit flat on the ground, with their legs straight out in front of them and with their big, white-soled bare feet pointing toward the porch. They fan themselves with cardboard-Jesus fans, just like the ones at Camp Meeting. Three more women and a little girl are coming across the ditch from the road, and they are carrying quilts, too.

"Who are they?" I ask.

"Just folks who come around when it's time," she answers and leads me to the porch steps. "You sit down right here and just be quiet. Don't go asking any questions."

"Why? And time for what?"

"There you go again," she says. "I never saw anybody in my whole life could ask so many questions."

"But how am I supposed to find out about things without asking?" I protest.

"I don't know," she raises her voice. "But you can. Just from watching, mostly. And listening."

So I think that it sounds like a fine game, and I sit on the bottom step and watch as more people come, one of them an old man who takes off his hat when he comes into the yard. Soon, there are twelve people gathered around, not counting two babies. Aunt Valley stands by the steps, nodding her head to them as they come and once in a while slapping away the gnats singing around her ears. But she doesn't say a word. On the porch, Old Auntie sits in the chair, talking softly, just like always.

In the yard, the people wait for something, but I don't know what.

So I watch them and wonder what it is you can find out from watching, instead of from asking. Like Aunt Valley says.

But watching for what? I look at the little girl who came with the three women, and she is picking tiny bits of bark off the crepe myrtle tree and

238

putting them in her hair. Two of the women are talking together in low voices, but the third woman is watching. She says something to the others, and they all look at the child, who is fully intent on putting bark in her hair. One of the women calls the little girl to her and pulls her into the big lap and laughs and starts picking the bark out of her hair. So nothing there.

The old man is leaning against the tree, smiling at nothing in particular and fanning himself slowly with his hat. Nothing.

"And listening," Aunt Valley had said. So I listen, but there's nothing to hear except locusts chirping in the tall grass in the ditch and the low, low hum of the people in the yard.

Then something else. An unreal feeling. Stripped of everything except for what it just is. The people sitting around in the swept yard and crickets chirping and the earth giving off the heat it's gathered all day from the August sun. All one thing and stirring in me the feeling of the old, vacant buildings. Something that gets gathered up and locked forever in one instant. Like the Great Mystery, only not sad. Maybe not even something to run away from, but to sit real still and just know is there.

Like gnats.

"Here we go," Aunt Valley speaks low, almost in a whisper, and when I look at her, she nods her head toward the porch.

Old Auntie looks out toward the ditch, as if she really can see all those people sitting in the yard, and she's still muttering to herself in tongues. Aunt Valley's papa comes from around back, totters across the yard, and comes and sits by me on the steps.

Everyone looking at Old Auntie now, and a feeling in the air that something's going to happen.

Her voice gets a little louder, and Aunt Valley's papa says "A-MAN!" and slaps his hand on his knee. Then Old Auntie's wavery, babbling voice gets even louder, and he shouts, "Praise the Lord!" I look at Aunt Valley, but she has her eyes shut.

All the while, Old Auntie's voice is getting louder and louder, and stronger and stronger until the sound of it lifts her right to her feet. So that when she stands, the people in the yard let out a moan together, like there's an invisible choir director telling them when to do it. White-palmed hands in the air, hovering there above the quilts and the shade from the chinaberry tree and the white-soled feet and the swept yard.

Old Auntie moves forward so she's leaning against the porch railing, talking so loud you'd think she's hollering to someone across the road, but not a thing she says makes a bit of sense. Not even to me. Not even though Aunt Valley says I can hear it right. The strange, chalk-white hands on the railing quivering a little, either from the hollering or from the standing up. The people saying Amen! and Hallelujah! all in and among whatever it is Old Auntie's saying.

And me watching and listening and thinking how it's just like Aunt Valley's church, except there are no walls, of course. And I watch and watch to see if maybe those golden sound-balls will start flying around. But they don't. Nothing but the August sun blazing away in the sky, looking for all the world as if it's gotten tangled in the branches of the trees. Somehow, I get struck with what the tree looked like early that morning, standing in the cool and peaceful yard. And what it would look like at evening. The people gone and the blazing sun gone and the strange sounds of Old Auntie's talking gone.

Even while I am thinking about that, I hear her let go with a final, long, loud string of sounds that still don't mean anything, and she leans back and sinks into the green chair just like she's a balloon with all the air gone out of it. And the silence is so much, it's almost like a roar. Then the people get up and pick up their quilts and walk away without a word.

I look at Aunt Valley, and she is looking at her papa beside me on the steps, and his cheeks are wet, like worn leather boots after someone's walked through damp grass in them.

"Now, can I ask questions?" I say to Aunt Valley.

She nods her head.

But—how strange!—I don't know what to ask. So maybe she's right, after all. Maybe I've found out things just from watching and listening, but I still don't know what they are.

Aunt Valley's papa gets up from the steps and totters around the house toward the backyard to see to his tomatoes, and Aunt Valley goes inside and fixes a glass of tea and brings it to Old Auntie, who is completely silent. In the green chair on the porch.

"So what is it I'm supposed to find out?" I ask, having finally found the question.

"I'm not sure," Aunt Valley says. "But maybe . . . just maybe . . . it's this: The Lord don't always talk to us in singing and shouting. Maybe sometimes He uses little bitty things—like chirren and real old folks. Those what aren't much like us. And Old Auntie is a lot like that—a old child. Always been a child, her whole life long. And I sure don't know what you're supposed to find out," she says. "Just whatever you're supposed to find, I reckon."

"But what's that?" I persist.

"I told you I don't know," Aunt Valley answers. "Different peoples hears different things. You just think about it for a little bit. Stop asking so many questions and just let it come to you."

So I sit quietly as I can and try to let it come, whatever it is. But all I can see is the little girl putting bark in her hair, and the three smiling women who watched her. And then the one who helped get the bark out of her hair. The way they were all there together on the quilt in the shade.

Caring about each other.

I think of Tulie's children and how they're never going to have some- one care about them, and here comes that strange feeling again, and this time I'm afraid of what it is. Something so strong, it makes me want to fling myself down on the ground and hold on tight, so I won't go flying off the face of the earth.

"It's like the gnats," I start to say, surprising myself. "And that little girl. . . ." I am talking, clutching at anything that makes sense, even words I don't care about or know. Anything.

Aunt Valley's eyes are half-lidded and a little cloudy, too.

"Does it . . ." Once more clutching at something.

"Lord only knows," Aunt Valley says, and her voice is sleepier and sleepier sounding—"No telling what-all chirren will do."

I don't know exactly what she's said because whatever came after "chirren," I don't hear it. Because of something coming up and over me so fast I don't even have time to think it.

So that Aunt Valley hollers, "Sweet Jesus!"

"Sweet Jesus!" again, only from very far away this time.

I start swimming upwards out of whatever has sucked me down and held me so long in the dark with dark children splashed with white. I open my eyes and see cans of pork and beans against the wall, their labels faded and faraway and a big jar of butter beans and Aunt Valley's broad face and furrowed forehead covered in tiny, little see-through pearls of sweat. A cardboard fan going back and forth, lifting the hairs at my temples and ever so slowly sweeping away the darkness.

"Sweet Jesus!" Aunt Valley says again. "She's coming back to us!"

Her papa's face, where he is leaning down and peering at me. The rub- bery mouth curves into a smile and then breaks into a toothless grin that's all pink, smooth gums and clouds of soft pink cheek-skin inside and a round, curled tongue.

"Here she be," he says, chuckling as if I'm a visitor who's just walked up on the porch.

241

"Honey, you done scared me half to death!" Aunt Valley says. "You want me to go call your mama?"

"No," I say, and my voice sounds strange and deep. "I'm not sick."

"You sure? You all right now?"

"I'm all right," I say. "I just forgot to run this time."

She pats me for a minute and then gets her pocketbook and rummages around in it, finds some change, and gives it to her papa. He goes out, to walk down the road to where there's a little country store and bring back a cold ginger ale that has beads of water all over the green bottle.

"You try and drink every bit of it," Aunt Valley says to me. "And I'll go make some biscuits and fix you some good milk and biscuits to eat. Make you feel better."

I've never had milk and biscuits mixed together before, and she brings it to me in a thick, white cup and with a spoon for eating it. Crumbled biscuits with fresh, sweet milk poured over them and stirred around until they're soft, and it's the best thing I've ever tasted.

I empty the cup and Aunt Valley takes it back to the kitchen and fixes more milk and biscuits for me, and I eat all of that while she sits on the foot of the cot and rubs my feet with her warm hands.

"Now can you tell me what it was happened to you?" she asks.

But I can't. Because I can't bear even to think it, much less say it. So I don't say a thing, but when I look at Aunt Valley, her eyes have water in them anyway, just as if I had told her everything I couldn't say.

"First day I ever came out to the Camp Ground to take care of you, you asked me about my grandchirren."

I nod, but I don't know what this has to do with anything.

"And then you said you knowed where there was chirren dying."

As soon as she says it, I can't even swallow the milk and biscuit I already have in my mouth.

"Well"—she pats my hand—"you just keep on trying to talk with my Old Auntie. 'Cause she feels it, too."

I swallow. And wonder, feels what?

How does she know? is what I'm thinking, because after all, if Aunt Valley can't understand what Old Auntie's saying, then how can she know?

"I don't know what it is," Aunt Valley says, as if she's heard me. "But it's what happens when the people comes in the yard some afternoons, like they done today."

"What?"

"She helps them carry they pain. All of 'em's pain. 'Cause they know she's carried pain, too, and come through it, thank the dear Lord."

"I don't understand," I say. And I don't.

"Neither do I," Aunt Valley admits. "But I understand one thing: You do the same thing."

"What?"

"Carry around feelings from other folks. And you just a child. A little bitty thing."

She clucks her tongue and shakes her head and says "Mm-mm," way down in her throat. I can tell by the way she's looking at me that it's something very important. At least to her it is.

She looks at me for a long time, and then her voice lightens. "But I been pondering considerable 'bout the gnats, 'specially since you was talking about 'em again." She nods her head in big, slow nods and raises her eyebrows at me and smiles.

"And?"

"And I 'spect it's one of the things we not supposed to get figured out."

"I thought so!" I laugh. "I thought all along that's what you'd say. 'Cause you plain old don't know!" For some reason, I'm delighted.

"Well, you don't know, neither!" she accuses, trying to act mad about it. But she's still rubbing my feet, so I know she isn't mad. Not really.

"Oh, I think you're right," I say, surprising her. And she looks at me so hard, like she's trying to decide whether I'm being truthful or not.

Finally, she says, "Well, He made lotsa other creatures, too, that day of creation, and them, I can figure out just fine."

"Tell me," I say, relaxing against the cool pillow.

"Well, like mules for pulling plows. And cows for giving milk. And cats for catching mouses . . ."

"What are mouses . . . mice for?" I ask.

She laughs and pats my foot one last time and gets up from the cot. Then she hesitates. "But it's an awful lot for a little girl to carry around," she mutters, as if she's not talking to me at all, but only thinking out loud.

It's the first time in my whole life that maybe someone knows how hard it is when the Great Mystery comes. Someone who doesn't think I'm strange or crazy. But of course, I don't tell her that.

"You try to rest," she says. "I'll be nearby do you need me."

So I close my eyes and listen to sounds of a truck shifting gears far away, and somewhere, a woman laughing for just a moment, like a splash of brilliant light against the twilight. And the clattering of dishes in the kitchen, where Aunt Valley is cooking supper. And knowing she will come if I call her.

*When I wake up again, it's in the middle of the night, I think. And some-
one has put a quilt over me and also left the door to my room open. Rain
is steady on the tin roof, and at first, I think that's the sound that has awakened me.*

*Then, "MEE-LIA?" The same up-note, down-note calling, the faraway,
crooning voice. So I lie awake in the dark, listening through the drumming of the rain. And I hear it again.*

"Mee-lia?"

Old Auntie. The wavering voice.

*Like a dream, to get out of bed and go through the kitchen and out to
the back porch and open the door to the preacher's room.*

*"Come on in," Old Auntie says just as clear as day. "I want to talk with
you about those children."*

"What children?" I ask, innocently.

*But still, I go into the tiny little room where that strange white colored
woman is waiting for me.*

22

"Storm coming up!" Mrs. Johnson yelled, scrambling up the steps and dragging the quilt behind her. "Y'all gonna sleep the whole afternoon?" she yelled at us.

"I wasn't asleep," I said. But I was surprised to see that while I had been sitting and thinking, the day had become nearly as dark as dusk and with a wind coming up that made the pine trees whisper and stirred up a dust-devil on the ground near the car.

"Then you sure was doing a good job a pretending," Mrs. Johnson argued. "Both of you. And I done said there's a storm coming!"

"Well, what are we supposed to do about that?" Maybelline asked, sleepy and more than a little bit irritated. "Run get the clothes off the line? Don't have any line. Run shut the windows? Don't have any windows, leastwise none that has any glass in them. So what're we supposed to do?"

A strong mutter of thunder and the wind growing.

Mrs. Johnson blinked vacantly at Maybelline. "Guess I forgot," she admitted. "Used to running around and getting things taken care of, do be a storm coming."

"We better close the windows to the car, at least," I said, but not a one of us moved to do it. Mrs. Johnson glared at me, just as if I'd suddenly suggested that she tote that barge and lift that bale. So I started to get up out of my chair, to do it myself.

"I'll get it," Maybelline said. And she did.

And we didn't even go inside during the storm, as perhaps we would have done, ordinarily. Although there wasn't such a thing as "ordinarily" for us. We hadn't been together long enough for that. But if I had been at home—in the house on State Street—I certainly would have gone indoors. To the safe, quiet rooms. To the beautiful, old rugs cushioning the rumbling of thunder. To the comfort of the gleaming silver tea service on the mahogany buffet. And to the almost indiscernible incense of beeswax polish and the gleaming mantel standing square-shouldered and solid, just as if it were holding up the wall against the heavy rains pounding against the roof.

But here, no difference, really, between being on the front porch and being inside the dark, cavernous old house with its empty windows and bare floors.

Mrs. Johnson leaned against the front door frame, still holding the quilt.

"What I missed most—living in a trailer like I done—was a porch. 'Specially when it's raining," she said in a musing voice.

So we watched as the first fat droplets pelted the yard, followed within minutes by a complete deluge. Then water pouring off the tin roof.

So that Old Auntie seems as if she's looking through the little window at the rain sliding off the edge of the roof.

"What children?" I ask.

And she just smiles.

"You know what children." Her eyes taking on that deeply sad look they had the first time I saw them.

So I know what's coming and I know I should run. But strangely, I stay right where I am standing, remembering how, one time, Mama had to "lift out"—that's what she called it—one of my baby teeth because it was so loose, she was afraid I'd swallow it in my sleep. How strange it felt to be afraid of that warm, gentle hand that had never touched me in anything but the kindest way. And after I'd squeezed my eyes shut just as tight as I could and opened my mouth—at that very moment—the tooth fell out all by itself, right into her waiting hand.

That's exactly what happens now. Because Old Auntie doesn't say anything out loud, and neither do I, but that everlasting image I've had of Tulie's children passes over to her. Falls right into the palm of her hand. Because just her caring about it and about me makes it all feel so much better.

And the strange relief of it, just exactly like me hearing Mama laugh and looking at her hand where the tooth is just lying there, all on its own.

"You feel better?" Old Auntie's voice surprises me.

"No," I say, trying to hold still, not let anything disturb the smooth, peaceful place where it used to be.

"Yes, you do." Not something to persuade me. Just a statement of fact.

"Yes," I say.

"Well, that's good." One of her hands caresses the small bulge her stomach makes under the blue quilt.

"What happened?" I ask most sincerely.

"Someone caring about you helps you carry it, is all," she answers.

"Why?" Because who on earth would help with something like that? Who on earth would look at those children on purpose? And who would sleep in the same bed with an old doll no one can tell is alive or dead. And it wearing a diaper?

"You got more?" Old Auntie asks, looking toward me intently.

"No," I say. "Not much, anyway."

"Well, you can do with that little bit, can't you?" She makes it sound like a question. But it isn't. It's an assurance, I know. But how is it I know that?

"It's a great mystery," Old Auntie murmurs.

"What is?" Suddenly, I am alert.

"What we feel for other folks. 'Specially their pain. You got a name for it?" she asks.

"No," I lie.

"I call it The Gift, but it's just Compassion, you know."

"Gift? Like a present? A birthday present or something?"

"Yes," she says. "Exactly like a present. And when someone gives you a present, you have to take it."

"But what if you don't want it?"

"Want it or not, you've got it," she pronounces. "Of course, the question is: What do you do with it?"

"Do with it?"

"Run away from it? Bear it with grace? Or maybe even thank God for it?"

Thank God? I am thinking. He's the One gave us this? What she calls a Gift? This Compassion-thing. He did this to me?

"It's only Love," she adds, as if she is telling me something I can understand. "Pure and simple, that's all it is. Not a mystery at all. And . . ." she adds, "whenever you're ready, Jesus will take all the hurt of it for you."

But I don't listen to her. Because all I can think about is that maybe God's the One did this to me.

"You think about it a little bit, and we'll talk again."

I am almost out of her room when I remember Aunt Valley saying, "Will you do it?" So I come back in and stand at the foot of Old Auntie's bed. Her eyes are closed.

"There's one more thing," I say, and the eyelids open. "You know anything about baptizing?"

"I know about baptizing," she says.

"Well, do you want to be? Baptized, I mean." And I am wondering where those golden balls of words are when you really need them.

The milky blue eyes shift up toward the ceiling, as if Old Auntie is looking at something up there. She smiles at whatever it is she thinks she sees, and she looks for so long and with such a smile on her face that finally, I must look also, even though I know there's nothing there.

And I am right.

"Do you?" I ask again.

"Do I?" she answers. And then in a voice that's almost like a little girl's, she says, "I lost my dress."

I say nothing. Just wait and watch those strange eyes searching blindly all around the ceiling.

"I know," I say. "But that was a long time ago, and we can get you a new dress."

"I lost my dress," she says again.

I say nothing.

"Get me a new dress?"

"Sure we will, if you want to be baptized."

"Oh, YES," she sighs.

And I am so happy thinking about being able to tell this good news to Aunt Valley that I run right out of Old Auntie's room and back to my own.

I am too excited to go back to sleep. Because I want to be able to tell Aunt Valley the good news the very minute she's up. So I lie on my cot and watch the small window way up high, waiting for the gray of coming light. Remember too how good it felt that time after my tooth fell out all by itself. And how I put it under my pillow so the Tooth Fairy would leave me a dime.

And when I look at the window again, full morning light coming through it, I can smell sausage cooking in the kitchen and hear Aunt Valley talking to someone. Her papa?

"Aunt Valley!" I yell and hear a loud clatter of plates, and then she's there by me. Just that fast.

"You feel okay?" Her voice and her face are anxious.

"I'm fine," I say. "And I have good news!"

"What?"

"Old Auntie says she wants to get baptized!"

Lizzie has come up behind Aunt Valley and they both stand there star-ing at me. Aunt Valley sits down on the foot of my bed, heavily and almost as if her legs won't hold her up. Lizzie stares at me without speaking.

"Old Auntie says she wants to get baptized," I repeat, as if to nudge them into saying something.

"When she say that?" Aunt Valley asks, at last.

"Last night."

"Whas going on here?" Lizzie demands, looking at us as if we've lost our minds.

"Melia here can understand what Old Auntie says," Aunt Valley explains, looking at me in a mixture of both wonder and disbelief.

"Nobody can understand her," Lizzie insists.

"Melia can." Aunt Valley is just as insistent.

"That's right," I pipe up. "She said she wants it."

"You'll tell this to the preacher?" Aunt Valley asks.

"Of course!" I am happy at the thought of seeing the big-man preacher again and maybe even getting to hear him yell "Praise JEE-SUS!"

"Now you're sure about what she said?" Aunt Valley checks with me one more time.

"I'm sure."

All this time, Lizzie leans against the doorway with her arms crossed over her chest and looking from Aunt Valley to me and back again.

"When did all this happen?" she asks.

"Night before last," Aunt Valley says. "I heard Melia and Old Auntie talking for the longest kind of time, and then I asked Melia to ask her about it. I guess that's what she did last night."

"You understand what she says?" Lizzie is still unbelieving.

"Not all the time," I confess.

Aunt Valley gets up off my bed. "I'm gonna go get the preacher."

Lizzie is still standing in the doorway.

"You finish up with fixing breakfast?" Aunt Valley asks her. And with-out a word, Lizzie turns and goes back to the kitchen.

"You get yourself dressed," Aunt Valley says to me. "I'll bring the preacher back with me, can he come that soon."

It's a quiet breakfast we have without Aunt Valley there. Her papa puts a whole fried egg in his mouth and chews it for the longest kind of time. Old Auntie just sits and looks at me and smiles. And Lizzie doesn't eat a thing, but just sips at her coffee and looks from me to Old Auntie and back again. Over and over.

Aunt Valley still isn't back yet, so I go and make up my bed. And when I pick up my pillow, to fluff it up, there's a shiny dime under it.

"Looks like it's not going to let up," Mrs. Johnson said. "Gonna rain all night long."

And I knew the dark that was coming wouldn't be a dark like at home—at my house—where the living room lamps made a yellow glow on the porch floor and lights from the house across the street marked the distance from one front porch to the other.

Not even dark like it was in Mrs. Johnson's daddy's little house, where headlights from an occasional car drifted across the yard at night. No. This was going to be a darkness so complete and so absolute that it would be like blindness.

But then, thank goodness, Maybelline found a kerosene lamp in one of the upstairs bedrooms and brought it downstairs, cleaned the chimney, and trimmed the old wick with my manicuring scissors. While Mrs. Johnson and I watched, Maybelline poured kerosene she'd found in an unmarked jar in the pantry into the lamp base, replaced the top, and carefully set the lamp in the center of the table in the dining room.

"You sure it's kerosene and not gasoline?" I asked.

"I'm sure," she said. But later on, I saw her sneak back into the dining room and take off the top and sniff at the liquid in the base, once again.

"Well, we've done the best we could, for one day," Maybelline said, as dark fell. "Guess we should have tried to get the bedrooms cleaned up, but we didn't."

"I don't wanta sleep up there without we've made sure about no rats or snakes or nothing like that," Mrs. Johnson said. "Sooner sleep on the floor down here and then get those rooms fixed up tomorrow."

Maybelline agreed. "We can put the quilts on the living room floor and sleep right here. Only got two pillows, though. Didn't you bring a pillow, Mrs. Johnson?"

Mrs. Johnson snorted. "Didn't bring nothing but me and my sack of ham and squash." Then she looked at us accusingly. "But you all shore was happy to help me eat 'em."

"You can have my pillow," Maybelline said. "She's right about the ham," she said to me, as if in explanation.

We finally lit the kerosene lamp—and it was, after all, kerosene and not gasoline, because it didn't explode—and sat around the table together, leaning into the pool of yellow light and drawing comfort from it. Like thirsty animals around a water hole.

"Tomorrow I'll go into town and get us some seeds for a garden and some canned goods and flour to hold us over," Maybelline said.

"'Most too late for a garden," Mrs. Johnson added.

Maybelline thought for a minute. "Maybe," she conceded. "But we have to try. We can still get collards. And pole beans. Not too late for those."

"I know how to butcher a hog and put up the meat," Mrs. Johnson offered. "But we got no hog."

"Next year," Maybelline offered.

And then there was nothing else to say. Only the dark outside the pool of light and the steady patter of rain. Without a word, I gathered the quilts and Maybelline picked up the lamp. We spread out the quilts on the floor. And that's how we spent our first night in New Jerusalem, sleeping on the hard floor and in a darkness that was just like pitch—once Maybelline put out the lamp—and wondering what tomorrow would bring. But just as I was about to fall asleep, I thought one last time about being there in a ramshackle old house way back in the woods. So far away from everything. And everybody.

"Not so very far away," I think I hear Aunt Valley say. "Just peaceful, that's all. Just mighty peaceful." I feel as if she's rocking back and forth right there on the front porch of Maybelline's granddaddy's old house. Back and forth. Back and forth. And she doesn't say another thing.

I awakened only once during the night when some nameless creature—probably a raccoon—went ambling through under the house, looking to get out of the rain, likely, and stirred up a cool and acrid aroma that came up through the wide cracks in the floor.

And then I go right back and start looking for that shiny dime the Tooth Fairy has put under my pillow. And she didn't even get a tooth for it!

251

23

The screen door slams, and Aunt Valley hollers, "Where is she?" so loud that her voice fills the whole inside of the little house like an explosion, and her big, fast-moving feet set up vibrations in the floor that I can feel all the way in my little pantry-room.

Before I can even get through the door, Aunt Valley comes into the kitchen, with preacher-man right behind her, and he just about fills up the whole room, all by himself.

Aunt Valley's papa jumps up from the table, nodding his head up and down and grinning so hard that all his gums show, and then, still nodding and grinning, he beats a hasty retreat right out the back door to his garden. Someone invisible inside of me says, "Yas'm, 'bout seben," nodding her head up and down just like Aunt Valley's papa.

Lizzie throws a baleful glance at me and goes out behind him. Old Auntie sits at the kitchen table, tilting her head to the side a little, as if she can tell that something is happening.

The preacher reaches over and puts one of his ham-sized hands on my shoulder and the other on Old Auntie's, and he's just beaming and looking from one of us to the other and giving off a glowing aroma of freshly ironed shirt and shaving soap.

"Ring the bells of Heaven! There is joy today!" Preacher-man halfway talks the words and halfway sings them, and his voice sets all the pot lids to rattling. Old Auntie smiles at the butter dish.

"Let us pray!" he commands, with his hands still on us. I bow my head and look down at the floor as if I'm watching a bug crawling across it. Or something like that.

He prays like that for a long time, but I don't mind, because the sound is so beautiful, it's just like listening to music. And once, when I have to shift my weight from one foot to the other—because his big hand is so heavy on my shoulder—I glance around a little, just to see if any of those big golden balls have started bouncing around the kitchen, but what I see is Old Auntie still smiling. I clinch my eyes shut again and my shoulder twitches a little under the preacher's big hand.

"Hea-ven-ly FA-ther!!" he yells. "I feel Your Spirit moving through this blessed little child right this very minute!" And that makes my shoulder twitch yet again.

Finally he says, "A-MAN!" And then Aunt Valley and the preacher and I sit down at the table with Old Auntie. Aunt Valley nods at me, and I tell him everything I heard Old Auntie say to me.

When I'm through, Aunt Valley reaches over and pats my hand, just as the preacher does the very same thing with Old Auntie's little doll-hand.

"Sister?" he says. "This child tells us you're ready to come to Jesus. To die with Him and be born again with Him on resurrection morning. Is this true?"

Old Auntie says not a word.

"Ask her again, sugar," Aunt Valley says to me.

"You want to be baptized? Like we talked about?" I say.

Still, Old Auntie doesn't answer, and I'm wondering if maybe she's back in some place where she can't understand what I say.

But after a long minute, she looks right at where I am sitting, smiles a big smile, and nods her head up and down enthusiastically.

For a breathless moment, no one says a thing, and then Aunt Valley breathes out the softest little hallelujah I've ever heard. It's just like something changes all of a sudden. Like when my stepdaddy gets over one of his headaches and I don't even know his headache's gone, so that I am still being very quiet. Then, from some far room at the other end of the house, I hear him laugh. That's exactly how it feels after Old Auntie nods her head.

After we all get done saying hallelujah—and just like I hoped, the big-man preacher shouts "Praise JEE-SUS!"—it's almost like a great celebration. Because Aunt Valley starts in to fixing the biggest breakfast for him that I have ever seen. Lizzie comes back inside to help, and she and Aunt Valley really go at it. They make a whole new panful of biscuits and another pot of grits and put on a fresh pot of coffee. Aunt Valley cooks up a skillet full of fragrant sausage patties and after they're done, she breaks four eggs into the grease and cooks them just the way Gus does when Mama orders her eggs "over easy."

It's certainly a fine thing to watch the preacher put away that big break-fast, relishing every single bite and sopping up the sausage drippings and egg yolks with his biscuit and washing it all down with cup after cup of steaming coffee. At last, when all the food is gone and the cup drained once again, Aunt Valley goes to fill it once more, but the preacher holds up his hand.

"No, ma'am! Thank you, sister," he moans happily, leaning back in his chair and patting his stomach. "That was indeed a most magnificent repast, but I must be going."

I'm not sure what it is he's said because I don't know what "repast" is, but it certainly does sound wonderful and makes the kitchen seem like a very special place where we've just had a wonderful party. He pushes his chair back and then looks over at me.

"Thank you for what you've done," he says in those rolling tones. Except when he speaks to me, his voice is softer and low.

"Is Old Auntie going to get to be with Jesus?" I ask.

"She certainly is," he assures me. "Just as soon as we get her baptized."

After the preacher leaves, Aunt Valley's papa goes to take "a little walk down the road." That's something he does almost every single day, and he must walk all the way to the little store where he went to get me some ginger ale, because every so often, he digs deep into his pocket and pulls out a stick of chewing gum for me. And I don't know of anyplace else there is to get chewing gum.

When he comes home, he's moving along faster than usual, and he comes in the door and tells Aunt Valley "telephone," and nods his head toward me.

"Hold my hand," Aunt Valley orders. And the thick fingers curl about my hand like a warm vise.

"Where we going?" I ask.

"Going over to Alma's, what I gave your mama the phone number for," she says. "Your mama called and when she does that, we're supposed to call her right back, soon's we find out about it. I 'spect she's telling us she's gon' be coming for you soon."

We go across Aunt Valley's backyard and then down the hill into a ravine, stepping over branches and crunching our way through dead leaves.

"Can't we get there by the road?" I ask.

"Sure can," she answers. "But this is closer by a good sight. And pretty, too."

She's right, of course. It is pretty, what with the land going down and down and the treetops high overhead filtering the sun so that even the very air has a green glow to it. And hushed, as if something is holding its breath and waiting for us to pass on by.

At the very bottom of the hill, a clear little stream that ripples along over rounded pebbles and white sand. We step right over it and keep going.

"Where's Old Auntie going to be baptized?" I ask, thinking of the shallow stream and how hard it would be to wash away someone's sins in that little bitty thing. And maybe just a little, I'm also hoping that Mama isn't going to come get me until I get to see that happen.

"Creek," Aunt Valley says, puffing a bit as we start up the other side of the ravine.

"A dark old creek where you can't even see the bottom?" I ask, picturing big-man preacher lowering Old Auntie down to where the bottom is strange and squishy, and we can't see her anymore.

"Why don't you wait, honey," Aunt Valley puffs. "Cain't walk and talk, too."

So I wait, while we scramble up the embankment and come out at the top right in the backyard where there's another small house, just like Aunt Valley's.

A woman is waiting for us on the back porch, with her arms crossed and hip thrust out.

"Gettin' too old to climb that," Aunt Valley hollers to her, breathing hard. We come up the steps and Aunt Valley puts her hand on my shoulder, leaning against me quite heavily.

"This here's Melia," she says. And to me, "This here's Alma. She's the one what has the telephone."

Alma nods her head at me, and I say, "How do you do."

"When she call?" Aunt Valley asks.

"'Bout a half hour ago," Alma says. "Good thing I saw your papa going along the road. Hate to have to go all the way over to youall's to get you."

"It's a ways," Aunt Valley agrees, and then we go into the dark, little house to where a telephone sits on a table in the living room. There's a doily under it and the table sitting against a bare wall, as if the phone's the most important thing in the whole room.

At the opposite wall is a brown couch with some of the stuffing coming out of it. It's so dark in the room that I almost don't notice the three brown children sitting on it, silent and sober-eyed.

"'Bout seben," someone whispers in my ear again.

255

"Whas the number again?" Aunt Valley asks me. Alma has followed us as far as the doorway to the living room, and she stops there. The children don't move a muscle, but their eyes swivel to look at her.

"Four-o-five," I say. *"In Savannah."*

"Well, I know that much," Aunt Valley says, picking up the receiver as if it's a snake that will suddenly come to life unless it's handled very gently.

Alma watches us for another moment and then turns and goes back out. The children's eyes swivel back to Aunt Valley and me.

"Operator?" Aunt Valley rolls her eyes toward the ceiling. *"Operator? Oh, there you are! I want Savannah. Four-o-five, please, ma'am."*

She listens, nodding, for a long moment. *"That's right. Yes'm. Yes'm."*

I watch Aunt Valley, but once in a while, I glance at the children, at their dark, unsmiling eyes. Then I realize I'm staring at them, so I smile, but they don't smile back.

"Yes'm," Aunt Valley says yet again. *"Hello? Hello?"* she says. Then, *"Yes'm. Aunt Valley here."*

So she's got my mama on the line, and suddenly I feel like I'm one of the children on the couch. Sitting real still and waiting for my mama to come and get me.

"Yes'm, she's just fine. Yes'm. She's right chere."

Aunt Valley holds out the receiver to me. *"It's your mama,"* she says, unnecessarily. I take it and turn so that my back is to the children, and I am facing the window that looks out over the backyard and the edge of the ravine.

Mama's voice makes my heart surge—such a clear and pretty voice and with a sparkle to it that reminds me of the little stream. *"Amelia? Sugar?"*

"Yes, ma'am?"

"We're back home from the hospital. Your stepdaddy's been so sick, but he's better now."

"Yes, ma'am," I say. But I don't say to her that he always gets sick if she goes away. Gets well just as soon as she comes back and straightens the covers on his bed and tastes his coffee when Gus brings it, to see if there's enough sugar in it.

"So I'll come get you tomorrow evening."

"Yes, ma'am." I am thinking about my still getting to see Old Auntie get baptized after all, because Mama won't come until later.

"You okay? You sound kind of funny. Everything all right?"

I turn so that I am once again looking at the children. *"Yes, ma'am,"* I say. *"You're coming tomorrow afternoon. Late."*

"I sure am," she laughs. *"Coming to get my baby. I sure have missed you."*

"I've missed you, too," I say.

"Oh . . . and honey? If you go to church with Aunt Valley tomorrow, you be sure and behave. It might not be the kind of church you're used to."

"Yes, ma'am."

"So just don't say anything," Mama adds.

I am thinking "Tell it, brother!" But I say, "Yes, ma'am. Bye now."

"Give me back to Aunt Valley, please," she says, and I do.

"Yes'm," Aunt Valley says. "Thas right. Pass right on by the road goes to Mount Horeb and go on 'bout a mile 'til you see a crossroads. That's Grayson's Corners. Third house on the right after you pass. Thas right. Settin' right out by the road. Got a green chair on the porch. Thas right. We be out on the porch waiting for you."

Aunt Valley pauses and looks down at me.

"No, ma'am," she says to Mama. "You don't owe me nothin'. Miss Amelia's been a welcome guest. A most welcome guest," she adds. "Yes'm, I know you 'preciate it. Yes'm. Yes'm. Good-bye now."

We leave the children sitting on the couch and go back out to the yard where Alma is hanging clothes on the line.

"Sure do thank you," Aunt Valley says. "When you get your bill, tell me how much." Alma nods and keeps on hanging clothes on the line.

Aunt Valley and I start back home, by the road this time. Because she says she's getting too old for climbing so much. And the whole time we walk, I am wondering how come Aunt Valley's house can be so close to the Camp Ground and yet seem so far away. Wondering, too, how long the dark children will sit silently in the dark room before Alma comes back inside.

"Whatchu got on your mind?" Aunt Valley asks. "You missing your mama now you've heard her voice?"

"Not that," I say, realizing as I say it that it's not quite true.

"Them chirren?"

As soon as she says it, I feel my throat trying to close up on me.

"Back to that again, are we?" she asks, slowing down in her strides and taking hold of my hand. And I'm glad she does that—takes my hand—because I can tell that my feet are ready to run. Run and run and never stop. What was it Old Auntie said? "When you're ready, Jesus will take it for you."

"I can't do it," I say.

"Can't do what?" Aunt Valley asks, perplexed.

"I don't know."

"You don't know, and I don't know," she says. "That's a fine kettle of fish. Let's just get you on home, cool you off a little. Awful hot this morning."

257

And I am thinking, *You too, Aunt Valley? You, whose name is so peaceful and calm?*

I don't say anything.

"One thing I do know," she says.

"What?"

"How scared you are."

"Me? Scared?" my voice isn't at all convincing, even to me. "Scared of what?"

"I can tell you, but you gotta be sure you wanta know," she says.

And what am I to say to that? Why, I've walked right into a trap! Because no matter whether I say yes or no, the fact of my being scared has already been established.

"You wanta know?" she asks again, and I am helpless to answer. "Well, I'm gonna tell you anyways," she pronounces. "Whether you like it or not."

I feel my throat getting tighter and tighter, and I can't say a thing. Can't get out a single word. Not even a croak.

"You loves folks—all kinds of folks—the strongest of any little thing I ever heard of. But you fight about it with yourself all the time. I don't know why. Mebbe something to do with losing your daddy. And your mama going off and leaving you. Mebbe something else, too."

Still, I can't speak, and before I can even think of it, my feet have sprung to life and I have wrenched my hand away from her and I'm running, but I don't know what from. Maybe the scurrying sounds in the tall grass. Maybe the dark children in the dark room. Maybe the devil, where he hides behind the tombstones on a moonless night.

"Oh, no, you don't!" Aunt Valley runs behind me, catching me by the shoulder, spinning me around. "Not gon' run this time," she pants. "Gon' stand and face it. Here and now."

"I won't!" I yell at her.

"You got to!" she yells back at me. "You done missed what I told you. You can't run fast enough to outrun love. And you can't throw it away neither. 'Cause it don't throw!"

"No!" I shriek so loud that she lets go of me in surprise, and I am running and running, all the way back to her house. But before I can get far enough away to where I can't hear her, she hollers at me, "Old Auntie loves you! Like it or not!"

When Aunt Valley finally gets to the house and comes up the steps, her papa and I are sitting in the porch swing together, like there's not a thing in the world going on. And Old Auntie in the green chair, talking

258

up a storm. Aunt Valley looks at us and goes on inside, muttering under her breath.

Nothing else is said about all those silly things she was yelling to me.

In the afternoon, Aunt Valley and I ride to town with Lizzie to find Old Auntie a baptizing dress. Aunt Valley says she isn't fond of store-bought dresses, but there isn't time to make one, so we don't have any choice.

While we are driving along, Lizzie looks down at me and says, "You know, I think Old Auntie and Amelia here are probably of a size." She's right, though I hadn't thought of that before. "But I 'spect we better get a size larger on account of . . ." Lizzie stops speaking.

"Yes," Aunt Valley says.

"On account of what?" I ask.

"Her sickness."

The inside of the store is dark and cool, especially after our ride in the blazing sunshine, and high up against the embossed tin ceiling, great fans paddle the air most pleasantly.

The child-sized clothes are all hanging on a circular rack near the back of the store, and among the dresses, only three of them are white, like Aunt Valley insists on.

"Don't matter she can't see it," Aunt Valley says. "It's gonna be just as close to what she was sewing on that time as we can get it."

Lizzie takes one of the dresses from the rack and holds it up, but it's way too big for either me or Old Auntie. But it does have pretty tucks on the bodice and a band of lace along the sleeves.

"Too big," Aunt Valley says.

"We could take it in," Lizzie offers.

"Skirt's kinda skimpy," Aunt Valley adds, and Lizzie puts it back.

The next white dress Lizzie takes out is nearer the right size, but it doesn't have any lace. Aunt Valley purses her lips and studies it carefully before she says, "Melia, would you try this one on for us?"

"Yes'm."

I take the dress and go behind the faded green curtain in the back corner of the store. Inside, there's a full-length mirror and a chair for me to put my clothes on. I watch myself as I peel off my dress. In the mirror, I see my pale body and my long, skinny arms and legs. For one startled moment, I look at my white face and freckles and muddy-green eyes that are like two burned holes in a pale blanket. And red hair.

And I do wonder why I look so strange—until I suddenly realize that I've become accustomed to seeing velvet black skin and dark, glistening

259

hair, so that seeing myself now, I look very faded and completely unin-teresting.

So before I put on the white dress, I know already that it's going to look pretty much the same on Old Auntie as it does on me, because of her being white. Sort of. And I wish with all my heart that she wasn't an albino person at all.

When I come out from behind the curtain, I go to Aunt Valley so she can fasten the buttons, and then I turn all the way around so she and Lizzie can see the dress.

"Pretty sleeves," Lizzie says.

"But not a speck of lace," Aunt Valley answers. "Plenty of room in the waist, though."

I stand there watching them while they study the dress. They are stand-ing in identical poses, each with one arm across her stomach and the elbow of the other arm resting in the upturned palm and the fist under the chin.

"Have to let down the hem. Wouldn't do to have her knees showing," Aunt Valley says.

"It's got a good deep hem. We can let it down tonight," Lizzie answers.

"Let's us go see if they got some little bit of lace we could whip onto the sleeves," Aunt Valley says, and they turn and go up near the front of the store where there's a big table loaded down with fabric bolts and wheels of lace.

While I stand there waiting for them, a neat little man comes from behind the hat counter and walks toward me. He is wearing glasses and a crooked tie and has his shirtsleeves rolled up.

"Aren't you Miss Kate's niece?" he asks, and I don't bother to correct him about me really being her great-niece.

"Yes, sir," I say. "I sure am. And my mama's daughter, too."

"Well, honey," he says, bending down and glancing over at where Aunt Valley and Lizzie are looking through all the rolls of lace. "I heard about you staying with Aunt Valley, and I know your mama's not here and nei-ther is your Aunt Kate, and . . ." he hesitates.

"Yes, sir?" I prompt him.

"Well, I don't think your mama would want you getting baptized, that's all. Not at their church!" Once again, he glances toward Aunt Valley and Lizzie. "No, sir!" he adds. "Don't think your mama would like it one little bit!"

"Oh." I look down at the white dress. "It's not me being baptized at all. No, sir. I've already been sprinkled. It's Old Auntie who's getting baptized."

"Aunt Valley's Old Auntie?"

"Yes, sir, she's the one."

"But I thought she wasn't quite right—in the head," he says easily.

"No, sir. She's just hard to understand is all."

"Oh," he says. "Well, all right then," and he goes back behind the counter.

But there's something about what he said that bothers me, and Aunt Valley and Lizzie are walking back toward me when I realize what it is: The way he says "their church" makes me think of what Carol Ann said about "their dishes."

Lizzie likes one kind of lace and Aunt Valley likes the other, so I stand there while they hold first one and then the other against the sleeves. And the whole time, I am thinking that I really do wish I was the one going to be baptized—and at "their church" as well. Because I could have a lovely white dress of my very own, and preacher-man himself would pick me up in his strong arms and carry me into the water—and if that happened, I wouldn't be one little bit scared. Just imagining it makes me smile.

"You're just being so sweet and patient," Aunt Valley says. "And I sure do 'preciate it."

"It's important about Old Auntie's dress," I say, and Aunt Valley and Lizzie smile and nod.

On the drive back to Aunt Valley's house, I sit in the middle again and Aunt Valley lets me be the one to hold the crisp paper package that has Old Auntie's baptizing dress in it and both kinds of lace. And all the way home, we sing at the top of our lungs:

> Whiter than snow, yes
> Whiter than snow;
> Now wash me and I shall be
> Whiter than snow!

That night after supper and after Aunt Valley and Lizzie get done letting down the hem of Old Auntie's dress and stitching all that pretty lace on the sleeves, and ironing it just so, Aunt Valley and I sit at the kitchen table together and she teaches me how to play bottle cap checkers. The board is one her papa made himself, and he sits with us and watches, but he never says a word. Aunt Valley tells me how he made the board by dividing it into squares and then burning some of the squares black so the whole board looks something like the black-and-white tile floor in the kitchen at home—at my stepdaddy's house. My bottle caps are all turned up and Aunt Valley's are all turned down, and that's how we play bottle cap checkers for the longest kind of time. And every time one of my bottle caps gets all the way over to the last row on Aunt Valley's side, I yell "Crown me!" and her old papa laughs so hard that his pink mouth curls up just like a little bow.

We have a grand time, and when I finally go to bed, it's very late, and I am too tired and sleepy to wonder if Old Auntie will call to me during the night.

She doesn't. Or, if she does, I don't hear her. Because I'm sound asleep.

The next morning, which is the day of Old Auntie's baptizing, I am already bathed and dressed and with my hair ribbons all freshly washed and ironed, and I am standing in the yard, waiting for Aunt Valley and Lizzie to get Old Auntie ready.

"Now don't you go getting yourself dirty," Aunt Valley had said to me, so I am standing by the tree and behaving myself. Just for her.

I am looking at the little house and I see Aunt Valley and Lizzie coming toward the screen door from inside where the room is dark. One of them is on either side of Old Auntie, and when Lizzie reaches out and pushes open the screen door, Old Auntie's new snow-white baptizing dress glows in the sunlight just like a white candle in a dark church.

She steps out onto the porch, still wearing her blue Indian-bead slippers, but in the sunlight, the beads seem to sparkle like little jewels.

Her face is turned upward, as if she is searching for the sunshine, and she is smiling like a tiny little bride.

Aunt Valley and Lizzie get Old Auntie to sit down in her green chair and then they get on either side, pick it right up with her in it, and carry it down the steps and across the yard, lifting it into the back of Lizzie's truck.

Aunt Valley's papa sits on the open tailgate, with his skinny legs hanging off, and Aunt Valley and Lizzie and I all get in the front seat together.

We go driving off to the creek, where Old Auntie's going to get washed clean of all her sins. So she can go to Jesus.

24

Maybelline and Mrs. Johnson were talking together in the dining room across the hall, their low voices in the cavernous room more like muffled drumrolls than words. And something from the dreaming left over, so that my hand is suspended between moving a bottle cap to the next square and reaching out to take the telephone receiver from Aunt Valley. From the dark side of the dark room, the children still watching.

"Well, I don't know. It's a long time, and she don't like me one little bit!" Mrs. Johnson's voice somewhat louder and very reluctant sounding.

For a moment, I thought I was getting dressed to go to Old Auntie's baptizing, and *where did I put my hair ribbon this time, is what I want to know!*

"Get yourself a pillow, while you're at it," Mrs. Johnson said in the dining room.

First thing they did so early that morning was drag the straw mattresses down from the bedrooms upstairs and take them out into the yard, where—I remembered from Camp Meeting—the mattresses would grow warm and sweet, take on the smell of sun and grass.

I'd been thinking that maybe I should gather more broomstraw and make another broom, just so we could have one to keep upstairs. But somehow, I didn't feel like doing it. Felt more like finding a small place where no one could see me, curling up into a little ball, and staying safe and warm. But of course, there was no such place like that in this house.

I felt something hot behind my eyes when I pictured the quiet house on State Street, the perfume of beeswax polish, and the comfort of the deep carpets.

Gone!

So all I could do was sit there on the porch with my chair as far back from the railing as I could get it, just being real still and quiet. Let Maybelline and Mrs. Johnson do all the work. That's how I felt that day.

Vulnerable.

After they got the mattresses out in the sunshine, all lined up in the tall, dry grass, I heard Maybelline say to Mrs. Johnson, "You sure you don't mind doing all the rest without any help?"

"It's all right," Mrs. Johnson answered. "You just go on and do what you gotta do."

So Maybelline came and squatted down by my chair, as I somehow knew she would do.

"I know you're not feeling very good today," she said. "Just wanted to tell you I'm gonna go on into town now and get us some supplies. And I might be gone a bit. But Mrs. Johnson's here."

"Why should you be 'gone a bit'?" I asked. "You said it wasn't far."

Maybelline glanced at the doorway, so I knew Mrs. Johnson was standing there, watching us. And listening.

"You two are up to something, I can tell," I said. "So don't you do anything silly, like bring a doctor back here with you. I'm just a little bit tired is all." Then I added, "It's been a lot—leaving my home and coming here."

"I know," Maybelline said. "Well, you just sit and rest—maybe I'll get the car checked over, too, long as I'm in town. It's running pretty rough."

Of course it's running rough, I thought. You ran it all the way down into that ravine, you know. Down near the creek where all the singing comes from.

But when I started to tell her, she'd already gone and gotten in the car. So I watched while she turned around in the yard and drove away, and I almost felt as I had when my stepdaddy came to the Camp Ground that time to get my mama. But not quite.

"You be okay sittin' here by yourself while I start in to cleaning upstairs?" Mrs. Johnson asked in what I thought was a suspiciously solicitous tone of voice.

"Of course!" I snapped. "Just you go on about your business."

She turned to go upstairs, and on an impulse, I called after her, "It'll be nice to sleep in a bed tonight. And in a clean room."

Then she was gone, and I was alone on the porch. Nothing to see but the pine woods and nothing to hear but crickets beginning to sing in the tall grass warmed by the long fingers of morning sunshine.

Once in a while, a thumping sound from Mrs. Johnson's working upstairs and a clumping of her feet on the stairs when she came down to get more water.

The sun warming up the ground so fast, and me sitting there watching while the earth began breathing long, slow breaths of yellow sun and green leaves, like something old and almost dead coming back to life.

"The city had no need of the sun," I was thinking and then wondering where it was I'd heard those words. And what city could it be, had no need of the sun? Nothing to warm the earth. And no moon, either, in that case. A moonless night and the devil looking out from behind the tombstones at Mount Horeb cemetery. No need of the sun?

Noontime came, and Mrs. Johnson stopped cleaning the bedrooms long enough to fix us the last of the squash, fried up in ham drippings. After that, she spread a quilt out under the pine trees and took a good, long nap before she went back upstairs. Then little by little, the hours passing and the shadows lengthening, and Mrs. Johnson went out in the yard and got each one of the heavy, sun-sweetened mattresses and dragged it back upstairs all by herself.

I didn't offer to help her. Because what I had it in my mind to do was sit on the porch and watch to see that nothing came along to surprise me. In the city with no need of the sun?

265

Then I must have dozed off for a while, because when I awakened, it was almost dusk and way past time for supper. The aroma of something good cooking. Chicken? Must be my imagination. And still no sign of Maybelline.

"It's rabbit," Mrs. Johnson announced when she put a plate heaped with golden-brown pieces of what looked like fried chicken on the table.

"Where did you get rabbit?" I asked suspiciously, remembering the coon or possum—one or the other—that had been roaming through under the house in the night.

"Caught him myself," Mrs. Johnson said proudly. "Made a rabbit snare just like my old daddy showed me how to do one time. And along come this big old fat bunny and WHOOSH! I catched him!"

In her voice, the age-old braggadocio of a victorious hunter. And whether it was because of Mrs. Johnson's "seasoning" of complete triumph or whether the rabbit had indeed been a good, fat one, I never did know. Just that it was absolutely delicious.

I ate three big pieces of fried rabbit and even licked my fingers.

"You sure got a appetite, anyway," Mrs. Johnson observed.

"It's so good," I told her. And what I didn't add was that my appetite for that good rabbit was like some kind of a terrible urge to fortify myself. But I didn't know why. Not back then I didn't.

"Where's Maybelline gone?" I asked, right out of a clear blue sky. And the question took Mrs. Johnson by surprise, as I'd intended it to do, so that she stared at me for long, silent moments before she answered.

"Dunno," she said, simply. But she diverted her eyes when she said it.

"Yes, you do," I insisted, trying to keep my voice as unaccusing as possible, because I knew if I made her mad or sounded the least little bit demanding, she'd clam right up.

"Just never you mind," she said, and her irritation was too thinly veiled.

"So that's the way it's going to be, then," I said.

"Thas the way what's gonna be?"

"You and Maybelline having secrets."

266

Well, of course, she didn't have an answer for that. And I didn't really need one. Because I'd about figured out exactly what was going on. And if they thought that's what was wrong with me, they'd missed it by a long shot.

"Come on upstairs," Mrs. Johnson directed. "I got something to show you."

And I couldn't have been more surprised when we got upstairs and went into the partitioned section toward the rear of the house. A lighted kerosene lamp sitting on an old but newly cleaned chest of drawers and casting a glow throughout the room, and too, the aromas of pine oil and sun-freshened bedding. My quilt on the freshly made bed. My dresses hanging in the chifforobe. And my window open to the singing of crickets in the pine woods, sweet and clear.

"She said you was gonna like this room," Mrs. Johnson explained. "You'd like hearing the crickets."

Well, I thought. This is one time she was right.

So for the first time since I'd slept in my own bed in my own room in my own home, I went to sleep under clean sheets and in a good bed. In a safe place, high up in the top of the stout old house, and with all the strong timbers to keep away the things that creep around in the dark.

During the night came a soft, steady rain and the sound of Maybelline and Mrs. Johnson speaking low in the next room. So wherever it was Maybelline had gone, she was back now, safe and sound. Then only silence and peace.

I dreamed of the road to Mount Horeb Camp Ground. No moon, but it was there somewhere behind the clouds, because from time to time a silver wave sweeping over the ground, casting a glow so bright it was almost like daytime. Kudzu leaves bathed in moonlight so that they cast shadows against the tangle of vines they grew from. The clouds moving low and fast, light followed by shadow followed by light over and over again, over the leaves, rapid and like the flickering light in a motion picture theater reflected on upturned faces waiting.

The faraway mutter of thunder and a brief, bright quiver of light in the belly of a towering cloud in the west.

267

Rain falling somewhere over there, not very far away, and maybe slapping hard now against a barn roof in the dark and startling the animals for a moment. A cow briefly shaking her ears back and forth—then, remembering that she is in a safe, dry place where the rain can't reach her, breathing deeply of the sweet, warm hay and going back to sleep.

From the edge of the woods, a sound. From the dark night where tiny, silver pearls of rain lined up on the long green pine needles.
"MEE-LIA?"
Old Auntie?

Right before dawn, when the rain had stopped. Because it was that most quiet time when night sounds are done and everything hushed and very still, waiting for the first easing off of the deepest night shadows.

"MEE-LIA?"
I'm coming!

I got out of bed and found myself in a dark, unfamiliar room, one much larger than it should have been. So that the door leading out of the cornmeal-smelling little room at Aunt Valley's and into the kitchen wasn't where it was supposed to be at all. Only a wall to be followed blindly and then a corner and another wall. And then a door.

Not the little pantry-room at all, but the upstairs of Maybelline's granddaddy's old house, and unfamiliar stairs to be so careful about, and to be quiet about, too. Because if Maybelline or Mrs. Johnson had heard me, they would have told me I'd been dreaming and take me back to bed and make me miss Old Auntie's baptizing.

I don't know how, but I found my way down the stairs and never made a single sound. It was almost as if my feet knew exactly how far to go down to find the next step and the exact distance from the foot of the stairs to the door. Then across the silent yard to the pines and far, far beyond. All the way back to where the creek was waiting. . . .

The way it is waiting when Lizzie parks the truck at the side of the road just before the wooden bridge, and Aunt Valley gets out and goes around to the back of the truck to lift her papa down from the tailgate and stand him on the hard, baked clay road. Then she and Lizzie get up in the truck itself and start lifting the green chair.

All the other people coming, walking along the road, many whose faces I know from the prayer meeting and from seeing them standing around in Aunt Valley's front yard when they came to hear Old Auntie. Among them and towering over them is preacher-man, wearing a flowing white robe as big as a bedsheet, laughing and bending down to listen to them, and then walking along just like a king among them.

He sees Aunt Valley and Lizzie starting to lift Old Auntie and her chair out of the truck, and he calls out, "Wait, sisters!" Taking giant strides, he comes to the truck, takes hold of the chair, lifts it out as if it's light as a feather, and sets the chair and Old Auntie on the ground.

"This is the glorious day we've all prayed for!" he exclaims, straightening up and looking up at the sky. Even Old Auntie chuckles at the sound of the big, joyous voice. "So let us go now to the River Jordan and baptize our Sister Evangeline into the family of the Lord!"

Evangeline! Old Auntie has a name! Why, I never even thought of that before. A name that all by itself sounds like singing and sunshine.

But I'm wondering, too, about this River Jordan he's talking about.

"It's a creek, isn't it?" I ask Aunt Valley, and she laughs and looks at preacher-man.

"Not today it isn't," he proclaims. "Today it's the River Jordan!" His voice booms out across the clay road, sending some nameless creature scurrying away in the dried grass.

"Amen!" shout the people, smiling and fanning themselves.

"AMEN!" yells preacher-man. Then he looks down at Old Auntie, where she's sitting in the green chair in the middle of the red clay road, smiling down at her Indian-bead shoes and wearing her beautiful baptizing dress. Somehow, my eyes fix themselves on the very back of her neck, right where the little braids begin, and I see that her head is nodding itself around a bit.

Preacher-man sees it too.

"Are you ready, sister?" he asks, and Old Auntie's head nods. So he bends down and picks her up out of the chair just as if she's a little child and walks away with her in his strong arms, following the crooked path down and down and sing-songing as he walks:

"We're bring-ing Evan-ge-line, Lord! To the Ri-vver Jor-dan for washing awayyy her sins! Yessss, Lord!"

Lizzie and Aunt Valley and me scrambling along behind him and the others following us in a long line and singing:

Shall we gather at the river,
Where bright angel feet have trod;
With its crystal tide forever
Flowing by the throne of God?
Yes, we'll gather at the river,
The beautiful, the beautiful river;
Gather with the saints at the river
That flows by the throne of God.

Down and down we go, into the deeper greens of shade trees and the smell of the creek—rotted bark and sweet, green leaves—drifting up to meet us. Down and down to where the water is as black as coffee. Slow-moving and silent.

I am thinking that it must be a great surprise to the creek when we all descend upon it, singing, where it widens into an elbow shape just below the wooden bridge. Because what's up top, at the bridge, is a blistering sun that's baked the red clay road into a hard crust. But down below, where the creek is, deep shade and the air soft to breathe.

Directly over the creek is a break in the high green canopy, like God has pulled back the treetops so He can sit on His throne the creek is flowing by and see what we're up to. And the creek itself coming from beyond the bridge and sliding past so slow and easy and then going off into the undergrowth.

Ere we reach the shining river,
Lay we every burden down;
Grave our spirits will deliver,
And provide a robe and crown.
Yes, we'll gather at the river,
The beautiful, the beautiful river;
Gather with the saints at the river
That flows by the throne of God.

Folks standing around on the banks, and the preacher looking above him at the trees and the green leaves and the people and then finally looking down at the deep and slow-moving creek. Just like that, he wades right into the water, with his shoes on and all, and with Old Auntie—Evangeline!—in his arms. Old Auntie with her thin, child-sized arms and the

270

round little stomach, like a baby ready to be born. As the preacher goes into the creek with her, she turns her face toward where Lizzie and Aunt Valley and I are standing on the bank and she waves her fingers at us just the least little bit behind the preacher's back.

"Sister Evangeline!" His golden voice fills the cavern below the high canopy of leaves and echoes back and forth across the dark water.

"I baptize you . . ." he begins, and as he speaks, he lifts Old Auntie higher. His arms are so strong, I'll bet he could fling her right up through the green-leaf canopy so she'd land right at the throne of God Himself.

That's what I am thinking when I see her face turned toward me from behind the preacher's massive shoulders. I stand there, looking right into her sightless eyes.

Suddenly she yells, "Quick! Give it to me! All of it! I'll take it to Jesus!"

"What'd she say?" Aunt Valley shifts her smiling gaze from Old Auntie to me. "What'd she say?" she asks again.

"No!" I yell—because I've just now realized what it is she's telling me to give her to take to Jesus.

"No!"

But it doesn't matter what I say, for it all starts happening, passing once again between Old Auntie and me—not silent and not invisible this time, but playing itself out like a flickering old movie right there in the air over the creek while everything else in all creation stops and waits for it to be done.

So that I watch while Tulie finishes scrubbing the floors with lye soap and washing the windows and airing out the curtains. So that Great-Aunt Kate's house is shiny fresh and clean and smelling like pine oil and sunshine.

Great-Aunt Kate gives her a little cash money, a big bundle of good clothes, a package of chewing tobacco, and a ten-pound sack of flour. And I know why.

I ride with Mama again when we take her back home. All the way down the bumpy road, only this time a very low and hot sun blazing through the cornstalks just like streaks of fire, and making even more tiger stripes in Tulie's yard.

But not the gentle ones of morning. Now a hot, hot orange only a little lighter than the clay.

The children still sitting on the steps, like they haven't moved the whole day long, and the little boy with no pants on still there, too. Mama and me watching while Tulie carries the sack of flour and puts it on the porch before she comes back to get the bundle of clothes.

Mama waving her fingers at the children and smiling.

271

"Wave at them, sugar," she says to me. But I never have a chance, because just like a flock of birds, the children lift silently and all at once off the steps and light on the sack of flour Tulie put on the porch and rip it open with their sharp claws and begin stuffing it into their mouths.

Their silent flurry and the little boy with no pants on coughing a cloud of flour dust. Snow white flour spilling onto his black stomach and his hands white as a ghost and the bleached mouth.

"Y'all stop that!" Tulie yells and starts running toward the porch with the big bundle of clothes bouncing against her leg. And when she gets to where the children are, her arm flailing up and down. Rising and falling over and over again.

Flour dust like a cloud all around the leaning porch of the crooked house in the middle of a yard full of hot tiger stripes.

"In the name of the Father!" preacher-man intones, and Old Auntie is smiling to beat the band, all of it gone over to her to take to Jesus, and going down and down with her as preacher-man lowers her into the black water.

When Old Auntie disappears completely, it is gone. Just like that.

"And of the Son! And of the Holy Ghost! A-MEN!"

He lifts her up out of the water, a wet little Old Auntie, and she raises her hands into the air and looks high up into the space in the green canopy and starts in to speaking in tongues, raising her hands even higher, palms up to the sky.

And I am free! Lifted until I think I'm floating around in the air somewhere just below the startled green leaves.

So that I can almost watch from way up there where all the Hallelujahs and Praise the Lords have gathered, and Old Auntie's speaking in tongues is a high, unending note over all. The people praising and singing and swaying together from side to side.

Preacher-man carries Old Auntie out of the black creek, out of the River Jordan and into the singing and clapping and swaying, standing there with her in his arms for a long time and smiling brighter than any sun that was ever in the sky.

I float back to the succulent earth. Clean.

Aunt Valley stares at me, and she's wearing wrinkles on her forehead like she gets when she's trying to figure out why God made gnats.

25

Maybelline hollering and holding me so tight I could hardly breathe. Both of us in the creek, strangely enough, and the black water cool around us and Maybelline shivering against me.

"Where are we?" I asked, coughing and shuddering in alarm at the ooze under my bare feet and the faint, scratchy feeling of submerged twigs and unspeakable things under the black water.

"You fell in the creek," Maybelline answered. "You coulda drowned!"

Mrs. Johnson up on the bank, holding the kerosene lamp high, so that Maybelline and I clutched each other in a glow that tipped each ripple of black water with silvery fire.

"Let go of me! I'm just fine!" I said, trying to push Maybelline away from me.

"No, ma'am!" she said. "You're not pushing me away this time. I'm gonna hold onto you all the way home."

"HOW COME YOU RUNNING AROUND IN THE WOODS IN THE MIDDLE OF THE NIGHT?" Mrs. Johnson hollered from the bank.

"What?"

"I SAID HOW COME . . . ."

"Where on earth were you trying to go off to?" Maybelline interrupted her. "Why, if I hadn't heard somebody or other calling your name way in the woods, I wouldn't even have known you were gone at all!"

Somebody calling my name? Old Auntie? Oh, my! Old Auntie?

I tried to pull away from Maybelline, but she held me in a death grip, so that I am powerless to join the people who are walking away from me, singing and clapping their way up the hill.

"No!" Maybelline bellowed at me suddenly, making me jump almost out of my skin. I stopped struggling and stood watching, as they all disappeared over the top of the hill. Maybelline whispered in my ear, "I think you're having a dream."

What on earth!

But even as I looked up toward the top of the hill, I could tell that there wasn't a hill there at all. Not at this creek. And not the blazing hot day of Old Auntie's baptism, either. Nighttime.

Maybelline must be right. It was a dream. But also not a dream. Memory!

"I'm so cold," I said to Maybelline. Because I didn't want to remember anything else, and I sure didn't want to think about how Maybelline could have heard Old Auntie calling to me from the woods. Not if it was a dream I was having. Not if it was memory.

We waded together toward the bank, where Mrs. Johnson held the lantern high with one hand and reached down with the other, to hoist me up as easily as if I were a doll. Maybelline scrambled up the bank and then held tight to my arm as we started back through the pines toward the old house. But as we walked . . . *we are suddenly surrounded by the clapping, singing crowd that follows preacher-man and a laughing Old Auntie as they top the hill.*

You're wrong, Maybelline. This isn't a dream at all! And I've got to go back until I get it right this time!

Preacher-man hoists Old Auntie and her green chair back into the truck and Lizzie gets behind the wheel. Aunt Valley starts to get in, too, but then she looks at me where I am standing as if I'm rooted to the clay road, and she motions to preacher-man to get in and ride. Aunt Valley picks up her old papa under the arms, sits him onto the extended tailgate, and takes my hand. We walk along, following the truck, and with all the people all around us and the singing starting up again out of the little yelps and praises it had broken into at the top of the hill. Coming together just like the pieces of a puzzle.

274

Old Auntie sitting in the green chair and with a towel over her head, smiling to beat the band and clapping her hands to the singing.

I'm marching right into all creation, and it feels good! My shoes start skipping along the clay road, two happy little dogs that are both named Blackie and having the very best time of their entire lives. And the shade from the pecan trees on either side of the road isn't sad at all. Just plain old shade. Nothing else.

I see a big, fat mockingbird in one of the trees. He's trying to imitate our singing, but he can't do it, so he tilts his head from side to side, watching us with his bright, black eyes and warbling a sound deep in his throat, maybe to try it out and see if it sounds like us. But it doesn't, because nothing can sound like us.

We pass by a crooked, gray house with sunshine coming through the roofless rafters, and the people who used to live there seem to come out onto the broken porch to smile and wave to us. I wave back at them.

> *We're march-ing to Zi—on,*
> *Beau-ti-ful, beau-ti-ful Zi—on;*
> *We're marching up-ward to Zi-on,*
> *The beau-ti-ful city of God!*

Eventually, all the marching and the singing and the clapping and the praising bring us right back to Aunt Valley's house, and all the people follow us right inside. So many people that the little house is bulging at the sides with them.

Lizzie takes Old Auntie into her room, to dry her off and help her into dry clothes, and the people begin squeezing themselves into the kitchen, laughing and sweating and reaching for the tall glasses of iced tea and for the plates they will load from the dishes of fried chicken and butter beans and potato salad and cornbread that are crowded onto every inch of the groaning table.

But Aunt Valley leads me right on through the people and out onto the back porch, where she kneels down, so that her face is even with mine.

"What happened back there?" she asks, and for an instant, I don't know what she means.

"Back there?" Meaningless. Because there is no such thing.

"Just before Old Auntie went under," she explains.

"Oh. That."

"Yes. That," she confirms. "Who was those chirren?"

"You saw them?" It's all I can say.

275

"I did indeed see them. I saw them! Those the chirren you been frettin' about?"

"Yes'm," I say, but somehow, I can't remember fretting so very much about them. Still, I wait to see if my throat is going to tighten up or my feet start in to running. But it doesn't happen. Then I remember that the Great Mystery is gone.

"Old Auntie took it to Jesus," I say, not really knowing the words, but trying anyway. Aunt Valley is still looking deep into my eyes, so I add, "And I'm washed clean in the River Jordan."

"Old Auntie took what to Jesus?"

"The hurting."

"Well . . . praise the Lord!" Aunt Valley whispers. "We've had ourselves a miracle sure enough this day!" She tries to get up off her knee, and she puts her hand on my shoulder and uses me to steady herself. Once she's standing again, she keeps her hand on me.

"This is very important. You do know that, don't you?" She is still whispering, and I nod. "It means you can love now."

I nod again. But the way she says the word love, I'm not sure what she means. But I'll figure it out later.

"Well then, you go on and get yourself some of that good chicken 'fore it's all eat up," she says. "We'll talk again after awhile."

For the rest of that whole, wonderful day, we are busy eating together and singing together and clapping our hands together. Lizzie helps Old Auntie out onto the porch and sits her in the green chair, and Old Auntie takes a long, peaceful nap right there.

I sit out on the back steps with Aunt Valley's old papa. He is gazing at his tomato plants, and I am eating another slice of sweet potato pie.

"You want some good tomatoes?" he asks me.

"No, thank you," I say.

"Well, Ezra! How you been doing?" The voice comes from inside the screen door to the back porch, and I turn to look at a big, smiling woman wearing a purple hat.

"Fine," he says, still gazing at his tomato plants.

"And who is that pretty little girl?"

I am thinking, ME? Me, pretty???

"Don't remember," he says, and then he looks at me as if he's never seen me before. "But she sure is pretty, come to think of it. You want some good tomatoes?" he asks, still gazing at me.

"No, thank you," I say.

ME? Pretty?

276

"I'll have some, Ezra," the woman says, and Old Papa grins and gets up off the steps and goes to picking tomatoes.

"He's a good man," the woman says to me in a low voice.

"Yes'm."

She's right, of course. He is a good man. And I'm pretty!

Late in the afternoon, the people quietly gather in the yard, waiting for Old Auntie to wake up and talk to them in tongues.

The sun is very, very hot, lying so low on the horizon and with all the heat of the long, hot day beginning to rise up from the earth.

The people rest in the shade and fan themselves while they wait. Some of them sleep.

Aunt Valley and I sit in the porch swing, and my suitcase is packed and waiting by the front steps. And still, we haven't talked again about what happened at Old Auntie's baptism. So our "after awhile" is slipping away. But I don't really mind, because my mama's coming to get me, and that's all that seems to matter.

At the very moment I am thinking about Mama, I see the black Packard coming far away down the road, with a big plume of red dust rising up behind it in the deep-gold sunshine, like the tail of a giant bird.

Mama!

Her riding along in the big car, and Gus driving it. Coming right down the dirt road and soon it will turn in at Aunt Valley's little house, where the people are sitting in the shade, some of them looking like statues.

Aunt Valley sees the car coming, too, and she reaches out and grabs my hand and holds it so tight that it surprises me and stops me from bolting out of the swing.

"Listen to me for just one little minute!" she says, but my eyes are on the car. It's getting bigger and bigger, and I can almost make out Gus's hands on the steering wheel. "Look at me!" Aunt Valley orders. I look at her. Something locks me in her gaze.

"We never got to the day of creation when God made man. And it's the most important." I am wondering why she's intent on telling this to me now. Now that my own mama is right there in the car, and it is getting closer and closer. My own mama will be waiting for me!

Aunt Valley talks so fast, I can hardly understand what she's saying. "God made man—you and me and Old Auntie and Miss Carol Ann and those chirren you fretted about so bad—made in His image, you hear me?"

I don't answer, but I start twisting my hand back and forth in her iron grip.

"Made in His image. Black as they are. And naked. And hungry—don't matter. Still in His image. All of us are, and that means we gotta love each other. Any way we can and no matter what!"

Suddenly, I am angry. So angry that I could slap her—just reach out and slap her hard. I wrench my hand back and forth, back and forth.

"Don't you never forget it!" she commands. "And don't you never try to throw it away. 'Cause it don't throw!"

Abruptly, I stop trying to pull away.

"Let . . . me . . . go," I say, in a voice that's so strong, the sound of it surprises me.

And she lets me go.

I grab my suitcase and dash down the leaning front steps into the yard, running past the people who are still sitting there, some of them leaning against the big tree and sleeping with their mouths open. The little girl who put tree bark in her hair is there, too, asleep now, and looking very much like a picture I have seen in a book at school—she is outstretched across her mother's knees, head back as if in death and one arm trailing on the bare ground. And the mother is looking down into her face in the most loving way. The picture in the book, a black-and-white picture with all kinds of gray in the hollows and crevices.

The big car purring and shiny in the sunlight, and Gus in his immaculate black suit, holding the door open, and his brief glance at the people in the yard before his face returns to the impassive gaze at absolutely nothing.

He holds the door open to the pearl-gray upholstery and Mama's feet, neatly crossed at the ankles, her perfume and warm hands and Gus closing the door behind me and the silence of the inside and Mama hugging me tight.

"I missed you!" she says.

"I missed you, too, Mama!"

"And what's going on out there?" Mama asks, as Gus closes the door.

"Oh, they're waiting for Old Auntie to wake up from her nap," I say, knowing all the time that whatever words I try to use to tell her anything won't work.

"Why?" Mama asks.

"She tells them things."

"Like a fortune-teller?"

"No, ma'am. Maybe like a preacher or something."

278

"Goodness!" she says, and then she reaches over and cups my cheek with a hand that is warm and sweet smelling. And suddenly, I love her so much I can hardly breathe.

"Look, sugar, . . . Mama brought you a welcome home present." She hands me a brand new overnight case—one that's a lot prettier and nicer than Carol Ann's.

"It's beautiful!"

The big car moves smoothly away, and I don't look back.

"And guess what? In only a week or so, we'll be going back to Great-Aunt Kate's for Carol Ann's birthday party, and you can use your new overnight case then. First thing tomorrow, we'll go downtown and find you a dress to wear to the party."

"What kind of dress?" I ask, because just for a moment, I think I see that little boy with no pants on standing off at the side of the road. So I open the overnight case and start looking in all the satiny little pockets it has in it so I won't have to look at him.

"Why, only the prettiest dress in the whole world," Mama says.

She laughs, and we look at each other, and I am thinking: Yes, a dress that will turn Carol Ann pea-green with envy!

I lean against her, breathing in her warm, clean aroma and watching out the car window to where the open fields are passing and the crooked houses are fading in the distance. But more. Something of myself, too.

"You okay?" Mama asks.

"I'm okay, now you're here."

I am silent again, because I don't want to think about Old Auntie or Aunt Valley at all. Not while my mama's right there with me.

"Anything happen back there to upset you?" Her voice is full of concern. "You tell Mama, you hear?"

I hesitate because maybe I should try to tell her. But instead I ask, "Do you believe in magic things?"

"Magic things?" she asks, just as if she's never heard the words before. "What kind of magic things?" I can tell she wants to know why I'm asking such a question. Because she can be very, very sharp about things like that.

"Magic things like thinking you see something that's not really there," I say. Because maybe it didn't happen. Maybe I dreamed every bit of it.

"What kind of something?" she persists, and her nose goes kind of pointy-looking so that she looks like a big mama bird all set for pecking at something until she gets it.

"I saw . . . blood . . . on Carol Ann's panties at Camp Meeting," I say, but I have no idea of why I'm talking about that. It isn't what I was thinking at all.

"Well"—no alarm in her voice now. But she speaks in a whisper, because of Gus. "That's a perfectly natural thing that happens to all little girls when they become young ladies. It's happened now to Carol Ann, and means she's old enough to have a child. That's what your Great-Aunt Kate was talking about when she said Carol Ann was becoming a woman."

We ride along in the smooth, quiet car, and Carol Ann seems very far away and completely unimportant.

"You could have asked Aunt Valley, instead of worrying about it since last week," Mama suggests.

"What kind of baby is Carol Ann going to have?" I ask.

"Goodness, none at all, right away. And I don't know what kind of baby," Mama says. "Just whatever kind she has, that's all—but only after she's all grown up and has a husband and a home of her own."

"A white baby or a black baby?"

"A white baby, of course!" Mama's offended. "And what does any of this have to do with magic things, anyway?"

Uh-oh. She's back on track.

"Because babies are magic things," I say, and she is visibly relieved.

"Of course they are, honey," she smiles at me. "Beautiful magic. All babies are."

No, Mama, I am thinking. Not all of them.

"Don't you try to throw it away," I hear Aunt Valley's voice just as clear as day. "'Cause it don't throw!"

But the big, quiet car just keeps moving farther and farther away every single moment, away from where the devil sits, grinning, behind a big white tombstone at Mount Horeb cemetery.

Maybelline and Mrs. Johnson helped me to my room, got my wet things off, and put me in a dry, clean nightgown before they tucked me into bed. They took turns sitting with me, probably because they were afraid I'd go walking off again. But that couldn't have happened, because my teeth were chattering and I drifted in and out of sleep and dreams such as I'd never had before. I felt so weak, I couldn't have walked across the room if my life depended upon it.

Once, when they were trying to get me to drink some tea, they offered it to me in a cup I could have sworn was part of my grandmama's china. But that was just the delirium, I supposed. At any rate, I couldn't stay awake long enough to ask about it.

Another time, I awakened to see Maybelline sitting by my bed, talking to Jesus. A long, steady stream of chatter.

"Raise her up," I heard her say, before I went back under—but not a going under to cool dark water, but to a hot, orange fever-sun and a dream in which I am still riding along with Mama in the big black Packard automobile, with Gus driving it. But suddenly there's a blazing beacon off to the side of the road, and a little two-rut path. Gus turns off and goes through a field of green corn growing shoulder-high to a big man.

And I know what's waiting at the end of it.

I look up at Mama, but she isn't there. Instead, Aunt Valley is sitting with me, patting my shoulder.

"You just don't listen," she mutters. "I told you it don't throw." Her words peal forth just like the old bell at Mount Horeb tabernacle calling everyone to come and sit on the hard wooden benches and fan themselves with their cardboard-Jesus fans.

I say not a word, just lean against her and watch through the window where row after row of tall green cornstalks slide past.

The car slows, as I know it will, and then stops. Gus gets out and opens the back door for me, his face careful and impartial and his gaze fixed, as always, on some indeterminate point in the distance.

Stupidly, I remain pressed against Aunt Valley, and finally she stops patting my shoulder. So it's time.

She sighs and whispers: "Every single one of us, we're made in His image, and we're worthy of love."

"Love?" I mouth the word as if I have never heard it before.

"Go on now," Aunt Valley urges. "It's time. Past time."

And because there's nothing else I can do, I get out of the car and watch in wonder as my feet—in old lady, lace-up shoes—move slowly across the sandy soil of Tulie's swept yard, right to the edge of the steps where the children are waiting.

281

I breathe the stench of their unwashed bodies and ravaged hair. Stare into their flat, unmoving eyes. See my own reflection in them—all the sad, white faces looking back at me.

"I've come back for you," I say.

"MAYBELLINE! COME ON UP HERE!" Mrs. Johnson bellowed, and then she stomped across the room and through the hallway and clumped down the first three or four stairs.

"COME ON UP HERE!" she hollered again. "SHE DONE BEEN MOANING AND CRYING AND HAVING THE WORSTEST STRUGGLE I EVER DID SEE. AND NOW SHE DONE COME BACK, RIDING A BIG WHITE ANGEL-HORSE AND LAUGHING OUT LOUD AND SHOUTING HALLELUJAH!"

"Did not!" I tried to yell, but the next thing I knew, Maybelline was right in my face. So close, I couldn't even focus on her. I waved her back.

"Now listen to me," I started right out. "This doesn't change a thing!" Because I knew they were probably going to start treating me like a crazy woman. Watch me all the time and such as that. Or worse, Maybelline would think I'd been "saved." At last.

"Oh, yes, it does. It changes everything," Maybelline said in a whisper.

"No, it doesn't!" I yelled back at her, but I didn't even know what we were arguing about.

"Of course it does," she insisted. "It means we're going to be able to love each other. Maybe be a real family even."

"What?"

"I shore ain't goin' love her," Mrs. Johnson snorted.

"Oh, yes, you are," Maybelline smiled.

"Now, look," Mrs. Johnson growled, putting massive fists on her hips. "I'm right glad she didn't drown in the creek, 'cause I wouldn't wish that on nobody. And maybe I'm even right glad she done got through whatever she was struggling so hard against," Mrs. Johnson admitted. "But that don't mean I'm goin' love no old white lady thinks she's so much better'n me."

"She won't think that," Maybelline pronounced.

"Who says? I sure ain't heard her say nothing about it." Mrs. Johnson's voice was low and suspicious.

"I don't even know what we're talking about," I said.

"Well, to tell the truth, I don't either," Mrs. Johnson admitted. "But before we go starting in on all this loving each other stuff, I suppose it's still all right for me to go all the way back down them steps, fix you a cup of tea, and then carry it all the way back up here to you."

"Please," I said.

Mrs. Johnson glared at me before she started down the stairs, clumping her feet hard and muttering in a red fury under her breath.

"Remember to bring a cup from her grandmama's china," Maybelline called after her, still smiling.

"I thought that's what you two were up to," I said. "But it doesn't change anything." Maybelline said not a single word, but just kept smiling at me.

It was quite maddening, you see. All that smiling Maybelline did. All the time. Took me a while to gain back my strength, and her smiling at me the whole time.

Mrs. Johnson made up for it by not smiling at all, by being just as grumpy as she possibly could be, and flying into tantrums about the least little thing. Maybelline made excuses for her, telling me her teeth were hurting her and that's what was making her so irritable. Finally, when I couldn't stand it any longer, I told Mrs. Johnson to go to town, find herself a dentist, and get him to make her some teeth—that I'd pay for them, because that's the only way I was ever going to have any peace.

"I thought you didn't have no money," Mrs. Johnson grumbled at me with a greedy gleam in her eyes.

"I said I'll pay for your teeth," I repeated. And that's all I would say, because I think it's really no business of hers whether I have any money put aside or not. But after all, my making all those plans for winding up next to Henry were premature anyway. Because I don't have any plans for going anywhere at all, at least any time soon. There's too much to be done around here, for one thing. Why, we have to put in a garden and get some glass to go in the windows and fence in a chicken yard. And do all the things it will take to move us forward a little bit.

Maybelline's trying to get her beauty parlor business started in town, and lots of folks here remember hearing her granddaddy's stories from their own granddaddies, so she has a right good number of ladies coming to her now. But the first little bit of money she got, Maybelline went out and bought a sow that's going to have babies, so now the sow lives under the kitchen. Come winter, we'll probably have a box of baby pigs staying warm under the cookstove. And when it finally comes time to slaughter them and put up the meat, I'll bet Maybelline will go into hysterics and not let Mrs. Johnson do it. We'll probably never have another bite of ham in our lives.

Mrs. Johnson's finally going to night school, like she said she wanted to do, and from time to time I help her out with her reading. It's really quite interesting, especially the history she's studying, but I do get a little tired of hearing her shout—right out of the blue—things like "FOUR SCORE AND SEVEN YEARS AGO!" Says she likes the sound of the words. I might as well like the sound of them, too.

And I have the children to think of. They are always sitting there on the steps of Maybelline's granddaddy's old house, but they aren't lonely anymore, because now they have me to care about them. Of course, I've got more sense than to say anything to Maybelline or Mrs. Johnson about them, but in a way I don't begin to understand, those children are a very great comfort to me—even if I do know that they are really only memories.

But I don't care one little bit, because it's all so lovely. And besides, every so often, Aunt Valley comes as well, to see me and the children. She usually stays for a long time, rocking in a chair and telling them how God made the world and everything in it. But when she gets to the part about Him making gnats, she comes right out and says she doesn't know why. And she always tells them about how every single soul in the whole world is made in God's image and worthy of love.

Sometimes, Old Auntie, wearing her beautiful, white baptizing dress, comes with Aunt Valley, but most of the time, she never says a thing. Just sits there and smiles at me and the children.

When I listen to Aunt Valley telling her stories all over again, I can sometimes hear dishes rattling far off in the kitchen and Mrs. Johnson and Maybelline talking and laughing together. Mrs. Johnson's right easy to get along with, now that she has those big, shiny, white teeth—and now that she's got it in her head she's the one jumped into the creek and saved me from drowning. Says she's a heroine!

Fall has come, and the evenings are cool, so Maybelline usually comes out on the porch, bringing me a sweater and putting it around my shoulders, even though I tell her I'm not one little bit cold.

When she does that—puts it around my shoulders anyway—the children all break into wide smiles and roll their eyes at each other, as if they have never seen anything quite as funny as Maybelline acting like she's my mama. Or something like that.

Old Auntie smiles, too, but I know exactly what she's saying—that it's just love in one of its terrible disguises. Not such a great mystery after all. Once in a while, Old Auntie stays after all the others have gone, and we drink tea from the beautiful cups and talk together for the longest time. And no one can understand a thing we say to each other.

Except Jesus.

Augusta Trobaugh, a native Southerner writing under a pseudonym, has her master of arts degree in English from the University of Georgia, with a concentration in American and Southern Literature. Her work has been funded through the Georgia Council of the Arts, and *Praise Jerusalem!* was a semi-finalist in the 1993 Pirate's Alley Faulkner Competition.